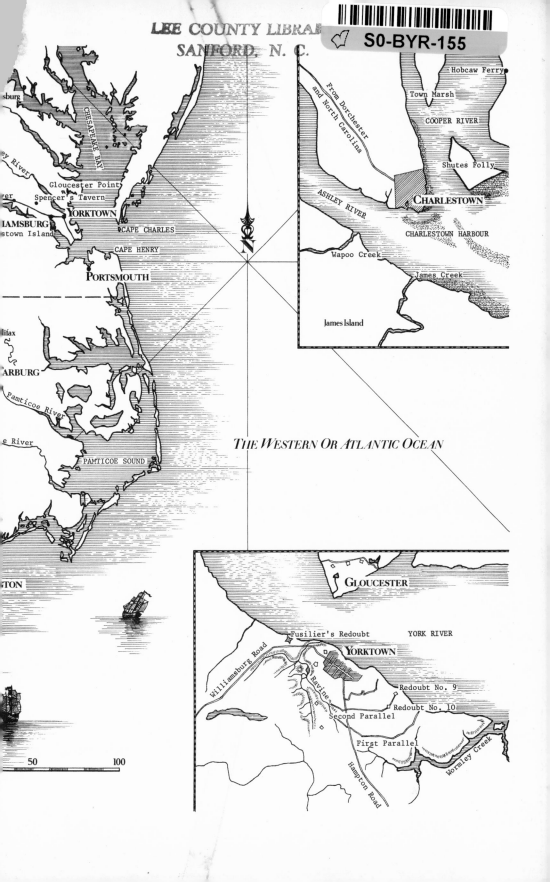

Hobcaw Ferry

Town Marsh

COOPER RIVER

From Dorchester
and North Carolina

Shutes Folly

ASHLEY RIVER

CHARLESTOWN

CHARLESTOWN HARBOUR

Wapoo Creek

James Creek

James Island

sburg

CHESAPEAKE BAY

Gloucester Point
Spencer's Tavern

YORKTOWN

ey River

er

IAMSBURG
town Island

CAPE CHARLES

CAPE HENRY

PORTSMOUTH

lifax

ARBURG

Pamticoe River

e River

PAMTICOE SOUND

THE WESTERN OR ATLANTIC OCEAN

N

GLOUCESTER

YORK RIVER

Fusilier's Redoubt

Williamsburg Road

YORKTOWN

Ravine

Redoubt No. 9

Redoubt No. 10

Second Parallel

First Parallel

Hampton Road

Wormley Creek

TON

50   100

Cato's War

Cato's War

A NOVEL OF
THE AMERICAN REVOLUTION

Guy Wheeler

MACMILLAN PUBLISHING CO., INC.

New York

Macmillan Publishing Co., Inc.
866 Third Avenue, New York, N.Y. 10022

Library of Congress Cataloging in Publication Data
Wheeler, Guy.
Cato's war.
1. United States—History—Revolution, 1775–
1783—Fiction. I. Title.
PZ4.W5618Cat 1980 [PR6073.H39] 823'.914
ISBN 0–02–626190–1 80–172

First Printing 1980

Printed in the United States of America

Endpaper map by Rupert Wheeler.

"A soldier's life is a joyful sorrow."
—RUSSIAN PROVERB

Author's Note

With the exception of Colonel Cato, Pvt. Matthew Ryan and the deserter Cook, all the major characters in the book are factual; the family of Lord Fairleigh of Lochdearn being modelled on the family of Lord Fairfax of Cameron. I have endeavoured to put their recorded opinions into the mouths of the factual characters; some of which, perhaps those of Gen. George Washington, may surprise.

Most English histories, not surprisingly, refer to the rebellion in the American colonies briefly and distastefully, ignoring the campaign of Lord Cornwallis' small army in the southern colonies which this story recounts. The neglect is unjust to an army, than which none have campaigned more bravely and behaved more honourably.

American histories, with some notable exceptions, tend to the mythological; firm in the belief that every colonist joined in the rebellion against the English King, that every man of them was both brave and a crack shot, and every woman of them virtuous. Sadly, this was not the case. The myth is unjust to the comparatively few colonists who did the fighting and the suffering.

For information on the colonists' view—both Loyalist and Patriot—of the political and social situation, I have relied most upon the histories of Mr. J. R. Alden and Prof. Daniel Boorstin; on military matters, upon the classic *Encyclopedia of the American Revolution*—the work of my erstwhile colleague Col. Mark M. Boatner III, U.S. Army, and upon Mr. Henry P. Johnston's history of the Yorktown campaign.

For a view on the political situation on this side of the Atlantic, I have relied on Profs. G. M. Trevelyan and J. H. Plumb; supported by Almon's *Parliamentary Register for 1780* and the *Royal Kalendar for 1780–81*—both of which I observed to report proceedings in Parliament markedly superior in content, cogency and style to those reported today in *Hansard*.

For the Royal army, Gen. Sir Henry Clinton's and Col. Banastre Tarleton's own narratives of the campaigns reveal an interesting contrast of personalities: Clinton too lacking in self-confidence to accept any blame—Tarleton too self-confident even to admit any error. Apart from these two and Mr. Edward B. Willcox's masterly dissection of Clinton's character, I have relied most upon Lord Cornwallis' papers and on the

Wickwires' biography of him, upon the *Journal* of Sgt. Roger Lamb of the 9th and 23rd Foot, upon the Regimental History of the 17th/21st Lancers and *The Exercise for the Horse, Dragoons and Foot Forces, 1727.*

Finally, on the ways of speech and accent in the colonies at the time, I have relied upon the definitive works on the subject by Mr. George Krap and Mr. Thomas Pyles.

I should like to record my appreciation for the assistance given me by the staffs of:

the British Army Museum

the Ministry of Defence Library

the Staff College Library

the Library of Congress

the Office of the Chief of Military History, U.S. Army

the Director of Research, Colonial Williamsburg

the South Carolina Historical Society.

Contents

Contents

Cato's War

Chapter One

*In which I am required to attend upon
the Secretary-at-War.*

The Right Honourable Charles Jenkinson, Member of Parliament for
Hastings and Secretary-at-War at the time of which I write, summoned
me to attend upon him, and thereafter upon Lord Germain, Secretary of
State for the American Colonies, and then upon His Majesty at St.
James's Palace, all on the same day, in a letter dated two days after that on
which he required my presence.

My wife remarked that if this was the way Mr. Jenkinson conducted
affairs little wonder the war in the American colonies was not progressing
well. The postboy arrived with the letter as I was about to ride to Forde
Abbey to join Franceis Gwyn in a day's fishing on the Axe. So, noting the
urgency of the summons, I went fishing.

That was the 8th April, 1780. The following day, being Sunday, I
spent attending divine service and preparing for my journey to London.

I always used to stay with Alexander and Georgina Popham when
visiting London, whether I came announced or not; and I arrived on the
Wednesday afternoon, with a great thirst, at their new house in Clarges
Street, beyond the Hyde Park Corner turnpike. Alexander sat as Member
of Parliament for Taunton; a genial, impetuous fellow, who held his Whig
views with such enthusiasm that they cost him his seat that year.

He had sent word from the House to expect him late that evening. I did
not object to that, because Georgina is as attractive as my wife; and knows
it. She uses it too, quite unscrupulously, to keep herself informed of all
that goes on in London, flirting with what the newspapers term
"authoritative and reliable sources" and she calls "political blabber-

mouths." She keeps her imagination well exercised in scandalizing her acquaintances with confidences on the frailties of the great; passing all reasonable belief but, perhaps, not all reasonable possibility.

So, for a whole hour, I was sat down and force-fed with China tea and affairs of state and major scandal. I was informed, in the strictest confidence of course, of the Prince of Wales' new mistress:

"A Mrs. Mary Robinson—an actress, my dear! She played Perdita in Mr. Sheridan's presentation of *Winter's Tale*. The Prince saw her and quite lost his wits. And poor Lord Malden!—he's infatuated with her himself and the Prince uses him to carry his billets-doux to her! Could anything be more cruel!"

Next was Lord Shelburne's duel. He had criticized in the Lords a Member of the Commons:

"He called him a clerk—which he is. But the newspapers reported it worse, of course, and he called Shelburne out. They exchanged shots and both missed—so careless. Even Mr. Burke—and you know he can't stand the sight of Shelburne—he said 'God forbid that gentlemen should be expected to answer for the gross misrepresentations of their speeches in either House which appear in the daily papers'—wasn't that thoughtful?

"Now what else? Oh, yes! Lord North was accused in the House of trying to buy the East India Company with public money for himself—and all his relations. They spring up everywhere, don't they, the North relations—like daisies on a lawn, but not nearly so pretty. Well, Charles Fox said he hoped the Prime Minister would be content with having lost America and not go losing India as well! Can't you see Charles saying it?—pushing out his pot and raising those enormous eyebrows, as if he was reprimanding an under-footman! I can't abide North! He's so everlastingly self-righteous and so everlastingly wrong."

Alexander brought home some friends, other Members of the House. Sir George Yonge, who sits for Honiton, I knew well, having voted for him. The others, the Members for Calne in Wiltshire—Col. Sir Charles Barre, a big, dour-faced man, and Mr. John Dunning, slight with the precise manner of a lawyer—were strangers to me.

Alexander greeted me as noisily as ever.

"Philip! Are you well? How good it is to see someone who hasn't had his wits corrupted from living in this madhouse of a city! Georgie, my dearest, for God's sake let's have some refreshment. We've had a most tedious day talking of taxes. And none of your China tea—damned yellow drench plays the devil with a man's bladder!"

Georgina gave a dutiful curtsy and stuck out her tongue. A well-matched pair, the Pophams.

George Yonge patted my shoulder.

"Glad to see you, Philip. What brings you to London?"

"To tell the truth, George, I don't know—"

"Hah, lad, you have that in common with any politician!" roared Alexander. "None of 'em knows why they're here, but they're all determined to stay forever!"

"Are you speaking of yourself?" I asked.

"Course not, m'dear fellow! Only describing that despicable rabble that poses as His Majesty's Government just now. Rest of us are noble, unselfish, incorruptible champions of the people's rights!"

As we supped, Georgina, sensing their air of weary frustration, enlivened the conversation with outrageous selections from her arsenal of scandal until even the unsmiling Barre was whooping with laughter. When she retired and left us to our wine we were all in a better humour.

It was a warm evening and Alexander pulled back the heavy blue velvet curtains and opened the windows, which looked onto the street. He brought two decanters of port from the sideboard, set one at his place and sent the second sliding across the polished mahogany to George Yonge.

"Keep it moving now, George," he said, "Man can die of thirst, y'know." He filled his own glass and pushed the decanter at me. "Well, Philip, you still haven't told us your news?"

"The Secretary-at-War wants me to see him, Lord George Germain and His Majesty, in that order, all on the same day."

"When? Tomorrow?"

"No—ten days ago." And I told them the story of the Secretary's letter.

"Bigod!" said Barre, disgustedly, "Exactly what I've been complaining about. No one in that damned Office knows what he's doing. Least of all that lick-spittle place-seeker Jenkinson."

"Oh, Issac," Dunning waved his clay at Barre. "He doesn't do so badly—I doubt there's many who could do better. He's a cool devil—and a clever one."

Barre grunted.

"He's a two-faced, canting vinegar-pisser! You can't admire the fellow, John?"

"Only his successful dedication to the advancement of his own interests. This man, Colonel Cato," Dunning's clay wagged at me now, "has crawled into the favour of Lord North and made himself indispensable to him—and the King too. A ruthless creature. I'd want him neither as friend nor enemy; though I doubt one would ever be sure which he was. He is one of the chief powers behind the excessive influence of the Crown in Parliament."

"I know that you've had petitions criticizing the influence of the Crown—"

"Indeed so, Philip," said Yonge, "And John Dunning here made a motion last week in the House based on those petitions; that the influence of the Crown has increased, is increasing and ought to be diminished. And we won it by fifteen votes. A famous victory over the royal cabal."

"Hear, hear!" Alexander rattled his glass on the table and slopped the wine over his cuff. "And, Philip, had you thought why we've been fighting our countrymen across the ocean for the last five years? Because they wished to be represented properly, to be taxed fairly and trade freely. Three reasonable enough aspirations for Englishmen I'd say; and that excellent Mr. Franklin, when he was here, claimed that they were all Englishmen and proud of it!"

"But, Alexander," I said, "the King has a responsibility to defend his people and possessions from foreign enemies, or rebellion in this country or the colonies. Surely this is what he's doing? Certainly our fellow-countrymen in the colonies should be properly represented—perhaps in Parliament?"

"And be permitted to manufacture and trade unrestrictedly?" Dunning broke in.

"Indeed. But in that case they should not resent tax levied for their own defence, as they have done."

"No," replied Dunning evenly, watching me intently over the tips of his fingers, "and I believe that would have been acceptable to the colonists five years ago."

"But, Alexander," I turned on him again, "the people confer authority on the King when they put the crown on his head—"

"And the people can remove all three—authority, crown, ay—and head if need be! They've done it before!" Alexander threw himself back in his chair and glared at me.

I must have looked as shocked as I felt. He wagged a finger at me.

"Shaken you to the roots to hear such talk, hasn't it? Well, my old country mole, you and your sort have been sitting on your behinds in your comfortable holes too long, preening your whiskers and telling each other all's right with the world really, the war will soon end and taxes will come down again. Well, it's not and it won't and they won't!"

"And what's to do about it then?"

He took a long pull at his glass and set it down unsteadily.

"First we must make our Teutonic monarch stop fumbling the levers of power."

"And if he won't?"

"Why, if he won't, we should pack him off back to his Hanoverian bogs. His father and grandfather were content enough there, bouncing around with their hideous mistresses, so why shouldn't he be? God knows why we ever allowed the breed into the country!"

"And who would you have in his place?"

"Do we need a monarchy? We've had Plantagenets and Tudors and Stewarts and Orange and now Hanover. Are we any the better for 'em?"

I sensed some embarrassment amongst the others at Alexander's outburst. There was some small talk but I could not heed it.

Treason—or what was called treason by those in power in this country in those times—has twice come nigh to ruining my family. Perhaps I judged too hastily that night—made too much of high words said in wine—saw treason where none existed. But treason is, for me, a ready ghost; made readier by the accounts of those of my family who fought and died for their beliefs under the Stewarts and the Protectorate. And Alexander's words had aroused the ghost.

Finally, I rose to my feet.

"Gentlemen," I said, "I suggest—with great respect—we remember that all of us hold positions of authority under the Crown, whoever wears it."

I looked at Alexander, slouched in his chair, chin on chest, lips thrust out, glaring at me under half-closed lids.

"And, Alexander, I may well be what you choose to call an old country mole; but I know treason when I hear it. And I have heard something very near it tonight. I would I had not heard it from a friend."

Alexander pouted the more and grunted. But John Dunning, still watching me over his fingertips, said,

"Colonel Cato, you have heard only what is being said openly over most dinner-tables in London tonight. And if the small-talk over dinner-tables is treasonous, then, sir, something is very amiss in the country." The beginning of a smile tipped the corners of his mouth. "I'm amazed the news has not reached you—in your hole."

I like John Dunning—one of the clearest and astutest minds in Parliament. Even though he is a politician—and a lawyer—he's a man to be trusted. I said,

[7]

"Well, sir, if it's as you say, then it is perhaps time for the moles to come out of their holes and vote this government out."

Dunning laughed.

"That's the way democracy should work," said he, "We must pray the rest of the moles are persuaded before our case becomes too desperate for some remedy short of what Alexander advocates."

I excused myself on the grounds that I had had a long journey and was very tired; which I was—but more confused by what I had heard. I wondered whether I had not been sitting in complacent idleness in Somerset too long. I had my excuses. Out of my twenty-three years' service I had spent only four in my own home. I felt the need, for the sake of my family, to establish myself at home for a proper period, and had asked to go on half-pay.

Previous to this semi-retirement I had always kept myself informed of affairs at home and abroad. But of late, newspapers had been my only informers; and they rarely give an unprejudiced record of events. To learn the truth of affairs one must consult regularly with those responsible for the shaping of them. I had neglected to do this; not wilfully, but out of apathy; an apathy which, it seems had seized the whole country.

Next morning I walked down to Horseguards, arriving there as the clock in the cupola struck nine. I was wearing civilian dress, so was ignored by the idle sentry-under-the-arms slouching in the stable archway. The entrance to the Secretary-at-War's Office was defended by a short, stout fellow in a gold-laced tricorne with a black cockade and a black redingote coat reaching almost to the ground, its heavy shoulder capes making him seem squatter and squarer than he was already; which was enough. He carried a small truncheon with a gilt crown atop it. I made to pass him but the truncheon blocked my way.

"And where d'you think you're a-goin," said he, all bristle and truculence, "and what's your business?"

His head came up to my top button. He strove to make up for that disadvantage by thrusting out his chin at me and bouncing up and down on his toes.

"My business is with Mr. Jenkinson," I said, pretty short.

My tone nettled him and his scrubby chin stuck out further.

"Ho, is it now! Well, it might be as you say, and then it might not be, all accordin'."

I was about to ask him, very plainly, what he meant, when a pleasant voice behind me said,

"May I assist you, sir?"

This was a neat little person, no taller than the guardian of the door, dressed in a brown velvet coat, red and white striped waistcoat and a small tricorne with a great brass buckle, worn well tipped forward on a high, tight-curled wig. A veritable macaroni. He bowed politely.

"Leonard Morse, sir. A senior clerk of this Department."

I returned his courtesy.

"Col. Philip Cato. Mr. Jenkinson has asked to see me."

"Ah yes, Colonel. We feared you had not received the letter since we did not see or hear from you."

"The letter was signed only seven days ago."

Morse tapped his chin with the amber top of his malacca cane and nodded.

"Ah—indeed? I fear some of our juniors are devilish idle, Colonel. However, you don't sail until the end of the month."

"And whither do I sail, pray?"

"Why, sir—Charlestown—South Carolina—" He looked surprised. "Was this not in the letter? Well—damme! This way, if you please, Colonel."

The black toadstool custodian had abandoned his defence of the door and leaned, grumbling, against a wooden booth within the entrance. Inside the booth sat an old crone in a mob-cap and shawl, looking no more pleasant than he did.

"Morning, Mrs. Fannen—'Morning, Stacey!"

Neither acknowledged Morse's greeting. It was not a good morning for them. He had done them out of screwing a shilling from me.

We crossed a small hallway, climbed a steep, curving flight of stairs and turned into a narrow passage. Here we met a sober-faced gentleman, his hands full of papers.

"Ah, Zachary, well met," said Morse. "Colonel Cato—Mr. Taylor, our Assistant Examiner of Accounts. He can discuss with you pay and allowances—entitlements for your horses and baggage—et cetera, et cetera. Meanwhile I'll inform the Secretary and Lord Germain you are arrived. His lordship asked to see you the moment you did so."

My business with Mr. Taylor did not take long. I learned early in my service not to argue with paymasters; you end by owing the Army money. Zachary Taylor had a mind like one of his ledgers; methodical, clear and exact. He had prepared a memorandum for me and explained every detail of it. I did my best to look as if I understood it; but my best was unconvincing, for he went through it all a second time. When he had finished I said,

[9]

"I'm grateful for your advice, Mr. Taylor. I don't yet know if I shall avail myself of it. I know nothing of the appointment, nor whether I shall accept it."

He smiled.

"Never mind, Colonel. We must ensure that we wring every penny piece due to you out of a niggardly Treasury. Shall we go to the Secretary?"

He halted at the door of the ante-room to the Secretary's office. His voice grated with distaste.

"His clerk is—a Mr. Boxcombe." And he bowed and left me.

Boxcombe is a former officer of Foot Guards whose acquaintance I own, but do not value. He had sold his commission on being offered this lucrative appointment in the Office of the Secretary-at-War. He was one of Lord North's relations. As he was the dullest-witted dummy they had ever suffered, the Foot Guards had eagerly assisted him to find a buyer.

Our conversation was short, to the point and one-sided. I told him I had an appointment with the Secretary and left him peering and bleating at my back as I went into the Secretary's office.

The Secretary was seated at his desk, dictating to two clerks who sat at either end of it. He looked up, frowning, but made no effort to rise or greet me.

I had not met Charles Jenkinson before and didn't like him when I did. He continued to dictate for a few minutes. The clerks seemed unconcerned by his unmannerly conduct, so I suppose it was the way he treated anyone whom he thought unworthy of his immediate notice. I took the opportunity to enjoy the view across St. James's park, with the King's new residence of Buckingham House standing at the end of the canal.

My nonchalance annoyed him. He dismissed his clerks curtly and sat at his desk eyeing me with cold dislike. I thought he could benefit from a little riling and I waved my cane airily at the open window.

"Fine view you have here, Mr. Jenkinson," I said affably.

He got to his feet. He is a smoothly elegant-looking fellow. He wore black with a chaste white frill of lace on his stock and at his cuffs and a cadogan wig neat with a black velvet bow. I thought his eyes cold, mean and calculating; jet black and heavy-lidded under thick black brows. He never blinked and his gaze never shifted from me. He has a queer, vicious twitch to his mouth when angry—as he was then, and a trick of licking his top lip with the tip of his tongue.

"And, pray, who are you, sir?"

"Colonel Cato, late of the North British Dragoons," I replied, equally short.

The angry twist of his mouth warped into a chilly smirk. I could willingly have put my cane across it.

"Ah yes—Colonel Cato." He drawled my name contemptuously. "I believe—since you disregarded the urgency of your instructions to report here—I believe the appointment we had in mind for you has been allotted to another; a Colonel Pelham—Lifeguards, I think."

Pelham—I know Percy Pelham, the old Duke of Newcastle's nephew. He served—when he felt inclined—in the Lifeguards for a few years. Then, to his distinguished Regiment's relief, he swaggered off to decorate the staff of any General, with a headquarters close to London, wishing to ingratiate himself with Percy's uncle—then the Prime Minister.

I took the letter instructing me to attend from my pocket and tossed it on the desk. "A little optimistic to ask me to report two days before the letter was signed. However, if you believe the appointment has been allotted we've no need to waste each other's time." And I picked up my hat and cane.

He could not know that Morse had told me that Germain wished to see me and that I was to sail at the end of the month. I suppose for his own self-satisfaction he thought to keep me in suspense a little. He let me get to the door before he spoke.

"Colonel Cato, one moment, please."

I opened the door, then turned to face him, looking as irritably bored as I could, which, since he still wore that ugly smirk, was not hard.

"Well?"

"Shut the door, if you please."

"Mr. Jenkinson," I said impatiently, "I'm told that Lord Germain wishes to see me at once, and that I sail to Charlestown at the end of the month. So I assume that the appointment you mention is under the direction of the Secretary for the American Colonies, and Lord Germain will be able to inform me whether it has, as you allege, been allotted to Colonel Pelham. Which, it occurs to me, by delaying your letter, you perhaps intended to achieve?"

That made him change legs. He slid smoothly round the desk and across the room, gesturing gracefully with both slim, well-manicured hands.

"Colonel, please, you have misunderstood me—" The devil I had!—and you'll note he blamed me for the "misunderstanding." "Pray come and sit down. We can discuss the appointment."

I stood my ground by the door. "What's there to discuss?"

He shrugged. "Perhaps I am misinformed—"

"How unfortunate to be both misunderstood and misinformed," I murmured.

"A common experience, I find, in dealings with lesser intellects, Colonel."

"Thank you."

The smirk crooked his mouth again.

"My dear Colonel,"—his voice something close to a purr—"I certainly didn't intend . . . But let me explain. Gen. Sir Henry Clinton—the Commander-in-Chief in the American Colonies—asked that Colonel Pelham be appointed to his staff. Naturally, I assumed that his wish in this personal matter would be acceptable to the Secretary for the American colonies. It appears I misjudged, and Lord Germain has recommended you to His Majesty as better suited for the duties Sir Henry Clinton has defined for his appointment."

"If Lord Germain's decision is so recent that you were unaware of it until now, sir, how was it that a letter was sent to me on the 6th—a week ago—instructing me to wait upon you on the 4th?"

He had his answer ready of course; with the faintest of pained expressions and the gentlest of reproachful tones.

"My dear Colonel, I do have important matters to attend to. Lord Germain asked that a list of suitable officers be compiled. I instructed that one be submitted to him and that the officers be requested to attend if required. The rest I left to my clerks, one of whom, I see, signed the letter,"—more graceful gesturing—"But I regret that they were so innattentive to their duties as to cause you inconvenience."

I'll say one thing for the Secretary-at-War. He can lie as fast as a dog can lick a dish; and every lie like truth—or near it. He smiled that twisted grimace and said,

"Well, let us have a glass of wine whilst we discuss your appointment."

"Your" appointment now, you see?—not Pelham's. You have to gallop round your corners to keep up with Mr. Jenkinson.

He sat down behind his desk—a most elegant affair of unusual, oval shape in a pale-coloured wood—and deliberately poured two glasses of wine exactly to the brim. With absolute steadiness he took one glass from the tray and, smoothly, set it down before me on the edge of the desk.

"Now, Colonel, to business." His manner was immediately brisk. "As you may know, Gen. Sir Henry Clinton has invested the port of Charlestown, the principal city of South Carolina, and is confident of seizing it shortly. He intends next to reduce the rebels throughout the southern colonies. He asked for a senior officer to be appointed to his staff to asssist in the coordination of these operations and nominated Colonel Pelham as his preference. Lord Germain is of the opinion that a senior officer of cavalry should be selected for the appointment, who could also be responsible for organizing the recruitment and training of militia cavalry and for the general direction of cavalry operations in those colonies."

"What cavalry does General Clinton have?"

"Little enough, unfortunately. A detachment of the 17th Light Dragoons and a provincial corps of cavalry and infantry—that is, they are recruited in the colonies, one of many such corps—entitled the British Legion. The Legion has provincial officers but is commanded by a Major Tarleton of the 1st Dragoon Guards. In fact he commands the whole cavalry force—about four hundred strong."

"And why is a senior officer of cavalry required to control a single major's command?"

"Exactly my question. Sir Henry is confident the fall of Charlestown will encourage loyalist elements to rally to him. He believes—and Lord Germain agrees with him—that he should be able to form two or three regiments of militia cavalry, which will need equipping and training and supervision in their support of his regular forces. Lord Germain considers the formation of these cavalry regiments to be essential to the success of the operations in the southern colonies." He leaned forward, a sudden grimness in his expression and his tone, to tap his forefinger on the desk in front of me, emphasizing each word. "Essential to the suppression of the rebellion throughout all thirteen colonies, Colonel!"

He paused and sat back. Still staring fixedly at me, he said slowly,

"His Majesty, who takes the closest interest in all such important appointments, has expressly ordered that this post must be filled by an officer of the widest experience and proven judgment."

"And you couldn't find one," I rejoined sourly. Recruiting militia and hammering them into shape for someone else to command didn't sound so attractive to me; dull louts who wanted only to come at rum, women and loot with as little effort and risk as possible. "My dear Colonel!" My self-esteem was somewhat gratified by his surprise. "You underestimate your high reputation. Lord Germain himself recommended your name strongly to His Majesty—" He broke off, suddenly appreciating from my frown that this was no welcome recommendation to any officer of the Army of my seniority.

[*13*]

The whole world knows of Germain's conduct when commanding the English cavalry at Minden. He was Lord Sackville then, only becoming Germain ten years ago, when he inherited the property of his aunt, Lady Betty Germain, and had to change his name to do so. At Minden he threw away the chance of routing the beaten French army by refusing to obey the orders of the Allied Commander-in-Chief, Prince Ferdinand of Brunswick, to charge their broken formations. Granby, second-in-command of the cavalry—I was on his staff—was furious, but could do nothing. The King—the present King's grandfather—wanted Sackville shot for cowardice, but he was never a coward. His court martial found him guilty of disobedience of orders, recommending that he was unfit to serve in any military capacity whatever; and George II ordered this finding to be entered in the Day Order Book of every Regiment in the Army. So you could ask what the devil Germain was doing, planning and ordering the strategy of the campaign in the American colonies, which was the responsibility of the Secretary for the American Department. And you could say the result confirmed the foresight of the court martial.

Jenkinson was, for a moment, at a loss for words; unusual for him, I'd think. I said,

"Who else has been considered?"

"No one—other than Pelham."

I got up and went to the window. The sun was warm on my face and all the lovely, gentle, happy sights and sounds of spring—the blaze of blossom on the trees, the patchwork of flowers in the grass, the sunlight on the water, the colour and gaiety of the crowds, the laughter of children playing below the window—all held me there.

Why should I leave this lovely country yet again on an errand like this? Most like to end fighting my own kin, long settled there; who now, it seemed, fought for those very causes for which our forbears had defied both kings and parliaments.

Jenkinson was at my elbow. "Colonel, this war has gone on too long. Opinion begins to go against it. The whole world is about our ears. The Russians and the Danes and the Swedes—and now the Dutch—are joined in armed neutrality against us to resist our search of their ships trading with our enemies. France and Spain seize our possessions. Our Navy and Army are stretched too widely around the world. The American rebels are the least of our enemies but consume too much of our strength. If we can reduce them, it will release troops and fleets to act against the French and Spanish.

"The rebels are become discouraged by their continued failures. One

[*14*]

victorious campaign in the south—which is strongly for the King—will destroy their spirit and their efforts will collapse. This is what Clinton intends. But he lacks cavalry. Without sufficient cavalry we cannot be certain of success; with it, victory is assured!"

I picked up my hat and cane.

"You shall have my answer tomorrow, sir."

His mouth was a thin, hard line. He sensed he had not succeeded in convincing me and resented it. He walked, stiff-legged, to the door and opened it.

"I am much obliged, Colonel, that you called. Pray forgive any inconvenience the delay of our letter may have caused. Mr. Boxcombe there will conduct you to Mr. Morse, who will escort you to Lord Germain's house—in Pall Mall, five minutes' walk from here, sir."

He gave me his hand, smooth, cold and firm; very suited to its owner.

"Good-day, Colonel. I shall look forward to receiving your answer tomorrow." His hand tightened on mine. "A satisfactory answer, I trust, sir."

He couldn't forgo that last, vicious, little snap. A hard, and friendless man.

Chapter Two

*In which I am taught my duty by the King
and witness the cost of being over-matched.*

Boxcombe slouched ahead of me to Morse's room. Corner-cupboard would be a more apt description of it, with its small, square, cobwebbed window, litters of papers piled in disorder on shelves, on boxes, on the desk and on the floor, and a fusty air compounded of the fragrancies of mouldering paper, burnt sealing-wax, stale snuff and the nearby privy.

Without knocking, Boxcombe stumped unceremoniously through the open door, glared at Morse—sitting with his feet on the desk, reading the *Morning Post*—grunted, swung round and pushed past me out of the door as gracelessly as he had entered.

"Charming colleague you have," I said.

Morse laughed.

"Biggest boor in London, Colonel. But a most valued colleague."

"Valued?"

"Well—valuable, to be more precise. We've a neat little cock-pit here in Horseguards, sir—in the cellars. It's no great size, so we confine our membership to friends of the Office. You must come and watch a main or two. Friend Boxcombe fondly believes he is a master of the game and a shrewd gambler. Fortunately he's neither. And, as he doesn't lack for loaves and fishes, his estimation of his own genius is yielding a few of us a tidy profit. Oh yes, a valuable colleague."

He threw down his newspaper and picking his hat off the unswept piles of paper, gave it a quick brush with his sleeve.

"Gad, the dust in here! Place never gets cleaned! That old hag, Mrs. Fannen—laziest bitch in Christendom! Well, sir, shall we shog, as Mr. Shakespeare says?—admirably expressive, don't you think? You've seen Mr. Sheridan's presentation of *The Winter's Tale* at Drury Lane? No?

Quite excellent, Colonel! 'Gad, a nice little filly that Mrs. Robinson! Played Perdita. There's a peach worth picking!—but, devil of a crowd in the orchard, what?" He winked. "According to *The Post* the Prince of Wales has plucked that fruit already, bigod! Well, no use being Prince if you can't help yourself to the pickings."

He prattled on as we pushed through the crowds along Whitehall and into Pall Mall. I lost most of what he said and there was no need to venture a word myself.

We stopped at a house about three-quarters the way along the street. I followed Morse up the steps to the door and as—still chattering—he turned to face me, he beat a tattoo on it with the head of his cane. The footman who opened it at once was fortunate not to have his eye knocked out.

"Where the devil have you been, fellow?" Morse demanded, "You've kept us waiting long enough. Now show Colonel Cato here in to his lordship. He's expecting him." He turned to me. "I'll bid you good-day, Colonel. Honoured to have made your acquaintance. Most interesting conversation. Trust we shall see you in the office again soon—" And he bowed himself backwards down the steps to the street.

The footman led me into a long, handsomely-furnished salon with windows opening onto a garden. I strolled over to a window and stared out into the garden. What could Germain add to what Jenkinson had already said? They didn't need *me*. I could name a dozen who would be glad to take my place.

Germain is not easy to get to know. The King likes and admires him, probably because his grandfather, George II, loathed him and wanted him shot. That's the way it seems to go with these Hanoverians; one monarch's friends are the next one's enemies, and vice-versa. He is not easily approached and was unpopular with the soldiers; not that he gave it a thought. He could never speak to any, nor ever showed any interest in their welfare; which is stupid in a commander. No soldier likes to fight—and maybe die—for a cold fish; even a brave, cold fish like Germain.

The trouble at Minden was that he and Prince Ferdinand had loathed and mistrusted one another. All the Army knew it. At Minden it only lost us the opportunity of destroying a beaten enemy. But, through history, such bad blood between commanders has lost battles; and not only battles. It played a great part in losing our American colonies.

Germain made his entrance—he hadn't changed that much. He is tall, about my height, but stouter, with large, strong features and bright, prominent blue eyes. He looks at you very straight—down his long nose—and speaks directly to the point in an overbearing manner. If you look as straight at him and speak as curtly you get along well enough. If you don't, he rides straight over you.

"Cato—I'm glad to see you well."

He shook my hand warmly. I had not expected so genial a greeting. We had last met at his court martial.

"You'll be wanting to discuss your appointment. Has Jenkinson informed you sufficiently?"

"He has, my lord. Why am I chosen for it in place of Pelham?"

"Because you are better suited for it. Why else? I believe you to be the best qualified of those available."

Very flattering. I said, "Are you satisfied, that sufficient volunteers will be forthcoming to form such a force of cavalry as Sir Henry requires?"

"I've no doubts on that. The majority of the colonists are loyal." He began to pace up and down the room as he spoke, his hands clasped behind him. "We must appeal to them over the heads of the agitators who are exploiting the people for their own profit. There's no bargaining with traitors, Cato. The rebel leaders' word is worthless. Look how they have forsworn their covenant to return the Convention Army—Burgoyne's troops—to New York. They've used every shabby pretext to avoid their agreed responsibilities. Those vulgar, muck-raking demagogues, Adams and Henry, and that devious fellow, Franklin—what can you expect of such rogues?"

"And what do you expect of Mr. Washington, my lord?"

"Hah! The rebels call him General now. But we hear there's many would as soon stab him in the back as pat it—dog eats dog! He's betrayed his oath and the commission he held from the King; a double-dyed traitor if there ever was one. Yet he could be useful to us if he had a mind, as some of his associates have been." The contempt in his voice was vicious. "They fear the rope if they fail, the lot of 'em!"

"There are some in the Commons who would disagree with your lordship's assessment of the situation—"

"There are damned traitors everywhere! Burke, Fox, Wilkes, Dunning—all treasonous devils! They impede the efforts of our administration, they betray the interests of their constituencies, they malign their country, they decry the successes of the Army—and all to gain power for themselves." He stopped and glared at me. "But you cannot be of their mind?"

[*18*]

"My lord, I am of a mind to serve my country as my duty requires; but not blindly or unthinkingly. I find it hard to accept that I may have to act against those of my own family who have lived in those parts for many years now. I can't believe they resist the King's authority without just cause, of which anyone who hasn't visited the country may not be aware—"

"Tcha! The very reasons why both Gen. William Howe and his brother Richard never prosecuted the war earlier with vigour. They knew the situation, was their cry, and we at Westminster had no appreciation of the difficulties of the business! Rubbish! They were protecting the interests of their friends. Don't you know the rhyme?:

> Awake, arouse Sir Billy!
> There's forage in the plain.
> Leave your little filly
> And open the campaign!

That was the truth of it. Just one year in those damned colonies and all our commanders seem struck by the palsy."

He began to stride up and down the room again.

"Take Clinton—you know him. He showed some spark when first he got there; though I know he's a difficult subordinate and Billy Howe could hardly be civil to him. But he did well enough at Bunker Hill and Rhode Island. Now he's in chief command he pokes around like some old granny gathering kindling from a stick pile.

"He says he hasn't sufficient troops for any decisive action. We send him troops—which we can ill afford—and he puts the action off until the morrow; which never comes. 'Fore God! If he devoted as much effort to action as he does to excusing his inaction he'd win that war in a six-month. He offers his resignation in every dispatch he sends. One fine day I'll surprise him by accepting it."

"And Lord Cornwallis—does he suffer from the palsy too?"

"Not him! There's another you know well—and like well too if I recall. You'll serve with him if Clinton succeeds at Charlestown. He'll have to leave Cornwallis in command in the Carolinas when he returns to headquarters in New York. That is one of the reasons I chose you, but—"

He halted and stared down at the carpet at his feet, rubbing it with the toe of his shoe. He looked at me out of the corner of his eye.

"But—you should know—the King—he mistrusts Charles Cornwallis a little. You remember Cornwallis voted in the Lords against almost every

[*19*]

measure proposed by the government against the colonies, and regularly spoke on behalf of the colonists. I could never support his arguments, but I'd never question his motives, as I would those of some who did the same. He has the highest principles and his loyalty is never in doubt. But—" he paused, "but the King is not truly an Englishman and he doesn't understand how a soldier can be loyal to his country and yet oppose the authority of the King."

"But Charles Cornwallis only voted against the government."

"True—true," the toe of his shoe dug deep into the pile of the carpet, "but—in the King's view—in the present circumstances—that is to dispute the prerogative of the King."

Alexander Popham's words came starkly to mind—"We must make our Teutonic monarch stop fumbling the levers of power."

I said—and I used the words of my great-grandfather at the time of our Civil War, which were held to be treason then and could be so now—and I could no more stop them than stop my breath—I said slowly,

"Then perhaps His Majesty should be advised that his view of his prerogative stretches beyond the limits set upon it by the people of England." I heard my voice becoming gruffer with emotion. "And that the precedents for such a view—are unhappy."

Germain stared down at the carpet in silence. Then he said very quietly,

"From my personal regard for you, Cato, I shall forget what you have just said."

He paced over to the window. His words came to me over his shoulder, curtly and, it seemed to me, with some menace.

"If you wish to serve your country you can best do so by joining Lord Cornwallis, whose opinions you seem to share in some measure. There you should learn that you have mistook both the origins of this wretched conflict and the reasons for its continuance."

I judged he was trying to bully me. I said,

"My lord, I shall not be threatened into acceptance of this appointment."

He whipped round.

"Threaten you? Good God, Cato, I'm the last person who would do that. I know I am too much in your debt. I know—I know what efforts were made to persuade some of you to say that I behaved with cowardice that day—at Minden. I know the King ordered you to state that I had shaken with fear and confusion. And you all refused. And I know too what must have befallen me had you not refused. They had a model in poor Admiral Byng."

He came across the room and gripped my shoulder.

"Cato, I do not forget my debts. Believe me a true friend, seeking only to advance your interests. I urge you to accept this appointment. I recommend you in the sincere hope that it would bring advancement—which I should be happy to recommend to His Majesty too."

Off he went again, once more round the room.

"Understand we can no longer find sufficient reinforcements in this country for Clinton. We are forced to recruit more colonists. If we fail in this we shall fail altogether. That is unthinkable."

"I've never known militia who would stand after a volley, my lord."

And, in truth, I've not known many who would stand to receive one either.

"Well, that may be true in some cases. But the militias we have there already—the provincial troops—corps like Rawdon's Volunteers of Ireland, Tarleton's Legion, Simcoe's Rangers—they are all well reported on. So perhaps they are not as poor soldiers as you think—"

I heard the door open behind me. Germain's gaze went over my shoulder, and I turned to see a large man framed in the doorway. He was a little above my height and heavily built; a few years older than me I thought. He was most elegant in a well-cut coat and knee-breeches of plum velvet. His white silk stock was tied high under his ample chins. He had a high colour, a large straight nose and his prominent, clear, blue eyes stared cheerfully and kindly. The face seemed familiar.

I looked at Germain. He was drawn stiffly upright, head bent. He said, "Your Majesty."

"Good day to you, my lord. Good day to you, sir." The words bubbled awkwardly out of the heavy-lipped mouth. "This gentleman, I suppose, is the Colonel Cato I've been waiting all morning to see—what? Thought I might run him to ground here. You've been instructing him in his duties, Germain, have you—what?"

Feet well apart and turned out, stomach leading, the King ambled, smiling, into the room; quacking away genially, for all the world like some old drake off the canal in St. James's Park. I mean this in no disrespect or derision; for though the King has his critics, I cannot believe that anyone acquainted with his natural modesty and courtesy can remain his enemy; other, of course, than that pot-bellied, lecherous little dunderhead of a son of his, who would happily see him dead. I know few men who give such an immediate impression of good-humour and kindliness. I'll own he is not the cleverest man I've ever met, but honesty and Christian principles are more than cleverness in a king. God knows, we English have had grief enough from our clever kings.

He patted Germain affectionately on the shoulder and extended a firm, plump hand to me.

"I've not had the pleasure of meeting you before, Colonel Cato. But I'm well aware of your distinguished record, sir. And how do you consider your appointment—what? A most vaulable service—most valuable, what?"

"I have not succeeded in persuading Colonel Cato to accept the appointment, Sire," said Germain.

"What? What? What's this?" The King turned on me. "Don't you understand the situation in our American colonies, sir? There are rebels, ruining and murdering my loyal subjects! My people look to me for defence against these evil men. Am I to refuse them protection, assistance, the support that is theirs by right? Am I to deny the responsibility which God and the people charged me with at my coronation? Never, sir, never—not while I live! What my people—whoever they are, wherever they are—what they ask of me they shall have. My treasure, my power, my strength, my life—it is all theirs. And they shall have it—all of it."

He may have said it all before, countless times to countless people; like any politician touting his principles of convenience from the hustings. The difference was that this man, with heart and soul, meant every word he said.

He had not finished with me. Wide-eyed, the veins on his forehead swelling, he loomed towards me, wagging a finger in my face.

"And, sir—and, sir—I look to my soldiers, especially those like yourself, with much knowledge and experience of war, to assist me in my duty to my peoples. I ask you to command them in battle against their oppressors. They are your countrymen as much as Germain and I. We are all Englishmen and proud above all else to be so! Should you not be as proud to serve them?"

He swung round on Germain.

"How is it that you cannot persuade Colonel Cato to accept this appointment? Why have you failed to convince him of its importance?—" and so on. I was not listening.

I felt suddenly and bitterly ashamed that I, an Englishman and a soldier, should need to be reminded of his duty by a German king; for so he was still regarded and resented, and not merely by those of the Jacobite

[22]

cause. My sense of shame was the sharper both because I liked him instinctively and because I knew, in my conscience, that he was right. It was my clear duty to accept the appointment. A man stands closer to his conscience than all else, and needs must live with it. So my mind was made up.

Germain's embarrassment showed clearly under the King's displeasure. I interrupted the royal tirade.

"By your leave, Sire,—his lordship has persuaded me both of the importance of the appointment and that I should accept it."

The relief and pleasure on both their faces was very satisfying to my conceit. Both wrung my hand furiously; the King with genuine pleasure and Germain with equally genuine relief. Germain had the last word.

"We place great hopes upon the moral effect of these forces you will raise, and great reliance upon the support they will give to His Majesty's cause."

I bowed and took my leave.

"Great hopes" and "great reliance"? Based on what? Guesses, promises, prejudices, opinions—and not an ounce of fact; the foundations for every politician's strategic fantasies.

Which is why the Army is forever pulling the politicians' chestnuts off the fire. We'd do better to pitch the politicians on to it.

I trudged back to Horseguards in a sombre mood. I thought I should inform the Secretary of my decision immediately, as much for my own convenience as his. I must have looked my thunderous, military worst as I strode through the yard, for even the sentry shuffled to a position of interest, if not of attention, and the doorkeeper, Stacey, leapt out of my way like a kicked cat.

"Mr. Jenkinson is a-gone, sir—some minutes ago," he ventured hesitantly, from behind the booth.

"Devil take it! Where? How long will he be?"

He grinned, delighted that his news was inconvenient.

"Well, it's all accordin'. Might be gone five minutes—and then it might be five hours—"

"Don't play the fool with me, rogue," I snapped, "Where's he gone?"

The grin faded sulkily.

"Gone to the 'ouse o' Commons. Won't be back today."

"Then where's Mr. Morse?"

A shifty look replaced the grin.

" 'Ard to say at this hour, sir—" A venal glint shone in the piggy eyes. "Might be able to find 'im for you—"

"Is he in the cock-pit?"

A long shot, but it dropped him. He disappeared, mumbling, behind the booth.

"Show me the way."

More mumbling from behind the booth.

"Come, man. Mr. Morse has invited me."

He emerged, but he was not to be hurried.

"Well, now, that's different, ain't it? If Mr. Morse invited you—that's all in order then, ain't it?"

"Just show me the way."

"Ah—can't be no 'arm in that, can there?" He thumped the side of the booth. "'Ere—Annie!" Old Mrs. Fannen came blearily out of her doze. "Annie, I'm a-conductin' this gentleman to the Treasury Office, see? Mind the door while I'm a-gone."

The crone nodded and dozed off again at once. Stacey leered at me.

"That's a good'un, ain't it? Treasury Office we calls it, the cock-pit, 'cause Mr. Morse says it's 'is best source of income. Always get a laugh from 'im."

We passed through a gloomy corridor into the yard, surprising the sentry, turned sharply through a large double door and down a flight of well-worn steps. To our left was a heavy wooden door, tight shut. Through it the sound of many voices echoed dully from the mouldering walls of the tunnel.

Stacey kicked the door.

"Open up, Danny! Got a friend for Mr. Morse 'ere."

A bolt rattled, the door creaked open a crack and a face, wrinkled and hairless—very like a gamecock's—peered out.

"Look sharp, then!" It squeaked, and we were in, with the door slamming and the bolt rattling home behind us.

The room was low and square, lit by four lanthorns hanging from the ceiling. A good two-thirds of the floor was taken up by the pit, about fifteen feet across, sunk below the level of the floor and enclosed by a solid wooden fence about two feet high.

A table and two chairs were set against the far wall; and on the table a handsome, five-branched silver candlestick, a silver inkstand with a long quill in it and a small ebony-handled silver bell. Behind the table sat the Assistant Examiner of Accounts, Zachary Taylor, the Master of the Main; eminently suited for the difficult post and obviously respected in it. Beside him, in the second chair, a wizened scribe scratched busily in a thick ledger—the match-book.

I looked about for Morse but could not see him in the crowd. The press was too great to allow me to push through it in search of him. I hoped that Stacey would find him for me.

The other occupants of that overcrowded cellar formed an amazing motley of the richest and the poorest; the noblest—in terms of rank only, you'll understand—and the meanest. A resplendent galaxy of extravagantly attired macaronis, scented handkerchiefs to their noses; other gentlemen of less exaggerated tastes, in coats of more conservative hue and chaste cut and soberly-striped waistcoats. And the rest—the ruck and refuse of the government offices, the waiters, the runners, the jockeys, the jobbers—out at elbows, split boots and broken hats; no scents or snuffs for them, but the neck of a gin bottle poking from the frayed pocket of a threadbare coat. "Friends of members of the Office" Morse had called them; and friends, doubtless, they remained whilst they had money to lose.

The blue tobacco smoke coiled thickly up to season the smudge of the flaring lanthorns. The shadows shifted and wavered in the changing light. The hubbub of shouted wagers and ribaldry deafened. And the stench—tobacco, lamp smoke, damp, spirits, chicken-dung—the steamy, sweaty stench; you could touch it.

Zachary Taylor banged a paper-weight on the table.

"Gentlemen—gentlemen, if you please—"

Silence fell.

"Before the main arranged for today we'll have a bye-match for fifty guineas a side, between Mr. Boxcombe's Black-breasted Red and Sir John Lade's Birchen Gray. Handlers—bring your charges to me directly!— You have three minutes, gentlemen!"

At once the clamour roared out again. In those next three minutes I heard as much money wagered as ever I had heard; and the greater part by the most out-of-pocket of the gamesters.

The two gamecocks were brought to Taylor, who examined each briefly against the details of the match-book and measured the silver spurs against an ivory rule. He nodded and both handlers moved to either side of the pit to await the signal to begin.

I felt a hand on my shoulder and Morse said,

"Glad to see you here, Colonel. Stacey tells me you were asking for me. Can it wait until after this match?"

"Certainly. I'm in no haste. What's your choice?"

"If anyone else but Boxcombe owned the Black-Red my money would be on it. But the clown buys expensive birds and then skimps on their

[25]

feeding. And he's got an idle rogue of a handler who cheats him. It's a good cock—one of the Knowsley strain—but it's over-big and in poor shapes for its task today. John Lade's bird has a great reputation as bloody-heeled—"

Taylor rang the silver bell briskly. The handlers clambered over the pit fence and kneeling, placed their birds down on the mat, facing one another, a couple of yards apart. They began to smoothe and fondle the birds, spitting on their fingers to wet the leather spur ties; whispering to the bird, pushing sharply towards his rival and pulling him back, enraging him to the fight.

"Ready, sir!" said Boxcombe's handler.

"Ready, sir!" said Lade's.

Taylor raised the bell slowly so that the mouth pointed upwards, poised it—and gave one sharp ring. The handlers loosed their birds.

At first the gamecocks stand motionless on the mat, gorgeous in the bright sheen of their colours, splendid in their pride and strength. There is a stillness in the room—barely the sound of men breathing—a wheezy cough.

Slowly each bird rises, stretching to its full height. It gives a throaty, menacing rattle, hunches its shoulders, shakes its head—then, up on tiptoe again, flaps its stubby, square-trimmed wings. Suddenly it crouches. The narrow head, dubbed of its comb and wattles, shoots out, like a snake's, to the full length of the lean, flexing neck with its close-shorn hackle. The sharp curve of the beak is poised like a drawn sabre. The eyes are unblinking, bright, vicious, evil. The duel begins—warily sparring, watching, dodging, measuring for the first cut—now almost beak to beak. Then—all at once—like twin puppets on their strings, they leap into the air to crash together in a whirlwind of red and grey and black and gold, with the lightning flash of the silver spurs striking and striking.

No one who has not seen two gamecocks fighting in the pit can envisage the colour and the beauty and the courage of the encounter. A tumult of sudden movement of vivid grace, more delicate and deadly than any duel between men. A duel between men plods only its formal course, through which, more often than not, both combatants can live. But in this duel-dance of death on the yellow mat one, at least, must die.

I like to watch two bantam cocks fight over their hens in the yard of my house. It is a natural act in a natural state and rarely is a bird hurt past mending. But this contest in the pit, with death the penalty for the loser, though colourful and brave, is not to my taste. So I did not enjoy the sight of the Black-Red gamecock struck down to die, its entrails staining the mat, whilst the victor strutted the pit, crowing, to the applause of its backers.

"The damnable, damned fool—" Morse, white-faced, stared down at the dead cock, cursing under his breath, oblivious to all around him.

"Over-matched," I said.

He glared at me.

"Over-matched?—of course it was over-matched! A fine, brave, honest bird—one of the best of its breed when properly matched and prepared. But try telling that to that slobbering, over-bred hogget Boxcombe. He knows better—the damned, blind fool!"

"Did you have any money on the match?" I asked.

"Oh, ay—I couldn't lose. Boxcombe owes me two hundred guineas— but I'd sooner have that poor creature alive; and that's the truth." He shrugged and turned away. "Well, let's off then. Will you come and share some cutlets and a bottle of claret with us, Colonel?"

The noise in the room rose again suddenly as the birds for the first match of the main were brought in. Morse turned to bellow at one of the soberly-dressed gentlemen.

"Edward! Come up on deck!"

I followed them up the stairs and into the yard.

"To the Lamb in the Strand," said Morse briskly, and we set off. I said, "I only wished to inform the Secretary that I had accepted the appointment."

"You have?" Morse stopped short. "Well, I'm damned! Who persuaded you? Well, perhaps I shouldn't ask. Wasn't the Secretary, I know. He was in a devil of a mood after you left. Had us all ferreting around for the records of other suitable officers."

"Did he indeed?" I said. We began to walk on again.

"Why, yes, of course. Old Poop-noddy Pelham wouldn't fit the bill—Germain wouldn't let him. We hadn't thought of anyone else. Now, Edward—" Morse took the soberly-dressed gentleman by the arm, "may I present Colonel Cato, whom we were talking about? And he is going to Charlestown, so perhaps you'll tell him what's planned for him? And, Colonel, may I present Capt. Edward Le Cras, lately commanding His Majesty's ship *Russell* and now a Commissioner of the Navy Board?"

The Captain's mahogany features cracked into a grin.

"Most convenient meeting, Colonel. Always say that cock-pit's a better place for business than any damned government office."

We arrived at the chop-house and sat round one end of a long, well-scrubbed table. Morse ordered the cutlets and claret.

"Well now," said Le Cras, "you'll take passage aboard the transport *Union*. The master is William Willis—good man. She joins the convoy at Spithead at the end of the month. The agent of the Navy Board at Portsmouth is a Lieutenant Parrey. Call at his office. If you can let me have a note of your needs I'll see he gets it. You'd do best to arrive in Portsmouth not later than the twenty-sixth of the month—gives you twelve clear days."

"I'm obliged, sir," I said. "I'll call on Lieutenant Parrey on the afternoon of the twenty-sixth. Do you happen to know whether the *Union* has good accommodation below decks for four horses?"

"I think not, Colonel. She's new built and roomly enough, but she's less height than most between decks. I'll make a note for Parrey on it."

"Very grateful, Captain." I turned to Morse. "Tell me, had Mr. Jenkinson not considered anyone else for this appointment other than Colonel Pelham and myself?"

"Never considered anyone but Pelham, Colonel, until he was told to invite you to come to London."

"By Lord Germain?"

"Well—matter of fact—it was the King who ordered it—about three weeks ago. Though I believe it was at Germain's instance."

"And Lord Germain asked for a list of other suitable officers?"

"A list?—no. That was the cause of all the trouble this morning after you'd left. Yours was the only name Germain gave."

"I see," I said. "But, if Mr. Jenkinson was instructed to write to me three weeks ago—why was no letter sent to me until seven days ago?"

Morse stared at me, straight-faced. "Perhaps Mr. Jenkinson forgot, sir."

"Perhaps. Who reminded him?"

The corner of his mouth twitched. "I made Boxcombe do that. Took him nearly a week to stop shaking after the Secretary had—er—thanked him."

"But why should the Secretary not wish me to take the appointment, Mr. Morse? He was doing his best to persuade me to it this morning."

Morse shrugged. "Well, as to that—it's hard to say." He began to scrape the bone of his cutlet slowly and meticulously. "He's not a man of any great personal means or influence, y'know. And the Pelhams have both—oh, very much of both—being related to the Newcastles. And Clinton being related to them too—perhaps our Mr. Jenkinson wasn't too averse to obliging that combination. He could only gain from it."

Le Cras wiped his mouth. "And what's Clinton going to say when he hears he's got the Colonel instead of Pelham?"

"Perhaps you will be good enough to inform me, Colonel?" Morse was even straighter-faced. "So that I can tell Mr. Jenkinson."

I got to my feet. "Mr. Morse, I'm most grateful for all your assistance—and my cutlets. Will you acquaint Mr. Jenkinson with my acceptance of the appointment?"

"A pleasure, Colonel, a pleasure I do assure you!" He sprung to his feet and wrung my hand warmly. "God speed! Leave the Secretary to me. We'll look forward to your triumphant return! God speed!—"

I took leave of them—with Morse still talking—and made my way down the Strand considering dispassionately the chances of my possible return, let alone a triumphant one. But at least, in the meantime, my encounter with Gen. Sir Henry Clinton should prove of interest.

Chapter Three

*In which I am instructed in politics and military
victualling, say farewell to my family and am acquainted
with a rank villain.*

I arrived back at the Pophams in a foul mood. Georgina saw this and, in
no time, sat me down, fed me China tea, and had my troubles out on the
carpet. I am no admirer of women as logicians, but sometimes, in their
own way—and God knows what that is—they arrive at the best answer, if
not the right one, quicker than clever men. She soon coaxed me into the
conviction that I had taken the best possible decision in the most vexing
circumstances.

Alexander arrived home a little before eleven, accompanied by John
Dunning. Alexander was in a worse mood than I had been.

"Beat, Georgie!—we were beat! Yesterday we had 'em scampering like
the rabbits they are. But North and Jenkinson have been at it, offering a
place here, a pension there—or the loss of either—and the rats leave the ship
in droves! It was merely an extension of John's motion against the influence
of the Crown that we won last week. But, we were beat." He slumped
into a chair, his head in his hands. "God knows what we can do. God
knows how we can rid ourselves of this Hanoverian hog-grubber and his
herd. He's made a eunuch of this Parliament. Can't generate anything but
wind and piss!"

Dunning smiled at Georgie and poured Alexander a large glass of claret.

"Here, Alex, this will improve matters." He turned to me. "Well,
Colonel, that's our news. What's yours, sir?"

"I sail at the end of this month to Charlestown in South Carolina, to join
General Clinton's staff."

"His Majesty called you to London to tell you that?"

"I am to raise and train cavalry militias from the colonists."

"Aha! So important is the recruitment of colonial corps become! Alexander, there is hope for us in this news."

"How so?" I asked.

"It can only mean, Colonel, that we can no longer find sufficient recruits for the Army in this country, which in turn could mean that we are closer than I thought to ending a war which should never have begun. You wonder why there is hope in that? Because, sir, the worse things become in the American colonies the quicker this administration will fall. And with the government will go the influence of the King."

"Do you not think you might, to some degree, be misjudging the King?"

Dunning's eyebrows rose.

"I see His Majesty has the same effect on you as he has on most, Colonel. Oh, I'll agree he probably means well and does all with a good conscience. But he is the tool of his mother and, worse, of his tutelary genius, John Stuart of Bute—whom some say is his mother's bed-mate, though I doubt that Caledonian pedlar is still capable of sustaining that service for Her Majesty. And then there's others who hope to profit from the King's favours."

"And you think it's impossible that some of those others act in good conscience too?—and believe that they serve the country as well as you might?"

Dunning's eyebrows rose higher still.

"Colonel Cato! Where would be the purpose in continuing in politics if I thought those who hold office today to be infallible?" He laughed. "Oh, there are some men of principle among them of course, though misguided. Germain, for instance, he has nothing to gain or lose. But then he's unsuited to politics. He is too direct, too straightforward, too dogmatic. It's his military training, I suppose!"

And he smiled disarmingly, sensing my rising ill-humour. But I was not to be put off my too direct, too straightforward, too dogmatic military course.

"And for your own personal advantage, you and your friends wish to see this war lost?"

"Don't be a damned fool, Philip," said Alexander, from the depths of his chair and his glass. That did it. I had had my fill of political polemics for the day and Dunning's slighting reference to soldiers infuriated me in my present circumstances.

"Thank you for the compliment, Alexander," I said, in a cold rage.

"From a politician, I count it as a compliment. As for you, Mr. Dunning, I take it that it matters not a whit to you and your friends how many of us damned fools of direct, straightforward, dogmatic soldiers die in the losing of this war so long as it ensures that you are returned to power to run this wretched country with the same blind, selfish stupidity with which you claim it is governed now."

Alexander sat, gaping and goggle-eyed, the wine spilling unheeded over his waistcoat. Dunning's face was chalk-white. He said haltingly, "Colonel Cato—I had no intent—to offend you, sir—forgive me." He was silent for a moment, then, in a voice stronger but still a little strained, "Sir, my friends and I wish to see this war with the colonists over. We wish to see a friendly and profitable association re-established between us. And we wish to see the government of England where it belongs—in the hands of the people."

He took a deep breath, then struck his fist into his palm.

"The war in America is being fought to establish autocracy—the supreme authority of the King and his faction over the colonies! Such a cause is barren and futile and suicidal and should be brought to an end now. Thereafter we should defend our countrymen in the Americas, whether they be colonists or no, to let them grow in peace until they become strong enough to join us willingly as our allies in that new world against all who seek to harm either of us there."

He paused and shook his head slowly.

"The first steps along this path will be painful and expensive. An admission that what we do now in America is wrong—wrong in constitutional law and in moral purpose. And entirely wrong if we were only trying to advance our own material interests! It may entail a difficult and dangerous withdrawal of our forces from those shores. It will certainly mean abandonment of our supporters in the colonies—for which they will justly condemn us. All those steps are painful. But I fear they must all be taken."

He stopped. Then, hesitant again,

"Colonel—I beg you to believe me—it is our chiefest—our deepest regret—that you—and many other brave men besides—should need to expose yourselves to danger—"

"No—oh, no—" Georgina burst into tears, ran to me and flung her arms tight around my neck, shaking with sobs. "You'll come safe home, Philip, won't you? You'll come home—"

I am very fond of Georgina, and I thought I knew her well; and this display of untypical emotion took me entirely by surprise. But I'm always being surprised by women's reactions. I held her close, thinking,

"Now where's the elegant, poised, exquisite, witty Georgina Popham—?"

And there she was—a little girl—sobbing her heart out on my shoulder. I was hard put to it to find words.

"I'll come safe home, Georgie,—I always do—" Not very clever, and not very effective either, for she still sobbed.

Alexander put his arm around his wife and pulled her gently away. He kissed her and patted her cheek.

"Georgie, my dearest, don't distress yourself. All will be well. The war may be over before Philip arrives! All *will* be well—"

Georgina tore herself free and struck him in the chest with her fist.

"All will be well? All will be well? Is that all you can say?" Now she was raging—and looking very fine in her fury. "You—you—politicians! You sicken me with your preachings! You—and John there—and the rest of you—you talk, talk, talk! No one is as clever as you—no one knows as much as you—no one is ever as right as you—never! And you never stop telling us so—all the time! But when something has to be done, something set right, what do you do? You send for the soldiers, men like Philip, to right it. They have to get us out of the mess your stupidity has blundered us into—in their too-direct, straightforward way! And when they die—" her voice choked, "—and when they die in battle—or of the fever—and their widows are left to weep—what do you do? You cluck 'How sad,' then turn your backs and go on talking, talking, talking. You—you hypocrites! You're all too cowardly to do aught yourselves! Cowards!"

Hands to her face, she ran out of the room.

Alexander was stupefied.

"What—what in Heaven's name ails her? For God's sake, Philip, what have you told her? Are you sent on some especially dangerous mission?"

He did not wait for an answer, but followed Georgina.

I turned back to Dunning.

"Mr. Dunning, you say you wish to see this war over—but not lost—and you hope to see us win trade and empire. Yet you would abandon our possessions in the Americas—and all our friends there, too, by God! Is that the way to win the war and trade and empire?"

He smiled sadly.

"Colonel, I said too that this war should never have been. It was always unnecessary. Had men of good-will on either side discussed our differences together, I am convinced it would never have occurred. Had we listened to honourable and far-sighted men like Mr. Franklin, had the King recognized and rewarded him and other gentlemen distinguished by their services—Mr. Philip Livingston in New York—Colonel Washington in Virginia—Mr. John Rutledge in Charlestown—" He sighed and shook his head, "But all that's past—and lost."

He turned and, leaning both hands on the chimney-piece, stared into the fire.

"Now all we can do, as Georgina says, is to ask the soldiers to set matters right—in their own way."

"And if we do not win?"

"No one can win now, Colonel. Both sides have already lost more than they can afford. The French and Spaniards are the only gainers."

"So, from the outset, some in authority never wished to win this war?"

Dunnning shrugged.

"Fairer to say they never wished to have it."

I was suddenly tired of Mr. Dunning and his politics. I said,

"I have a long ride tomorrow, sir, and start early. Pray excuse me."

Dunning took my hand in both his. He said quietly,

"God speed you, Colonel, and bring you safe home. For when this war is done we shall need all the good soldiers we have; to requite ourselves with France for all the evil they do us now, throughout the whole world."

Pleasant to be told that you are both a good soldier and needed. But who believes politicians?

I was up and away early the next morning. I left a note for Georgina and an armful of spring flowers I had bought in Piccadilly. I rode that day as far as the White Hart in Whitchurch, and on the morrow to Dinton, five miles west of Salisbury, where Anne's cousin, William Wyndham, lives; so that I arrived home on the afternoon of Sunday the 16th April.

God knows how fortunate I count myself to have such a wife as my beloved Anne. You might, with good reason, have thought that the week of preparation would for her have been a time of tears and regrets. It was never so. She made it a time of laughter and gaiety. Of busy sewings and launderings and stitchings and pressings; of preserving and packing food and wine into hampers to relieve the dullness—and foulness—of food on board ship. She had the whole household washing and polishing and waxing and greasing—with the children all running errands on their ponies—to have all ready in time.

She had friends come in to dine or sup, and stay to sing and dance and drink and laugh with us. The days—the few days—passed too quickly, and all the time she was smiling and loving; and I marvelled at it. Until one night I woke to hear her sobbing—oh, so quietly—beside me, her face buried in her pillow so that I should not be disturbed. And, as I lay there, holding her in my arms, I cursed the war, I cursed the King, the government, the rebels and any and everything that took her from me, until she kissed me into silence. Men have said that I was brave in battle—that's no boast, what profit is there in boasting at my age?—but I would God I possessed but a part of her steady fortitude and loving spirit. Oh, it's easy for those who go to the wars: the pain is theirs who sit and wait at home.

I was not alone in damning the eyes of all who would take me from my love and home. There was Matthew Ryan, my soldier-servant, who had stayed with me after I had left the Regiment. He had taught my five sons to ride, and to shoot straighter with a fowling piece than ever I could. He had taught them to take all manner of game and fish—sometimes by means of which I did not entirely approve. He had taught them to drive the gig—much to their mother's alarm. And he had taught them the songs of all countries in which he and I had soldiered together, playing them on the little guitar he had come by serving with me.

He and Kitty—Katharine Dowsett—Anne's maid, had been very close and loving a while before our departure. So there were two of us damning all eyes.

I had arranged for the heavy baggage to go by cart earlier; to wait at Portsmouth until I arrived there with Matthew on the 26th with two led horses carrying the rest of it. Then all—cart, our hacks and led horses—could be brought home together. For I have long decided never to take my own horses on shipboard unless they have good accommodation and proper head-room; else, on a long voyage, the poor beasts stand crouched, barely able to move, wasting to sacks of bones in foetid holds.

We left on the Monday morning, and I can scarce bear to recall those moments even now. The noise and bustle of the past week were gone. All was prepared, all was packed. Naught remained but to get on our horses and ride off to war. Anne and the children stood on the front steps—all brave still, but the tears were there openly now. Matthew and I were in uniform for the first time for a long while, so I suppose we looked gallant enough, but, God's life, that's not how we felt.

Our farewells done—Kitty clung to Matthew as long and as close as Anne to me—we mounted and rode off with the children running beside us, holding on to our stirrup leathers, shouting and laughing in excitement. God bless them, they had no real understanding of what my departure could mean for them. They were happy and gay and, at that moment, that was all that mattered to me. Friends and village folk had gathered at the gates to wish us God-speed. They shouted pleasantries— not all of them polite—which eased the moment. And away up the London road we went.

As we climbed the hill on the far side of the valley we looked back at the house, rising above the trees. Everyone stood on the lawn, waiting for us to reappear, and they all waved and we heard them shouting. Then we were over the crest of the hill—and they were gone.

For some time we rode on in silence, full of our own thoughts. But before we reached Crewkerne, Matthew had recovered his spirits enough to draw out his guitar and begin to sing. No foreign songs now, only good English ballads—and an Irish one about a "fair Kitty".

We rode through Yeovil and Sherborne and Milborne Port to Shaftesbury, where we put up at the Grosvenor Arms in the High Street. Mr. Jeremiah Miles, the landlord, is a good, honest soul, well-known to me from many such journeyings. When we left, early next morning, he gave me a bottle of the light Rhenish wine, wrapped in a wet cloth to keep it cool, to wash the chalk dust out of our throats wherever we dined on the way. For it was warm and dry that spring and the chalk dust on the Dorset and Wiltshire roads rises easily in the air and hangs long in it.

We came out of Shaftesbury by the turnpike on the valley road, climbed Whitesheet Hill, over Swallowcliffe Down, past Fovant Hutt, cursing the London coach as it rumbled by in clouds of white dust, past Wilton, watching the spire of Salisbury cathedral rise gloriously against the green banks of Old Sarum and Castle Hill, and down Harnham Hill into Salisbury. Salisbury is one of my favourite towns, but we had no time to dwell in it and rode out along Castle Street and by Stockbridge to Winchester.

Here we put up in the George in the High Street, travelling on the next morning through Farham and Cosham and the fort beyond, down the hill to Hilsey and Portsey and so into Portsmouth. And as we descended the hill we saw, stretched out before us across the shining waters of Spithead, the spring convoy, forming for the passage to America.

As we drew down to the docks, the light breeze off the sea carried the sound of drums, the cries of men working on the lighters and in the rigging of the ships at the quayside, the rumble of the casks rolling over the cobbles and of guns being run out at drill, the clatter of the hooves of the horses pulling wagon-loads of stores and of troop horses moving to board the transports, and now and again, through the medley of discords, the eerie shrill of a boatswain's pipe. The same breeze carried the smells of the dockyards to us; the rankness of fresh paint, the acrid stink of pitch and the wood smoke from the braziers on which the great kettles fumed, the bitter reek of white-hot iron in the smithies, the redolence of woods, the pungent mustiness of new cordage, and, spicing it all, the brackish tang of the sea. Craft of every shape and size crossed and re-crossed the crowded spaces between the ships, which were in every state of preparedness. Some were bright with new paint and metal work gleaming in the sun; others showed patched and stained canvas, cordage hanging disordered, their upperworks scarred by storm and shot. On every side there was activity and bustle.

The office of the representative of the Navy Board was easy to find, but desperate difficult to arrive at. The whole of Portsmouth appeared to be seeking it. I dismounted at the door and told Matthew to lead all off to the nearest inn and wait for me there.

To my relief, most of those crowding in the doorway only sought to speak with the clerks in the large offices on both sides of the entrance hall. I walked the length of the hall and through a door leading into a long passage, running the length of the building, with doors leading off it at intervals. The question of which of the many doors to try was made up for me by the sound of angry voices. One voice thundered above the rest:

"Mr. Fish, I don't give a damn where you get your men! Lock-ups, gin-kens, whore-shops—where in hell you will. But don't press any more men from the transports, or we'll have no crews to man the bloody convoy. You know as well as I do they're mostly protected men. I could have you broken for taking them. And, by God, I *will* have those buttons off your cuff if I have another complaint against you!"

A low, hoarse voice began to answer, mainly with obscenities, but was cut short by the first voice.

"Out of here you sodden, gotch-gutted gowk—out! And take your rabble of toss-pots with you! Now—OUT!"

The door flung open and a half-dozen burly louts in sailor's dress surged towards me, led by as gross and evil-looking a rogue as ever I've seen. They brushed past me, grumbling among themselves, and swept out into the main hall.

I looked into the office from which they had come. I expected to see a giant form capable of producing the stentorian roar which had quelled and overawed the surly crew I had met in the passage. At a table by the window sat a scrimpy little scrog of a man in the faded uniform of a lieutenant of the Navy, a size too large for his narrow shoulders. He looked up. His one bright, blue eye glared at me. The eyelid of the other eye was stitched closed by the livid tear of a scar running from under the front of his balding scratch-wig across his forehead and eye down to the point of his jaw.

He leapt to his feet. "Colonel Cato?"

"Yes. You are Lieutenant Parrey?"

"The same, sir! Forgive your reception. Usual trouble with the press-gangs. All damned crimps should be hanged at birth—'specially that gang of hell-kites. Wretched transports—arrive here with a bare minimum of hands—lose half to His Majesty's ships through the tender care of those boozing body-snatchers! Now—" He shuffled a mass of documents around on the table. "Where's that paper?" He shuffled some more. "Had it this morning—from Captain Le Cras—put it in a safe place so's not to lose it, damn it!" He sighed, defeated. "Well, anyway, Colonel, Mr. Willis awaits you aboard the *Union*. He's got places for you and one soldier. And there's something about four horses—but you might not be taking them?"

"I shan't be."

"Ah—room for some remounts for the 17th Dragoons." And he made a note on a bill of lading he found in the pile. "So much damned paper round here nowadays! Y'see, Navy Board controls victualling to the American colonies now. Treasury used to do it, and o'course, right damnation muck they made of it! Provisioning yards moved here from Cork. So now we've got the local crafty downies to deal with. Shifts and dodges they get up to!"

He threw himself back in his chair, waved at a broken one for me, grinned misshapenly—only one side of his face moving—and poured a couple of glasses of tawny liquid from a stone jug.

"Will you bring your arse to anchor then, Colonel? An' you'll take a little rumbo to fumigate your pipes, I'm sure?"

I wasn't sure, but I did; and wished I hadn't. Parrey sank his dose in one, with all the euphony of a well-scoured drain, and gave a gusty sigh.

" 'S'better! You'd never believe it, Colonel. Condemned a load of beef this morning—agent's—name o'Dawkins—sharp bastard. All in good, sound casks it was. 'Open up a couple,' I says. 'Surely that's not necessary, Mr. Parrey,' says he. 'You can see they're all well packed. You don't pack rubbish like that.' 'I'll have a look anyways,' I says. Sure enough, it was all bloody shin and marrow-bones! Bigod, I give it him!

'You know the terms of the provision contract for beef, Mr. Dawkins,' I says, 'Where's your thirty pieces each of seven pounds weight, making two hundred and ten pounds of good sound meat in all per cask?' 'You struck on bad casks, Mr. Parrey,' says he. 'Right,' I says, 'I've forgot what good, sound meat looks like. Let's have a sight of some,' I says, 'Open 'em all up!' He looked at me! Blood and 'ounds!—thought he'd cooper me up with the marrow-bones!"

He stared through the dirty window at his elbow, his eye suddenly blazing like a port-fire, his face tautening in a hideous grimace. He jumped to his feet, flung open the window and delivered a devastating broadside.

"Mr. Dawkins! Get your shiftless, scuffle-hunting doddy-polls to move your damned carrion before I turn you into some yourself!" He slammed the window shut, but grumbled on. "Fine thorough-going churchman he'd make!—in through the north door and out through the south without stopping—'cept to screw the bloody alms-box!"

"Are all contractors so dishonest?" I asked.

"No, not all. Most of 'em try it on at first, and if they're caught out deal pretty square thereafter. If they don't—they're out. It's their agents I blame—like that Dawkins; got more to gain—less to lose. So they're always out to make."

He got to his feet again, poured and drained another glass from the stone jug in quick time, rammed his hat on and snatched up a heavy ebony cane topped with a large and battered silver knob.

"Now, Colonel, let's get—" His gaze went past me to the window. "'Od's belly and bones!—look at yon gallows-cheating by-blow!" The window screeched open once more. "Mis-ter Daw-kins! 'f ye can't make your caudge-pawed brothel-bravos move your bloody casks faster than that I'll batten ye down in one, bung up!" The window banged down and he turned and bustled through the door, snarling in his throat like a terrier in a fox-earth.

We went out through the crowded outer office very much faster than I came in. Lieutenant Parrey used his cane freely and indiscriminately on any who stood in his way, and all who suffered from it were either too surprised or too horrified by his expression to retaliate. We collected Matthew from a nearby inn and plunged into the thronging mass of soldiers, seamen, carters, porters, labourers, beggars, whores and hucksters all busily pushing every way like ants in a broken nest. In the wake of Parrey's flailing cane, Matthew and I, leading our horses, found the crowd parted like the waters of the sea before the children of Israel, until we came to where the *Union* lay. The way was rough and tortuous, the noise was stunning and the stench—even the horses coughed.

Aboard the *Union*, I went with Parrey to the after-cabin to meet the master.

Mr. Willis is of middling height, broad and barrel-chested, but quick and neat in all his movements, and with an easy, confident air of command. He wore his own hair tied back in a small queue and dark blue coat and breeches cut in uniform fashion and bound with black braid. His naval-style tricorne, with its black cockade, was similarly bound with braid. All very smart and workmanlike.

The *Union* was a neat, smart, well-ordered and shipshape barque. All was scrubbed clean, polished or fresh-painted. The hands went about their duties in a lively fashion and whistled and sang at their work.

Mr. Willis was studying a lading plan when we entered, but at once came forward to greet us.

"Colonel Cato? Welcome aboard, sir, and you too, Mr. Parrey. Your baggage being properly attended to, Colonel?"

"Yes, sir, thank you."

"Good—and your horses, sir?"

"I'll not be shipping them, Mr. Willis."

"Well, there's space for deck cargo then, Mr. Parrey. Have you anything for me?"

Parrey nodded.

"Four remounts for the 17th Dragoons."

"Well, let's have them aboard today, if you please, Mr. Parrey. You'll send a couple of soldiers to mind them, I suppose? And extra rations?"

"Be on board this afternoon, Mr. Willis. You know *Mercury* and *Northampton* and you are to pull out on the afternoon tide tomorrow to take station in convoy? Good. Escorts are expected tomorrow—*Centurion* and three frigates. Wish you an easy passage, gentlemen! Good fortune in the wars, Colonel!"

Willis returned to his lading plan and I went to examine my own quarters. It was a cabin, perhaps six feet by eight, with a bunk set upon a sort of chest of drawers at one end. I could not stand upright in most of it, which was a vexing inconvenience. It was lit by a small window, set high up in the bulkhead at the foot of the bunk, overlooking the deck amidships; and by a lantern, secured to one of the two beams supporting the deck, which formed my ceiling.

On shipboard I invariably strike my head against beams like these with such painful and depressing frequency, that I take to wearing my military wig in my cabin to save my skull. I am not fond of wigs on campaign, I find them a time-wasting hindrance; apart from becoming filthy and verminous. However, for the next six weeks, I was grateful for it.

My quarters were luxurious compared with those of the five other officers travelling aboard the *Union*, so I had no cause to complain. Matthew had already begun to arrange my things and had secured the miniature of Anne, which travels with me wherever I go, to the bulkhead beside the bunk. At that moment I found this of especial comfort.

I was happy to find that the accommodation in which Matthew and all other rank and file lived was well-planned and far better than I had seen before. The Master's sense of good order was apparent there as elsewhere in his ship. We ask too much of our soldiers to allow them to be treated like cattle for the profit of a few tight-fisted ship-owners, in ships more suited as slavers than as transports for His Majesty's troops. That evening, unheedful of the rattling and thumping and rumbling and shouting and chanting which accompanied the loading of various stores aboard, I was writing a letter to Anne, the last she would receive from me for at least five months, when Mr. Willis knocked on my door.

"Will you be joining us for some supper in the after-cabin, Colonel? I like my mate and myself to meet together with all our guests as often as possible—makes for company and variety—and mealtimes are the best for it. But if you prefer to have your meals in your cabin, sir, that can be arranged."

I put my pen aside.

"I'm not so solitary in my preferences, Mr. Willis. I'll be honoured to join you."

The after-cabin was plainly but comfortably appointed. The other officers were already seated at table with Mr. Fellowes, the mate; a great, solidly built man, rarely smiling but imperturbable and, for all his bulk, as nimble as a cat.

They had all risen as we came in, and now stood in that courteous but critical silence in which junior officers receive senior officers strange to them.

I dislike undue formality in any mess and am ever quick to dispense with it. I smiled, bowed and said,

"Good evening, gentlemen," I was still in uniform, as they were themselves, "My name is Philip Cato. May I ask yours?"

The senior of the four, a major of the 33rd Foot, a tall, erect, red-faced, paunchy fellow with a smiling face, bowed first,

"John Conyngham, Colonel, rejoining my Regiment."

A Captain of the 71st Highlanders was next. Short, slight, dark, also very erect with head held well back, his black eyes—a touch hostile, a touch contemptuous—very steady in their proud gaze over a nose like a hawk's beak. He gave the shadow of an inclination of his head.

"James Macdonell of Keppoch."

My service has chanced to bring me into contact more than most with these Highlanders. They are brave and prickly prideful for their honour, which makes them good soldiers in battle; and these qualities must be recognized if you will have them for friends. I said,

"I am well acquainted with the high reputation of the Clan Donald."

I used the word "clan," though it is still illegal to do so. It had its effect. Macdonell's head bowed courteously this time.

"I take reinforcements to my Regiment, Colonel."

The ensign of the 71st Highlanders standing beside Macdonell represented the popular concept of a Highlander. A tall, ruddy-faced, broad-shouldered lad, with the brightest blue eyes under a fair thatch. His square, raw-boned hands fumbled his belt as he ducked his head shyly,

"Alexander Fraser—I'm with Captain Macdonell, sir."

The last of the four was a surgeon. A neat, precise, young man with the air of cheerful confidence that Army surgeons customarily possess; and need. He wore the facings of the 76th Foot.

"James Hawkins, surgeon to the 76th, Colonel,"—with more of a nod than a bow, but a beaming smile to go with it.

We sat down and set to. The food was good, plain stuff, well cooked and well served.

"I was told there would be five other officers," I said, "Whom do we lack?"

"Charles Russell of the 17th Dragoons, Colonel," answered the surgeon, "He's taking reinforcements to his Regiment. Unfortunately, he took too much brandy and then too many liberties with a young lady of this town, the daughter of an Excise officer—and they reckon to represent God in Portsmouth. In reward, the Provost Marshal set him in charge of three deserters from another corps aboard a ship of the convoy which has already put out."

"What was Charles' piece like?" asked Conyngham.

"Charlie said she's as much a maid as her mother, and even more ready to tumble than he was—that's unbelievable—and most nimble in the hips. But when her ma found her with Charlie playing a paradiddle on her kettle-drums she started to bawl she was misused, the silly giglet."

We all laughed, but I noted that Alexander Fraser's prominent ears grew very red.

[*42*]

I retired early after supper, but was soon awakened by an uproar on deck. I looked out of the little window at the foot of my bunk.

In the unsteady glare of the lanterns lighting the deck amidships, a few yards distant with his back to me, stood a tall officer, feet apart, hands on hips, a short, heavy-headed cutting whip in one fist.

Opposite him, in manacles and leg-irons, restrained by six troopers, I made out three dishevelled creatures, their breeches, leggings and shoes identifying them as soldiers, though they wore no jackets. One hung limply in the grasp of his guard, as if exhausted and in pain.

"Now, my beauties," said the officer cheerfully, "We've had enough fun getting you aboard, but now you'd best give over. There's food and water below and your accommodation is better than mine, I promise you. Behave fair and you'll be treated fair. Take 'em below, Sergeant Hawes."

As they began to move, the exhausted man stumbled in his leg-irons and fell to his knees. His guards helped him to his feet, relaxing their hold to relieve him. Suddenly he thrashed his hands from side to side, striking both guards in the face with his manacles so that they staggered back, loosing him altogether. Snatching up the chain of his leg-irons, he ran awkwardly to the head of the gangway. The officer grabbed him, but the man, clenching his fists together, struck him full in the face with the cuffs, knocking him to the deck. The fugitive began to clamber down the gangway, but his leg-chain caught in the decking and, for a moment, he bent, struggling to release it. As he straightened, the officer, his face streaming blood, was on him. The man struck at him again with his manacles, but missed. He overbalanced and, as he did so, the officer brought the head of his whip down hard across the side of his face. The man toppled backwards down the gangway, rolled under the rail and fell, screaming, into the narrow space between the ship and the quay. The splash cut off the scream.

There was no help possible—the heavy chains saw to that. All stood spell-bound by the horror. Then, one of the two remaining prisoners, a huge fellow, bigger than either of his guards, broke out raving and swearing at the officer.

"You bastard, you killed 'im! I saw you. You murdered 'im!"

"Gag him," ordered the officer, curtly.

A wooden peg was thrust into the man's mouth and secured by a cord round his head. He still mumbled and groaned and, suddenly exerting all his considerable strength, heaved himself free from his guards and hurled himself at the officer. Both crashed to the deck, rolling over and over.

Feet rattled down the ladder beside my window. The mate, a belaying pin swinging from his hand, ran across to the struggling forms and ended the fight with one terrific blow on the man's head. He helped the officer to his feet and picked up his hat.

"Lord bless you, Mr. Russell, you was having some uncommon pretty milling with your friend there!"

"Much obliged, Mr. Fellowes," said Russell, brushing himself off, "but we were just beginning to enjoy ourselves."

"Seen that poor sod fall from the gangplank," said the mate, "Naught anyone could do for him."

"Don't waste your pity," Russell mopped his face tenderly and twisted his head from side to side, grimacing with pain. "Raped some threepenny-upright and took her earnings. When she began to howl he strangled her. And when her pimp came running, he stabbed him. No loss." He looked at the inert mass at his feet. "Nor would this one be either."

The troopers threw water over the big man and dragged him to his feet. His head rolled sluggishly until they jerked his head back by his hair. His eyes came open slowly. Russell and he were face to face, a yard apart. The man spat, fouling the officer's jacket.

"Cook," said Russell, unmoved and unmoving, his voice as cold as ice, "Cook, we'll have the fat off your back ribs for that. We'll cook you, Master Cook."

Chapter Four

*In which a self-styled rebel introduces me to true
beauty, I attend a punishment and our cause
is put in question.*

I did not sleep easily that night and so overslept. I entered the after-cabin
to breakfast late and found myself alone with Lieutenant Russell. His face
was one large bruise and he had one hand in bandages. He got to his feet,
bowed, introduced himself and added cheerfully,

"Forgive my appearance, Colonel. Had a little trouble with some
deserters."

"I saw it."

"Oh—well—it was unfortunate. But he was a murderer, Colonel, and
was resisting arrest."

"It certainly wasn't your fault, Mr. Russell. No trace of him, I
suppose?"

"No, sir. They say there won't be even at low tide." He sounded
relieved. "But the Provost Marshal's clerk forgot to have me sign for the
irons on the man, so they say they'll have to fish him up. Trust the
Ordnance Board—"

"How's that man Cook?"

Russell grimaced.

"He's survived that tap Mr. Fellowes gave him."

"And what will you do with him?"

"Five hundred lashes, Colonel—with your permission."

There was no emotion in his voice; his decision was a matter of course.

"I see," I said. "Well, do as you see fit; he's your man. You'll have to ask
the Master's permission if the punishment is to be carried out on board."

I sounded tolerably discouraging. To use the lash on a common villain
to discourage him from further villainy is acceptable. But to use it on a

soldier or sailor degrades him to a common villain, whilst still demanding that he be prepared to die fighting courageously for the authority which flogged him. No discipline induced by fear and brutality ever withstood the serverest test in battle. I said,

"Hasn't he done enough for a court martial to give him a hempen halter?"

"Nothing I'd like better, Colonel. But the magistrates ordered him to be delivered to his regiment."

"What have the magistrates to do with deserters?"

"Well, a few nights ago, Cook found an old hag in some back street selling pies. He took her money—fourpence. She ran after him, screaming, so he struck her—killed her. The watch arrested him, after a bit of a battle. Drunk, of course."

"In God's name! Why weren't he and the monster who murdered the whore not hanged then and there?"

"Oh, the magistrates thought they should save themselves the expense of keeping them until the assizes by ordering the Provost Marshal to get them to their regiments. The damned old hypocrites blethered piously that they hoped they would make into good soldiers—if their regiments didn't hang 'em first. They didn't appear to think the Spithead fairy and her free-holder and the old pie-vendor much of a loss."

"And what of the other one, the small man? Is he another murderer?"

"Crowder? Oh, no. He's a sneak-thief, a pickpocket and a sharper. Quick with his fingers, his tongue and a pack of cards. He'll give no trouble."

Matthew came in and whispered to me at the top of his voice.

"There's a gentleman asking for to see your honour. Says he's a cousin of yours—not one that I know. Wouldn't give me his name."

"What's he look like, Matthew?"

"Sure, he's a tall, queer stick of a fellow, your honour, with a face on him like the devil himself. Looks as if he'd slit your weasand as soon as give you good-day. Shall I be telling him your honour isn't wishful to see him—?"

"Where is he?"

"In your honour's cabin. I'm in there a-tidying, when in he comes, quiet as a ghost—never heard the step of him. I looks round—there he is. Bigod, he give me a turn! Beelzebub himself—"

"I'll go now. You bring Mr. Russell some more ham. He needs restoring after all the exercise he had last night."

"Restoring, is it?" Matthew studied Russell's face with professional interest. "It's not ham he's after wanting then; it's some good beef for the poor face of him."

I left them discussing the alternatives.

The self-styled cousin was a stranger to me. Matthew's description was exact. He had the look of the devil—a wily, genial, old devil. He was sitting on my bunk with Anne's miniature in his hands. He peered at me searchingly with the intentness of a wild animal—or a fugitive. Then he relaxed and the devilish countenance softened into a smile of great charm.

"It is! Thanks be to God, it is!" He set down the miniature carefully on my pillow. "Ye will not know me, cousin, though my name may be familiar to ye. I am Alexander Fairleigh of Croachy, first cousin to the Fairleighs of Lochdearn, related to your mother through the Grants of Glenmoriston. Man, I could never mistake ye! Ye've not changed o'ermuch from the little painting Katharine Fairleigh had of her favourite nephew, which she showed so proudly to everyone. Ah, it's good to see you—even if ye do wear that damned red coat!"

He wrung my hand soundly, then nodded at Anne's picture.

"And yon's your fair lady?" He poked a finger in my ribs. "What the devil possesses ye to go off to the wars when ye've a wife like that at home?—man, you're crack-brained! And I hear ye've five braw sons, forbye." He took up Anne's picture again and shook his head. "Och, lad, it's a sore pity you've not a daughter like her."

"Indeed," said I, "We both dearly wished one. But—she cannot have more children."

He replaced the miniature carefully and sat down on my bunk once more. Then, staring hard at me he leaned forward, and smiled that devilish smile.

"Well, now, ye'll be wondering why I am come."

"You're very welcome whyever you're here, sir. May I offer you some refreshment?"

"Nay, thank'ee, lad. I cannot stay and I'll not keep ye. Now—d'ye know that my cousin—our cousin—Lochdearn lives at his settlement in the colony of North Carolina? He calls it Belhaven—after his family home in Strath Dearn."

"I knew this from Lady Katharine Fairleigh," I said.

"Ay, well, he still lives there with his sons, Jamie and Charlie—braw lads. I visited Belhaven four years agone." He paused and looked down at his hands. "Just after Katharine's ship was lost at sea; she was returning home from one of her visits to Croachy." Another pause; then he added gently, "Ye knew she had died, Philip?"

"I knew," I said.

As often as I hear her name the hurt revives. I had idolized the Lady Katharine Fairleigh—the wife of Fairleigh of Lochdearn. She was beautiful, she was brave and she was devoted to her family. Lochdearn was one of those excluded by name from the general pardon granted to the Scottish rebels of the '45 rebellion, and, until recent years, would certainly have been arrested and arraigned for treason had he set foot in Scotland. So Katharine Fairleigh had come in his place to do what family business had to be done in this country; though liable herself to arrest as her husband's accomplice.

On those visits she was often in our home, and her beauty and her gaiety and her spirit transformed it for us all whilst she stayed. For no reason that I can imagine, she was lovingly proud of her soldier nephew. And I dreamt of her—though older than me by fifteen years—those calf-dreams that some women, confident in a serene, mature beauty, can inspire in foolish young soldiers; and not only in foolish, young soldiers.

"Ay, I thought ye'd know." Alexander Fairleigh nodded. "She loved ye dearly. And that's the reason I'm here, lad. When I was at Belhaven then, Lochdearn asked me to take their daughter to her real home in Strath Dearn, to bide with her own kin until the war was over. There are lawless gangs in all the colonies now who burn and murder and loot in the name of liberty or the king—whichever suits—and Lochdearn feared that such a mob might attack Belhaven; and the mountain men in those parts—they're worse than any animals. So I brought the lass home to Croachy—she was no more than fifteen; but now she's nineteen she's wishful for to go back to her father and her brothers."

"But why?—the war's not over—the danger's not passed."

He leaned back and folded his arms, eyeing me solemnly.

"The official reason is that since Lord Fairleigh of Lochdearn holds the trust and confidence of both sides in the Carolinas in the same manner as Lord Fairfax of Cameron does in Virginia, he could provide a stabilizing and reconciling influence in the southern colonies after the King's rule has been re-established, as it looks soon to be. And to allay the suspicions of those who might think that Lochdearn was acting under some personal pressure, his only daughter should not be residing in Scotland; but, being the age she is, she should be at Belhaven in North Carolina, managing his household—and, bigod, it would not surprise me to see her managing the colony besides! That's what I told old John Bute to tell the King's mama, so, if ye know how that household wags, ye'll understand that that's how the King himself thinks now. And it makes sense anyways ye see it. So your friend Germain had his orders."

He smiled again.

"But if ye were to ask me my personal reason—it's because the hell-cat's driving me into an early grave forever nagging at me to send her home!"

"Didn't she wish to come to Scotland?"

"Well, I'll not say she struggled and screamed the whole journey over. And she liked it well enough in Strath Dearn not to wish to travel out abroad. But we'll have no bother to get her back across the ocean."

"And she's to travel back with this convoy?"

"Ay."

"But where?—how?"

"On this ship. How else? I tell ye she's gey better than the coble we came on!"

"But this is a military transport. What authority—?"

The smile spread in triumph over his lean features. He produced and, with great deliberation, unfolded a paper and held it out to me. It greeted all the loyal subjects of His Majesty King George the Third—and instructed them to afford every assistance to his trusty and well-beloved Col. Philip Cato in the escorting of the Lady Lucy Fairleigh etcetera, etcetera. It was dated the 23rd of April and signed by Germain.

I exploded. "In God's name—why am I to escort her?"

"Lord save us, lad—ye'll mind she's your own cousin!"

"And yours too!"

Croachy shook his head.

"I'm still proscribed by this German Elector ye've took for a King."

"Proscribed? Rubbish! The general pardon—"

He blazed up at once.

"I'm not minded to take any oath to yon Hanoverian usurper!" He jabbed a forefinger at me. "Look ye, lad—I was but ten when I first went out with my father to join the Earl of Mar in '15. I fought at Sherrifmuir and they looked to hang me—me, ten years old! I was forty when I took my claymore and my sons and my people to join the Prince and Lord George Murray in '45, and they looked the harder to take off my head along with Lovat and Kilmarnock and Balmerino on Tower Hill. And now I'm seventy-five and not worth the looking for—I know it. But I'll not take pardons from any of them!"

There's no arguing with Croachy. He lives for his memory of a life of rebellion and a devotion to a lost cause; though he'll never think himself a rebel, nor his cause lost. Sad that such steadfast loyalty should be squandered on what remains of the gallant Young Chevalier—Charles Stewart, a sponging, leching, fuddled hulk, a miserable pensioner of the throne he sought to usurp.

I studied the paper he had given me.

"How did you hear I was ordered to Charlestown and aboard this ship?"

My angry frustration seemed to amuse him, for he grinned, tapping the side of his beaky nose with a long-nailed finger.

"I have my friends, cousin; some of them in places that would surprise ye. When I knew ye were sailing to take up your appointment, I just happened to meet yon Lord Germain and mentioned in conversation your relationship to Lucy. And—intelligent body that he is—he remarked on the extraordinary coincidence that ye were about to take passage to Charlestown, and suggested you might escort her. I did not think it proper to gainsay so important a gentleman."

This little story of petty intrigue did not help my temper. I said coldly,

"You say, sir, that you are proscribed still, and yet you confer on confidential matters of state with this Hanoverian usurper's ministers!"

"Och, well—och, well," He waved an airy hand, "Ye ken there can always be understandings between gentlemen when there's cause enow."

Matthew tapped on the door.

"The Master's compliments and regrets, your honour, and he hopes that it won't inconvenience you to move to another cabin. The Lady Fairleigh—"

Furious now, I turned on Croachy.

"By God, sir, I'm deeply obliged to you! First you saddle me with the chit—then you turn me out of my quarters—"

"Now, lad," he patted my shoulder, trying to placate me, "Ye'd not have her sleeping in the bilges! Ye'd best come and renew your acquaintance with her—"

"I've never met the girl yet," I fumed, "And if I'm to be kicked out of my cabin to suit her convenience I'm not so damned eager to meet the baggage now—"

Croachy's hand tightened on my shoulder, his eyes on the door behind me. Matthew froze like a statue, staring past me. There was suddenly in the cabin the gentlest suggestion of a perfume I had once known well—Katharine Fairleigh's.

I turned to the door. A man's heart may miss a beat for many reasons; but rarely for the sight of real beauty, as mine did then. Lucy Fairleigh was the loveliest woman I had ever seen or ever shall see—simply that.

Her presence dominated the cabin; for me, all else faded into shadow around her. Every slightest move she made was a joy to watch. Her eyes were on me, bright, gay; even a little pleading, like a child's seeking approval. I bowed, speechless, my mind incapable of framing the simplest courtesies. She curtsied. After my ill-tempered outburst, which she must have heard, I expected some anger in her gaze, but there was none.

Of a sudden the weights fell from my tongue, but my wits were, somehow, still not my own. I said, softly,

"I rejoice to see that the Lady Lucy has inherited all her mother's beauty—and yet more. Though I never thought there could be so much more."

For at that moment I knew in my heart, my mind, my inmost being, that if ever I felt love for any woman at first sight, I felt it then. We looked into each other's eyes—for how long?—God knows. But for long enough for me to think I recognized in hers some suggestion of the emotion which I felt must blaze like a beacon flame from mine. And, at that, I took fright.

"I'll move out of the cabin at once, ma'am," I said abruptly. Oh yes!—I was put out, caught off balance, bitterly ashamed of my rudeness, and hopelessly, incurably shy—as I always am—in the presence of a beautiful woman. But, much more than any of these, despite my tangled senses, I knew again what I was and whose I was. I rapped out,

"Matthew, get these things out of the way and attend to Lady Fairleigh's at once." I bowed, stiffly this time, "You'll excuse me, ma'am. You'll be wishing to make your farewells." I strode out on deck and paced back and forth for a few minutes, which helped me to regain my composure. A well-appointed carriage stood at the foot of the gangway and Lieutenant Parrey and Mr. Willis stood conversing with a gentleman who was directing the unloading of Lucy Fairleigh's baggage from it.

"Philip," said a soft voice. It was my unbeloved kinsman. "She's your cousin, man. Maybe she's inconvenienced ye a mite, but could ye not show her a wee bit more consideration?"

I had recovered myself, but was still not in much of a mood to discuss the matter.

"Yes, of course. I was thoughtless, I'll admit. When she's settled and rested I'll make my apologies. I'll see she's comfortable—and look after her—never fear."

"Ay, that's good. I hope your new cabin will—"

"It will be perfectly adequate."

"Have ye seen it then?"

"No—but I'm sure it will do very well."

"Ay, I hope so." He was contrite now. "I'm sad to put ye to trouble, Philip—"

"It's no trouble—none at all."

We stood in silence for a moment, then, almost timidly, he touched the cuff of my jacket.

"Ye know—Lucy has a book of your mother's letters to Katharine?"

"Indeed?"

"Ay—she cut out the bits about you—the journeys you made—the battles ye'd fought in—all your mother's tattle about ye. She used to write little stories about them—draw little sketches and colour them—"

"Why should she do that?"

His hand pressed heavier on my cuff. His voice pleaded.

"Why?—lad, ye've been Lucy's hero since she was eight—when Katharine first had yon wee picture of ye—in your uniform. Did Katharine never tell ye?"

My mouth was suddenly dry. I found it hard to say—

"Never."

"Well, maybe Katharine thought it only a child's fantasy. Indeed, Lucy was a clever lass and she'd little enough to occupy her mind in Carolina or Strath Dearn save her own imaginings."

He took my hand in both of his and pressed it.

"Be kind to her, Philip. She has her mother's love and courage—and the Fairleigh temper to match it—but there's aye something of that child in her yet."

We walked to the head of the gangway, where he turned and nodded at me, looking more cheerful again.

"God bless ye, lad. Ye'll take good care of her. And God bring ye back safe to your loved ones. Farewell, cousin!"

He turned up the collar of his cloak, pulled his hat down over his eyes, and was away down the gangway and into the carriage like a black ghost; the image of a conspirator.

I went to Lucy Fairleigh's cabin to make my apologies for my rudeness and found Matthew standing like a sentry at the door.

"Her ladyship's resting, your honour. Been a-travelling most of the night. Asked that she shouldn't be disturbed."

"Has she had anything to eat?"

"A little soup—says she's not a good sailor, your honour."

"Well, let me know if she needs anything."

Back on deck, Lieutenant Parrey was still talking with Mr. Willis. I asked if Cook was to receive his punishment in the town gaol, as Russell had asked.

"No time, Colonel," answered Parrey. "You sail within the hour."

Willis frowned. "Does Mr. Russell know this?"

"Looks as if he does now," rejoined Parrey.

Russell was striding along the quay. He came up the gangway and, seeing the three of us, approached and saluted Willis. He spoke painfully through swollen lips.

"Mr. Willis, sir, I'm afraid the Provost Marshal says there's insufficient time for the man Cook to receive his punishment in the prison here."

Willis, hands behind his back, nodded silently.

"I hope, sir," Russell said, irresolutely, "You will permit it to be carried out on board, sir—if you approve, sir—"

"I suppose so, Mr. Russell. Please make your arrangements with the boatswain. Tomorrow will be best."

Russell saluted again, tried to smile politely—it obviously hurt—and went in search of the boatswain.

Parrey slapped Willis on the back.

"There you are, Mr. Willis—there's your entertainment for your guests' first day at sea all arranged! You'll have other diversions for every day too, I'm sure! Flogging, mast-heading, plank-walking, keel-hauling—all the parlour games! A most amusing passage you'll have, Colonel! Well, I'll wish you gentlemen a pleasant voyage and leave you to your festivities!"

With an elaborate salute he was off.

We put out that afternoon on the tide. As they worked, the hands sang a cheerful ditty, of which the chorus, as much as I can remember, ran—

> "The girl that I adore—ore—ore,
> She is a Portsmouth whore—ore—ore"

whilst the verses described their heroine and her attributes and activities in intimate detail. I remarked on the appropriateness of the song to Mr. Fellowes, standing by me at the rail. He grinned.

"The lads ring the changes. If we was putting out from Plymouth, she'd be a Plymouth whore."

We took our station and that evening, Thursday the 27th April, under a cloudless sky of the palest blue, the convoy sailed. A gallant sight, as any great number of ships sailing together in order must be.

Wrapped in my cloak, I watched, entranced, the ever-changing scene.

[53]

With the wind astern, all the ships, in close order, held steady on their course into the lurid glare of the setting sun. The mastheads swung wildly against the darkening sky. The wind thrummed and whined through the rigging. Every timber of the ship groaned in discordant unison. The spray hissed over the rail to patter on the pale decks. And whilst I gazed, forgetful of all time, the lights ashore on the Isle of Wight faded behind us into the dark blue mists of the evening. We sailed on, out into the Channel, and saw no more of England.

The next day the wind blew harder and keener from the northeast, bringing showers of sleet. The *Union* moved more gaily than many of the stomachs aboard could abide. Matthew reported Lucy Fairleigh to be one of those so affected, and she stayed in her cabin. I am fortunate never to have been subject to sea-sickness myself; it must be one of the unhappiest conditions.

At seven bells in the forenoon watch the drummers of the 71st beat the muster, the rolls sounding dully on the wet drum-skins. The soldiers were ranged on three sides of a square, facing inwards. The grenadier company of the 33rd in their tall, scarlet caps, the bonnets and plaids of the 71st, the 17th Light Dragoons, in their red-plumed helmets—they made a bright splash of colour on this grey day. But I've never seen an unhappier looking lot of soldiers. The colour of the faces of most matched the colour of the seas surging past the rail—a dirty green.

I stood with Mr. Willis on the poop, the rest of the officers, except Russell, in line behind me. There was a querulous mutter from John Conyngham.

"My fellows are going to lose their damned hats overboard before we're finished. All new on Monday."

I decided to take a hand.

"Mr. Russell!"

The drum-major of the 71st, standing stripped to the waist, stirring the lashes of the cat-o'-nine-tails round in a butt of salt water, touched Russell on the arm and nodded in my direction. Russell clambered stiffly up to the poop-deck. I turned to face the officers.

"Gentlemen, under these conditions your soldiers can gain no benefit from witnessing the example to be made of this man. Many are very evidently sick and they're all getting wet and cold to no purpose. And, as Major Conyngham fears, they may all lose their hats. You will remain on deck yourselves, but the quicker you dismiss your soldiers the better.

"Mr. Russell, you'll keep such men as you require to administer the punishment. I suggest the surgeon examines the prisoner after each hundred lashes to advise you whether he's fit to receive more. If he isn't, you can administer the remainder later. Now, please get on with the business."

The soldiers crowded down the companionways and the decks were swiftly cleared.

Mr. Willis, the officers, the drum-major and a guard of a sergeant and four troopers of the 17th Light Dragoons remained on deck. Russell ordered,

"Fetch up the prisoner!"

The guard clambered down a ladder to the deck below, to re-appear heaving Cook and the other deserter, Crowder, a scrawny pinch of a man. As Crowder was not to be flogged, I supposed he was attending just for his instruction. He was at once sick over the side, loudly and at length, after which he collapsed, moaning, into the scuppers.

Cook was fettered hand and foot and his hands were bound behind his back. A wedge of wood was still tied in his mouth.

"Why's this man still gagged, Sergeant Hawes?" asked Russell sharply.

"Your honour, he's never given over a-swearing and abusing the guard since he come round. So we stuffed yon in his gob to quiet him. It'll do for him to bite on when the cat bites on him."

Russell nodded.

"Secure the prisoner."

The guard unbound Cook's hands one at a time and lashed him by the wrists to hang from the shrouds. Most soldiers, when securing a prisoner for punishment, try to make things as easy for the poor wretch as they may. The guard were not inclined to be so charitable for Cook. They pulled the lashings tight enough to cut, and he mumbled and groaned at them through his gag. Sergeant Hawes tore the ragged shirt from his back. The great muscles of his shoulders, straining from his own weight, showed dark red weals—old scars—where the cat had clawed him before. And much good it had done him.

"Make ready," said Russell.

The drum-major of the 71st was a great ox of a fellow. He was also, according to Capt. James Macdonnell, an artist with the cat; and he wanted to show it. He took a few leisurely, careful practice swings, letting the lashes flick caressingly over Cook's bare back. Then he reported to Russell.

"Ready to commence punishment, your honour."

Russell's voice was clear and dispassionate.

"Five hundred lashes. The surgeon will please to inspect after one hundred. Sergeant Hawes—count the strokes."

"Sir!" said Sergeant Hawes.

"Lay on!" said Russell.

And the lashes—hissing like the nine cats themselves—struck with that peculiarly horrible, flat thud; not at all the noise you'd think they would make. And the breath came out of Cook in an agonized grunt.

"One!" Sergeant Hawes' voice rang sharp.

"Two!"

"Three!"

Anyone who can watch unmoved the bloody disintegration of a man's body under the effect of one hundred lashes for the twelve minutes or so it takes to lay them across the wretch's back has a stronger stomach than I have. Surgeon Hawkins examined the prisoner after the hundred strokes, conferred with Russell, and came to whisper to me.

"He's a strong fellow, Colonel, but this highlander lays it on. Russell's restricting it to two hundred lashes today."

And so it went on—

Thud!—"One hundred and five."

Thud!—"One hundred and six."

Thud!

—and on.

If you wish to strip the flesh off a man's back there are easier ways of doing it than by flogging it off while he's unconscious. It's all so damned pointless and repulsive.

At the two hundred they cut him down. He collapsed in a senseless, bloody heap and they lugged him below like a fresh-butchered carcass.

"Have that other prisoner scrub the deck until it shines, Mr. Russell!" I hardly recognized my own voice for the anger and disgust in it.

Russell glanced doubtfully at the moaning heap, huddled in the scuppers.

"I fear he's unfit for any such duty, Colonel."

"Then kick his damned, idle backside until he is!"

I had observed the miserable Crowder covertly watching his accomplice being flayed, and clearly enjoying it. Russell had not. He stared at me, puzzled.

"Very good, sir. Sergeant Hawes—!"

Sergeant Hawes nudged the prostrate body with a fastidious toe and stepped back quickly when it retched violently. He shook his head at me, a little reproachfully.

"Drum-major!" My voice carried as I meant it to do. "Put the cat across that misery a couple of times—"

Crowder's recovery was remarkable to behold.

"No, your honour! No, for Gawd's sake! I'm fit enough—"

A furious Sergeant Hawes grabbed him by the scruff and dragged him, stumbling over his gyves, to fling him down with his nose in the blood. Crowder was promptly and substantially sick.

I went below to the after-cabin and called for brandy; other officers following suit. Poor young Fraser looked very pale. I felt sorry for him as I had felt for myself the first time I ever saw a man flogged.

"Never seen that sort of punishment before, Mr. Fraser?"

"Never, sir—I hope I never shall again!"

"You'd best get used to it, Alex," said Conyngham cheeringly, "Discipline's got to be maintained."

"If I could not maintain discipline in my company without the lash, I'd not soldier," said Macdonnell, coldly.

"Nor I." Russell's tone was very sour. Conyngham laughed.

"Charlie, how can you say that? You've just ordered this fellow five hundred touches—"

"He's not my soldier. If he were he'd be decorating a gallows in Portsmouth. We don't want his sort in the 17th. There's only two punishments worth a damn. Drummed out down the gauntlet or the drop off the cart tail. And I believe all our good soldiers would be glad to be shut of the bad ones either way!" He got to his feet. "I'd better see if that devil's still alive."

"You can't use the gauntlet where we're going," said Conyngham. "The next time you see the fellow he'll be a sergeant in the rebel army! Their General Greene reckons they get all their best recruits from our deserters."

"But they don't flog in the American army—" burst out Fraser, "So why should we?"

"They don't flog!" scoffed Conyngham, "Lad, they've been flogging as heartily as Hessians for years—and old 'Mad Anthony' Wayne, one of their best generals, has a hanging once a week to keep his lads up to scratch. They had mutiny after mutiny until Washington told their Congress there's no other way of keeping discipline in their rabble. And he's right! He's a damned good officer, old George W. Doesn't stand any nonsense."

"I heard he badly wanted a commission in the Regular Army."

"That's right, Colonel. He was always petitioning the Virginia

Governors to be given one. We junior officers reckoned he'd earned it—and more. But the senior officers never gave the provincial officers the credit they deserved, 'specially any of 'em who had wiped their eye as clean as Washington had at the Wilderness. Pity—he could even be serving with us now." Conyngham looked at me curiously. "You've never served in the colonies, Colonel?"

"Not in the American colonies. But I've served with General Clinton in the Low Countries and Germany—and with Lord Cornwallis."

"Cornwallis—ah, there's a soldiers' soldier for you!" Conyngham said. "They say he was on the side of the colonists all along until he was sent out to fight them. And they reckon it was the separation that killed his wife. He must feel very bitter."

"It's not in him to be bitter," I said. "He's the sort who will always give of his best."

Conyngham looked down into his glass.

"I know his wife's family well," he said. "Her father was Colonel of the 3rd Foot Guards. She was a sweet girl, damned attractive, full of mischief and always teasing you—never to hurt, always to make you laugh. Cornwallis adored her—and she him. They had children—lots of friends. Hadn't got much money, but they used to laugh a lot together." He took a long pull at his brandy. "They say he doesn't laugh much now."

There was a silence. I had known Jemima Cornwallis. Jemima—a funny little name. And she died last year—of a broken heart, just that. Charles Cornwallis was near mad with grief; told me he had nothing to live for now but the Army.

Alexander Fraser said, hesitantly,

"It must be very difficult to do something you believe is wrong. I mean—not just doing it once—but to go on doing it. Like Lord Cornwallis—to fight for a cause in which you don't truly believe—and never have believed—"

Macdonnell dipped the tip of his forefinger in his brandy and flicked the drops at Fraser.

"Careful now, Alex. Don't go in too deep."

Fraser reddened. Macdonell looked at me with the half-angry, half-mocking smile, too often on his lips.

"You see, Colonel, Fraser's grandfather and my grandfather died at Culloden fighting for Charles Stewart, of course."

"And you have never believed in the Stewart cause?"

"It died before ever I was born. And good riddance."

He drained his glass and slammed it down.

"My family have taken the oath to King George—and we'll keep it."

"But why do you fight for an English king?" said Conyngham.

Macdonell laughed sardonically.

"To earn my bread, to be sure! Why do you fight for a German one?"

The door of the cabin flew open and Surgeon Hawkins stamped straight across to the brandy decanters.

"How's Cook?" I asked.

"He'll live, sir,—under the tender ministrations of Lady Fairleigh—"

"But she's sick."

"She's been down there in the cell, bathing and tending his back. Stopped him swearing! After she'd finished with Cook, Russell took her back to her cabin."

"Where's Russell now?"

"Looking round his troop deck and horse lines, Colonel." He kicked the leg of Macdonell's chair. "Like a good officer should, Captain Macdonell!"

"Away with all pox-ridden pintle-smiths!" Macdonell got to his feet and stretched. "You've interrupted an interesting philosophical discussion with your chattering teeth and clacking tongue." He put on his cloak and bonnet. "Alex, bide still, lad. You're too pallid round the chops. Now, Major Conyngham, you'll agree we'll need the surgeon's advice on the condition of our troop decks?"

"Indeed," Conyngham shrugged himself into his cloak, "He must certainly accompany us."

"To the devil with the both of you! I've just been round your damned decks!"

"Ah, then, his advice will be positively essential, Major Conyngham, don't you think? Pray take his other arm!"

"For God's sake! Let me have a sup of brandy first—I'm perished with cold—"

"Drinking before going on duty!" Conyngham cried reproachfully, "God save us! Did you hear that, Captain Macdonell? Heaven defend the poor 76th from this idle, drunken whore-tester!"

They pushed him through the cabin door and it slammed behind them. Fraser sat down again. He looked very white and drawn.

"I don't feel very well, I'll admit, Colonel."

"Sea-sickness. It'll pass."

"Not just sea-sickness, sir. I was—it's the•—I've never seen a man flogged—it sickened me, I'm afraid. How d'you think I'll be in battle, sir? I can gralloch a beast—but—that—" he shuddered. I put my hand on his—it was ice-cold.

[59]

"I felt the same. I always do. Battle's not like that at all."

He looked up at me incredulously.

"You do? I never thought—well, I feel—a little better then—" He smiled wanly.

I mixed him a strong, hot toddy.

"Hold the mug in both hands—and sip it slowly."

After a few sips he looked at me again, over the top of the steaming mug.

"May I ask you a question, Colonel?"

"Ask away."

He took another sip from the mug, then—

"Colonel—sir—do you believe we're fighting for a good cause? I mean, sir,—for the good of our country?"

So there it was. I was being made to answer the question I had never ceased to ask myself. And, for the sake of this lad, I had to answer it convincingly.

"Mr. Fraser, if I did not believe so, I should not be on this ship now. History may prove me wrong. But, as soldiers, all you and I can do—is our duty—as our conscience directs us, and as best we can. No one can ask us to do more. No one can criticise us for doing as much."

He lowered the mug slowly to his knees. After a moment he looked up at me again and smiled.

"Thank you, sir, for being so patient with me," his voice was still unsteady, "I wasn't sure—in my own mind. And when you spoke of Lord Cornwallis—I thought—I know how ignorant I am of these things. Jamie—Captain Macdonell—tries to help me understand. But—I'm not very clever at it. It helps me to be—to hear it from you, Colonel."

He looked down into the mug. I saw his mouth open and shut once or twice. Then he said, still looking down,

"I'll always try to give of my best, sir—like you said Lord Cornwallis does."

For a few seconds his words took my breath away. I said,

"I think you'll do very well, Mr. Fraser." And I spoke the Gospel truth.

But his straightforward question and his straightforward trust in my answer set my own doubts once more astir.

Chapter Five

*In which I have an audience of
the Commander-in-Chief.*

In no time at all Lucy Fairleigh had them all eating out of her hand. After she had recovered from her sea-sickness she took all her meals with us in the after-cabin. When we were all engaged in our daily administrative duties, she would accompany James Hawkins on his rounds of the sick, assisting him with a skill which surprised him.

"She tells me that her home in Carolina was attacked by Indians when she was young and a few times since by reiving gangs, so she's experienced in tending wounded as well as in the care of the sick in their settlement." He reported to me. "She's a capable young lady, your niece, Colonel."

"Your niece" you'll note, not "your cousin". Lucy called me "uncle" from the start; I think to tease me for my early ill humour. She seemed put out when I accepted the title without comment. So then she played the part of a spirited wilful niece to the full, and, with everyone on her side, she soon had me established in the role of a tedious, strait-laced and unsociable relation; which, perhaps, I was, but she made me a damned long-suffering one.

She liked to feel her power to dominate others by her beauty and her spirit, and used a sharp and ready wit—and a wonderful gift of mimicry—to provoke those who would not submit to her domination. And, since all save myself were content to be dominated by one so fascinating, I was her chief butt. This I accepted willingly too—which irritated her the more—because it made our relationship the easier for me.

However, after two weeks, she was deposed from her imperious rule of us all by two separate occasions. On the first, she had accepted a challenge from Charles Russell that she would not climb to the crow's-nest, and, having borrowed a pair of breeches from the cabin-boy, climbed near to the mast-head.

After Mr. Willis had informed both most clearly of his opinion of them, and they had apologized, I took it on myself to have an additional word with them in my cabin. I saw Russell first and my interview with him was short; but I doubt he'll forget it. Then Lucy stormed in.

"Why did you not speak to me before seeing Charles?"

"Because he is an officer in command of men, and so he is important to me."

"And I'm unimportant to you!"

I let her wait, glaring at me, a few moments before I answered.

"More important than my own life, Lucy. And, for your family's sake, I beg you not to hazard your own so stupidly again."

All the fire went out of her in a puff. She stood looking at me like a scolded child, sad-eyed, twisting her fingers in each other nervously.

"I'm—I'm sorry, Philip."

She ducked her head and turned to leave, but at the door she looked back at me. Of a sudden she ran and threw her arms around my neck.

"Philip—Oh, Philip—I'm being so horrid. Why don't you hate me?"

I smiled—dazedly, I expect.

"I do," I said, "I loathe you!"

She kissed me lightly once, full on the lips, then ran to the door. There she spun round, and with that glorious smile—

"I'll be good!" she cried, "I'll be a good girl now! You'll see!" She blew me another kiss and was gone. I sat down on my bunk, my heart thumping like a smith's hammer.

The second occasion, a day or so later, was a grimmer affair. Under James Hawkins' guidance, she had dressed Cook's back for two weeks. Russell and Hawkins decided between them then that Cook was fit to suffer the rest of his punishment—three hundred lashes. You may well imagine her opinion of the decision; I didn't need to imagine it—I heard it clear through the bulkhead separating my cabin from the after-cabin. Naturally, and properly, Russell and Hawkins were politely adamant in holding to their decision. Lucy came rushing to my cabin.

"They're going to flog that man again—"

"I know," I said, "I heard."

"But, Philip—it's brutal—horrible." She was near hysterical, "You can stop it—please—"

"Lucy, he deserted, he murdered a helpless old woman, and he tried to kill Charles Russell."

"But he's been punished!"

"Only partly; and only for part of his crimes. I hate flogging. But it's got to be done."

"His back—all gashed and torn—ohh!" She covered her face with her hands, "It makes me sick—"

I took her hands.

"You use these, very bravely, in helping James to nurse the sick—and Cook—and we all admire you for it."

She began to shake with sobs, gripping the lapels of my jacket.

"Oh, Philip—I'm frightened—"

"Frightened? Why? Has he threatened you? I'll—"

"No—it's just his hate. He's so full of hate, all the time. He never says anything—he never thanks James for his care—I think he hates us for it. He just hates—everybody—everything. It's so—" She began to shudder violently and I held her against me to steady her.

"I don't think you should go on nursing him—"

"Oh, but I must—now I've begun—I'll go on—"

She started to recover herself now and the shuddering and sobbing slowed. She borrowed one of my large handkerchiefs to mop her eyes and blow her nose like a trumpet. She looked a forlorn fifteen. I kissed her cheek and sat her down on the bunk beside me and put my arm round her. She rested her head on my shoulder and we sat like that for a couple of minutes. I felt her begin to relax.

"Oh, Philip, I wish I had come to visit you in Somerset," she said, her voice muffled in the collar of my coat.

"We should have liked you to. I didn't even know you were in Strath Dearn. For the last four years I'm afraid I've been living—like an old country mole."

She laughed a little at that.

"You—an old country mole!"

She nodded at Anne's miniature hanging beside the head of my bunk. "Is that Anne?"

From the hollow of my shoulder she studied the picture.

"Pretty—I've never met her—and she looks fun too."

"She is."

"Do you always have it with you—that miniature?"

"Yes—wherever I go."

She looked up at me, wide-eyed, a little quizzically.

"Does she know?—that you take it, I mean?"

"I—I don't know. I just take it. I always have."

She started to smile, then bit her lip in a line of white, even teeth.

"How like you," she said. She smiled properly now and kissed my cheek. Then she stood up and saw herself in my looking glass.

"Oh, heavens! What a sight! Look at my face!" And she was gone from my cabin like a bat out of a bedroom.

So Cook had the rest of his punishment before the whole ship's company. Lucy shut herself up in the after-cabin so as not to hear it, and I posted Matthew at the door to ensure that she didn't interfere. And, when it was over, she went down to the cells at once with James Hawkins, and began to nurse him again. James and Charlie Russell reckoned she saved the devil's life.

Thirty days out from Spithead we parted from the larger part of the convoy and, with our escort, sailed directly for Charlestown. It became very hot and I hated to think—for, from experience, I knew very well—what conditions were like on the other transports, not so well equipped. Burial services were held most days on one or other of them. Carcasses of horses were, of course, never put over the side; even with the little flesh remaining on them after four weeks at sea, they supplied the galleys with welcome fresh meat.

One morning the thud of a gun brought us all on deck. A curl of smoke hung astern of the scout sloop, a mile ahead of the convoy, and a flutter of bunting on her halyards told of the approach of an English frigate from the west.

The frigate ran alongside our escort—the armed store-ship *Camel*—to pass messages aboard. As she turned away on her course and passed close by us, we hailed her asking for news. They shouted back—

"Charlestown is ours—surrendered twelve days ago—" So we cheered her as she sailed on to England.

That night was one of celebration. John Conyngham had been present at the miserable disaster of the last attempt to seize Charlestown four years since, commanded by Gen. Sir Henry Clinton. After Lucy had retired, Conyngham, well-wined, gave us the benefit of his opinion of the abilities of Sir Henry and his naval subordinate Comdr. Peter Parker.

"They rarely spoke to each other—never understood one another when they did. Clinton distrusted Parker—Parker despised Clinton. Happy confluence of martial genius, bigod! Clinton never able to make up his mind, and Parker, pig-stupid, with all the patience of a monkey with a poker up its arse!" He drained his glass and belched thunderously. "Well, at least the noble Sir Henry hasn't made such a right muck of it this time!"

Early on the evening of Tuesday, the 6th June, the outlines of Sullivan's and James islands showed black against the setting sun. At dawn we moved through the Ship Canal into the fine, natural harbour, full of the transports of Clinton's force and its supporting squadron preparing to leave in convoy.

A clammy heat had enveloped us as we drew near land and my cabin became unbearably stuffy. I went out on deck and watched the shadows on the hills change in the morning light, and the seagulls circling and swooping around each ship of our line. The birds screamed and jostled and fought as they dived and snatched the garbage pitched over the side; the only sound in the stillness of the morning as we moved slowly into the harbour. I was so engrossed in watching them that I did not notice that Lucy had joined me until she tugged my sleeve.

"I couldn't sleep," she said. Her eyes were shining with excitement and her dark auburn curls tumbled in enchanting disorder over her white shawl. "It's so wonderful to be nearly home again!"

We stood silent, side by side, for a while, watching the gulls and the ships we passed. Then she tugged at my sleeve again.

"Philip, you will come and see us at Belhaven—?" She was looking down at my sleeve. "Father would be so happy if you could—" She looked up at me now. "Please—you will come, won't you?"

If it made her happy, why not say yes? So I did. After all, it seemed very unlikely that I should be able to do so. Even if I did, she would by then have happily renewed all the local acquaintanceships of her family. The close association of the weeks aboard ship would be a fading memory. I should be almost forgotten—just an old friend; and, on reflection, that thought did not please me.

She took my arm then and I looked down at her young loveliness, and the happiness in her eyes. Suddenly, forgetting all else, I bent and kissed her lips. But her mouth stayed pressed to mine—and her hand tightened on my arm—harder and longer than I intended.

I panicked—not for the first time in such circumstances. I've said I'm always hopelessly shy in the presence of a beautiful woman; and usually behave like an idiot. I straightened up, ashamed with myself. I should never have kissed her. I had never intended—certainly, I hadn't!—she had entirely misread—or had she? I took her hand from my arm and held it. "Lucy—" I said.

"Ow!—Oh, hell and damnation!" A trumpet of oaths echoed up the companionway. It was John Conyngham's voice and he clumped up on deck still swearing.

I let go of Lucy's hand. Whatever I had been about to say—and I hadn't much idea what I was going to say—would have to wait. Conyngham joined us, rubbing his head. "Those damned beams are going to be the death of me 'fore we get off this godforsaken bumboat! Hit me head twenty times a day." He stared around. "Well, Charlestown looks better than when I was here last time!" And he began to whistle "The girl I left behind me"—flat.

I avoided Lucy's eyes and turned back to the rail. At that moment a cutter ran alongside us and an army officer seated in the sternsheets hailed us.

"Is Colonel Cato aboard?"

I went down to meet him as he came over the side. A slimly elegant young man, middle-sized and very upright in bearing, with a ready smile and an easy, brisk manner. He swung neatly-booted legs over the rail, came smoothly to the attention, swept off his hat and bowed. All a little theatrical.

"Maj. John Andre, 26th Regiment, Colonel—acting as Adjutant General for the Commander-in-Chief. Welcome to Charlestown. The Commander-in-Chief presents his compliments and wishes to see you at once, sir."

"Where is the General?"

Andre waved a hand at one of the frigates.

"Aboard *Romulus*, sir."

As we were rowed across to the frigate I asked how he had known my name and that I should arrive on the convoy.

"Brigadier General Dalrymple arrived to relieve William Cathcart as Quartermaster-General on the 10th of last month. He mentioned that Lord Germain had recommended your appointment."

"And how did the Commander-in-Chief receive that piece of intelligence?"

Poor Andre—his composure deserted him. Scarlet in the face, he stammered—

"He—he—expressed his interest, Colonel—"

I nodded. I could guess the expression he used too. After this Andre maintained a tactful silence until he ushered me into the main cabin of *Romulus*, to stand before the desk at which His Excellency Gen. Sir Henry

Clinton, Commander-in-Chief of His Majesty's Forces in the American colonies, was busily scribbling.

They called him Pussy in the Coldstream Guards and the nickname had followed him into the 1st Foot Guards. I met him later, when I was serving on the Marquis of Granby's staff and he was an aide to the Allied Commander-in-Chief, Prince Ferdinand of Brunswick. A pudgy little fellow, humourless and conceited, so he was teased fairly regularly, and his jaggy little temper only made his persecutors tease him the more mercilessly. "Puss, puss," they would cry, "Put your naughty claws away like a good pussy!" And he would stump off, blinking and muttering.

He clung close to any generals about, and made it abundantly clear that I was too junior to be worthy of his notice. He can't ride to save his tubby life—his short, fat legs and buxom behind don't help, but he insists on buying big, common horses, on which he thinks he cuts a fine soldierly figure, but looks like a petrified ape on an elephant. He's a randy little monkey too. They say he chooses his whores like his horses—big and common; and if he rides them the way he rides his horses I shouldn't think they stay sound for long either.

After a minute or so he deigned to notice us. He looked as if he expected me to genuflect.

"Colonel Cato, your Excellency," said Andre. He glanced from one to the other, plainly uncomfortable in the atmosphere of mutual dislike, and slipped away.

Clinton began to scrabble around in the papers in the trays on his desk. Each tray was neatly labelled for its proper contents, but it was plain this meant nothing to him. At length he found the paper he wanted. He scanned it silently. Then—

"You're not the officer I should have chosen."

There's a damnably encouraging welcome for you at the end of a seven weeks' voyage. I said,

"I understood your Excellency required a cavalry officer of some experience."

He glared up at me. "Who told you that?"

"The Secretary-at-War and the Secretary for these colonies—"

"Jenkinson and Germain! Those—humbugs! They never listen to a damned word I say!"

"—and His Majesty." I smiled affably.

"H'mph." He reddened, then grumbled, "Don't recall asking for a cavalry officer. I thought—"

[67]

"I saw the letter, General," I said. I hadn't, of course, but I was sick of his fussing.

He bent lower over the paper.

"Well—perhaps I did. Can't recall it—" he shuffled some papers in another tray. "Don't seem to have a copy—" Then, in a sudden fume of irritation, "I told that fool Jenkinson I wanted Pelham!"

I said, "With great respect to Colonel Pelham's abilities—" which was a damned sight more than they deserved—"I believe he has not seen much service with troops, and none at all overseas."

Clinton's expression was coldly spiteful.

"I wanted an officer I can trust."

He watched me struggle for words. I said,

"Then, perhaps His Majesty should be informed that he has made the wrong choice."

"The King? What has the King to do with it?"

"He informed me personally that he had chosen me as the officer best qualified to assist your Excellency in the recruiting and training of militia cavalry in the southern colonies."

He smacked both hands on his desk petulantly.

"And who told him we should find such recruits in these parts? And in numbers meriting the attention of an officer of your seniority? Germain, of course! That man tells me—from three thousand miles away he is good enough to inform me—" he took on a fatuously pompous tone—"That I am assured of finding a multitude of loyal subjects of His Majesty, who need but a word to leap to the defence of their homes against the rebels." He smacked his desk again. "And what do I find?" He screamed the words. "A louse-ridden rabble of layabouts, sick of being drilled by Steuben, flogged by Washington, hanged by Wayne and starved and cheated by Congress, straggle into our lines, and an identical gang of our rubbish is bribed by agents, seduced by whores and suborned by agitators to join theirs. A pretty exchange! We get their bog-Irish and they get our rebel Scots with a few English felons thrown in for good measure!"

"General, I understood that you claimed you could recruit two or three regiments of militia cavalry in the south. It was the reason for this appointment."

"I said no such thing!—" he suddenly checked himself, "Well—perhaps I did. I had my reasons. I wish to God I could. We'll never end this business until we do get such support—never. The rebels grow daily stronger and Jenkinson demands daily that I send troops to fight in the Indies, Gibraltar, Minorca, India—everywhere but here in these colonies.

[*68*]

And when I ask for reinforcements, what do I get?" His voice rose again, almost hysterically. "An acknowledgment—yes, by God,—an acknowledgment! Along with a rag-bag of cretinous plans, dreamt up by pot-valiant idiots who've seen no service outside a harlot's boudoir! They want me to fail! I'm certain of it!"

I began even to feel sorry for him.

"And how may I assist you, General?"

He got to his feet and stared hard at me.

"I am compelled to trust you, Cato." He began to pace up and down, head bent, hands behind his back. "You know Lord Cornwallis is my deputy?"

"Yes."

"And that he has in his pocket a dormant commission to command in these colonies if I am killed, or resign—or am relieved of my command?"

"No, General."

"And how does that—arrangement—strike you?"

"Very unsatisfactory—for both parties."

"For both parties? Well—maybe so. But for me it's damnable. Because I can't trust Cornwallis to discharge my orders as I wish."

"But his lordship is a most loyal officer—"

"That hasn't deterred him in the past from interpreting my orders differently from my intentions."

This did not surprise me. Clinton's orders are notorious. Few people have ever understood them. They say he has trouble with them himself.

"General, how is this relevant to my appointment?"

He faced me squarely. He spoke slowly, unemotionally.

"I shall attach you to Lord Cornwallis' staff. But, understand, Cato," an edge came into his voice, "your duty is to me! You will report to me regularly and fully each month on Cornwallis' actions and plans, and immediately in the event of any change of policy or plan deviating from the letter of my orders."

I had hoped I had not heard aright. My hesitation betrayed my misgivings. Clinton's jaw thrust out truculently.

"D'you hear me? D'you understand?"

"I certainly hear you, General—very clearly. Whether I understand you as clearly—I doubt."

The disgust in my voice was plain. His button of a mouth slackened. What he was asking me to do was indefensible, but, stupidly obstinate, he tried to brazen it out and overawe me.

"Doubt? You report to me regularly—that's all!"

"Do you think I shall provide a reliable channel of information, General?"

"No, I don't. But, in the circumstances, can you think of a better?"

"Does Lord Cornwallis not report to you regularly?"

"Of course he does—" he waved a peevish paw at me—"but never fully enough—"

"And, of course, you have informed his lordship of this failing?"

"Well—" he caught my unsympathetic eye and flared up. "Yes— Yes!—on many occasions! Oh, God damn Germain for sending me an idiot!"

I forced myself to keep my temper and speak slowly.

"And I am not to discuss my reports with his lordship?"

His embarrassment was almost pathetic.

"Well—you—well—you may need to discuss some point—but you must be discreet—"

"And you will not inform Lord Cornwallis of the true nature of my duties?"

He gaped at me, uncomprehending.

"What?—of course not—what do you mean? Of course—I shall—not betray your—"

"Betray me!" I hit the desk so hard the inkpot flew into the air and overturned into one of the trays, and Clinton recoiled before my sudden rage. "Betray me? Who's betraying whom here, General? By God, I see why you wanted a man you could trust! That dunder-headed dolly-mopper, cousin Percy Pelham! No one else would ever trust him. Well, sir, nowhere in my orders am I required to spy on Lord Cornwallis for you; nor on any other of your commanders. Nor shall I accept any instruction from you to do so. If those are the duties for which you brought me here—then, to hell with them!"

I burned my boats with a good blaze. Then I pulled myself up. I said, most formally,

"I must ask your Excellency to order that I take passage home by the next ship, to inform the Secretary-at-War and His Majesty of the true nature of the duties you intend for this officer you require for your staff; and for your predilection for Colonel Pelham as best suited for the appointment."

I bowed, turned about and was halfway to the door, when Clinton said impassively,

"Colonel Cato, I have not yet dismissed you."

I turned back expecting to see him either fulminating or blubbering. He was neither. He is a strange fellow. He can go from mood to mood quicker than anyone I know. He stood behind his desk mopping at the ink with a napkin, looking morosely relaxed.

"Come, Cato, we know each other too well to shout at one another. Shall we forget it?" As if we were just beginning our conversation.

"I'm content, General."

"Good. Now, I want your advice. But you must understand the situation here first. Too many people think they do—and too few do. And that goes for both sides."

He fumbled a silver snuff-box out of his pocket, helped himself generously—and put it away again.

"The rebels. If they had half the pluck of a wooden-legged louse they could have run us out of these colonies four years ago. But they haven't. There are gentlemen of courage and ability among them, but too few for their purposes. Their chief strength is the French support; without it they would be lost. Admittedly French and American forces operating together have achieved only frustration and disaster for themselves so far, but that could change. And the French will support the rebels whilst it profits France."

"Will it profit France to regain Canada, General?"

"Not in the least. They know there are more valuable possessions for them to regain outside this continent than within it."

He began his pacing again.

"For ourselves. Well, Germain fondly believes I have some thirty thousand soldiers here. If I could lay my hand on twelve thousand effectives, fit to ride a horse or hold a musket, I should count myself fortunate.

"Both the King and Germain insist that the majority of the colonists are loyalist at heart—God knows on what evidence—and it needs only the encouragement of a success or two of our arms for thousands to spring to our side. I've just destroyed the rebel army in the Carolinas. Five and a half thousand prisoners we took, seven generals, three hundred and fifteen cannon. A success? So where are all these loyalists rushing to join our colours?

"The truth is ninety-five out of a hundred colonists only want to be left to their own businesses. Had they been on the rebel side we could not have lasted here a six-month. Were they on ours the fighting would stop tomorrow. We're fighting maybe five per cent of the people and maybe two per cent are active loyalists. The rest help either side, or both, when it suits them—or when they have to."

"So how will this end, General?"

"Depends on who first tires of the game. If Jenkinson demands more reinforcement from my strength here, we could become too weak to avoid a defeat at sea or on land. The government might decide the American colonies less of a loss than the sugar islands and India—their trade is far more profitable than any with these colonies."

"But what if the rebels suffer more defeats—as here at Charlestown? Won't that weaken and discourage them sufficiently to accept the King's authority again?"

"You have it arsy-varsy, my dear Cato. We must discourage them before they will weaken." He leaned across his desk, his expression lively and animated. "We must strike everywhere we can, at any rebel community within our safe reach. And the secret of that safe reach is sea-power. While we maintain control over these seas, we can land, at will, anywhere along the length of this coast. We can put ashore brigades, with cavalry and guns, at different places, to a prepared plan. They will strike at rebel communities nearby—destroy ships, stores, forage, tobacco—anything of value to the rebels. Provoke the local militia to attack them, defeat it, re-embark and strike again elsewhere—"

He ran out of breath. I said,

"What if we lose control of the coastal waters?"

"The day we lose control of these seas we lose all. Any force we cannot extract by sea will inevitably be overwhelmed—eventually—by a greater enemy force. We must always support every operation by an adequate naval strength. That will be my constant and chief concern."

He saw my misgivings in my face and bristled. He never could listen to criticism of his own ideas, though ever quick enough to damn anyone else's.

"What have I overlooked?"

I wondered how best to put my criticism without provoking another argument. We had had trouble enough for one day—he and I. I used the points he had given me himself.

"General, you complain you have too few men, yet you're prepared to deploy them in pennyworths up and down this coast, their whole support—their very survival, as you say—dependent on our naval forces; whose operations are entirely dependent on favourable weather. But the enemy, on land, will attack them in any weather, and may indeed overhwelm them so."

"Do you doubt the ability and devotion of our naval commanders?"

An irrelevance, of course—typical of his style of arguing; but,

[*72*]

considering his own disastrous experiences of naval co-operation, an interesting remark.

"Not a whit, General. But the ablest and most devoted naval commander can't drive in against an off-shore gale to embark me and my soldiers off a beach on which I am hard pressed."

No point in arguing with him. He had set his mind on his strategy of "Conflagration," as he called it. Not even the enemy was going to dissuade him. Sir Henry Clinton and my dear wife argue from the same premise; they are right and the facts are irrelevant.

And so on he raged, for another ten minutes of his valuable time; full of the proper use of sea-power—with no mention of its misuse. Finally he dropped into his chair and muttered,

"Well, let us leave that." He rested his elbows on his desk and dropped his head in his hands. After a moment he said despondently,

"Cato, you're a friend of Charles Cornwallis. You know him better than I. He wants independent command—which I suppose I must give him if I leave him in command here. But then—how do I command him? How do I control his actions here in the Carolinas from New York?"

Again I could not believe my ears. Did I really have to tell a Commander-in-Chief this?

"General—you give him his orders—clearly—and trust him. How else?"

And again he exploded.

"Trust! Trust! Trust!" He hit the desk each time with a clenched fist. "Why is it that I forever have to trust everyone else when no one ever trusts me? Not Germain—not Jenkinson—not Howe—not Cornwallis—not the King himself—none of them trust me! How can I trust Cornwallis?—How?"

"Why can't you trust him, General?"

"Why? Why can't I trust him—?" He mumbled, barely audible. He clutched at the desk edge. As I watched the fear and doubt clouding back into those bulging eyes, the answer to my question came clear to me with a horrid plainness; and a horrifying significance. Here was a man who could not trust his own judgment; who could not trust himself. How could he bring himself to trust anyone else? And he was the Commander-in-Chief.

His face seemed to fall apart before my eyes. What strength and resolution there had been now crumbled into the indecision, the suspicion and the petulance of Germain's description of him—"an old granny, poking around, gathering kindling from a stick-pile." He had scrabbled his way up to this high responsibility, for which—and he knew it too well now—he was inadequate.

My feelings must, as usual, have shown too clearly in my expression. He dropped his eyes to the paper before him and began to stutter,

"Colonel Cato—you will be attached to the staff of Lord Cornwallis—to advise him—on the recruitment, training and employment of militia cavalry—and assist him in—such other matters as he may require." He paused and took a deep breath. Then the words came out in a rush—"You will report to me regularly and fully—on all Lord Cornwallis' plans for the conduct of the campaign in these southern colonies. That is all."

I waited a few seconds, then I said,

"May I have your Excellency's permission to leave?"

No answer. So I left. But, at the door, I turned and bowed. Military courtesies, when executed punctiliously, are an exercise in self-discipline very steadying to the nerves; and also the most effective rebuke to the rudeness of a superior officer. I never neglect them, especially when I'm in a flaming temper. Which I was. Why? Because it had all been so pointless.

Unbelievable that a Commander-in-Chief—the Commander-in-Chief, God save us!—had been at such pains to cobble up this sordid little plot to suit his own tortuous intrigue and offset his lack of self-confidence in his dealings with his subordinate, whom he knew to be—and envied—as a stronger and better commander than himself.

I was to be his informer in Cornwallis' camp. Cornwallis, suspecting this, would be careful to obey the letter of his orders. If, resenting my presence, Cornwallis sought to dismiss me, Clinton could defend me; if he chose to do so. If, because I had failed him in some way, he did not choose, then I could be dismissed; probably in disgrace, if it suited Clinton better. A pretty scheme, from which the only possible gainer would be Clinton. But one point he had overlooked, and his shabby artifice wrecked on it. A point of which he had reminded us both. I am a friend of Charles Cornwallis.

Chapter Six

In which I encounter the rank villain again
and suffer until assisted by a swamp fox.

On deck a member of Clinton's staff awaited me; a tall, thin major of the 17th Light Dragoons.

"Oliver de Lancey, Colonel—Deputy Quartermaster-General. I've arranged for a cutter to wait on you, sir. Accommodation is prepared for you in Brigadier-General Pattison's headquarters in the Brewton House in King Street—he commands in Charlestown. A carriage and a wagon for your baggage will meet you on the quay if you will instruct the midshipman in charge of the cutter as to your needs and the hour you intend to go ashore."

"Very kind. Is the cutter alongside?"

"Manned the moment before you came on deck, Colonel."

"Immaculate timing. I suppose the progress of my conversation with the Commander-in-Chief was—evident?"

"It usually is," said de Lancey, dryly.

"I'm escorting the Lady Lucy Fairleigh—"

"Oh yes, Colonel. The Admiral made his barge available to Lord Fairleigh so that he could meet her. There's the barge returning now, so I suppose she'll already be ashore."

"How the devil did the Admiral know she was aboard the *Union?*"

De Lancey smiled that patient smile good staff officers use on senior officers overtaken by events.

"Lord Fairleigh had a letter by hand of Brigadier-General Dalrymple, who arrived last month, and *Camel* made a signal to the flagship as you came into harbour this morning."

My first thought was to go ashore myself, in the hope of seeing Lucy

[75]

before she left Charlestown. My second was that Lord Fairleigh was, unwittingly, doing precisely what had to be done; what I had lacked the wit and courage to do. Lucy and I would now part with—well, affection. If we should chance to meet again, I hoped it would have matured to friendship—a fond friendship. That is what I told myself. But my day was suddenly become drab and colourless; though there was an irony about the efficiency of the arrangements for Lucy's reception which made me smile, if a little sourly. I said,

"Never underestimate the influence of a proscribed Scots rebel, Major de Lancey."

He hadn't the faintest idea of what I was talking about, but being a good cavalry officer, smiled politely, said, "Very good, Colonel," and saluted as I went down to the cutter.

Back aboard the *Union* I was met by Conyngham.

"And how did you find His Excellency the Commander-in-Chief, Colonel?"

"Much the same as ever."

Conyngham sucked his teeth.

"Then God help us all," he said glumly.

I instructed the midshipman of the cutter to report back at nine the following morning, and it was there most punctually.

It could not take all our baggage and, at the quay, Matthew stayed to unload the first part into the waiting wagon and return to the *Union* for the second load.

Along with the baggage-wagon was a shabby gig, beside which stood an immaculate sergeant of the 23rd Foot. His salute was as smart as his appearance and his brogue as broad as Matthew's.

"Begging your honour's pardon—Sergeant Lamb, 23rd Regiment, sir. General Pattison's compliments and regrets, sir, no officer is available to meet your honour. May I be permitted to escort your honour myself?"

The gig was better suited for carting rubbish and looked uncomfortable besides. I said,

"Thank you, Sergeant Lamb. Please dismiss the gig. I'd like to stretch my legs after being aboard ship for seven weeks. Is it far to the headquarters?"

"Fifteen minutes' walk, your honour."

"Well, perhaps we may take a little longer, and you can show me the sights as we go."

We picked our way through the gangs of dock labourers—prisoners and

Negroes—loading the stores from the newly arrived transports into the wagons, which waited in a tangle of endless columns stretching the length of each quay and out into the street beyond. On each wagon a Negro driver huddled fast asleep. In each tenth wagon lolled a sentry of the local militia, supposedly a guard against pilfering, and as vigilant as the drivers. Each sentry we passed received a smart rap across that part of his anatomy convenient to Sergeant Lamb's cane and an injunction to—

"Be alert there!"

The streets through which we passed were filled with people of every sort and style. No one hurried, nor seemed to have need to do so. All was leisured amiability. Everyone appeared to have all the time in the world with naught to do. Which is probably why Charlestown was the centre of intrigue and sedition that it was. But the air of unhurried ease was infectious, and I found it so pleasant to move about again freely with Sergeant Lamb, who knew and spoke about the city so well, that it was over an hour before we arrived at the headquarters in King Street.

The Brewton House was a most elegant building, standing back from the roadway behind a high, brick, stone-topped wall. The Union flag flew above the gate, beneath which a sergeant and sentry of the 7th Foot saluted smartly as we entered. At the tall front door, at the head of a semi-circle of white stone steps, a second sentry saluted and we passed into the wide, flag-stoned hall.

The room allotted to me, at the back of the house on the ground floor, was small and furnished as a library. A bed had been put in it and Matthew was arranging my things to his liking. After my quarters aboard the *Union* it was palatial.

Matthew seemed somewhat out of humour. He had a badly grazed hand and a cut under one eye.

"What the devil have you been doing?" I asked. "Been rousting in the gin-kens already?"

"Devil a bit I have then!" said Matthew indignantly. "Would I be doing that before I'd seen your honour to rights here? No, it was that whoreson gibbet-fruit Cook and his trimmer, Crowder. They've got clear away. I tried to stop 'em and got this for me pains."

"They escaped? When? How did it happen?"

"Well, they'd had the leg-irons took off aboard, so there was only the bracelets on 'em. Mr. Russell sends 'em ashore under guard in the cutter that brought the rest of our baggage, but there was no guard on the quay to meet them. The officer in the cutter don't want to take them back to the ship nor hang about, so he leaves them there to wait for the other guard to arrive. There was only Corporal Finnis and another of the 17th with them. I was started to load the cart when I hear a shout and there's Crowder a-racing along the quay and Cook in a mill with Corporal Finnis and the other lad out, cold meat, on the ground.

"I trips Crowder and fetches him a chatterer and runs to help the Corporal. But before I gets there, Cook cracks his nut with the cuffs of his clinkers and he's cold meat too. I goes for Cook and we has a bit of a barney, but he's twice me, your honour, and I'm ends up under a cart soon enough. I shouts to the wagon-guards for to stop him, but devil a man moved. They say deserters find friends easy enough around these parts, so we'll not be seeing them again I'm thinking."

"Poor old Matthew! Leave those things and go and get those cuts dressed now. Is Corporal Finnis all right—and the other soldier?"

"Finnis' nose is broke, but I don't know of the other fellow, your honour."

"Are they searching for Cook and Crowder?"

"Oh, they'll search. That's what the officer said. But as to finding 'em—" he shrugged and nodded at a letter addressed to me lying on the table. "That was left by the General's orderly."

The note informed me that Brigadier General Pattison requested the honour of my company at a small reception to be held at nine o'clock that evening in the ballroom of the house. And would I be kind enough to come a few minutes before nine to permit him to have a word with me?

So, a little before nine, I climbed the great mahogany staircase to the ballroom on the upper floor. The tall double doors were opened for me by a sentry. I strode in—and tripped on the carpet; which gave me, on my hands and knees, the opportunity to observe that it was an Axminster. The carpets in my own house come from this same manufactory—only eight miles away—and this small touch of the familiar restored my equanimity somewhat. It needed it; I don't make a practice of approaching generals on all fours.

Officers of the artillery are—in the main—precise gentlemen; which is just as well for the rest of the Army. Brig. Gen. James Pattison is no exception. Standing, very erect, beside a large table at the far end of the room, he gave me time to regain my feet and observe my surroundings before advancing at a steady pace, hand outstretched, to greet me. He is a tall, fine-looking man, with long, narrow, aquiline features and very blue eyes. His manner is modelled on David Garrick playing Hamlet. He doesn't speak to you—he addresses you, pausing between every few words. He opened fire at extreme range.

"Ah—Colonel Pelham—permit me, sir—to welcome you—to Charles-town."

He is a trifle short-sighted, which makes him adopt that supposedly aristocratic style of peering frown. As he came close enough to discern the details of my uniform the frown became puzzled.

"You have changed—your regiment, sir?"

"Not I, sir," I replied, "but I can't answer for Colonel Pelham."

A little off-hand? Well, I didn't much care for being taken for Percy Pelham. For a moment he was at a loss for a declamation. I thought I should clear the air.

"My name, General, is Cato—2nd Dragoons—the Greys." His style of speech was infectious.

His nose rose higher as he peered the harder, the furrows deepening in the frown.

"But why then—did the Commander-in-Chief—give me to understand—that Colonel Pelham—of the Lifeguards—was to be appointed—to the staff of Lord Cornwallis?"

"I believe—" I began, but then thought better of it, "I have no idea, General."

"I see. Strange. A misunderstanding. Well, Colonel Cato—in that case—permit me to welcome you—to Charlestown."

That was the sum of our introductory conversation. He had clearly lost interest in me; doubtless appreciating, precisely, the degree by which his career would benefit from acquaintanceship with the Catos, as opposed to association with the Pelhams. He gave me a starchy, little bow, turned abruptly on his heel and paced to the door to greet his first guests. I walked to the far end of the room, which is small for a ballroom but handsomely decorated; the walls panelled in mahogany and the ceiling painted, very strikingly, to represent the evening sky—dark blue, with silvery clouds and stars. A large and fine chandelier hangs opposite the great fireplace set in the inner wall. On the chimney-piece is a marble plaque depicting a hunting scene and above it an over-mantel, supported on white columns, frames a portrait of a man, which I judged to be by Mr. Reynolds.

I was attempting to identify the constellations on the ceiling when John Conyngham tapped my shoulder. "Well, Colonel, you've a pretty snug roost here! Do they find you a well-shaped warming-pan as well then?

Lud! Damned good-looking women in this town! Always heard there were. My head's been turning one way and t'other so fast coming here, it near came unscrewed!"

"They don't hold your sort of warming pans in Army Board stores, John. You have to find your own. Matthew tells me Charles Russell has lost his gallows-bait."

"Ay, but not his fault. And small chance of ever finding them again. They'll hide up in one of those cunny-cloisters down by the docks and get the resident nuns to fend for them awhile. There's many a deserter gone to earth in those warrens, I'm told."

Pattison manoeuvred through the crowd towards me, beside him a dapper little fellow to whom I took an instant dislike. A long, thin, grey face set in a permanent, cheerless smirk—long, thin, grey hands, everlastingly massaging each other—narrow, cold, grey eyes, forever flickering round the room, but never meeting anyone else's.

Pattison addressed me.

"Colonel Cato—may I present—Mr. Secker. A gentleman with whom you will have—much to do. He keeps us—" and his voice dropped dramatically—"well informed!" He nodded portentously and left us.

Secker shook his head disapprovingly.

"I fear the General is a little indiscreet on occasion, Colonel." He took my elbow and breathed unfragrantly in my ear. "As you are a member of Lord Cornwallis's staff, sir, let me hasten to assure you I am so myself—in a certain capacity. You will appreciate, I'm sure, how essential it is that we know who are our friends."

I retrieved my elbow.

"You have a difficult and dangerous occupation, Mr. Secker. Do you operate widely in the colony?"

"Widely enough, Colonel. I have friends up-country whom I visit regularly. But I avoid penetrating into North Carolina. That would be too dangerous—I'm too well known there, you see. Even here, sir, in Charlestown, my life is in constant danger. But I have the satisfaction of knowing that I do my duty."

And doing very well for himself too, I supposed, for his clothes were of excellent material and well-cut. I guessed he told Clinton what Clinton wanted to believe; and probably did the same for any rebel commander too.

He washed his hands thoroughly and gave a little bob.

"If you will forgive me, my dear Colonel. Not wise for me to be seen talking to senior officers too long—people jump to unfortunate conclusions, you know. Honoured to make your acquaintance, sir—we shall meet—" And he bowed himself off into the throng.

Pattison had said that it was to be a small reception, but the room was crowded. I found the heat unbearable and the air scarcely breathable. These southern ladies, pretty, charming, gay and witty as they are, seemed to apply their various perfumes with a jug. A little scent titillates and tantalizes a man's sensibilities; too much only suffocates them.

I paid my compliments to Pattison and thankfully struggled my way out of the sweaty mêlée and downstairs to the peace of my own room. Matthew had not lit my candles and, as I entered the darkness another perfume came to my nostrils.

"Lucy!—Lucy!"

There was no answer. I fumbled for the tinder box, dropped it, swore, scrabbled around on my hands and knees for it, found it and finally managed to light a candle. I stared round the little room—it was empty. But the scent hung, mocking me, and on the little table by my bed lay a note.

"I had hoped to thank you for your kindness and say goodbye. They said you were engaged in the reception and did not know when you would come. I waited but must go now. We leave early tomorrow. My father and I hope that you will visit us at Belhaven. Please come. Your loving cousin—Lucy."

She had been here, in this room. She had sat here, on my bed, waiting for me. And I was within feet of her—being bored by Pattison and repelled by Secker. I hit the poor little table so hard, it shattered. Then I saw Anne's picture—on the floor—and cursed myself for an infatuated fool.

Cornwallis was not due to return to Charlestown until the 17'th June—another ten days. I decided to wait until the 19th and, if he had not returned, to set out for his forward headquarters at Camden.

Then followed, despite the comforts of the Brewton House, ten of the longest, most miserable and homesick days of all my soldiering. They were enlivened only by the charming amiability of the family of the owner, Mrs. Rebecca Motte. She is a widow and a sister of the Miles Brewton who built the house, and whose portrait hangs over the fireplace in the ballroom. Her three daughters were all married or affianced to officers of the rebel army, but were all the soul of kindness to the officers of Pattison's headquarters. Perhaps they were trying to suborn us from our duties; but I doubt it.

None of Cornwallis' staff was left in Charlestown, and Pattison's few officers were fully engaged in the administration of the port and city; now the major base for our operations in the southern colonies. So whilst all to whom I spoke were very ready with their advice on how to recruit militia cavalry, they were as ready with their regrets that they were unable, personally, to assist me in reaping the harvest, which—so they assured me—was there for the taking.

I had been supplied with horses taken at the surrender of the city. They were soft and out of condition; quite unfit for campaigning. I thought some slow work each day through the country around Charlestown would improve them, and, at the same time, afford me the opportunity to test the temperature of the loyalist fervour and estimate the size of the recruiting harvest. I was overwhelmed by the number of those who protested fulsomely their loyalty to His Majesty; but not with the number of those prepared to put their professed loyalty to the test of military service. However, a few followed me back to Charlestown, and these I attached, according to their preference of arms, to Charles Russell's detachment, or to the 7th Foot, who were very much weakened by sickness.

Saturday, the 17th June, came and went with no news of Cornwallis. I had expected this and had already arranged to ride to Camden with Charles Russell, who had been ordered to move with his reinforcement draft of the 17th Dragoons to join Colonel Tarleton's British Legion there. Russell reported that, despite careful exercise since coming ashore, his horses could march no more than fifteen miles a day; and that, in this climate and with their campaign loads, only at a walk.

"Can't even mount all my draft, Colonel. Some of 'em will have to ride in the baggage carts, with the unfit animals led behind. The voyage has taken the stomachs out of the poor beasts. They're bags of bones. Got sores that just won't heal in this awful, damp heat. A couple more days of slow work could help."

"We'll be at your stables on Monday morning then," I said, "At seven."

"Very good, Colonel. I'll be happy to leave this town for a while. The girls are like the weather—too hot for comfort."

Monday morning saw Matthew and I riding up King Street to the stables of the 17th Dragoons. It was not the smartest area of Charlestown, and as we passed through, a few whores were out refreshing themselves after their labours of the night. They greeted our uniforms with spirit and imagination.

"Come on, Captain, then! It's a lovely morning for a paddle up my creek—"

Another unlovely, unlaced baggage calls to Matthew—

"Ah, lookit the 'andsome soldier-boy! I'll wager 'e's got a gristle like a bull! Come 'ere, natty lad, I ain't a bleedin' virgin but you can 'ave what's left—"

"Arrah!" cries Matthew. "You're a generous lot o' lasses, you Charlestown girls!"

"That's me ballocky boy!" screeches the baggage, " 'e appreciates us gals!" And they all shout and cheer and wave and urge us to hasten back to their pleasures.

The detachment of the 17th were drawn up on the road outside their quarters. The men, standing at their horses' heads, looked very well. The horses looked dreadful. Russell saluted.

"Daren't go further than Dorchester today, Colonel. That's fifteen miles. I can't ask my poor beasts to do more."

"Fifteen miles will do," I said. "Please carry on."

Russell saluted again and turned back to his troop. After years of civil idleness it was pleasant to hear again the familiar orders and watch the well-drilled movements of these regular cavalry troopers; nothing wooden or strained about them, only the alert, relaxed confidence of trained soldiers.

Russell's voice rang out clear, even gaily.

"Stand to your horses—Prepare to mount—Mount—Tell off by threes—Prove—Threes right wheel, march—Halt—Dress—Column . . . March—" and on that command, as the drill book says, "By the aid of both legs pressed gently against the horse's sides, without drawing up the heels, every man puts his horse into a walk." And so they did. And it was indeed all that the feeble animals could manage under their campaign loads.

I looked at Matthew. "We're off to war again, Matthew."

He grinned from ear to ear. "Sure, and it's altogether like coming home again, your honour!"

We arrived in Dorchester that evening with all the horses still sound. On examining them the next morning, we decided to move another fifteen miles on the Georgetown road to Bonneau's Ferry on the Cooper River. Sergeant Hawes and the detachment were accommodated in the barns of the Loyalist Mr. Harlestan, whilst Russell and I were hospitably welcomed by the local minister.

Travel in this unfamiliar land would have been impossible without the maps of the colonies, fortunately produced in the years immediately before the war. I had found, at Sayer and Bennett's in Fleet Street, one of these—a map of North and South Carolina, drawn by Mr. Henry

Mouzon; a rebel, living in Georgetown, whose map, published in London, impartially served both sides.

On inspection next morning, the exercise and better air appeared to have improved the horses' condition, and we decided on a longer march. We chose to ride by Biggin Bridge to Monks Corner, whence the road led over the cross by Coram's Plantation to Nelson's Ferry. Crossing the Santee River there, we could approach Camden along the road between the river and the High Hills of Santee.

After passing Monks Corner the road became difficult, crossing countless steep-sided, swampy ravines. This slowed us so that we did not climb out of the last of these obstacles until near dark. We passed one farmstead, which, in the failing light, looked deserted and badly damaged by fire. Two miles further down the road we came to the plantation of a Mr. Whitten, who offered us the freedom of his barn readily enough but begged to be excused accommodating Russell and me in his house, saying he had some guests already. I thought his manner odd, but he offered his son as a guide for us to the house of a Mr. Carey, two miles on. I was prepared to roll up in my cloak in the barn, but Russell protested,

"Colonel, why refuse comfortable beds when they're there?"

So, leaving Sergeant Hawes in charge again, we rode off into the dark behind Whitten's son—a sullen-looking clod—taking with us a corporal and three troopers as a guard.

Mr. Carey's house stood back from the road at the end of a quarter-mile of sandy track. He welcomed us with uncommon warmth. Young Whitten left us unceremoniously, ignoring our thanks.

"Surly cub," said Mr. Carey, shaking his head after him, "only seen him smile once—flogging one of his father's runaways. Keeps bad company and he'll come to a bad end."

The Careys' hospitality was as warm as their welcome. The beds were only truckles, but the supper Mrs. Carey and her two daughters set before us was excellent; and the peach brandy accompanying it better still. Corporal Mills and the guard, as well accommodated in a small cabin at the back of the house, received the same generous treatment—including the peach brandy. Russell and I went early to our beds, too weary to do more than throw off our jackets.

I woke with my bed on top of me and a boot in my ribs.

"Come on, rouse, bloody-back!" The bed was heaved off me and I was rolled over with another kick. "D'you want to sleep all day then?"

I raised myself on my elbow, my head spinning. I peered up at my assailant, straight into the muzzle of one of my own pistols. Somewhere in the house women were screaming. Russell and I together scrambled to our feet and tried to force our way to the door. We were tripped and pinned down; and the screaming went on—and on. Our attackers sneered,

"Never you mind to them, lobsters! Them Tory bitches is being 'tended to by our lads well 'nough—"

Our hands were bound behind us and we were dragged to our feet. There were four filthy, mean-looking ruffians, all in tattered remnants of uniforms—British and American. One of them snatched up my hat and coat with a shout.

"Godamighty, lads! Lookee 'ere then! 'E's a bleedin' colonel!"

The screaming had stopped now. We were pushed down the stairs and out through the back porch. Beyond the cabin where the guard had slept sprawled a 17th Dragoon, face down, the back of his head crushed in by a heavy club; which lay, spattered with blood, beside him.

Behind the house was a small clearing. Here, still in their night clothes, Carey and his wife were tied to one tree. At their feet lay their two daughters, naked, the one sobbing hysterically, the other unconscious; children of fourteen and fifteen years.

Corporal Mills and the two remaining troopers of the guard were standing under a branch of a great oak, their hands tied behind them and ropes around their necks. The ends of the ropes hung over the branch above them.

In front of them stood a group of eight men, a ragged, down-at-heel rabble. One of them, a big, burly fellow in a dirty, white uniform jacket with green facings stained with blood, shouted hoarsely at the two troopers of the 17th.

"You join us lads—there's good pickings for all. Doxies and rum—all you want!" The soldiers were silent. "Join us—or, by God, you'll swing else!"

"Captain!" The leader of our group shouted, "Look 'ere then—we got a colonel—a real, live colonel!"

All heads turned our way. The group stood, grinning, around the big fellow they called captain and a small man standing beside him. The captain was Cook—the small man, Crowder.

Crowder recognized us first. His teeth bared in a yellow snarl—like a rat's. He ran across, halted in front of me and saluted with a flourish.

"Welcome, Colonel Cato, sir! What an honour to 'ave you with us! 'Ow can we entertain your honour? Per'aps you'll dance a Tyburn jig for us, sir? We got strings to suit you!"

[*85*]

Laughing and shouting, he and my captors jostled me across to where the soldiers were standing under the oak tree.

"Hold your noise!" Cook's voice silenced the hubbub at once. They were obviously very frightened of Cook. He stared in silence at Russell—and Russell at him. Then—

"Good morning, Mr. Russell," said Cook quietly, "unexpected pleasure this, sir. But I owe you a lot and I'd hoped we'd meet again." He breathed deep, keeping tight control of his voice. "You killed my mate, Jack Parkes, Mr. Russell. And you had that Scotch bastard take my back off—in two doses. Well—" he paused, "we can't oblige your honour by cleaning you off to your backribs in two doses—but if you'd consent to us trying it in one—" His voice choked in his throat. His eyes narrowed to vicious slits and he spat out the words. "Get that bleedin' shirt off 'im an' fetch me a whip! Lash 'im up to that tree. Spread 'im good and wide. I'm goin' to carve every bit of hide off 'im I can see!"

They lashed Russell, spreadeagled, to a big pine. A man came running from the barn.

"Can't find no whip anywheres, Captain—"

Cook's backhander sent him spinning and the wretch scrambled to his feet and fled headlong back to the barn.

"Where's Ryan?" I whispered to Corporal Mills.

"Weren't with us. Might 'ave got away—if 'e ain't dead."

Crowder struck him in the mouth.

"Shut yer gob, you—or I'll stop yer breath an' all!"

He picked up a rope, made a noose, put it over my head and tossed the end of the rope over the same branch as the others. He screamed with laughter.

"Look'ee 'ere, boys, the Colonel's going to dance for us!"

He and two others heaved on the rope, the noose closed and I was swung up. I had dropped my chin on my chest and the noose closed over it, so I did not choke. They saw this and, loosing the rope, let me fall, then heaved on it again immediately. This time the noose slid under my chin. I tried to tense my neck muscles, but too late. My head, eyes, throat, tongue, chest—all were consumed in one blaze of agony; and the world ended.

At first, when I regained consciousness, only the pain told me I was alive. Things came slowly into focus. I lay propped against the tree, the noose still around my neck. A blowsy, young woman, her fat face framed in a tangle of yellow hair, hung over me, grinning, relishing my torment. She wore a thin blouse, barely covering her very ample bosom, and over that my coat. I recall considering, hazily, whether, with her yellow locks and flimsy bodice, she was an angel. I decided she wasn't, for, even to my benumbed nostrils, she stank.

" 'Ere 'e comes!" she squealed, " 'is eyes is open! There, love—got yer breath back? Ready for another swing? Come on, Crowdy—let's see 'im do a jig!"

The rope jerked me to my knees. I doubled up, retching and shivering. The hag bent down and leered into my face.

"Cold are you, dearie? Like your smart coat, would you?"

She made as if to pull it off, but the facing hooks caught in her bodice and tore it open, exposing her breasts—large, flabby and dirty. She giggled and wobbled them in my face. Unangelic. Crowder pulled her back.

"Get out of it, Bess. You won't get naught for sporting yer blubber' fore 'im—"

She caught him a ringing slap.

"Get yer claws off of me! Yer don't own me." She simpered down at me. " 'E's a nice-lookin' feller—reckon 'e'd give me a better jerkin' than you do with that bleedin' fiddle-stick o' your'n!"

They all laughed at this and Crowder, furious, struck her. She stumbled and fell on top of me. I thought, bemusedly, that if I was fated to be suffocated, I should prefer the rope. I was still not really in the world—Corporal Mills told me most of what followed my elevation.

Crowder, swearing at the prostrate Bess, was himself knocked to the ground by a tall, fine-looking, quadroon girl; a Charlestown prostitute, known—according to Mills—as Big Kate.

"Lousy little shy-cock," she said contemptuously, and, as Crowder got up, she knocked him down again.

"Shut that bloody squalling," said Cook, coldly.

They had made him a whip of sorts; a stock with four rough cut strips of leather and four lengths of knotted whipcord bound to the end of it. He held the whip where Russell could see it.

"You'll have to pardon the roughness of this here instrument, Mr. Russell. But I'll do my duty as best I can, sir." He called to his gang. "Get a couple of buckets of water here, with some salt in 'em. We don't want Mr. Russell falling asleep."

He waited in silence for the buckets and a sack of salt to be brought.

"Now then, Mr. Russell, we're ready. We'll tell you when you've had your five hundred and after that just you say when you want us to stop,

[87]

sir, and we'll stop right away. Then we'll hang you, along with the Colonel there. O'course, if you wants us to, we could go on and take your heart out through your back ribs. But it's a hot and sweaty business that, this time o' year, sir; so we'd be much obliged to be saved the trouble."

His tone was entirely unemotional; and so the more horrible. He unbuttoned his jacket, flexed his shoulders and made the whip lashes whistle through the air. Then he said, respectfully,

"Permission to begin punishment, please, Mr. Russell."

Russell ignored him. Cook said again, grinning viciously,

"Permission to begin punishment, please, Mr. Russell."

Russell did not answer. Cook's grin faded.

"Are you ready, Mr. Russell?"

Still no answer from Russell.

"Are you ready, Mr. Russell?"

Cook's voice shook with anger; but still he waited. And Russell waited too—in silence. Cook snarled,

"God damn you, you stiff-necked swine!" And brought the first stroke down—and another—and another. The instrument may have been rough, but it was effective enough, as the blood on the lashes soon showed. Russell made no move or sound, and this enraged Cook the more. His arm had swung like a machine some twenty times, when a voice from behind us said,

"And what, pray, is this?"

They had all been so intent on Cook and Russell that no one had noticed eight horsemen ride out from the trees behind us, to sit now half surrounding us. All rode good horses, all wore dragoon uniform; seven had carbines covering Cook's gang. The eighth, the commander, was a small man, neat in appearance. He sat squarely on his big, bay horse. His crimson jacket and white leathers fitted well; his horse furniture was immaculate. The pistols in his saddle holsters showed silver mounted butts. The face under the visor of his dragoon cap was lean, with a high-bridged nose and jutting chin, unsmiling, dominating. He said again,

"And what, pray, is this?"

Cook tucked the whip under his arm and buttoned his jacket.

"We caught some British soldiers," he said sullenly.

"So I see," said the horseman, "And that gentleman—and those ladies?" He pointed at the wretched Careys.

"He's a bleeding Tory farmer—he was a-entertaining of 'em."

"Indeed? And who are you?"

Cook hitched a thumb in his waistband and his tone became bolder, "Captain Cook's my name. We're South Carolina Militia."

"Indeed?" The officer's gaze raked Cook from head to heel. "And pray, Cap-tain—" he drawled the word—"Cook of the South Carolina Militia, why do you wear the jacket of an officer of the 3rd Continental Dragoons?"

Cook glowered at him.

"Don't see it's any o' your business. I lost my uniform in Charlestown. Found this one. Do till I get a new one—"

"And where did you find it, Cap-tain—"

Cook's temper blazed at the officer's contempt.

"What the 'ell's it got to do with you? Who d'you think you are—"

The officer raised his hand. At once, from all sides of the clearing, more horsemen rode out from the trees; among them an elderly man with a bandaged head. The officer called to him.

"Is that your nephew's jacket on that man, Mr. Monk?"

"It is, Colonel. See the blood from the wound he took at the fight at Biggin Bridge, sir. That's the man who murdered John—"

"He's a damned liar! He's a traitor Tory—"

Cook strode forward a pace—but only one pace. The officer's hand moved like light and the long barrel of his pistol pointed very steadily at Cook's head, with the hammer cocked. His voice had a new edge.

"I have lived all my life in these parts, Cap-tain Cook. I know who favours the King's cause and who the revolution. And I know murderers when I see them. And I see them now. Mr. Monk here is a loyal American and an old friend. Mr. Carey there as loyally supports King George, and I respect him for it. You and your cut-throats treat them both the same. You murdered Mr. Monk's nephew, an officer of the 3rd Dragoons, wounded and helpless in bed. You raped and butchered his daughter. You thought you had killed him. You looted and burnt his house. You would now do the same to the Careys." He looked round his command. "Captain Milton, escort Mr. Carey and his family into the house, please. Take Surgeon Hart with you. Major Gamble, have these ruffians bound—and loose that soldier they were flogging; Surgeon Hart can tend him too—"

He suddenly noticed my jacket on Bess. He stared.

"How did you come by that jacket, woman?"

Bess, crouching by me, whimpered with terror. Corporal Mills spoke out,

"If you please, your honour, it's the Colonel's there."

"What Colonel's? Where?"

[*89*]

"There on the ground, your honour. They was a-hanging of 'im. He's near dead, sir."

The officer was off his horse in an instant, limped across to me and dropped on his knees beside me. He raised my head gently and removed the noose, exposing the rope burn round my throat.

"God's teeth!" His fury exploded like a grenade. "You murdering whore! You'd treat an officer so! Sergeant Bland—bind this hell-hag and put this rope on her—"

Bess's snivel changed to hysterical screaming.

"No, your honour, no! I never touched 'im. It were 'im—" she pointed at Crowder, "Stike me dead if I lie, sir!—"

Now it was Crowder's turn to howl.

"She's lying, your honour—she wanted to watch 'im 'anged—she made us do it, your honour—"

"Us?" said the officer.

"Them two what's with 'im there, your honour—them's the ones what done it." Bess pointed at the two men with Crowder. I hadn't had the leisure to observe the identity of my intending executioners earlier; it hadn't seemed a matter of any consequence. But now I noted that one of them was the unsmiling, young Mr. Whitten. Perhaps he had smiled pulling on my rope.

The officer turned to Corporal Mills.

"Who did this?"

"Them three, your honour."

"Then you and your two lads can hang them—and that whore."

"Oh God! your honour—" Bess clutched at the officer, shrieking, "You wouldn't 'ang a girl—"

He shook her off.

"I'd hang a murderess as soon as a murderer," he said, dispassionately.

I was carried into the house, where Corporal Mills later told me that they had hanged Crowder, Bess and Whitten with his fellow executioner all on the same branch on which they had hoisted me. I felt no pity for any of them.

"Then them fellows bound Cook's lot," said Mills, " 'cept Kate, an' she cut Cook loose. She makes up to one of them what was 'olding the horses an' takes 'is free 'and and shoves it in 'er tit—er—puts it in 'er bosom, sir. Then she trips 'im an' grabs a nag. Cook jumps on it and is off with 'er a-holding to 'is leg. But 'e kicks 'er off and gets clean away. They drags Kate back, kicking and screaming, 'You'll never catch 'im, 'e'll come back for me!' "

"The officer looked at 'er like she was a cowpat. "'E'll find you easy enough,' 'e says, 'along with your sister strumpet on that tree!'"

"Then she starts shouting she was with child. 'You damned ditchdrab!' 'e says, 'Don't plead your poxy belly to me! Its fruit will be as foul as you!' So we strung up the lot—with Kate along o' the fat tart. Good riddance!"

The executions were accompanied by a fair amount of noise. Russell asked the officer the cause of it.

"We're destroying the sweepings of the old world and the new together, sir. When I catch gangs of deserters from either army—or from both, like these—I destroy them. I hope the King's troops do likewise."

"And the women too, sir?"

"Women! They assist in murder and rape—and you call them women? We'll manage without such sluts."

Mr. Carey brought him some drink and we had time to examine our deliverer. I saw he wore a boot on one leg and a thick stocking on the other. Unable to speak, I pointed at the stocking. He laughed.

"I broke my ankle in Charlestown some six weeks ago, Colonel. They took me home, fortunately for me. So I wasn't in the city when you took it. Shan't get a boot on it for some time yet, I fear." He smiled at us. "May I ask who you gentlemen are?"

"This is Col. Philip Cato," answered Russell, "a member of Lord Cornwallis' staff. I am Lieutenant Russell, 17th Light Dragoons. And you, sir?"

"Thank you, Mr. Russell. My name is Francis Marion, Colonel of the 2nd South Carolina Regiment of the Continental Line."

"Well, Colonel," said Russell, "I suppose we are now your prisoners?"

Marion's smile widened.

"Mr. Russell, please! Today we are allies, sir! I assure you I'm delighted to have been of some assistance—"

One of his troopers clattered up to the porch.

"Colonel Marion, sir—party of King's troops coming fast from Nelson's Ferry way. Over a hundred, sir—an' some o' Tarleton's Greens among 'em."

Marion got to his feet leisurely and sighed.

"Ah, yes—Tarleton—he's ever with us. Here's to his confusion!" He drained his glass and, hobbling over to me, took my hand gently.

"It's been my honour and pleasure, Colonel—a quick recovery, sir. And you too Mr. Russell—pray don't move, sir." And to the Careys—"Mr. Carey—Mrs. Carey ma'am—farewell. Be prudent, I beg you. You know me for a friend. But I'm not always here to aid honest folk."

[*91*]

He bowed, limped down the steps of the porch and clambered awkwardly into his saddle. Then he cried to me—

"Colonel Cato—you're both cavalrymen; so I suppose you're foxhunters as well. As I must play the swamp fox now, pray favour me with a few minutes' law before you put hounds into this covert!"

And, with a wave, he swung his horse about and he and his command vanished into the shadows of the woods.

Chapter Seven

In which my concept of my duty is supported by
Lord Cornwallis and I accompany a fighting patrol.

"Well, them fellows come along very 'andy." Corporal Mills' voice rang through my throbbing skull. "Now lads, you get and put poor Trim 'ere to bed with a shovel, whilst I gets his kit together."

"What we'm a-doin' wi' the rest on 'em, Corporal?"

"Leave 'em to the crows. They're welcome to 'em."

A sound of hooves along the track and a voice called,

"Bigod, it's Paddy! Corporal—Ryan's back! Where ye been, Paddy? Back to bleedin' Charlestown?"

Matthew asked anxiously, "Is the Colonel all right?"

" 'E's inside the 'ouse. They damn near done for 'im. Would 'ave done for us an' all afore you give us the pleasure of your bloody company again!"

"Och, what ye yammering about? Ye sound alive enough!"

"Ain't no thanks to you, ye bog-trotting bangster! We reckoned you'd piked off. Them bastards could 'ave strung us up like a lot of 'ams 'fore you got back."

"What if they had? Sure, I'd have avenged ye."

"Ye would? Ah well—did ye hear that Jack? If them whores' gets 'ad 'anged us, old Paddy would 'ave avenged us. Ain't that nice of 'im?"

"Ay, bless 'im—'e's always the thoughtful one—the—"

"Hold your blether and get that 'ole dug!" Corporal Mills sounded irritated. "Ryan, you go an' tend the officers. 'Ere, where's Sergeant Hawes then?"

An ominous pause. Matthew said nervously,

"I—I couldn't find the house, Corporal."

[93]

"Ye couldn't find—What d'ye mean? It's straight down the bloody road! Which way did ye go on the road—left or right?"

Silence. Corporal Mills again,

"Godamighty, man, don't ye know yer left from yer—? Well—did ye turn to yer sword 'and or away from it?"

"I—well—I turned towards it. Bedad, it's away I should have turned—we turned to it a-coming in here. I plain lost me way—"

Mills spluttered venomously.

"Lost yer way, ye witless pigwidgeon—ay, by God ye did! More's the pity ye found yer bloody way back! Bigod, if yer bleedin' arse were loose ye'd lose that an' all!"

A very crestfallen Matthew came hurrying in to me.

I was given a draught, left for me by Surgeon Hart, and slept soundly all day, waking only when it was dark. The pain had eased. My boots and some of my clothes had been removed, my neck was swathed in a great poultice and I lay under a blanket.

A lamp, shining dimly, outlined the cloaked figure of a man sitting by me. For once the night air was cool and full of the sounds of cicadas and frogs. The pale moonlight lay aslant the yard, silvering the roof-shingles on the barns and the tops of the trees beyond. Stars pricked the dark blue sky and the fireflies danced in the shadows.

I shifted on the bed and the man in the cloak leant forward.

"Philip—" A voice I thought I knew. I grunted. He placed his hand on mine. "Philip—it's Charles Cornwallis. Don't try to speak. Must hurt like the very devil. Thank God that crafty rascal Marion got here when he did. Your man, Ryan, found our advanced guard and they came on at the gallop; but they might have come too late. I've had the story from Russell. I have to be in Charlestown tomorrow, so I must be off. I'm leaving a surgeon here to look after you and some dragoons of the British Legion as escort." He rose and hooked the throat chain of his cloak. "Russell says he'll be fit to ride on tomorrow—he's a good lad—so he can take his detachment on to Camden." He pressed my hand. "I'll see you in Charlestown in a few days." And was gone.

Matthew came out of the shadows.

"Surgeon said to move you indoors when you waked, your honour." He called to the guard commander for men to help carry my bed. "Good to see his lordship again. He don't change—nor never forget a soldier. Remembered me at once, your honour! Four o'clock in the afternoon he arrived here, and it's near ten now. Been sat all the while on that chair.

[*94*]

Forbid us to wake you. Just sat there waiting for you to wake. That's a friend."

For three days I remained at the Careys'. The British Legion troopers buried poor Private Trim of the 17th Light Dragoons in the Careys' neat little cemetery, in a clearing in the woods close by the house. The bodies of Cook's gang were flung into a pit deep in the woods.

"Sure and it's a sad thing that devil's brat Cook weren't among 'em," said Matthew. "He'll be after raising hell wherever he goes."

Unable to move easily or comfortably, I devoted my time to writing a long letter to Anne, short ones to the children and imagining myself at home in Somerset on these midsummer mornings. I saw the flocks moving slowly along the hillside, with the lambs' plaintive bleating and the ewes' anxious replies. I saw the horses and the cattle grown fat on the summer grass, their coats sleek and shining, and I heard the foals whinnying to each other across the paddocks. I smelt the sweetness of the new hay and heard the rumble of the carts as they carried it to the barns. I felt the soft grass of the lawn under my feet and breathed the scents of flowers and herbs, blending and changing as I passed. And I heard the sound of the church bells, as on a Sunday morning and evening the gentle breeze carried it, rising and falling, up from the green, green valley with its silver stream.

And, whilst I lay there, wretched and sweating in my swaddling poultice, heart-sick for my loved ones and my home—I thought, too, of Lucy.

After the three days, though still unable to speak or swallow comfortably, I decided that I was fit enough to ride and, after a fond farewell to the Careys, we began the journey to Charlestown at a slow pace. On arrival in my room in the Brewton House I was again put to bed. But the journey and the exercise had done me good, and the following day I felt nearly recovered.

The day after that, Cornwallis came to see me. For a little we talked of my home and family; I knew he could not bear to speak of his. After a while he said,

"I hear Pussy wanted that booby of a nephew of his—what's his name—to tell him when I was being naughty, but he had to give you that honour, you lucky fellow. To be in the personal confidence of the Commander-in-Chief—what distinction!" He laughed a little bitterly. "Wish to God *I* was—he might let me know what he intends to do! He's left me four pages of his contradictory mumble-bumble as a guide.

Doesn't trust me, of course. Far as I can see, I'm free to conduct affairs in any way I wish—so long as I don't actually do anything. How did you find him?"

"About the same as ever."

"Oh, he's changed, Philip, more than you think. He used to have spunk enough—not much, but enough. Now he's as spunkless as a shotten herring. He can't make a decision and hold to it. To tell the truth, he can't make a decision!"

"He mentioned a plan he called 'Conflagration.' "

" 'Conflagration'—ay, he's had that bee in his bonnet for some time now. We can never win this war that way. We can win only by beating every army they send against us. And do you know how many soldiers Pussy has left me to do that with? Three thousand! Three thousand to keep Georgia and South Carolina in peace, to persuade the dissidents in North Carolina into submission and to reduce the rebellion in Virginia if I ever get there—all without leaving Charlestown. That's all he wants.

"He told me that he had conquered both the Carolinas at Charlestown; I had only to hold them. Then he paroled all the rebels we took here; none of whom have any intention of honouring their paroles, of course. They'll have their knives in our backs within the month.

"He's always had a genius for getting everything into a bloody muddle and blaming everyone else for it. Don't bother to tell him I said so in your report—I've already told him!"

He looked at me dejectedly for a moment, then threw himself back in his chair and laughed.

"Oh, what's the use of complaining? Thank God, I've a good staff and some of the best commanders you could wish."

I said, "Charles, why are you fighting this war? You voted against it in Parliament. Why did you agree to serve here?"

He was solemn again, looking down at his hands.

"Just to keep myself sane probably, Philip. I couldn't bear the thought of living alone at Culford without Jemima. I'll get used to living without her in time. I must—for the children's sake. But not just yet—not at Culford.

"As to the war—why, yes, I voted against it. I voted against the Stamp Act, and the Declaratory Act, and every damned fool, misguided measure Grenville and Rockingham took against these colonies. There were only five of us in the whole House of Lords who voted against the Declaratory Act—and we were right! And, by God, we're still right! There was never any need for this damned war. There was never any need for me to serve over here—" his face twisted and his voice grew harsh—"there was never any need for Jemima—" He covered his face with his hands and took a long, deep breath. Then he dropped his hands to his lap, his face emotionless. "Forgive me, Philip—when you love that much—it takes time."

We were both silent for a moment. Then I said,

"But you volunteered to serve here before Jemima died. Why?"

He gave a sort of gasp and spread out his hands.

"Why? Well, why are you here? On half-pay—you had no need to come. You may even fight your relations here. As for me—well, for as long as I could I tried to discharge my duty, as I saw it, to the people in these colonies—my countrymen—to defend them against what I—and many others—considered to be injustice. My rank and position demanded that. Why else am I privileged to sit in the House of Lords? Perhaps I was wrong on some points—perhaps I could have acted more wisely in their interests. I tried to do what I thought to be right—" he shook his head, "and I failed. So when these countrymen of ours revolted, what was left for me—for either of us—but our duty as soldiers?"

You will know why I forced myself to ask, "Would you have rebelled if you had been in their place?" He looked at me intently, his head cocked on one side. "Would you?"

For my peace of mind I had to state my creed.

"Charles, I own I don't know all the circumstances, but from what I know—yes, I believe I would."

He smiled.

"I know some of your forbears were a touch impetuous in their loyalties. But, would I have done the same had I been a colonist?—say, if I'd been in Washington's shoes?" He was silent for a moment. "I would have done all in my power to effect an understanding, a reconciliation—as the Fairfaxes and Fairleighs have done. But in the end—I think I would have ridden with you, Philip—I think I would—" He broke off, almost as if he regretted his admission.

After he had left, as I lay in the dimness of my little room, his words resounded again in my mind. A man who had worked heart and soul to prevent this useless war; who had ruined his political career defending the interests of the colonists; who, had he been a colonist, could himself have defied the King. And he had said,

"Why are we here? We have our duty as soldiers. What is left for us?"

My duty had been made plain for me. I thanked God, and prayed for His guidance in the discharging of it.

I improved so fast that on Sunday the 2nd July, the surgeon agreed that I should move to Cornwallis' headquarters at Drayton Hall. There I resumed planning my inspection of such militia cavalry as we had and examining how we might recruit more. I decided to start by observing the operations of the militia throughout the colony. I proposed to go first to Camden to confer with Colonel Lord Rawdon, who commanded there, and thence to such outposts as he advised. Cornwallis agreed to this. On leaving him, I handed him my first report to the Commander-in-Chief. He read it and shook his head.

"You'd best criticize something, Philip, or he'll not believe a word!"

"I'll only tell him the truth. He can believe what he pleases."

"Well, if you'll allow me, I'll be interested to see his comments." And so we left it.

I rode out from Drayton before dawn on Wednesday the 5th July and arrived at Camden on the afternoon of the Saturday.

Camden had prospered in its fifty years as a centre of trade. It is well laid out with wide streets and several handsome houses. It forms almost a complete rectangle, about one hundred chains from north to south and fifty from east to west, the whole enclosed within a system of defences remarkable in their efficiency and strength. As it was the chief market town in that half of South Carolina it provided our main centre of supply.

I had never met the commander of the Camden garrison before. All I had heard of him was that there was little love between him and Clinton since he had told the Commander-in-Chief that he was sick of being his Adjutant-General. Only Clinton thought the less of him for it.

At first sight I would not argue with the description of Col. Lord Francis Rawdon as the ugliest man in Europe, but I would add that he is one of the most unselfish and modest. There is some nonsense traded about nowadays by over-imaginative gibble-gabbles that, in the Headquarters in Charlestown, Mrs. Rebecca Motte kept her three attractive daughters locked in the loft of Brewton House to protect them from the licentiousness of our officers; particularly, so the fable goes, from the lustful clutches of Lord Rawdon—for God's sake! Francis Rawdon—that insatiable seducer of maidens!—who, if a girl only smiles sweet on him, blinks and stammers and blushes to the tips of those barn-door ears of his, sticking out like a pair of inn-signs from his noddle.

It was characteristic of him that he should at once inform me, apologetically, that he is fourteen years younger and junior to me, and that his appointment as Colonel related only to his own provincial corps, the Volunteers of Ireland; which he, an Irishman himself, had raised largely with Irish deserters from the rebel armies. He suggested that he should hand over command of Camden and his district to me. I said that I was very content to act under his orders, and that if Cornwallis had wished any change he would have ordered it.

Rawdon advised me to visit the outpost of Rocky Mount, thirty miles north of Camden, at the junction of the roads to Kings Mountain and Charlottesburg in North Carolina; and, from there, to visit the fort at Ninety-Six, eighty miles to the west, on the border of the Cherokee Indian country. These two patrols and visits would meet my purpose very well.

I left Camden at dawn the next day with a party of the 71st Highlanders commanded by James Macdonell, and a detachment of the 17th Light Dragoons, commanded by one of their own officers. Charles Russell was attached as supernumerary to this detachment.

I mention that the detachment of the 17th Light Dragoons was commanded by an officer of the Regiment; this was not always the case. The Regiment had provided a draft to reinforce the British Legion "as a pattern for the provincial recruits of which that corps is formed," to quote Clinton's instruction. In addition, a troop of the Regiment, usually some sixty strong, commanded by its own officers, was attached to the Legion. Inevitably the men of the detachment and the attached troop were interchanged, and, at times, the regular soldiers of the 17th were commanded by the provincial officers of the Legion, not always to the liking of the soldiers of the 17th.

Tarleton, admitted by both sides as the ablest commander of cavalry in either army, admired them greatly and tried to persuade them to wear the green jacket of the Legion cavalry. They declined the honour, preferring to patch their own faded scarlet with its white facings and the death's-head motto of the 17th Light Dragoons. I know no better or braver light cavalry.

We arrived at Rocky Mount that same evening. The main strength of the garrison was found by one of the battalions of New York Volunteers. The commander, Lieutenant-Colonel Turnbull, was conferring with his officers when we presented ourselves.

"You come most opportunely, Colonel," he said, "we've just now had news of a gathering of some of the most stubborn rebels in these parts." He gestured at a tall, gib-faced captain, wearing the white summer jacket of the British Legion dragoons. "I was instructing Captain Huck here to seek them out and destroy them. He is to take a troop of his own dragoons, a platoon of my battalion as mounted infantry and a company of the local militia. May I continue my orders?"

"Please do," I said.

"Thank you. Now, Captain Huck, I suggest your best way to Clem's Creek is by—"

"I ken the country," Huck broke in impatiently, "and the sooner I'm away the better, I'm thinking."

He spoke with a strong Lowland Scots accent and a surly contempt for Turnbull's orders. Turnbull said patiently,

"Very well. But you will not move before dark. It's in your interests to conceal your move, and it's in mine to conceal the fact that you are removing a third of my strength."

Huck grunted, "Oh ay, midnight will be soon enough."

Turnbull looked at me. "Will you accompany the patrol, Colonel?"

Huck blazed up at once.

"I'll not be taking visitors with me! It's no firky-toodling inspection we'll be doing—"

"I shall accompany the patrol," I said.

Huck was now raging. "I command this patrol—"

"And I command you, Captain Huck," I interrupted him, "and all other cavalry in this colony." I didn't, of course, but Huck wasn't to know that. "I accompany you on this patrol, or you'll return to Camden under escort. There are others who can command it as competently, I suppose."

There was no further argument. But it was a sullen Capt. Christian Huck who marched his command out of the fort at midnight. James Macdonell and Charles Russell had asked to accompany me and I had agreed; which had not made Huck any happier.

We moved in silence and in single file on a narrow path leading from a postern gate of the fort down to a track in the low ground to the north, which ran parallel to the road leading to the main junction below Kings Mountain. The night was hot, humid and noisy with insects and the scent of the pines overpowering. On arriving on the track we formed as silently into close column, sent forward a point to cover our advance, and marched until dawn through an unending tunnel of pines, whose overhanging branchs enclosed the dust we raised, letting only the faintest glim of starlight into the sweaty, grimy, suffocating depths in which we rode.

As dawn paled the few patches of sky we could see through the trees, we halted, dismounted, formed in defensive square with the horses linked together in the middle, made a breakfast and marched on.

At this time of day the air is cooler and, as it grew lighter and the country opened out, with fewer pine brakes and many small plantations and farms, we rode more comfortably and at ease. Though now it was necessary to move more tactically, and we put out van and rearguards, which, small as they were, reduced our main body to a mere half-strength of the whole.

I had questioned the wisdom of sending so small a force on such an errand, in a district which, according to information, abounded with rebel communities.

"Oh, Huck will pick up reinforcement on the way, Colonel," said Turnbull. "You'll find a good few militia will tag on."

And, indeed, a good few did come to join us. And left again as quickly when they became bored, tired, thirsty or too far from home; or when Huck cursed them.

"How can I stop 'em?" he growled, "Ye can never ken who comes to support ye or who to spy on ye. That's the devil o' it. Militia!" And he spat.

We rode on through most of that day, occasionally stopping at some house to seek information and refreshment; or to demand it, more often than not, with threats and obscenities from Huck and his dragoons. I grew quickly tired of the abuse which they showered on all to whom they spoke.

"Why all this foulness and bullying?" I asked. "These people are ready to show kindness, without threats and abuse."

"Ready to shoot us in the back too, the bastards. You don't know them. We do." Huck was unrepentant and made no effort to control his troopers' tongues, or their fists and boots.

Towards evening he rode up beside me, with a sinister grin.

"We've news of a meeting of rebels in a house close by, belonging to a man named McClure—a rebel. Early tomorrow."

"Can we trust the information?"

"We have to take what information we get. If there's no meeting—" he shrugged and rode off to give his orders.

We bivouacked in a large wood and slept for a few hours; then, leaving our fires burning, crept quietly out of the back of the wood and marched in silence, with no lights, some four miles to a position overlooking the McClure plantation. We waited, concealed, until dawn. Fires were lit in the house and the slaves went out to their work. Still Huck made no move. The men breakfasted on biscuit and rum and water. I did without the water.

Two hours after dawn six men, all armed, dismounted at the house and went indoors. Now Huck moved, swiftly, silently, efficiently. Two parties of dragoons rode by routes concealed from the house, to cut it off from the road. The New York Volunteers moved into positions within range of it. The militia closed in to surround the house, the slaves in the fields and outbuildings being too terrified to give warning.

With all in position still unobserved, Huck led a dozen of the militia into the house. There was shouting, screaming—and some shooting. All over very quickly. Huck knew his trade.

We rode down to the house. Huck strode out of the front door and wiped his sabre with a petticoat from the clothes line hanging in the veranda. He shouted into the house.

"Bring 'em out! We can hang 'em out here."

The bodies of six men were dragged out and flung onto the grass in front of the house. A girl ran out, sobbing hysterically. There was blood on her long, blonde hair and on her dress and hands.

"You filthy, murdering beasts—you butchers—"

"Whisht, girl," snarled Huck, "I'll tear your tongue out!"

She ran at him, raving, tearing at his face with her nails. He struck her, knocking her into a sobbing heap against the wall.

"Fetch 'em out! Bring a couple of halter ropes here!"

They brought out two young men; one little more than a boy. Huck grabbed the elder by his shirt.

"This is Edward Martin, Colonel—a murderer—married to a McClure whore. And this," he shook the boy by the hair, "is a McClure cub. They were moulding bullets from pewter plates. Have 'em up, lads—on that hickory there—"

"God's wounds!" I said, "Aren't there enough dead here already? Why not take them prisoner?"

Huck grimaced. "We canna burden ourselves with prisoners on a patrol like this. Only fit for hanging—dogs like these."

A woman came out onto the porch. She saw the bodies lying in the grass and fell on her knees, sobbing.

"Dinna fash yersel, Mrs. McClure," sneered Huck. "Ye ken well enough they'd have served us the same 'an they had caught us so!"

A soldier put a noose on young James McClure. Mrs. McClure, seeing this, flung herself at Huck's feet.

"For God's sake, sir, he's naught but a boy yet—a boy—"

She clung to Huck's arm. He shook her off. She clutched his arm again, and he struck her with the flat of his sabre, knocking her to the floor. Young McClure cursed him for a coward. Huck jabbed the boy's throat with his sabre.

"Curse me, would ye? Ay, crow my bonny cockerel—crow! Shall I spit ye on this then?—or stop your cluck with a wee bit hempen collar?"

"Captain Huck," I said, "you'll not hang either of those men here—or today."

He glared at me, furious. "Ah, well," says he, "since we may not hang them here today—maybe we'll hang them elsewhere the morrow."

He rammed his sabre into the scabbard, called for his horse and rapped out orders to secure Martin and McClure, to search the house and to re-form his command.

His salute, when all was ready, was perfunctory.

"We needs must haste, Colonel. I've left a party under Lieutenant Munro to search for aught of use to the rebels."

"Lieutenant Munro will see that there is no looting."

Huck's mouth twisted into something between a smirk and a sneer.

"He has his orders. We'll march on—if you please, sir." His tone made it clear that he didn't give a damn if I pleased or not.

Our road led round a hill. I looked back after we had gone a mile. A column of smoke curled into the sky from behind the hill. Some minutes later Munro's party rejoined us, their saddle bags bulging. I called to Munro,

"Is that smoke from the McClure house?"

"I'm afraid one of the slaves assisting us to search the loft dropped his light on some straw mattresses, Colonel. We tried to dowse the flames, but these timber houses burn like tinder." He shrugged, expressionless. "A nice house—very sad."

In mid-afternoon we came to the house of another plantation.

"This place belongs to a William Bratton, Colonel," said Huck, "a damned Whig. We may pick up something of use here."

I knew that I should avoid occasion to rebuke Huck yet again, so I sought escape. I had noted a chapel on the hillside a mile further on.

"I'll go and call on the minister there," I said. "He may have some news for us."

There is little any minister of religion does not know of affairs within his parish; and the majority of ministers in the colonies were for the King. Huck appreciated this.

"Ay, Colonel—ye'd best take an escort."

"Give me a file of the New York Volunteers," I said.

Huck was almost smiling now. "Ay, I'll do that—and I'll send word before we move." And off he rode, whistling gaily.

As we waited for the escort to join us, James Macdonell said thoughtfully, "I think I should stay with Huck, Colonel. For one thing, it may help to know what he's about when he's out of your sight; and also, for all that he hails from Philadelphia now, Huck is still a Lowland Scot, whilst I see that the most around these parts are Scots of Highland origin. That's a good setting for a massacre, one way or the other." He grinned his peculiarly wolfish grin, which usually forbode trouble.

"Very well, Jamie, we'll await you at the minister's," I said. He saluted and trotted off to the Bratton house.

In the manse, beside the chapel, we received a warm welcome, a good meal, some excellent peach brandy—but no information. The minister was a very frightened man.

"It's hard for us who stay loyal to the Church and the Crown, Colonel," he confided. "In some places ministers have already been dispossessed— some murdered even. We are sadly persecuted."

After an hour Macdonell trotted into the yard of the manse.

"Huck is moving back down the valley to another house—Williamson's. Old Mrs. Bratton wasn't the soul of Highland hospitality. Says her husband is at Clems Creek with Sumter—but, by God, if I were Sumter I'd send her husband home and take her campaigning! She's worth a platoon of grenadiers! Went for Huck hammer and tongs! Worth a guinea a minute! He's threatening to hang one of his dragoons too. They'd got cut on peach brandy they'd looted from the McClures', and one took a swing at Mrs. Bratton with his forage hook. When I said it was lucky he hadn't hurt her, Huck said he wouldn't have given a cuss if he'd cut her into collops—but he wasn't having one of his soldiers drunk on duty and he'd hang the sot when he was sober!"

"When do we leave?"

"Early tomorrow. He'll send word. Old Mrs. Bratton boasted that everyone had gone to join Sumter at Clems Creek. We'll get after them tomorrow."

The minister offered us beds in the manse. We went to them early and I woke just at dawning. I felt restless, so got up, went round the sentries, and then walked on the little terrace in front of the manse, which looked out over the valley. It was the only time of day I found pleasant at that season in the Carolinas. Up in these hills the air was fresh and cool. The barest breeze brought the scent of the pines which covered the hill sides, and gently flirted with the leaves of the oaks and hickorys surrounding the manse. Under a sky of the palest blue, a thin mist hung flat and still below me, like the surface of an inland sea, along the length of the lower valley. All was utterly calm. Only the dawn bird calls broke the sleepy silence.

A sudden, tearing crash of musketry echoed and re-echoed through the hills. One volley. And another. And another. Confused shouting, faint on the still air. Another volley. Then an almost continuous rattle and clatter of shots, dull and muffled. All from the direction of the Williamson house.

We were out, saddled up, weapons checked, on our horses, formed and cantering down the road within seven minutes. James Macdonell led us by a track onto a wooded ridge overlooking the Williamson plantation. Halfway down the ridge the forward edge of the wood made the boundary of the plantation. We halted in its cover.

It was at once clear that the fight was as good as over—and lost. Two small groups of the red-coated New York Volunteers and white-jacketed Legion dragoons still stood together, firing volleys. The whole militia had surrendered; not that that saved some of them from being shot or bayoneted where they stood as the rebels came up to them. Soon all firing ceased, and the rebels swarmed through the small encampment between the rail fences lining the road to the house.

Suddenly, from the shadows at the back of the house, a party of five Legion dragoons galloped into the morning sunlight. Out over the rail fence they came, then, bent over their horses' necks, at full stretch up the track leading to where we stood. A few shots were fired after them, and a dozen rebels ran to their horses and rode whooping after them.

The leader of the dragoons was Lieutenant Munro. Dazzled by the sunlight, it was a moment before he saw us in the shadows under the trees. He called hoarsely,

"All's lost, Colonel. The devils caught us at dawn. Stood off and shot us down like ducks on a damned pond."

"Where's Captain Huck?"

"Dead, Colonel. They knocked him down as he came out of the house. Damned fool place to bivouac—"

I road forward a few paces to look for the pursuing rebels. They had started to halloo as they came up the track and the reason for their bloodlust was clear. Two of our militiamen were running for their lives a few yards ahead of them, one with a musket, the other unarmed. The unarmed man turned and raised his hands in surrender.

"Cut him down! Cut him down!" one of the riders bellowed. And so they did. Wheeling their horses round him as he stood, his hands still above his head, slashing and hacking at him like the bungling butchers they were. Covered in blood, he reeled through the ring of plunging horses and tried again to stumble up the hill. They rode him down. He staggered to his feet once more and the swords flashed again and again—his murderers screaming and laughing like madmen. Down he went, into the dust; and they rode over him and after the other man.

He, too, tried at first to surrender, but they gave no quarter. So, whilst they circled him, slashing at his head and shoulders, he fought them bravely with his clubbed musket, knocking one of them from his saddle. But, in the end, they served him the same as the other; led by the same man who had shouted to cut down the first poor devil.

After they had done with him, they all sat laughing and cheering, waving their bloody swords over their heads and leaning down to thrust them into the body of their victim.

You can condemn them. But remember that these men were civilians and that this may have been their first such encounter. The thrill of danger and victory and the sight of blood can turn a man to brute beast if he is unused to them. A professional soldier, with some experience of victory and defeat, views surrendered prisoners with an unemotional—usually kindly—detachment; remembering that he might be in their shoes one day. It's the amateurs who do the murdering in war; but you'll never get civilians to believe that.

Anyway, I didn't like the look of this lot of amateurs and thought to teach them a lesson. Munro was at my side, cursing, urgent for action.

"Shall we charge them, Colonel? We outnumber them—"

"No. We might suffer further casualties and not dispose of all of them. Anyway, they'd see us from below and come after us in greater strength. No—let them come to us. You take two of your men and ride down towards them. Make sure they see you and then, at once, pretend to panic—shout—and gallop back to us here. Keep well ahead of them—we don't want to knock you down."

Munro grinned excitedly.

"Yes, Colonel. Jamieson, McClellan, you heard that—follow me, turn when I do—and for God's sake stay close!"

It was a perfect setting for an ambuscade. As it passed over the top of the ridge, the narrow track, deep in shade, ran between high banks, turning sharply to the left halfway along their length. I placed four of the New York Volunteers as a front stop twenty paces beyond the bend; and four more, concealed in the undergrowth, at the entrance to the cut, to close the trap as the back stop. The rest of us—those who were not holding horses—lay with our pistols or carbines along the tops of the banks. We heard the howling of the wolf pack suddenly renew, and checked the primings of our weapons.

Up into the shadow of the trees galloped Munro and his troopers, through the ambuscade, then wheeled back, unslung their carbines, and joined us on the banks.

Out of the sun and into the shadows, hallooing and tantivying, came the rebel troop, urging on their horses with the flat of their swords; fooled by the oldest ruse in the history of war. As the leading pair rounded the turn between the banks, the four men of the front stop put two one-ounce balls into each of them. Their horses, taking fright at the fire in front of them, reared and whipped round, oversetting those behind. There was a hideous convulsion of rearing, screaming horses and tumbling, shrieking men. We picked them off as they crawled from under their horses. One, unscathed, ducked under the bank and ran round the turn, straight onto the bayonets of the front stop. A few cried for quarter and got the same quarter they gave the militiamen—what else? Their loud-mouthed leader, riding at the back, turned his horse, spurred back down the cut and met the fire of the four muskets of the back stop point-blank. He pitched off on the near side, his left foot stuck in the stirrup, and he was dragged some way, face down, before they caught his horse. All done inside the half-minute.

These swashbuckling moss-troopers—some no older than young James McClure, I noted—had gathered eager for the fight. They had got one; a quick and easy skirmish, and had won it handsomely. They had careered after the five dragoons, bent on blooding their swords, and had done so—on two unarmed prisoners. Now they had learned the other side to war.

We caught the horses; all well-made, strong beasts in good condition, the sort we had been scouring the country to find. I particularly liked the big, bay mare belonging to the leader of the gang—a kind eye, nice head and neck, good shoulder, deep and short-coupled and a bottom like a cook's, clean legs and good feet and a little above sixteen hands—the best sort for an officer's charger. I took her myself and called her Williamson; which everyone thought a strange name for a mare. Everyone, that is, but Charles Russell, Jamie Macdonell, Matthew and I.

I sent Munro back to the wood's edge to see if our firing had alarmed the enemy. But in the confusion surrounding the shooting and hanging of some of our militia—I suppose those whose homes were in those parts—our few shots in the wood had gone unnoticed.

There was naught else to do now but ride back fast to Rocky Mount.

This we did, all that day and night; being joined by fugitives from Huck's force on the way. So we came to the fort a little before dawn on Thursday the 13th July.

Jamie Macdonell stayed at Rocky Mount with his detachment. Charles Russell, Sergeant Hawes and seven troopers of the 17th returned with me that same afternoon to Camden.

At Camden, Francis Rawdon muttered fretfully,

" 'Ecod, near a hundred men lost—and all those Legion cavalry. That fool Huck—oh, brave enough, but no common sense. How could Turnbull think of sending him on such an errand? Sumter would have eaten him! And Tarleton's going to be livid! He'll say his precious dragoons are being wasted on unimportant and dangerous missions. And he'll be right. But I wish he wouldn't be so damned self-righteous about it. He can make mistakes too, I suppose."

I had not yet met Lieut.-Col. Banastre Tarleton.

"I suppose so," I said.

Chapter Eight

*In which I become acquainted with Banastre
Tarleton and we practise a little deception.*

After a day's rest at Camden, I began my journey to Ninety-Six on the
morning of Saturday the 15th July. Ninety-Six was the most important
trading post in South Carolina after Camden. It stands on the Charlestown Path, the road from Charlestown to Fort Prince George in the
country of the Cherokee Indians, whence it was supposed to lie ninety-six
miles; until the actual distance was found to be sixty-five. But this was
considered only as evidence of the incompetence of the surveyor, and no
cause to change the name.

The garrison was commanded by Lieut.-Col. Nisbet Balfour of the
23rd Regiment, who had under his command, apart from the regular and
provincial troops, about four hundred militia commanded by Maj. Patrick
Ferguson, late of my own Regiment and now of the 71st Highlanders.
Clinton had appointed Ferguson Inspector of Militia in the southern
colonies before I arrived in Charlestown, so, naturally, I sought his advice
on the prospects of recruiting militia cavalry.

Patrick grinned, "Recruit militia, Philip!—you're out of your mind!
Untrainable in arms, undisciplined in conduct, unsteady in action,
unvaliant in adversity—and unwanted in general! That's the opinion of all
regular commanders of both sides on militia. Washington calls them a
damned hindrance to his operations!"

"You don't regard them so."

"True—but then I try to understand their difficulties and I encourage
them; which is a better way of recruiting them than ignoring their
difficulties and damning them. Oh, you'll find a fair number who will
serve—but it will be on their terms; for two months—until harvest and

after that again until Christmas—only in the Ninety-Six precinct—and so on. Ridiculous, you'll say—but look at it from their side. They have farms and businesses to mind and families to protect. How enthusiastic would you be in their case? The rebel recruiters can be rough with those who don't 'volunteer'; we can't be."

And it was as he said. My chief obstacle was that I found no leaders among the Loyalist communities who could arouse the purpose and the devotion that men like Marion and Sumter inspired amongst the rebels. Without such native leadership and local example very few of them would hazard themselves. I found one hundred and sixty recruits, and Clinton's pessimistic estimate re-echoed in my ear—"A few—a few, but in no sort of numbers that warrants your attention—"

The entirely inexperienced I left with Balfour and Patrick Ferguson, to be trained as mounted infantry for duties in the Ninety-Six precinct. The others—eighty-seven recruits of varied experience—I gave to Charles Russell and Sergeant Hawes, to be taught the skills of a light dragoon. These, with my escort of the 17th Light Dragoons commanded by Charles Russell, marched with me when I left Ninety-Six to return to Charlestown. We drilled and exercised all the way home, finally arriving in reasonable military order at the New Barracks in Charlestown on Wednesday the 26th July.

I reported to Cornwallis—and Clinton—confirming what they already knew. That there were too few recruits of the quality needed for service as light cavalry to form even one effective militia regiment in South Carolina.

"But militia can act with courage and resolution if led by good officers, Charles," I said, "Patrick Ferguson's force gives an example of what can be achieved by a regular officer with a bent for such service."

"That's right," rejoined Cornwallis, gloomily, "and that's why every rebel militia leader wants to see him dead. He's been altogether too successful. And now he's getting rash. He'll end up in trouble one of these days—I've warned him."

"Don't you trust him?" I asked—and wondered what Clinton would have answered. Cornwallis answered it characteristically.

"Trust him?—of course I trust him. I've given him command, haven't I?" He frowned. "It's just that he's too damned over-confident on occasion." He waved a hand at the map hanging beside him. "He's forever asking to be allowed to go plunging off into the back country—Tryon County, up there—into what he calls rebel recruiting areas. I can't always be telling him no."

"But, Charles, he has a strong enough force to support such forays."

"I know, Philip. But God's wounds, man!—even Patrick Ferguson can make mistakes! What if he's killed? I take it he doesn't claim any measure of immortality? Then what happens to that force of his? They rely too much upon him and his reputation. If he's killed and, as a result, they are badly cut up, what happens then to Loyalist enthusiasm for support for us?"

I had no answer for that and Cornwallis nodded ruefully. Then he said, with an acid smile,

"Well, your report will please old Pussy anyway. I can just see him gloating over it. He'll send it on to George Germain with one of his usual illegible, unintelligible moans!" He sat back in his chair and stretched. "Well, what will you do now, Philip?"

"Whatever you wish. I suppose I'm still on your staff, until you dismiss me."

"God forbid I should ever do that. I need my friends around me. And I need someone on my staff to supervise all the cavalry and mounted infantry we have—regular, provincial and militia. They're spread all over the country and suffer for want of an experienced officer to keep an eye on them. You'll control their operations and administration."

"I hope I can do justice to the task."

"You will. You'll have trouble from Ban Tarleton though. He's another such as Ferguson. His command rely too much on his presence as well. They can't do much right without him. Look at that wretched affair of Huck's. And he's very touchy about his corps. After the Huck affair he came raging to me that his dragoons were being misused. He's right. Should have thought Francis Rawdon and Turnbull would have seen that it was unwise to trust a man like Huck with such a mission—but they're both inexperienced in the use of cavalry." He looked at me, frowning a little. "Couldn't you have controlled Huck?"

"I thought you'd ask me that," I said—and told him the whole story. At the end he nodded thoughtfully,

"Yes, you're quite right. Over-confidence and impulsiveness. They're Banastre's faults—and his inexperienced officers catch 'em. And Huck was a cross-grained boor into the bargain."

He studied his map, chewing his lower lip.

"You know, Philip, at the back of my mind I've always had a fear—as I've had of Ferguson too—that one day Ban will make a really bad mistake. And that will cost us all dear. I'm at fault, of course. I rely too much on him as well. Doesn't do his conceit any good—but what else can I do?"

[*111*]

He picked up his quill and wagged it at me.

"But you can help me. Tarleton will respect you as an experienced cavalryman, though he'll pretend not to at first. Make him stop his soldiers' rough handling of civilians who give no offence. Make him restrain his own possessiveness about the Legion. And, for God's sake, get him to improve his reporting and his interpreting of the information he sends me." He pointed the quill at me like a sword. " 'Men's faults do seldom to themselves appear'—so make his clear to him!"

Tarleton was convalescing from fever in Charlestown, quartered in the house of some notorious rebel. He had deservedly established a reputation as a brilliant and courageous commander of light cavalry. As I rode into Charlestown I wondered how I was to impress his faults upon him—and have him admit them.

The noise could be heard from the end of the street. The front door of the house was open and half Charlestown was wandering in and out. Every room was a bedroom of sorts. At least they all had beds in them; and a colourful selection of the ladies of Charlestown reclining on most in varying states of undress, along with gentlemen—officers of the Legion, I supposed—similarly clad, or unclad. July in Charlestown is very warm.

I was directed upstairs to a large room with a bed at one end. On the foot of the bed sat a startlingly pretty girl, playing a lute and singing "The girl I left behind me"—a little sadly, I thought—to the young man lying on it.

He was well-built, broad-shouldered, slim in the waist and hips, with a face of almost feminine beauty—save for a hawk nose and a hard mouth—topped by a shock of red hair. He wore a silk shirt, open to the waist, the tan breeches of the Legion and white silk stockings. He lay back against the cushions, resting a glass of wine on his knees, listening intently to the song.

"Col. Banastre Tarleton?" I said.

He looked a touch displeased at having his idyll disturbed and made no effort to rise.

"Colonel Cato, I believe? Forgive me for not rising. I still feel as if I'm hamstrung."

"I apologize for disturbing you," I said, and bowed to the girl.

"Your pardon, sir," Tarleton exclaimed, "Miss Sarah Pinckney, Colonel. Her father is a good rebel. He doesn't know she's here!"

I wondered whether her father had sent her. But I wanted to speak to him alone and asked to do so.

"Away, Sarah, my love!" cried Tarleton, "Colonel Cato and I are about to confabulate most secretly. And for God's sake bring us some more wine—"

To my surprise, Miss Pinckney rose at once, kissed him fondly, curtsied to me and closed the door behind her gently.

"Do you maintain such an admirable discipline in all your relationships?" I asked.

"A strict but amicable discipline, Colonel." He leaned back on his pillows and smiled. "Now, you've come to tell me that I do not sufficiently control my soldiers when they deal—as you think, harshly, and as I think, properly—with rebels, that I am jealous of my Legion and over-critical of officers who mis-employ my soldiers. Correct?"

He laughed mockingly.

"You forgot one other point," I replied.

The smile left the thin mouth. "And what is that?"

I thought he needed taking down—hard.

"Your reports and intelligences are sometimes inaccurate, often inadequate, usually ill-interpreted and always too few."

"God's death!" He exploded off his bed, stamping with rage. "Who says so? What do you know of my reports? I've never sent you one—"

I was surprised to see how short he was—a little below middle height; he had seemed taller lying on the bed. I happened to glance down at the boots by his bed. The heels were a good two inches higher than the average. He caught my glance and flushed. I had his Achilles heel. I relaxed in my armchair and stretched out my legs—they're long—saying in the mildest of tones,

"Gratifying to see my remarks revive your hamstrings."

"Tcha!"

He slumped in a furious, sullen heap on his bed. Then he caught my smile. And, suddenly, he was roaring with laughter, his anger gone in the instant.

"You win, Colonel, you win! Now, stop bullying me!" He shook his head reproachfully. "I'm only a poor little fellow. You ought to be kinder to me. Now, have some wine. Here's ruin to the Hero of Saratoga, Horatio Gates, the fat, renegade, little sot—and may we be the instrument that achieves it!"

I felt I had earned a drink.

"Now," said Tarleton, "my reports, Colonel. Firstly I operate in rebel country. A number of my couriers have been caught and—killed. So I can't put too much information in my reports."

"You have ciphers?"

He grimaced. "Oh, ciphers—yes, I've got ciphers. Only I can never find the damned things. And it takes so long to encipher—Oh, all right, Colonel, yes—I'll do better!" And he grinned. "As to being jealous of my command. Well, who trained this Legion? Who fights the Commissary for its stores? Who stole its horses from the train? We have so little good cavalry and it makes me mad to see my dragoons worn to shadows on missions which any mounted infantryman could do. I must stop this misuse. Is that wrong?"

"No. But you're a little loud about it."

"Loud? Bigod—you've got to shout loud to get anything into the noddles of some of the rockheaded dandiprats here!"

"You'll be glad to know you're succeeding." I took a breath, for I sensed a storm to come. "And on the charge of brutality—by yourself—and your men?"

For a moment he sat, tense and still, staring down at the floor. Then, in a strangely quiet voice, he said,

"This is not the sort of war you're used to, Colonel. There's no honour in it. It's a filthy shambles, like every civil war. My men are all colonial born—all Americans—like thousands of others in our provincial corps and militia." He breathed in through clenched teeth. "Colonel, I'll wager you've never sent off a courier—with one of the reports we were talking about—and found him, days later, spreadeagled, naked, on a hurdle, with the soles of his feet and his parts burnt to make him talk.

"I'll wager you've never sent out a small foraging party, and found them two days later, foully mutilated, all hanging from the same tree. Oh, they have pretty tricks, some of these rebels.

"What do I say to one of my soldiers who goes home on leave to find his family's farm burned to the ground, his father and elder brother hanged nearby, and his mother and sister turned out in their nightclothes, with everyone too scared to aid them?

"What do I say to a lad of twenty whom I let home to see his wife and finds her raped to death, their six-month-old baby impaled on a fence-post, and the cabin he built for them in ashes?

"And this happens not once, Colonel, but all the time! My men—my Americans—see what happens to their homes and families. Am I to prevent them retaliating when they can?" He struck his knee with his clenched fist. "I'm damned if I will! I've seen all these things—and worse, God's blood, far, far worse! And where I can punish, I'll punish!"

He got to his feet and limped towards me, shaking his fist as he spoke.

"You may say the rebel generals regret the brutalities, the murders, the rapings, the burnings by their supporters. Well, tell me why in hell they don't do something about it? Why don't they hang their murderers, their rapists, their baby-butchers? I'll tell you why! Because they benefit from the terror and know it! Name me one rebel general who has hanged one of his men for murdering or looting a loyalist; or for murdering a British prisoner to rob him. Name me one! You can't. And don't tell me they don't encourage it. They call it 'patriotic fervour' and 'the righteous protest of the people against the oppressor'. Oh yes, I know all the snivelling, hypocritical claptrap they spew. They exaggerate our reprisals out of all recognition, and call them acts of brute oppression. Well, by God, in return for their acts of patriotic fervour and righteous protest, I'm ready to give them some brute oppression to complain about!"

He stood glaring down at me.

"And mark my words, Colonel. You ride with us and you'll be thinking the same before you've finished. We all come to it in the end!"

He collapsed back on his bed, panting, the sweat streaming down his face. He was still very angry. But his tone now was almost nonchalant.

"Not guilty, Colonel—on grounds of extreme provocation."

"And your men?"

I got the answer I hoped for.

"My men are my men. I, alone, am answerable for everything they do. If any of them deserve correction, I shall dispense it. And, believe me, I do."

I finished my wine and got to my feet.

"Thank you," I said, "for clearing my mind on several points. I trust our conversation won't retard your recovery. Because Lord Cornwallis had news yesterday that—as you appear to be aware—General Gates has taken over command of the rebel army in North Carolina from General de Kalb, and is marching south with a considerable force of Continental troops."

Tarleton was at once alert, his fever forgotten.

"When does he wish me to ride?"

"When you're fit. Say, in a week's time?"

"Three days, Colonel. Today's Saturday—we'll march on Tuesday. May I ask for my orders by tomorrow? And—" he cocked an eyebrow, "will you ride with us?—to supervise us?"

"I'll be glad to ride with you. I look forward to receiving some instruction in this form of war from the best of authorities."

[*115*]

He heaved himself to his feet again and bowed.

"It will be my pleasure to show you the rules of the game, Colonel. One final point, sir. We ride very light." He smiled again, grimly, "We pick up our comforts on the way."

And so, on Tuesday the 1st August, before dawn, Matthew and I rode, in company with Tarleton, out of the north gate of Charlestown. I have never returned there. In the column were Charles Russell and his dragoons, thirty dragoons of the Legion and the eighty-seven recruits I had brought from Ninety-Six—now embodied in the Legion. Our orders were to ride through the country between the Pedee and Santee rivers, encouraging the loyalist element, and suppressing all signs of rebellion in the town of Kingstree. Thence we were to join Francis Rawdon at Camden.

Moving by unfrequented tracks, we would have travelled fast but for the weather. Shortly after dawn it began to rain heavily, and so continued for four days and nights. It stayed close and humid; far too hot to wear cloaks or tarpaulin jackets. So we bumped along on our dripping horses, plunging into hidden holes, sliding into gullies and scrambling out of them and shambling unsteadily through the muddy torrents of the fast-rising creeks. It took us four and a half days to cover the forty miles to Lenews Ferry on the Santee River. Each night we halted under the cover of some broken-down barn or burned-out farmhouse. There were many such. In these we stripped and tried to dry our soaking clothing by our fires; whilst we crouched, coughing, and with our eyes stinging in the acrid smoke, seeking refuge from the myriads of insects seeking to satisfy their appetites on our naked bodies. A scene suited in every torment for inclusion in Dante's "Inferno." Indeed, one of my conceptions of Purgatory is to march in such misery through the swamps of South Carolina until eternity.

On the afternoon we arrived at the Santee River the rain stopped. We halted in a plantation belonging to a Loyalist, to dry and clean ourselves, our horses and our weapons. The following morning, having been joined by a troop of thirty local militia commanded by a Col. Elias Ball, we crossed the Black River below Kingstree, and, making a gallant sight and a lot of noise, cantered into the centre of the little town; the very heart of the rebel community of the area.

Patrols were at once sent round the town and surrounding farms and plantations to search for rebels in hiding, weapons and ammunition. Four men were found who were known to have broken their paroles given at

Charlestown. Two resisted and were shot; the other two were hanged. The houses in which they were found were burned, along with all others in which caches of weapons and ammunition were found. All was done dispassionately, thoroughly and with dispatch.

Tarleton was everywhere. His manner surprised me. Even in the face of the anger and the agony of those he punished or destroyed he was always courteous, always imperturbable and invariably ruthless. And his soldiers followed his example.

"I tell them to remember that they're masters of the situation," he said, "I tell them a man who loses his temper loses control of himself—and the matter in hand; and that makes trouble. I tell them to stay calm—stay polite—and hit hard."

The evening sky was clouded with smoke from the burning buildings and stores and standing crops. I had seen enough of such futile waste in other wars; but never done with such terrible efficiency. Sad to see that none were more active in the work than the wretched victims' neighbours—the militiamen of Col. Elias Ball; who, of course, had suffered the same way themselves.

Our little force was bivouacked on the town green, with the officers billeted in two houses facing onto it. I was in the same house as Tarleton, along with Colonel Ball and some officers of the Legion.

At a little after ten o'clock, one of the sentries brought in a woman dressed all in black, a heavy veil over her head. She dropped a brief curtsy and threw back her veil. She was strikingly good-looking, with a brave air about her.

"Gentlemen," she said, breathless, "You are all in the greatest danger here. Messengers went from Kingstree this afternoon to Major James, who commands the rebel militia in Williamsburg, that you encamp here tonight. My maid was told by a friend—a slave of a rebel family in this town—that Major James will be here at midnight with five hundred men."

"We're much in your debt, ma'am," said Tarleton, at his suavest, "May we know your name?"

"My name is Hamilton, sir. My husband I think you know—Maj. John Hamilton—?"

"Of course," said Tarleton, warmly. "We've been thankful for his help before. And now it's you who come to our aid." He studied her for a moment, then asked, "Do you have children, Mrs. Hamilton?"

She stared at him, frowning, puzzled. "Why yes, sir, I do. But—they're far too young to ride with you—"

"I'd no thought of that, ma'am. But you risk your life and your children's lives by coming here with this news."

Her eyes widened—they were very beautiful.

"It was my duty, sir."

Tarleton said slowly, "Ah—yes—your duty." He took a deep breath. "And all we can do in return, ma'am—is to express our almighty admiration for your courage, your devotion to your duty—and your beauty!" And he bowed low.

Mrs. Hamilton blushed scarlet. She pulled the veil over her head and went to the door. In the doorway she turned and curtsied again. Her voice shook,

"God bless you, gentlemen, and bring you all safe home." And she was gone.

"Bigod!" exclaimed Tarleton, "No offence to you, Elias, but if all Tory gentlemen who demand that we protect their property had half the courage of such wives, this damned war would never have started!"

"Oh, it's difficult for some—" mumbled Ball.

"Difficult!" stormed Tarleton, "Difficult! God's wounds, man, d'you think after what we've done here in Kingstree today it was easy for her? Difficult!"

He snorted and emptied his glass. Then he grinned and slapped the disconcerted Ball on the shoulder.

"Good old Elias! You're not quite as lovely as Mrs. Hamilton, but, God bless you, you don't find it difficult! And you're all we've got to guide us out of here! Come on then, lads,—to horse and away! But do everything quietly. We don't want the whole damned town watching the way we go."

We moved fifteen minutes later, at a walk, and rode north out of the town and over the Black River at Kingstree Bridge. We were seen, of course. Curtains were part-drawn and shadows moved in the alleys as we passed. Colonel Ball took with him a Negro servant of a friend of his, resident in the town. After we had crossed the bridge, he gave the Negro a shilling, posted him at the southern end of the bridge, and told him to shout to the rebel militia that we had galloped off to the south, towards the Santee River. And we turned north, along the west bank of the Black River.

We rode through the darkness, still at a walk, with little noise. After a few miles the track narrowed and turned down to a ford over the river. The water at the ford came only to the horses' bellies, and the current being slow and the bottom hard gravel, there was little danger of horse and rider falling, provided they accomplished the steep descent down the high bank into the river the right way up. Not easy.

We practise a little deception

The moon had already set, and, in the darkness under the overhanging trees, the near vertical descent through the poached black mud of the track was one of the most hazardous exercises in horsemanship I have ever performed.

I was relieved to find that such perils held no terrors for Williamson; she seemed well practised in their passage. For, with no assistance from me—unable to see my hand before my face—she came back on her hocks, settled her handsome bottom into the mud, and slid sedately down into the river as if on a sledge.

Within the quarter-hour our whole force was assembled on the east bank of the Black River; whilst, as we learned later, a Captain McCottry and his company of the Williamsburg rebel militia were, to the best of their belief, hot on our heels on the west bank of the Santee.

"Where now?" I asked Tarleton.

"I want to get to Salem at the head of Black River as soon as we may, Colonel. Then we can cross north of the Santee Hills to Camden. But old Elias is going to call on an acquaintance to repay an old score—and you can guess what that is!"

Colonel Ball rode up cursing, slapping his hat on his thigh.

"God damned branch knocked me hat off into the water. Catch me death of cold—"

"Better than an overdose of lead," said Tarleton, shortly, "Elias, this is where we part company. Apologise to your friend that we were unable to join you in paying our respects—but no doubt your's will be enough for him. And safe home!"

"Ay—safe home, lads!" Ball waved his hat over his head, "And—God save the King!" And his troop all cheered.

We rode north without halt all that day. We came to Salem almost unrecognizable even to each other under the dust which had settled on our sweat-stained faces and shirts; for we had long discarded our uniform jackets in the heat and stuffed them in our saddle-bags. As, in the early evening, we rode past the first houses, a young fellow ran from one to watch us. He checked his stride and stared.

"Jings!" he whooped. "Dragoons!"

He ran to the point troopers, who waved him back down the column to where Tarleton and I rode.

"Are you Continental troops, sir?" he panted.

"And what if we are?" said Tarleton.

"Sir, we heard you was a-comin'." His eyes grew round with wonder, "Sir—are you—Colonel Washington?"

[119]

The idea made Tarleton's smile crack the dust-mask on his face. The lad was entirely misled by it. He shouted to the houses,

"It's him—it's Colonel Washington!"

People waved from the houses and we waved back. The boy ran beside us. "Sir, Mr. Bradley is at his house. He is expecting of you. Shall I guide you?"

"Well, I doubt we've time—"

"Oh, I'll go get my horse, sir. Won't keep you but a minute." And he was off like an arrow.

We halted. Tarleton looked at me.

"Well, what do we do now, Colonel?"

"I think we must play the farce through and go on to this man Bradley. We can say we're returning from a patrol and are in haste to report to Gates."

"Ay," said Tarleton, thoughtfully, slouched in his saddle. He began to grin. "If they believe us, maybe we can get a guide!" He called quietly to the nearest officers. "Ride down the column. Make sure every man understands that I am Colonel Washington and we're all Continental dragoons—Bland's Regiment and—what's another one—Baylor's. Say the Legion are Bland's and the 17th are Baylor's. Keep their jackets hidden and make sure no one sees our badges too close. And don't let anyone knock the dust off his saddle-cloth or valise."

The boy returned, bouncing about on a great, coffin-headed chestnut. He clutched a bell-mouthed fowling-piece and wore a rusty hunting sword, without a scabbard, stuck in his belt.

"Ecod, young man, you're well accoutred!" said Tarleton.

"I'm a-goin' to join the Williamsburg militia!"

"You are? I'm sure they'll welcome anyone so well-armed! Well, let's be on."

And we trotted on smartly in the dusk to the Bradley house.

Old James Bradley was a Member of the South Carolina rebel Assembly and was as self-important and pompous as most representatives of the people are; not only in America. Whilst entertaining us nobly, he continually demanded to be allowed to assist us in our operations.

"And where will you ride, Colonel?" he asked Tarleton. "We heard that General Gates was at Mask's Ferry two days ago."

Tarleton nodded and murmured confidentially, "I should like to be able to creep round behind Lord Rawdon there in Camden and strike at his supplies on the Santee road—even into Camden—"

"Splendid, Colonel!" Bradley bubbled with enthusiasm, "If you permit me to ride with you, I could guide you to the Santee road. There's some desperate treacherous places at the crossings on the Black River."

Tarleton nodded slowly, as if giving the matter careful thought. Then he shook his head.

"No, sir. I recall that I heard you are on parole. What would happen if you fell into enemy hands?"

Bradley thrust out his lower lip. "A fig for the parole! Not worth the paper it's written on! If I'm caught they'll only make me sign another one—and I'll treat it the same!"

"Indeed?" said Tarleton, genuinely surprised. "Egad, interesting to hear that British paroles are held in such slight regard. What would you do, sir, to a Tory who breaks his so?"

Mr. Assemblyman Bradley never hesitated. "Why, hang the rogue! What else?"

"Exactly," replied Tarleton. "As you say—what else?" And both our consciences felt the easier for that.

We decided to leave Salem at dawn on the morrow; and secretly set double sentries and relief picket officers on duty all night. But there were no alarms, and at dawn we marched to Bradley's ford on the Black River, accompanied by Mr. Bradley himself and a half-dozen of his friends, all well-mounted and well-armed.

We rode all that day and most of the next. As we approached the Santee road late in the afternoon, Tarleton ordered a file of dragoons forward to do advance guard in front of our guides. We all halted to allow them to take up their stations. Having passed through us, the file turned about, unswivelled their carbines and levelled them at the rebels. Tarleton and I had ridden to one side from the rebel group, and now we each drew a pistol and cocked.

"Gentlemen," said Tarleton apologetically, "I must ask you all to throw down your weapons, if you please."

Bradley burst out angrily, "Colonel Washington, what jest is this, sir? Are we not to be trusted?"

"Mr. Bradley, believe me," Tarleton was still more apologetic, "Were I Colonel Washington I should certainly trust you with my life. But since you have all broken your paroles I obviously cannot trust you. So now, please, throw down your arms."

They did so in sullen silence. Bradley said furiously, "Well, you have tricked us, sir. So, you're an officer of the King. If you're capable of telling the truth, pray tell us who you are."

Tarleton said, very patiently, "Mr. Bradley, I'll remind you that you all

[*121*]

have lied to the King's representatives who took your paroles. And you will recall the penalty you recommended for that. As to my name, gentlemen, it is Banastre Tarleton."

There was a horrid silence and some very white faces among them. They huddled behind Bradley, who sat his horse square, fist on hip, glaring at Tarleton under the flopping brim of his hat.

"I see," he said, more furious still. "I have had the honour of entertaining the bloody-handed Tarleton. And now you will hang us; as I recommended—yes, I recall it, sir. So, Colonel Tarleton, that oak behind you will suit me very well—and, if you are ready, sir, damn you, so am I!"

Tarleton smiled and shook his head.

"Never at my hand, Mr. Bradley. But I must deliver you to the Provost Marshal in Camden. In return for your kindness to us, you each have ten minutes to pen a note to your wives. Then the youngest of you may ride back to Salem with your letters, and the rest of us will ride on to Camden." And so we did.

In Camden we learned that Rawdon was with the greater part of his force, covering the crossing of Little Lynches Creek, fifteen miles to the north-east of the town; and that the outposts of Rocky Mount and Hanging Rock still held, despite attacks by rebel militia led by Sumter.

I returned from a quick tour of the defences of the town to find Tarleton in a pretty rage.

"What in hell's name does Rawdon think he's doing with my dragoons? I find them digging graves, on prison guard, grooms to his staff—anywhere but where they should be! Who's patrolling the flanks? Who's watching the river crossings? Who's guarding his supply route? I'll tell you who! My poor, bloody forty dragoons he has with him—that's who! Working day and night until they and their wretched nags drop dead of exhaustion. While everyone else dawdles around scratching their arses!"

He kicked a chair, hurt his toe and swore horribly.

"He's even dismounted some of them and given their horses to his staff—all poxy foot-wobblers who can't ride one side of a rocking-horse! They'd all look better riding around in a cart—a dung cart for preference!—Well, what now?"

A trooper had entered and saluted.

"Your honour, Major Hanger's compliments—ready to move."

Tarleton sighed with relief. "Thank God! You'll ride with us, Colonel?"

We found Rawdon in the shade of some trees overlooking Lynches Creek and the ruins of the bridge on the road from Camden to Hillsborough. Beyond the creek, stretching away into the dust and distance, dragged the long disordered straggle of the rebel columns.

Rawdon welcomed us warmly. "Thank God, you bring some more dragoons! Can we get patrols out to the right and rear, Ban? Every dragoon I have is covering Charles Corbett's withdrawal from Hanging Rock. Sumter attacked it on Sunday—got a bloody nose, but we lost a good few—some of your Legion infantry, Ban—you heard Kenneth McCulloch was killed?—"

Tarleton's mouth was a very thin line. "I hadn't heard." He took off his helmet and wiped his forehead with his sleeve. "Kenneth McCulloch— that's one Sumter's going to pay me for." He rubbed his palm round the browband of the helmet and rammed it on his head again. Then he said, sharply, "Well, Colonel, I'll send patrols to your right flank and down to the Santee road, then I'll discover how Corbet's doing. I'll leave George Hanger here—he's my second-in-command now—with a reserve for you."

"Thank you, Ban," said Rawdon, "I feel a lot safer when you're around."

"So do my men," said Tarleton, sourly.

Rawdon bit his lip, "I'm sorry about McCulloch, Ban. He was a good officer."

Tarleton looked down at his boots. He nodded.

"Yes—he was."

Then he turned on his heel and strode off to his horse.

"He's not very pleased with you, Francis," I said.

"No. I'm not very good at using his dragoons," said Rawdon, "But I do my best. Now you're here, maybe I'll do better."

For the next three days we withdrew slowly on Camden. There was some minor skirmishing all the while, but no real set-to. In the cavalry, who were the most engaged, casualties came more from the heat than from the enemy. Falling back on our own base of supply, we were well provided. Though we had many sick—about one-third of our whole strength—the men were well-rested, well-fed and in good order; but all too few, for we numbered less than two thousand effectives and the reports of Gates' force ranged from five to twelve thousand.

Save for a cavalry screen, we were withdrawn entirely into the town itself by the evening of Sunday the 13th August. And on that same evening, there arrived, to everyone's relief and satisfaction, from the west, a reinforcement of four companies of light infantry from Ninety-Six; and from the south, travelling night and day for three days from Charlestown, Lieut.-Gen. the Lord Charles Cornwallis.

Chapter Nine

*In which, being informed of his plans,
we discomfit General Graves.*

"'Rumour doth double, like the voice and echo,
The numbers of the fear'd,'"
said Cornwallis. It was the early afternoon of Tuesday the 15th August.
We were sitting in his headquarters in the Kershaw house in Camden in a
fairly informal council of war; and a fairly depressed one too. We had just
heard that, the same morning, the rebel militia leader Sumter had
captured Fort Carey, the redoubt guarding the Wateree River ferry, with
its entire garrison. "We" consisted of Rawdon, Tarleton, James
Webster—commanding the 23rd Regiment—myself and Maj. Richard
England, the Deputy Adjutant-General, acting as secretary.

Cornwallis' quill moved slowly down a column of figures. "So
now—we stand—with 122 officers—and 2,117 rank and file—four
6-pounders and two 3-pounders—h'm." His quill tip moved to the bottom
of an adjoining column and scratched the paper impatiently. "7,100—I
don't believe it! The rebels can't raise above 5,000 Continentals anywhere.
Say Gates has 2,000—he can't have more—and it's 2,000 more than I'd
trust him with—then the rest must be militia—and he can't have more
than 3,000 of those—"

England peered over Cornwallis' shoulder, "Armand's Legion, my lord,
are 350 cavalry and infantry by report—and you haven't entered the
Virginia Militia—1,500, under General Stevens, joined the rebel army
yesterday—"

"Well," Cornwallis scratched in the figure, "say 6,000 over all. Three to
one against—not bad—"

"And, my lord, Sumter is being reinforced by General Gates with 300 of the Delaware Line, which makes him over 1,000—"

Richard England, though a nice fellow, is not much given to optimism; well-suited for appointment to the staff or the company of Job's comforters.

"For God's sake, Richard," said Cornwallis impatiently, "300 Continentals with Sumter means 300 less with Gates! Whose damned side are you on?"

We all sat silent for a while. Finally England said, glumly,

"Shall I prepare orders for withdrawal from Camden, my lord?"

Cornwallis stared at him blankly, "Where the devil to?"

England coloured up to his wig.

"My lord, I thought—to Charlestown. I thought it prudent to prepare such a plan against the need—I thought it—prudent—"

Cornwallis smiled, "Richard—Richard, thy name is Prudence."

Poor England. He was always called Prudence thereafter. Cornwallis wagged his quill under England's nose.

"And I'll tell you why we can't withdraw from Camden. Because if we do we'll forfeit all we have gained since winning Charlestown. Do we do that without a fight? And, more important still, I have eight hundred sick men in the hospitals here. I'll not leave them to rebel mercy—look what happened to the poor lads after Saratoga. So, my prudent Richard, you can start preparing an order to march against Gates instead."

"So we're to fight?" I said, "Good enough. When? Where?"

"I'll know when Secker gets back," replied Cornwallis, "If he gets back, that is."

"Secker!"

"I know, Philip, I can't trust him either. But we've nobody else. I sent him off to find Gates and discover his strength and intentions. I doubt he can tell Gates much about us that he doesn't know already, so we've little to lose and a lot to gain. It's my guess that if he thinks we can beat Gates, he'll be back—"

At that moment—all very timely—Secker was announced. He sidled in, looking very pleased with himself.

"Now, Mr. Secker, well returned!" said Cornwallis, "What news?"

"My lord," Secker smirked at us, "Gentlemen, I can present you with the entire order of battle of the rebel army and its commander's resolves for its future actions. And, my lord,—you'll not believe it—all given me, word for word, personally—along with a bottle of very reasonable claret—by the noble Horatio himself, sitting in his own tent! My lord, I have in my life met with some remarkably gullible creatures, but never yet with the like of this hero of Saratoga!"

"How the devil did you get into General Gates' tent?" asked Cornwallis.

"My lord, nothing easier! I presented myself, all openly, at his camp. I informed the officer commanding his guard that I was a Marylander, and that I had heard that the Maryland Brigade of the Continental Line was present. I said I wished to pay my respects to the Commanding General and to my fellow Marylanders engaged in so noble a cause. That opened all doors! I was taken by the officer straight to Gates himself—after I happened to mention that I'd been in Camden the day before."

"And what did Gates have to say?"

"My lord, he sat me down, gave me a glass of claret and asked what I knew of the army in Camden. I asked him what he already knew. So, he told me—and it was surprisingly little; but I confirmed it, though much of it was inaccurate. This pleased him mightily—very naive, my lord—and I enlarged a little upon it. I said some infantry had arrived from Ninety-Six. He asked me how many. I said I thought they brought our strength to around three thousand. He pooh-poohed this as too great. So I said his information was better than mine—which he readily believed. Then he said that he had heard there were over a thousand sick in Camden. So I said I thought the true figure well above that—and this time he was ready to believe me! The man's a fool, my lord. He believes only what he wants."

"H'm—" Cornwallis' eyes never left Secker's face, "aught else?"

"My lord," Secker leant forward, as if anxious not to be overheard, "he inquired most anxiously whether you were in Camden. I said that you had not arrived and were not expected before Friday." Secker clapped his hands. "Oh, that pleased him, my lord! 'Excellent!' he cried. 'We've two clear days. Well, now we must move fast!' "

"Move fast?" Cornwallis stiffened, "To do what? When?"

"To assault Camden, my lord—at dawn tomorrow!"

The tension in the room was suddenly electric. Cornwallis fell back in his chair. His eyes still on Secker's face.

"Gates said that?"

"His very words, my lord."

Cornwallis nodded slowly and pushed his paper across the table. "Does his force bear any resemblance to those figures?"

"Gates' own estimation of his strength is around seven thousand effectives, my lord. Now, let me see—" Secker perched a pair of gold-rimmed eye-glasses on his nose—"Two Maryland Brigades—900—Delaware Line—yes—Porterfield—Armand—that figure's a little high, I believe—North Carolina Militia, 2,000 of those—Virginia—arrived as I was there—Gates said twelve hundred at least—and artillery, six guns only, my lord; short of horses, he said. Yes, these are much the same as General Gates gave me." He pushed the paper away.

Cornwallis' stare was unmoving and emotionless.

"Did no one regard you with suspicion, Mr. Secker?"

"Certainly Gates didn't, my lord. But his Assistant Adjutant-General—a Colonel Williams, from Maryland—showed some concern on the General's freeness with me. But I mentioned a few names of his acquaintance—though, I'll own, not of mine—which appeared to satisfy him."

"You were fortunate, sir," said Cornwallis, dryly. Then he smiled and added, "But you showed most commendable courage and skill." Secker smirked and bowed from his chair. "But, of what quality are those rebel troops? In what state are they?"

"My lord, the Continentals—both the Maryland and Delaware Lines—looked like soldiers and their officers looked like officers. Armand's Legion seem brisk and the cavalry well-mounted. But for the rest, I would not set great store by them. Of the staff, apart from the Colonel Williams I mentioned, who struck me as a very competent officer, the rest seemed inexperienced and in awe of the General. As to their state, they have had very many sick of the flux, by reason of their poor diet on the march here—green corn, green peaches and molasses was all, they claim!"

"Very interesting." Cornwallis made a note.

"My lord," Secker ventured hesitantly, "would it be impertinent to ask what your lordship's intentions are now?"

"Not at all. I called this council to decide them. We'll give you the opportunity for a little rest and refreshment and will inform you when we have agreed our course of action. I am most grateful to you." Cornwallis nodded his dismissal.

Secker departed reluctantly, but still smirking. After the door closed behind him, Cornwallis said,

"That fellow's backing both cocks in this main. He'll go straight to Gates once he knows our intentions. So we'll give him some. He can have your notes for a withdrawal, Richard. But don't give them to him before dark and don't let him leave before he has them."

England looked puzzled. "Shall I arrest him, my lord?"

Cornwallis cocked an eyebrow. "If we're going to use him again, to arrest him might not be—prudent."

England coloured up once more. Tarleton got to his feet.

"I'll see to it," he said and slouched out of the room. He was back within a minute and sat down without a word.

"Well?" said Cornwallis, frowning.

Tarleton looked surprised. "It's done."

"What's done?" Cornwallis' frown deepened.

"My lord, one of my corporals has gone to tell Secker that his horse has lost a shoe."

"And has it?"

"Well, no—not yet, that is."

"I see. And when will the horse lose the shoe?"

"The corporal will say that he has taken the horse to the nearest farrier. That will be one of mine."

"And what will the farrier do? Take the shoe off and put it on again? That won't take very long."

"No, it shouldn't, my lord—but this farrier is a ham-fisted clod and he's sure to prick the horse. And, just in case he doesn't—he'll be ordered to—"

The room shook with our laughter.

"Very good, Ban," said Cornwallis, "but if we're to let him away later, you'll have to find him another beast."

The tension in the room was relaxed for a moment. I said,

"Do we still fight?"

"Of course," said Cornwallis, smiling. "Odds are better than I thought. But, Ban, I want confirmation on the time of this assault. I want prisoners and I want them here before dark. Richard, issue an order warning all commanders of a move tonight, but don't give any destination, and prepare orders for an advance on the road to Rugeley's Mills. That's all, gentlemen. I'll send word when I need you again."

He sent for us at seven o'clock. Tarleton had found his prisoners; and a sorry trio they were. Filthy and ragged in civilian clothes, though all three had military waist-belts and knapsacks of sorts; one had a round hat with a broken cockade and another a flopped hat with no crown. And they stood, miserable and terrified, between two dragoons of the Legion.

"Banastre found these men three miles this side of Rugeley's Mills," said Cornwallis. "Two of them claim to be North Carolina Militia, and the third—with no hat—Virginia Militia. They've lain sick at Lynches Creek and were rejoining their corps." He studied the men with a kindly air. He has always held soldiers in high regard; even makeshift ones, like these. "Now, you've been sick, you say. What ailed you?"

The man in the flopped hat answered for all three, "If it please your honour, we 'ad the bloody flux."

"Flux?" Cornwallis stared. "Indeed? Have many had it?"

"Precious near the lot, your honour, they're starvin'."

"Are they?" Cornwallis nodded sympathetically. Flopped Hat took heart and spoke with more confidence.

" 'Course, old fatgut Gates ain't starvin', your honour. 'E ain't the boy for 'ardship, they say. Always got a bottle, an' a blow-out an' a blossom in 'is tent, they do say—"

Straight-faced, Cornwallis continued to nod in sympathy.

"But us, your honour, we've starved most of our way 'ere. Most what we've 'ad was unripe corn and 'ard peaches. Turns your guts to swash, your honour."

"I should think it must," murmured Cornwallis. "And are many in that state even now?"

"Dunno 'bout now, your honour. But when I fell out from the North Carolina, four days agone, most on 'em was so loose they could shit through the eye of a needle an' not splash the sides—as the sayin' goes, your honour."

"Does it?" mused Cornwallis, "I must remember it." He smiled. "Tell me, when did you lads last have a proper meal—good roast beef, dumplings, pease and a fair measure of rum to wash it down?"

The poor devils were slavering at the thought.

"Crimes, your honour!" said Round Hat, "Oi a'nt 'ad nothing loike that sin' oi left 'ome!"

"Well, you'll have it tonight and all you want, I promise you," replied Cornwallis cheerily. "But one last question before I send you off to your beef and dumplings. What were your orders about rejoining your corps?"

The encouragement of the beef and dumplings was enough for them to answer all together, interrupting and confirming each other.

"We was ordered to wait to join our corps on the 'ighroad from Rugeley's Mills, your honour—we was told they'd be marching that way tonight—that's right, your honour, gospel truth—the army's a-marchin' from the Mills tonight—they be a-goin' fer to attack the town ter-morrer morn, your honour—ah, that's what they tell us, your honour—that's so, surely—"

Cornwallis let them babble themselves into silence. They all stood, open-mouthed, their eyes going apprehensively from one to another of us as we sat watching them. The man in the flopped hat took it off and held it in front of him, shuffling it round by the brim in his filthy hands. He said nervously,

"We told the officer what took us what we was a-doin'," he looked across at Tarleton, "Didn't we, your honour?—an all what we'd 'eard—" his eyes came back to Cornwallis. "We ain't a-lyin', your honour—"

Cornwallis smiled encouragingly at them. "I believe you. Now, away to your dumplings!" He wagged his finger at the cornet commanding the guard. "See these men get what I promised."

When the door had closed behind the prisoners, Cornwallis said,

"We'll march at ten o'clock tonight. Richard will give you the orders. We'll march in silence—no noise or lights. Every man who can march, to march. We need every sabre—every musket. I intend to move on Rugeley's Mills along the high road. I hope to surprise Gates before he moves himself. If we can't do that, then we'll meet him on the way and still surprise him. I'm leaving Major M'Arthur in command of the town."

"What will you tell Secker?" asked Rawdon.

Cornwallis grinned. "Oh I'm a dabster at fairy tales, Francis. You can leave it to me." He looked round the table. "No queries? Very well, gentlemen—have your corps stand to arms now, please."

We moved off through the north gate at ten o'clock precisely. Cornwallis and his staff rode with Lieut.-Col. James Webster, who commanded the first division. Twenty dragoons and twenty infantry of the Legion formed the advance guard, and behind them the four companies of light infantry from Ninety-Six marched in close column. We rode behind these. The rest of the division comprised the 23rd and 33rd Regiments. Behind Webster's division marched the second division, commanded by Rawdon and composed entirely of provincial troops—the Volunteers of Ireland, the North Carolina Regiment and the Legion infantry—together with the South Carolina Militia. The two battalions of the 71st Highlanders formed the reserve, marching behind the second division. The cavalry of the Legion and the 17th Light Dragoons acted as rearguard.

We marched in silence, but we might as well have let every man sing. The hot, clammy night was filled with hubbub of night animals, birds and insects; so that a man could scarce hear himself speak.

A little before midnight we arrived at Saunders Creek, four miles north of Camden. The crossing, wide and muddy, occasioned some delay and much subdued swearing. As we moved slowly up the hill on the north side, the militia guide said, "Low sand hills here, my lord—few trees—some scrub. The gum swamps close in on both sides just ahead—"

A shot rang out in front. And another—and another—single shots—no volleying. There was a cheer, shouting, a scream cut short, a ragged volley, another rattle of shots. With James Webster I trotted to the head of the column of light infantry. The leading company had shaken out into skirmish line on either side of the road. The infantry of the advance guard fell back through them in good order, carrying two wounded. The dragoons followed them back through the line and at once moved out either way to cover the flanks.

"Where's Lieutenant Donovan?" Webster called.

A Welsh voice answered coolly, "Wounded, sir, in the charge. We struck their advance guard. They was more than us, so we charged them. They fell back, but they aren't gone far. The Lieutenant's here, sir. We can get him back on his horse."

"Who is that?" I asked.

"Sergeant Davies, your honour, Legion cavalry."

"Well done the Legion. James, I'll take him back to report."

The light infantry companies were deployed in line and I was turning to ride back when a low cry came from the dark.

"Enemy advancing, sir,—on the right!"

Webster was unmoved. "Let 'em come, then give 'em a volley."

The centre company volleyed first. Then the volleys continued along the line. Dark masses of enemy swung from left to right across our front and back again, like a herd of sheep headed by a dog, and then withdrew. The firing ceased and the light infantry companies lay down, silent, in their positions. We could hear the rebels cursing freely as they stumbled about in the bracken, picking up their wounded and retreating.

Cornwallis was sitting easy on his horse, hat off, brandy flask in hand, chatting quietly to Francis Rawdon.

"Well, Philip, what's the news?"

"James has the light infantry and the 23rd in position across the road. He has driven off what looks like the rebel advance guard. Sergeant Davies here was in our advance guard and can tell you how it started."

Cornwallis listened to Davies' report of the skirmish and thanked him for it. "Is Lieutenant Donovan sore hurt?"

"A ball in the shoulder, my lord. I think it's not broke."

"And these rebels—were they resolute?"

"They ran at once, my lord—the dragoons that is. We chased 'em and cut a few down, but some infantry took us in flank. Them dragoons seemed not to be expecting us; most on 'em had their carbines slung."

"Thank you," said Cornwallis, "as I hoped. Ask Colonel Webster to be so good as to report to me here."

Rawdon, Webster, Tarleton, Captain Campbell of the 71st and Lieutenant McLeod of the artillery gathered to receive their orders. In brief, these were that, shortly before dawn, Webster's and Rawdon's divisions would form line to the right and left of the road respectively, with their inner flanks on the road and their outer resting on the swamps which—fortunately for us—constricted the ground here to a narrow frontage. This constriction prevented the rebels taking advantage of their greater strength to outflank us. Four guns were placed centrally in the line, between the two divisions. The two battalions of the 71st, with the remaining two guns, formed the reserve. The cavalry was stationed behind the reserve, ready to exploit any success.

It wanted three hours to dawn. The troops were ordered to rest with their weapons beside them and try to get some sleep. There was naught else to do. With no moon, it was now too dark for any reconnaissance. We weren't entirely sure where we were, nor what the ground was like, nor how large the rebel army was, nor how near. The only thing we knew for sure was that we should have to fight in the morning.

Matthew had unsaddled Williamson, brushed her over and fed her, and unrolled my cloak for me under a bush. I sat down on the cloak and wished with all my soul for a dram. Tarleton came out of the dark and dropped onto the cloak beside me.

" 'Ods teeth! No sort of a battle for us. Can't move a step to either flank without going up to our bellies in stinking bog."

Matthew appeared with a bottle wrapped in a dripping cloth.

"A bottle of the General's German wine, your honour."

"Wonderful, Matthew! How did you get it so chilled?"

"Och, I took and wet it whilst we was paddling in the creek."

"Why don't you let this genius join the Legion?" asked Tarleton.

"You've rogues enough in it already. Matthew did you ask Lord Cornwallis' servant for this wine?"

"Well, as to that, your honour, I did not exactly ask him. It was stood there on the table—all alone—"

"What did he say when he couldn't find it?"

"Well, I wasn't there then, your honour."

What could I say? "Bring yourself a mug, Matthew!"

"Ah, that's very kind of your honour. It's partial I am to the German wines. And his lordship has the most elegant taste for the choosing of them. It's only the best he'll have."

[*133*]

Tarleton was helpless with laughter. I said,

"For God's sake, Banastre, stop giggling! It was you who said that we pick up our comforts on the way."

"So I did! And, bigod, we could all take instruction from Matthew in the art of it!"

It was a good bottle and it helped to pass the time. Later I walked across to the 71st and found Jamie Macdonell sat on a stump in front of his company, his drawn claymore across his knees, whetting away with a stone at the cutting edge of the point.

"Where's Alexander Fraser?" I asked.

"Och, the young laird!" Macdonell grinned cynically and chucked his chin. "He's over yonder, Colonel, communing with his ancestors. And a damned, plaguy, blackguard lot they all were—but only heroes to him!"

And there was Fraser, sitting motionless on a tree stump, his claymore point down in the ground between his knees, his chin resting on the basket, gazing fixedly toward the east, willing the sun to rise on his first day of battle.

As the night wore on I strolled through both divisions, talking to the soldiers, following a practice I had adopted on a similar night before some action I had long forgotten. They lay or sat in little groups, talking quietly, smoking their pipes, waiting for the dawn. I came back to my cloak to find Tarleton playing dice in the dim starlight with his second-in-command, George Hanger, and Charles Russell.

"Finished doing your grand rounds, Colonel?" said Tarleton. "We've no more wine, I'm afraid, but there's some brandy and water in George's canteen there."

"Good," I said, and took a long pull at George Hanger's brandy and water. It was lukewarm and tasted foul.

Half-an-hour later the divisions moved into line of battle. The reserve battalions closed up and the guns were manhandled into their positions. There was very little noise. The steady shuffle of feet—the swish of bracken and reeds trodden down—a clink of a buckle on a musket barrel—a quiet order as a file straggled—a muffled oath as a man stumbled in a bog-patch. In a few minutes it was done, and all was still again.

It was hot and sweaty and airless, and now the first light in the eastern sky showed us in what dismal desolation we stood. A thousand low sand hills, covered in dry grass and bracken. A few miserable, crooked pines and meagre, haggard oaks. To our right and left the bog—patches of sickly, yellowed reeds, blotched with pools of stinking black mud, out of which the stumps of long-dead trees poked like rotten teeth. A place of death and decay.

I clambered onto Williamson, settled in the saddle, looked to the priming of my pistols, loosened my sword in the scabbard and rode forward to report to Cornwallis. The brandy had soured in my mouth. My jacket hung heavy and close on me. The sweat ran down from under my browband and stung my eyes. I felt filthy and sticky and irritable.

I hate to fight in a clammy heat. A cold, dry day is best, with no wind. With a wind blowing it's hard to make out the orders, calls and drumbeats. But a wet day is worst. The horses slip and flounder in the mud, so that the speed and weight of the charge are lost, and, with them, its shock and effect.

Charles Cornwallis was his usual, imperturbable self. We rode together to the top of a sand hill, from which we could see across the whole battle field. Our compact lines of scarlet looked so thin before the masses of the rebel army. But then you noted the looseness and lack of order in the formations on their left, in front of Webster's division.

"Militia," said Cornwallis with satisfaction, peering through his spy-glass. "North Carolina and Virginia Militias—and unhappy they look too!" He swung his glass to inspect the other flank; a solid phalanx of blue, well-formed and spaced in good order. "Continental Line—Maryland and Delaware Regiments. That will be the German general—de Kalb. They look as good as Rawdon's lads—"

At that moment the rebel guns, in the middle of their line, opened. Too high, the round shot kicking up the dust in the road between the battalions of the 71st. Our guns joined their thunder as the sun laboured into the sky, a yellow ball in the morning haze. In the still, sultry air the cannon smoke hung in heavy coils, scarce moving, between the lines.

An officer rode forward to the rebel left shouting orders. A slow shuffle began, the troops on the far left falling back and the second line straggling forward to fill their place. Mounted officers rode through the confused mass shouting. Dismounted officers and sergeants joined in the bellowing and flailed about with their spontoons, trying to bring some regularity into the movement. It was not a tactical manoeuvre of formed companies. It was an unorganized mob, shambling aimlessly without understanding or purpose into chaos.

Cornwallis watched for a few minutes, whilst order and counter-order compounded the disorder. Then he shut his glass with a snap. "My compliments to Lord Rawdon and Colonel Webster, the line will advance and engage. And to Colonel Tarleton, the cavalry to prepare to move round our right flank to take the enemy in flank and rear."

"I'll go to Webster," I said. "Russell can go to Tarleton."

"Thank you, Philip. Major England, will you go to Lord Rawdon, please? I shall keep to the line of the road."

I trotted off, accompanied by Matthew, to the left flank of Webster's division.

"Advance and engage, James," I said.

"Not a damned moment too soon! Drums!—beat 'Advance!' "

As I rode along behind the line, drum after drum picked up the signal. The officers strode out in front of their companies. The swords flashed from the scabbards and the bayonets sprung, glittering, above head-high, in an unbroken screen of steel along each rank. Then, as one man, the whole line stepped off at the unhurried pace beaten out by the steady throb of the drums.

The sight of our advance produced different reactions in the two halves of the rebel line. On their right, the Continental troops stood firm, awaiting the assault. On the left, opposite Webster's division, the shouting became desperate and the spontoons flailed more fiercely, knocking men into line. Some men struck back with their musket butts and fighting developed within the rebel militia battalions themselves as they surged incoherently forward.

Charles Russell rode alongside me. "Colonel Tarleton will be two hundred paces to the rear of the right flank—" And there he was. Sitting square as a jockey on his big horse; his enormous sabre, which he always carried, lying across his saddle-bow, his command in close column behind him.

The steady beat of our drums ceased abruptly. The line halted some fifty paces from the rebels. The orders rang out—

"Make ready!" Hammers clicked back to full cock.

"Present!" The front rank dropped on one knee. The bayonets flashed gold in the morning sun as the muskets rose to the aim.

"Fire!" An even scarlet flame spat from every musket in the line. Russell's horse whipped round in fright. Williamson snorted and put her ears back. The powder smoke rolled in thick clouds between us and the rebel line.

"Charge bayonets!" the Drums thundered the "Charge" and the familiar growling cheer of the British infantry started somewhere and ran along the ranks into a terrifying crescendo as the whole division ran forward into the smoke. We followed them, unable even to see our horses' ears, so thick was the reek, guided by the shouts of the sergeants bringing up the rear rank, "Hold together—close up to the left—hold together, lads—"

A ragged volley pattered from the unseen enemy. A ball clipped my hat. Williamson shied from the body of a Welch Fusilier, face down in the bracken. The cheering rose to a roar—a fierce triumphant roar—and as we rode out of the smoke we saw the reason for it. The whole front of the rebel force facing us, both the Virginia and North Carolina Militias, was falling back in utter disarray. Some threw away their loaded muskets and ran; some flung them down and cried for quarter; some stood, herded into forlorn little groups by their officers striving to withstand our charge, and were swept away.

The fugitives ran headlong through the gaps between the companies of their own second line. Some, confronted by the ranks, tried frenziedly to hack and batter their way through; a few being shot or cut down by their own compatriots as they fought to escape. But now, as our line of scarlet and steel, reformed after the first charge, advanced steadily and inexorably against them through the smoke, these reserve companies themselves began to break. A ripple ran along the front ranks. First, one man turned—then another—flinging down their muskets—pushing their way back through the ranks behind. The whole front of one company—in an instant—crumbled. Men ran back from the flanks of another. Officers and sergeants struck at them with their spontoons. Mounted officers rode through the struggling, panic-stricken mob—for now it was nothing more—shouting and slashing with their swords; all to no avail. Fear had run through the whole left wing of the rebel army like fever in a body, rendering it palsied and impotent.

Tarleton rode up beside me. "Colonel, I'll leave George Hanger and half my force here. The rebels are holding on the right, but when we've swept this rubbish off the field, George can take them in flank. I'll take the other half in pursuit—"

"Don't go too far then," I ordered. "We only need make sure this wing can't re-form. A mile down the road should do you. Then come straight back here. If they fight hard on the right there, George won't be strong enough with only seventy dragoons. We'll need every man you've got."

Tarleton saluted and was off with half his command within the minute. As they came up with the embrangled mass of militia the column slowed to a trot and deployed with parade-ground precision into two lines. Over their heads, I saw Tarleton's sabre wave—then, bent low on their horses' necks they charged.

At once the rabble before them began to run—anywhere—every way—in any direction out of the reach of those gleaming, slashing blades. The screaming of the terrified wretches, cut down and trampled under the iron-shod hooves, came to us above the sounds of battle around the rebel right wing—isolated now, for the left wing would never re-form.

The 1st Maryland Brigade, the rebel reserve formation, moved up along the west side of the road to reinforce their right wing. James Webster wheeled the 23rd and the light infantry and attacked the Marylanders' flank. The rebel brigade turned to fight back, but were shattered by repeated volleys. George Hanger's dragoons, racing round behind them, stormed in to cut a swath through their rear files. Their agony was completed by the bayonets of the 23rd and light infantry, and the survivors broke and ran, or surrendered where they stood.

I sent Russell with orders to Hanger to prepare to act against the rear of the rebel right wing. The action on that flank was now close-joined, hand-to-hand. The 2nd Maryland Brigade and the Delaware Regiment were fighting with the stubborn determination of regulars. The battle there would not be so easily won. I rode off in search of Tarleton.

We passed a few fugitive stragglings of militia, stumbling aimlessly away from the battle. They offered us no offence; content that we ignored them.

A mounted officer was shouting at one such group of Virginia Militia, "Get back to the line, you men! Where are your officers?" The men ignored him and made off towards some bushes nearby. He rode after them, but they ran the faster and disappeared into the bushes, save two whom he caught great whacks across their heads and shoulders with the flat of his sabre, knocking them to the ground. He cursed them for craven curs and rode off towards another group.

The two men, picking themselves up, levelled their muskets at his back. Matthew and I were ten paces from them and still unnoticed when I heard their hammers click back. I shouted to the officer and rode straight at them. They turned, but I was on them before they could aim at me. I took the nearest on my off side with my point between his eyes, then, whipping the mare round, took the other on the near side with a cut at head which split his open. Matthew, galloping on, made the officer prisoner.

The officer saluted me courteously, "Most grateful, sir—saved my life beyond a doubt. Trust I'll be able to repay your kindness. Just now—fear I can't oblige you as a prisoner—" He wheeled his horse towards the battle, struck in his spurs and, crouching low, was off like an arrow. Unthinking, I had ridden between him and the muzzle of Matthew's carbine. Matthew brought his carbine to the aim, but I knocked up the barrel.

"Let his own men shoot him if they must, Matthew."

We turned to ride after Tarleton, but saw him returning at a steady canter with his dragoons again in close column behind him. I rode alongside him. "George Hanger dealt very well with their reserve brigade, Ban. I've ordered him to re-form to attack the rear of their right flank. There was a devil of a scrimmage going on there."

"Sounds as if there still is," Tarleton grinned happily.

The smoke hung thick where the main battle raged. The roar of the cannon was silenced, but volleys crackled unevenly—though how the men aimed through the stagnant, sooty reek, God only knows. Now there was the noise, hideous and overpowering in its intensity, of men fighting hand-to-hand, knee-to-knee, body-to-body, with sword, spontoon, bayonet and butt; thrusting, stabbing, hacking, clubbing—screaming, shouting, raving, bellowing—falling—dying.

England came to us at a gallop. "Colonel—" breathlessly, "Thank God I've found you in all this damned smoke! The General wishes the Legion cavalry to form about two hundred yards to your right—there. Major Hanger is thereabouts—if you could see him. You are to strike the rebels in rear—that will be about two hundred yards in front of where Major Hanger is drawn up. Your trumpeters are to continue to sound the charge until you close with the rebels, so that the infantry will know to cease volley firing to their front. At once, if you please, sir."

We cantered on and—out of the smoke—found Hanger sitting in front of two immaculate lines of dragoons. Tarleton led his column to the right of Hanger's troop and turned into line, two deep. The 17th Light Dragoons moved to their proper station on the right of the line.

"Banastre," I said, "I'm charging with you. I'll ride with the 17th. You're in command."

He grinned from ear to ear, saluted with a swinging flourish of his sabre, and trotted out in front of the centre of the line. I rode down to join the 17th. As I came to them, I saluted them. "First time I've had the honour of charging with you, gentlemen. Trust it won't be the last!"

They all grinned too, and I fell in to one side of Capt. Henry Talbot, commanding the troop. I said, "I'll accompany you, Captain Talbot, if you've no objection."

"Very welcome, Colonel," replied Talbot.

A long note of the trumpets and we were off—at a walk; a few quick notes and we trotted—straight into the smoke.

"Hold together—knee to knee—close in—close in to the centre." The orders ran up and down our invisible line. Then, suddenly, we were out of the smoke, and, fifty yards in front of us, the rear lines of the rebel troops. Men carrying wounded, surgeons tending them, soldiers filling cartridge bags or water canteens, others opening cases and sacks of cartridges and shot; all the business of the immediate support of the fight.

Our trumpets rang out the urgent notes of the charge. All heads turned towards us, bewilderment and fear on every face. Some ran for their weapons—but all too late. Sabres swinging, we were amongst them, scattering them, and through them with overwhelming force and shock into the rear files of the rebel regiments. They, too, had not seen or heard us until too late. Most were still facing front when we came upon them; so that the first man I took with my point between his shoulder blades. He slid off my blade as Williamson went over him, and I swung my sword free to cut at the men on either side of her. Poor devils, they were now so close-packed with the force of our charge that they could scarce move hand or foot, let alone fire their muskets or thrust at us with their bayonets. They were cut down where they stood, like sheep in a slaughter pen.

Williamson began to half-rear and plunge forward through the serried ranks as if fording a deep stream. Frantic at being so confined, she lashed out with her front feet and kicked out behind in a sort of capriole; causing more injury and havoc with her flying hooves than ever I could with my sword.

After a minute of lunatic hacking and cursing we were through them. I rode clear, turned and shouted to rally and re-form. The bugles sounded the "Rally." We formed again quickly—more loosely than at first—and charged in again. This time we sliced straight through them and most began to run back.

The fighting was now in little groups and knots. Pockets of blue-coated rebels were fighting bravely, back to back, surrounded by a wall of scarlet, until they were overborne or, as most did, flung down their arms and asked for quarter. One such group, larger than the rest, fought on fiercely with a stubborn courage. In its front rank stood a large man, bareheaded, in the uniform of a general. He was covered in blood from several wounds and his sword broken. But he fought on, with his broken sword, shouting encouragement to those around him.

I rode at the group and one of them thrust at me with his bayonet. I parried the point on my offside, riposted along the barrel of his musket and thrust into his throat. He tumbled backwards and, my point catching somehow in his jaw, I could not free my sword. Another stabbed at me on my near side. I fended off the blade with my left hand, so jerking the rein that Williamson's shoulder knocked him off balance. He thrust again as he reeled and, this time, the bayonet pierced through my left thigh and into my saddle, where—being of French pattern, weak in the blade—it broke off just above the socket. He scrambled to his feet and came at me with his musket clubbed. But as he swung it round, Matthew's sword sliced through his wrist, his hat and his head down to his ears.

The dead man hanging on my blade would have pulled me from my saddle had I not been skewered onto it. I stamped my foot on his chest and heaved on the hilt and he fell away. I felt no pain from the wound in my thigh, and looked around for an enemy to ride at—but, suddenly, there was none. The rebel general had been struck down and those around him had surrendered. All at once the firing and the shouting ceased. Now there were only the sounds of anguish—the agonies of the wounded and the dying. The battle for Camden was over.

There is an awful weariness which seizes upon you at the end of such an action. I looked down at the mess of blood over Williamson's shoulders and in her mane, all up my sword arm and on my breeches and boots. I thought my saddle damp and slippery under me and my left boot oddly full of water, until I realized that my saddle was soaked—and my boot filling—with my own blood. I still felt no pain from the wound, but I was suddenly dizzy and a burning vomit rose in my throat. I must have swayed, for I felt Matthew's arm come round me, holding me steady in the saddle.

"Holy Mother of God! Are ye right now, your honour? Och, I should have got to that devil quicker. Shall we ride over to the surgeons there?"

We did. Stapleton, the surgeon of the Legion, gave me some brandy, which helped. Then I rode alongside his wagon and, with Henry Talbot's arm round me and Matthew holding Williamson's head, Stapleton and his assistant, from the wagon, heaved the bayonet blade out of my saddle and me. They washed the wound, poured rum into it, plugged it at both ends and bandaged it. And I travelled back into Camden in the same wagon as two officers of the 2nd Maryland Brigade, a sergeant and private of the Volunteers of Ireland and a private of the Delaware Regiment; all feeling very sorry for ourselves.

We had won. Gates' army was utterly destroyed. Gates himself, so we

[*141*]

later heard, fled a headlong hundred miles without stop—riding like a race jockey all the way—though he's hardly built for one. Seven hundred rebel dead counted and near fifteen hundred prisoners—the most of these from the regiments of the Continental Line; besides three thousand militia scattered to the four corners of the Carolinas. And our own losses—seventy killed and two hundred and forty wounded.

But these are mere figures. Look at the returns of casualties published by the rebel Congress and in London. Other than General de Kalb and his aide, de Busson, there is not one name that is not British. Dead in a futile struggle between fellow-countrymen.

Chapter Ten

*In which I arrive at Belhaven and
a singular welcome.*

I was a little feverish from my wound, and Cornwallis forbore to see me until four days after the battle.

"We've just buried de Kalb. I hear you were wounded attacking his bodyguard."

"That was de Kalb? The general with the broken sword?"

"Yes—a brave man. He died of his wounds, eleven of them, all in front. God! when I think of a man like that—not even a colonist—battling like a lion to the last; whilst that creature Gates scuttled away before the battle had barely begun—!"

"And what will you do now?"

"What can I do but push on into North Carolina? If I simply remain here, which is what Pussy intends that I should do, if I understand him aright, the rebels will build up their strength again and all that we won last Wednesday will be lost."

But he was forced to delay to build up reserves of stores, to call up reinforcements and to recruit more militia; and he was further hindered by the heat and the numbers of wounded—from both armies—in the hospitals of Camden, and the fever, which struck down many more than ever fell in battle. I, myself, was one who suffered so.

For recovering well from my wound, I had been fit enough to stand to drink Tarleton's health on his return to Camden after destroying Sumter's force at Fishing Creek, thirty miles north of the town; recovering all the prisoners, sick, and stores taken by Sumter at the Wateree Ferry. He had surprised the rebels in bivouac, and Sumter—called by his followers "the

[*143*]

Gamecock"—had scurried into the bushes in his undershirt before the fight.

"All I ever see of these rebel commanders is their bare arses vanishing into the shrubbery—like a lot of rabbit scuts flitting down a burrow!" Tarleton said contemptuously, "Ecod! the old Swamp Fox wouldn't go off and leave his men to fight that way. He'd make ten of this shy-cock Gamecock!"

The very next day I was, of a sudden, delirious with a fever and stayed so for six days, wasting to a skeleton. On the seventh day the fever broke, but left me so weak that I could not get about easily without a stick until mid-September. Matthew tended me carefully until he too fell ill of it. But he suffered less than I by reason of some potions he was given by a fugitive Negro slave, who attached himself to us and served us in return for food, rum and some worn-out clothes of mine.

Whilst Matthew and I were still recovering, the army marched out from Camden to Charlottesburg in North Carolina. Thence, at the end of the month, being fully restored, I marched with a party of men from various corps who were also lately recovered from wounds or sickness.

Cornwallis greeted me as cheerfully as ever; but he looked very tired and was much cast down by his lack of success in curbing the rebels in North Carolina.

"They grow in strength every day, but, despite every encouragement, scarce a single self-styled loyal subject of the King raises a finger to assist us. They want it all done for them."

He clearly needed some encouragement and I hoped I might provide it. I decided to propose a plan I had had in mind for some time. "If you have no employment for me here for ten days or so, I should like to visit my cousins, the Fairleighs, at Belhaven. They say old Lord Fairleigh is influential in Tryon County. He might be persuaded to assist us."

I made no mention of Lucy, but I'll admit she had not been beyond my thoughts at the conception of the plan; nor was she now.

"A good idea, Philip," he nodded, brightening at once. "You might find us some recruits. And you could bring me word from Patrick Ferguson. I let him go up there a month ago to encourage the loyalists and I've had nothing from him. I was going to send Tarleton to him, but now he's ill with fever. Where is Belhaven?"

"In the Montague Hills—on the Catawba River."

"Is it, bigod! Then you'll need to take a strong escort!"

The next day—Tuesday the 3rd October—I left Charlottesburg with a troop of the 17th Light Dragoons, thirty rank and file. The most of their officers were sick, and those that weren't were fully occupied with patrols. Tarleton and Talbot, both on sickbeds, apologized for the deficiency of officers.

"Don't fret yourselves," I said, "Sergeant Hawes and I won't get into any trouble. We may even catch Sumter!"

"If you do," scoffed Tarleton, "ask him if he'd like his breeches back."

The Fairleighs had first come to Belhaven in 1716, immediately after the rebellion led by James Stewart, the Old Pretender; though, God knows, he did more pretending than leading. Then, after the rebellion led by his son, Charles Stewart, had failed bloodily at Culloden in April of 1746, most of the remainder of the Fairleigh family and their people came here. Not all clans, nor all Highlanders, had rallied to Charles Stewart, and, of those that did, many did so unwillingly. But, willing or no, for all those who marched with him to Derby and back and did not die on the bayonets of Cumberland's army, there was no place in Britain but prisons or the grave.

Belhaven faces north-east on a flat-topped hill in a bend of the Catawba River, in a position well-chosen for defence. A freestone wall, over head-high, encircles the entire hill halfway up its height; though somewhat decayed, it showed how the defence of the little community had been provided for in the first planning of the settlement. From a distance the square front of the house has the dour look of most great Scottish houses; but, as we drew close, we observed how the tall columns and graceful proportions of a portico softened the severity of its appearance. By this time we were within shot of the wall, which appeared to be under repair. This made me doubt the wisdom of riding too unwarily through the great gates guarding the approach.

I halted the troop and sent the point on ahead to secure our passage through the defile of the gate. They found nothing. Nor could I, through my glass, discover any movement about the house. We moved forward up the hill and through the gates; the troop with carbines unswivelled and I with a pistol out and cocked. The house appeared to stand solitary on its crest with no out-buildings around it. Still no life showed; not a dog barked.

Suddenly one of the point troopers raised his carbine above his head. As one man, the leading four files formed skirmish line, turned left, dropped off on the near side and rested their carbines, aimed at the house, across their saddles.

A figure appeared in the shadows of the portico and the trooper's challenge echoed in its columns. "Halt there! Stand still or I fire!"

"Halt, is it? And who bade you give orders here? Where's your commander, fellow?" It was a voice of unquestioned authority, with that precision and peculiar lilt I find so pleasant in the speech of Highland Scots. I had found Lord Fairleigh.

I rode to the foot of the broad steps leading up to the portico, giving myself time to examine the house and its surrounds. Now, close to, the whole impression of the house, with its well-balanced, uncluttered proportions, was one of grace and elegance utterly unexpected in so desolate a situation; but of greater interest was the domestic area of the settlement, lying behind and sheltered by the house.

The house itself stood a little off from the centre of a circular plateau. Before it, for a third of the area of the plateau, stretched a lawn encircled with great oaks. Behind it, over the remaining expanse, the hill had been excavated to the depth of a full storey below the ground level of the house. Within this space were ranged shingle-roofed, stone cottages, with stabling and barns for cattle and the storage of implements, grain, hay and straw. I noted workshops for a farrier, a saddler, a potter and a carpenter. There were a bakehouse and a brewhouse, with a cooper working alongside. There was a butchery and, dug into the hillside beside it, what I judged to be an icehouse. In all, a small self-supporting and self-sufficient village; and over all there was an air of well-ordered industry and prosperity.

Around the outside of the village, along the edge of the plateau, ran the freestone wall and within it a wooden sentry-walk, fallen away in places. Embrasured musket-ports were cut in the wall, both above and below the walk. At one end of the wall, where it adjoined the front, raised portion of the plateau, stood a small, square, stone tower, the top embrasured at both outward corners for cannon, though none were emplaced. I supposed there was a similar tower to complete the other end of the wall. And wherever any part of the fortification of the settlement was dilapidated, repair was evidently in hand.

The man I presumed to be Lord Fairleigh was of middle height, thick-set but very upright in his stance. I judged him to be in his middle sixties. His face was thin with high cheek bones and a long, straight nose. His eyes were the bluest I had seen in any man, set deep beneath straight, bushy eyebrows. His expression was kindly but his manner courteously chill. A full-bottomed, curled, unpowdered periwig fell over his shoulders. His coat, as old-fashioned as his wig, was of brown velvet bound with gold lace. At his throat a knot of lace was secured by an elaborate, silver plaid brooch set with a great yellow stone, on which was engraved a boar's head—the Fairleigh arms. Fifty years out of fashion, I thought. But what's fashion to such a man? He'd have looked lairdly enough in a mobcap and an old horse blanket.

I uncovered and bowed from my saddle, "Pray, sir, do I have the honour of addressing Lord Fairleigh of Lochdearn?"

He answered coldly, "Col. Philip Cato, is it ever your practice to ride up to a kinsman's house as if you intended to take it by storm?" Then he burst out into a great laugh. "Get ye down, nephew, and come away in. I was sad not to see you in Charlestown. I'm much in your debt for your care of Lucy."

I gave my horse to a young Negro, a nice, smiling intelligent-looking lad neatly dressed in drab livery. Lord Fairleigh spoke to him in the Gaelic and the boy bowed and trotted away, leading my horse and calling, in English, to my troopers to follow him.

We mounted the steps of the portico.

"How did you recognize me, my Lord?" I asked.

He laughed again, "How could I not? Your picture stood ever on my Katharine's table. I came to know your features as well as those of my own sons! And Lucy told me that you might visit us."

"Ah, yes. And how is Lucy?" I tried to make it sound nonchalant.

"Lucy?—She's well—well." As we paced across the pavement of the porch he stopped, took my arm and turned me about. We looked across the broad stretch of the lawn and over the hills lining the Catawba valley. He sighed. "Beautiful, is it not? It ever puts me in mind of my home. I love this place—but my home is Lochdearn. Please God one day my heart will lie there with my forbears. James is of my mind too—but Charles, my younger son, and Lucy want none other home than this. We have been left in peace here, and though I served the Stewarts, my kinsmen at home have not suffered; and I still hold my title from the King's hand. For these mercies I owe him my gratitude and my duty—and I strive to pay that debt." He patted my shoulder. "But this is no way to greet a welcome guest! Come now, nephew, this way—I believe I may have a surprise for you!"

He flung open the door of an ante-room. Surprise there was indeed. Standing in the window bay, watching my troopers as they formed and moved off down the driveway were three gentlemen. All wore uniforms of senior officers of the rebel army. Having observed my arrival, they were obviously expecting to see me. However, our surprise seemed mutual. For a few seconds of silence no one moved. Then Fairleigh laughed gaily and said,

[*147*]

"Now, gentlemen, let the world wait awhile. We'll have done with wars for to-day." He took my arm and led me to the senior of the three; a short fellow with a high, bald forehead, cold, ice-blue eyes which bored into you like gimlets, and a grimly jutting jaw below a mouth like a gin.

"General, may I present my kinsman, Col. Philip Cato. Philip—Gen. Mordecai Gist, commanding the 2nd Maryland Brigade."

Fairleigh's words met with a slight inclination of the bald forehead; but the eyes never shifted from mine. My acknowledgement matched.

"I observed how bravely General Gist's brigade fought in the engagement near Camden," I said.

The gin creased slightly round the ends; and that, I learned was the nearest Mordecai Gist ever came to smiling.

"Honoured to make your acquaintance in less exacting circumstances, Colonel Cato."

The officer on the General's right bowed and offered me his hand, "Delighted to meet you again, Colonel. Otho Williams is my name. Though I doubt that means aught to you."

"Are you not General Gates' Adjutant-General, sir?"

The thought, apparently, gave him no cause for enthusiasm. "Yes. But you don't recall our earlier meeting? Well, I have more cause." He paused, then turned to General Gist. "Colonel Cato perhaps chooses not to remember, General. But it was he who saved my life during the battle, as I described to you."

"Was it, indeed? Well, sir, it was a noble act and we owe you gratitude!" Now Gist wrung my hand vigorously, whilst the third officer, a tall stoutly-built man, florid-faced and dark-haired, near broke my back thumping it, crying, "Damned noble, bigod, damned noble!"

I remembered. "You were rallying the militia—"

"And you cut down the two who were set to shoot me."

Now all was smiles and cordiality, and Fairleigh introduced me to the third officer. "Cousin William, Philip Cato being a kinsman of mine is, thereby, a kinsman of thine too. Philip, may I present our kinsman Col. William Washington, commanding the 1st and 3rd Continental Dragoons, who, incidentally, is a cousin of the Commander-in-Chief; so you are well connected in the Revolutionary Army!"

Washington shook my hand warmly and pounded my already numb shoulder. "Damnation delighted, cousin! See you've an escort of regular cavalry—none of those damned ruffians of Tarleton's. By Heaven, it was a joy to watch how they moved! Wish to God I could get my men to look so well. Why don't you let me have a few, hey? We'll pay 'em well—give 'em a grant of land too. What d'you say, hey?" His great bulk shook with laughter. Then, suddenly appreciating that his suggestion was hardly tactful, he spluttered in scarlet embarrassment, "Don't take me amiss, my dear fellow, hey? Wouldn't dream of it. I'd hang the rogues first, what?" He turned back to the window. "Now, where's me glass?" He sighed and mumbled on. "Could do with some, though. Dam rag-tag lot I've got now—"

I went then with Lord Fairleigh to see to the needs of my soldiers and our horses. I found all well-housed and fed, the men messing together on the most amicable terms with the escorts of Continental troops accompanying the three rebel officers. This done, Fairleigh excused himself to attend to his affairs and I rejoined the others in the ante-room. The time passed quickly in talk until, of a sudden, the double doors opened and Fairleigh stood in the doorway, smiling and bowing to us.

He was now dressed in a long snuff-coloured coat, heavily brocaded. A fall of fine lace frothed from under his chin and more lace showed at his wristbands. An order glittered on his left breast—French or Jacobite. He made a splendid, noble figure. As one man we all rose, but our eyes were not on him. Beside him stood Lucy.

She wore a pale-blue pannier-style gown, very plain, with a low-cut square neckline edged with lace. A narrow, pale-blue velvet collar supported a brilliant diamond star and her hair hung loose in ringlets over her bare shoulders.

Her presence dominated the room, as it had dominated my cabin aboard the *Union*. She looked for me as she entered, but then, almost as if afraid to recognize me, looked away at once. With a charming grace she curtsied to Mordecai Gist—deep enough to reveal sufficient of her lovely figure to make him blink. Otho Williams she greeted in similar style. Then, running to William Washington, she reached up to throw her bare arms round his neck and kissed him warmly. Washington was taken aback. "Bigod, what good deed have I done to merit such a cousinly greeting?" And he returned it as warmly.

And then it was my turn. We stood looking into each other's eyes as we had before. But where before I had seen smiling, teasing affection, now I saw only defiance. I put out my hand. "Lucy—" I said. And at that the fire went quite from her eyes, and all at once they were full of tears. Her hand went up to her throat, and she turned and ran from the room.

"You must forgive her," Lord Fairleigh's voice seemed to come from a distance. "Since she has been home she has heard too much against the King's troops and the ravages of Tarleton's dragoons and the loyalists—"

I came to earth with a bump. "Indeed I understand very well," I said. "Has she heard too of the work of the Sons of Liberty and the Mountain Men?"

It was a stupidly vicious thing to say to him, but he answered me gently. "Ay, ay—but she will not believe a word against such—patriots; though they have done foul enough work even in these parts. She is young and impressionable still—all is black or white—"

Gist said sourly, "You're right, Colonel. God damn them, they do no credit to any of us, these gangs of so-called patriots and loyalists. Deserters from both our armies or mere common villains, out only for murder or loot. Cut-throats, no one is safe from them. It's as much a cause of worry and embarrassment to us as it is to you."

"Indeed, General," Lord Fairleigh was obviously anxious to turn the conversation away from his daughter. "And you should know that there are many in these parts who fear that, if the King's authority disappears altogether, this Congress will be powerless—or unwilling—to control such evils."

Gist coughed uncertainly, "Well, h'm, I'd suppose the militias could be mustered to deal—"

Colonel Williams snorted. Washington threw back his head and laughed, " 'Fore God, General! They're the devils that do the raping and murdering—after they've run like rabbits from the battlefield!"

"You should know that after Camden," Williams added, dryly.

"And that is why I am renewing the defences of this house," said Fairleigh. "If the King's authority is dispersed, no colony can maintain order on its own. You will need a standing, regular force, such as the Continental Line is to-day—under command of some central authority such as Congress—"

"Never! By God, never!" Gist exploded. "Damnation, my lord! Exchange one tyranny for another worse! Where's the sense in that? Rid ourselves of a King to saddle ourselves at once with that pack of scheming, slandering, money-grubbing thieves who preen themselves in Philadelphia to-day? That's a government worse than those clowns in Westminster! 'Fore God, I'd sooner welcome back my sovereign lord King George the Third, with all his taxes, than submit my state to that damned cabal of charlatans in Congress!"

Hooves clattered on the carriageway. Fairleigh went to the window. "Ah, Jamie and Charlie are returned, with some friends, I see—officers of the Virginia and Carolina militias." He turned to us. "Gentlemen, you have made your opinions of the military qualities of the militias very clear, but I must ask your forbearance now. These young men are not practised in war, perhaps were not well led—"

"Only way to lead 'em is with a bayonet up their backsides," muttered Washington.

"William," said Fairleigh, reproachfully.

"Oh, ay, never fear—I'll not say a damned word to 'em—"

Seeing I was now well out-numbered, I suggested that I should withdraw to my room to refresh myself after my journey.

"Come with me," said Lord Fairleigh. He led the way into the hall. "My dear lad," he said as we climbed the broad stairs, "I trust you will not be distressed by what is said and done by these young militia officers. They—well, I should not have chosen them as my friends were I their age."

"Remembering how silly and awkward I must have been thought when I was their age, I may find them congenial company," I said.

He chuckled. "Ah, you do my heart good, lad, I wish my dear Katharine were here to talk with you."

We mounted in silence to the wide landing and he led me on through the tall windows opening on to the balcony over the main entrance. We looked down the length of the valley. The mists of the hills were patches of rose in the last light of sunset, and in the dim blue depths below the golden reflections of the first stars trailed their wavering streamers over the smooth surface of the waters.

Fairleigh said, diffidently, "You'll not be hurt by Lucy's coldness?"

I was quite unable to reply. After a moment he led me to the door of my room, and, at the door, he took my lapel and whispered in my ear, "Be gentle with my poor Lucy," and closed the door softly behind me.

I stripped off and got into a great tin bath, washed away the sweat and dust, had Matthew add more hot water, and sat imagining Lucy's face forming and fading a thousand times in the intertwining coils of the steam. In time the coldness of the water brought me out of my foolish dreaming. Matthew had laid out my civil clothes; a dark blue frock coat and the waistcoat which Anne had so lovingly embroidered. That brought me to my senses.

I hoped to join the other guests unobtrusively, and studied them, gathered in the hall below me, as I descended the stairs. Gist, Williams and Washington had all changed out of uniform, and two other men, whom I guessed to be James and Charles Fairleigh, were also dressed as civilians. Both were tall, and I judged the elder, James, the dark one, to be in his late twenties, and Charles, the fair one, a couple of years younger.

James, neatly dressed and with a mature and confident air, was listening to Washington. Charles, not so composed a picture, was talking animatedly with Lucy and a burly, coarsely handsome, young man in the uniform of the Virginia Militia; whom, I noted with a twinge of jealousy, Lucy appeared to regard with more than a casual affection.

The rest wore the uniforms of the Virginia or North Carolina Militias; with one exception. Clad in a black coat of oddly clerical cut, smiling humourlessly at Washington's banter, was Mr. Secker.

Lord Fairleigh espied me. "Ah, well-timed, nephew!—" At once all heads turned towards me. I bowed to Lord Fairleigh, which, since he was standing beside him, allowed me to observe that Secker's smile had been displaced by an expression of dismay. I bowed to Lucy, to which she turned her back. I was walking through the company towards Lord Fairleigh when, through the murmur of conversation, a voice called from behind me,

"Hey, where's the red coat? Do lobsters come out of their shells at night then?"

There was a roar of laughter from the militia officers, but, close to Gist and Williams, I was encouraged to see their evident displeasure at this bumpkin wit. I looked the speaker up and down slowly—it was the large officer of the Virginia Militia—and turned away.

He called after me, "Oh, you've seen me before, sir! You can be brave enough in here, but wait until we meet in a proper set-to. You'll recognize me then all right!"

Otho Williams broke in. "Mr. Chawton, if you wish Colonel Cato to recognize you, turn round and show him your back. That's all he can have seen of you so far." I did not turn to see the effect of this on Chawton, but I heard no more from him.

Neither Secker nor I made any sign of mutual recognition on being introduced, but he slid away immediately thereafter, eyed closely, I noted, by Williams.

As we entered the dining-room Charles Fairleigh took my arm and asked to sit with me. Lord Fairleigh sat at one end of the long table, flanked by Gist, Williams and Washington and, after a few words with his sister, James Fairleigh, looking puzzled, went to the bottom of the table: whilst Charles led me to a seat midway from either end. Then Lucy, with Chawton beside her, placed herself exactly opposite me; and the expression on their faces made me wonder whether my positioning had been the aim of a neat little plot. I had hoped for a quiet, uneventful evening and an early bed. I had reckoned without Lucy.

Oh, she was clever in her torture—for that is what it was; taking every advantage of the respect and courtesy properly due to her, and allowing none to me. At first we exchanged, formally and coldly, the insignificances of polite chatter. Then she began—oh, so lightly—to turn what I said against me in a gentle, bantering fashion. She made little quips against the King, and more vicious ones against Cumberland and the Army's suppression of Charles Stewart's rebellion—aimed at getting her father's and brothers' sympathies, and succeeding.

She even had me laughing at some of her earlier remarks. But, as I began to find less humour in her wit, I noted that, though at times she had the whole table in a roar, she never laughed herself and her eyes never left me. She wore all the while a sort of angry half-smile, near to tears, as if she forced herself to do what hurt her too.

And now she gained the support of Gist and Williams, with gibes about the military disasters of Lexington and Saratoga, and the disgraceful shambles of Clinton's first assault on Charlestown.

At last, with every one round the table on her side—save James, who now, apparently, saw her purpose and sat grimly silent,—she came nearer home. Her lash stung from every angle. She denounced the inhumanity to prisoners in Charlestown, the hanging of prisoners of war taken at Camden, the evil reputation of the British Legion, the theft of slaves and goods, the recruiting of what she called "poor whites" into the Army by promises of loot. For all these charges—she alleged them proven—she piled all blame and censure on my head.

After our first innocent exchanges I had said not a word, but continued my meal in silence, leaving her to rage and sneer on; which had made her rage the more. But the meal ended and having no other means of occupying myself, I decided to return fire. For the first time in all that evening's pillorying I gainsaid her.

"Ma'am," I said, as courteously as I was still able, "after the action near Camden we found among General Gates' papers letters from persons you describe as peaceable, honourable gentlemen of Charlestown, proposing and plotting treachery and murder against the King's forces. And in the very pockets of those prisoners taken at that battle who were afterwards executed, we found the same paroles they had sworn on being released after surrendering during earlier actions. What would General Gates have done with such persons had the position been reversed?"

"Lies!" She bent forward, raging at me across the table, "Lies, lies, lies!" she hissed, all restraint gone, "All lies on your lying redcoat tongue!"

"Ma'am, this land was won from the French and the Indians by soldiers wearing red coats."

She leapt to her feet and struck the table with both clenched fists. She looked beautiful beyond all words, but I was in no mood to appreciate it. Had the table not been between us I believe she would have struck me. There was an awful hysteria in her fury, as if she were intent on destroying herself—or something within herself.

"How dare you contradict me in my house! How dare you speak in my house! How dare you crawl into my house! You are not wanted here—you have betrayed us—"

Another fist crashed on the table. James Fairleigh was on his feet. "Father, will you not tell this stupid child that she will not insult our kinsman under our roof before our guests?"

"Who are you to correct me? You cringe before these thieves and murderers!" Lucy turned on him like a wildcat. "You are not your father's son—" and there she went too far.

"Lucy!" Lord Fairleigh's voice came gruffly down the table. She turned and looked at the old man. "Sit down and be silent, girl. Remember your duty to your guests—" a little querulously.

'Fore God! I thought "sit down and remember your duty to our guests"—is that all he can say? He should have put her over his knee and thrashed her.

Lucy did not budge. She stood staring at her father. Now it was plainly a struggle of wills; and plainer still which was the stronger. Fairleigh lowered his head and cleared his throat noisily. He flapped a hand at her, feebly. "Sit down, my dear, sit down, please."

Still she did not move and her face hardened. She knew she was the master and, still inflamed by passion, now wilfully and openly shamed her father's weakness. It was pathetically embarrassing. I rose to my feet.

"My lord," I said, "I have no wish to be a cause of dissension in your family. I loved the Lady Katharine too well." I heard Lucy catch her breath at that. She stared at me now, her lips parted, gripping the table until her finger-nails were as white as her cheeks. I said slowly and quietly,

"Lady Lucy blames me for a host of ills. But it is clear that I myself am the cause of her displeasure. If you permit, my lord, I'll withdraw now."

I waited a moment for some reaction from Fairleigh, but he gave no indication that he had even heard me. I walked towards the door. A chair scraped back.

"And I come with you." James came from the end of the table.

"And I." Otho Williams got up from his place.

"And I—And I." Gist and Washington rose to join me.

This—at last—roused Fairleigh. "Gentlemen—gentlemen, please—sit down. My daughter was joking—Lucy, say you meant nothing—please—"

James and I stopped, hoping that Lucy would, somehow, apologize for her outburst. Gist, his hand on the door-handle, waited for her to speak. She glared at him like a defiant child. Gist—and Williams and Washington beside him—stared back, their faces expressionless. Her nerve broke. She glanced frantically around the young militia officers for support; but they behaved like true militia. Finally she turned to me. Throughout dinner I had persevered in treating her courteously and respectfully, though God knows how I managed it. But now I must have looked as disagreeable as I felt. So she whipped round on her father again, and, with a deep curtsy—

"Father dear," she said, all soft and breathless, "I beg that you will forgive me. I see that I have offended the shallow sensibilities of some of our guests. It is I who should withdraw." And she went with flags flying and guns blazing.

She stormed over to the door like a ship of the line running under full sail. At the door she halted, very erect, both hands on her skirts, looking straight in front of her, and waited for one of us to open the door. But at her remark about "shallow sensibilities," Gist's hand had gone from the door to behind his back, and he had stepped a pace away. She waited. No one moved. She glared round at each of us in turn—met cold unconcern in every eye. She stamped her foot and ran to the door, but, letting go of her skirt to grasp the handle, tripped on the hem and fell heavily against the door. Still no one moved. She pulled herself to her knees by the handle and wrenched at it with both hands. It was large and slippery and stiff and she could not turn it. Now her breath came in sobs and I saw the tears on her lashes. Still none of us moved. Only Charles half rose from his chair, but sank back on meeting his elder brother's eye. Still she struggled with the handle, tears falling freely now, stubbornly refusing to cry for quarter. And then—thank Heaven—the handle was turned from the other side by a servant, and she fled—sobbing—through it. James kicked the door shut with a slam.

"I think we may sit down again, gentlemen," he said.

Lord Fairleigh rose quickly to his feet and came to grasp my hand. "Nephew, forgive me. I should have checked the silly child. She is overwrought, poor bairn." Still obviously more concerned for his daughter than for her discourtesy, he called to his younger son, "Charlie, go to Lucy, lad, she may need comforting." He looked round the militia officers. "And any of you gentlemen who wish to leave may do so."

All the militia, and Secker with them, bowed to Lord Fairleigh and left the room.

Lord Fairleigh was in a dither. "Perhaps I should go to her myself. She was very—"

"Sit down, uncle, for God's sake," said Washington impatiently, "There's enough young bulls out there to keep that tetchy little heifer happy."

Fairleigh sat down slowly, not best pleased at the inelegant metaphor. But he got no sympathy from any of us and sat silent whilst more wine was brought and poured. Washington drained his glass and promptly refilled it. "Ahhh—damned good claret this, uncle."

Fairleigh came out of his ill-humour. "Thank you, William,—yes, a good claret. Be wasted on those boys."

I thought to relieve his embarrassment at Lucy's behaviour and moved up to sit beside him. He bent across to me and put his hand on my wrist. He said, very quietly so that only I could hear, "Philip, believe me, what Lucy said tonight has no bearing on her regard for you."

I shrugged. "It's of no consequence," I said.

"You don't believe me. Philip, permit me to know my own daughter. She was much—disturbed—when I told her you were here. Now, she is—distraught." His hand closed tightly on my wrist and he looked at me straight. "Can you tell me why?"

"I—" Again I could not make myself answer—and I couldn't meet his gaze either. He loosed my wrist.

"Ah," he sighed, "It's as I thought—

> 'Love's tongue is in the eyes,
> And most concealed, doth most itself discover.'

I cannot blame you, Philip—her mother loved you like her own son."

We sat silent, both, in our own ways, sunk in thoughts of Lucy. The conversation flowed round us, lively and noisy. Washington was denouncing Gen. Charles Lee—a rebel renegade, late of the 16th Light Dragoons—as a traitor to the Revolutionary Army.

"Traitor?" Fairleigh looked up sharply, "That is an ill-judged term for you to use of any man, William."

"But, uncle—look—" Washington protested, "he was taken prisoner at

Basking Ridge—by his old regiment—coincidence, d'you think?—and offered to betray our army to General Howe. So if he's not a proper traitor, show me one!"

Fairleigh leaned back in his great chair. Above his head the candle-light gilded the carving of the coat-of-arms of the Fairleighs of Lochdearn—arms borne at Falkirk and Bannockburn and Flodden and Culloden against the English power. He smiled at Washington and shook his head. "Dear William, you are ever saying that reading hurts your head, but you really should inform yourself more exactly of your own situation." The smile faded. "You ask to see a proper traitor. Go look in your glass, nephew. There you will see as damnably treasonous a traitor as ever drew breath—as I, too, see in mine. We around this table are all proper traitors, William, save two." He pointed at me. "No traitor there." He pointed at James. "And there is the son of a proper traitor, William, who will, God willing, purge our family's name of its treason, so that we may again walk with honour in our true homeland."

Otho Williams broke in, "But Lord Fairleigh, how can you call us traitors? We are Americans—"

"Marylanders," interjected Gist.

"Very well, General," said Williams, patiently, "Marylanders and Virginians and New Yorkers. We've cast off King George's authority."

"All rebels claim to have cast off their sovereign's authority, Colonel. But your galaxy of windbags in Philadelphia can do naught in law to set aside King George's authority until he himself acknowledges that it has lapsed."

"But, my lord, we're in treaty with France and Spain."

"And much damned good it's done us," said Gist morosely.

"Agreed, General—but perhaps the Frogs won't run the next time."

Gist frowned. "Why do we want a next time? That idiot D'Estaing failed us at New York and Newport in '78 and at Savannah last year. Isn't that enough? Anyone can see they're only using us for their own ends."

"But what choice have you?" demanded Fairleigh. "How could your defiance of the English King stand were it not propped on French crutches? Your cannon are French, your muskets are French, the money you are paid for your services—"

"The money we're not paid, you mean," grumbled Washington.

Fairleigh waved an impatient hand. "But—have you considered who will become your enemy if you should succeed in your defiance? Do you think the French will ignore the opportunity to regain what they have lost on this continent in the last war? And to whom then will you turn for support?"

"Why, to our English cousins!" cried Williams, and raised his glass to me. "We must hide behind Britannia's skirts awhile until we grow strong enough to fight the bullies of Europe by ourselves."

"Ay, maybe," Fairleigh nodded. "But for now you cannot survive without the French."

Washington refilled his glass. "Well, at least we can do without that perfumed popinjay Lafayette forever telling us how brave and unselfish he is to come and help us," he growled. "Fellow slobbers like a girl over poor cousin George—damned embarrassing. George is very good about it though—"

But Williams was not satisfied. "But Lord Fairleigh, the Kings of France and Spain have both acknowledged our independence by treaty—"

Fairleigh shook his head at him, "Sir, you cannot really believe that they do so solely for your benefit?—and that if they cease to benefit they would not condemn you as traitors and applaud your execution for treason against the established monarchy? They know full well the fevers of rebellion are catching, and have their own reasons for fearing such infection within their own estates. In time they may even have cause to regret that they have assisted you this far."

"You're being deuced encouraging this evening, uncle," said Washington gloomily. He peered down the table. "Let's have some more of the claret up here—only good thing that comes from France!"

Fairleigh glanced round his guests, "If you would not be accounted traitors, gentlemen, you have no alternative—but to win." He smiled, "Remember,

> 'Treason doth never prosper. What's the reason?
> For if it prospers, none dare call it treason!' "

That cheered them. Washington shouted with laughter and clapped his hands. "Capital! Capital! Ay, that's what we'll do—we'll win and prosper!"

Outside in the hall there was a rush of feet and a babble of voices and laughter. The noise moved out on to the portico and along it. Someone started to sing, strumming a zither. Washington stretched back in his chair and heaved a long sigh, "Damme—we've finished the claret! No point in hanging about here!"

We all walked out onto the portico. The air was fresh and cool, and on it soft scents, strange to me, mingled with the sharp tang of wood-smoke from the village behind the house. Before us, stretching clear to the newest risen stars, lay a country wilder but lovelier now than by day, the hills and trees etched in alabaster in the moonlight. Lord Fairleigh and the others descended the steps and walked out across the lawn. I stood, still bewitched by the enchantment of the scene.

There were footsteps behind me. Two figures had left the group gathered round the singer at the far end of the portico; one was Chawton, the other Lucy. Chawton stopped,

"Look there—damme, if it aren't the lobster." He swayed and staggered a little. "All alone—poor ol' lobster—" Lucy whispered at him, and they disappeared through the door.

You would have supposed with me, wouldn't you, that after her behaviour at dinner, Lucy Fairleigh would have had little attraction for me, and the thought of her with another man a thing of no consequence? What chemistry is it that turns a man's bones to water at the sight of one particular woman and sets his senses ablaze when he sees her with another man? I stared distractedly at the scene before me, uncaring of its beauty; my ears straining, of course, to hear what was passing in the hall.

A little shriek—Lucy's laugh, an uneasy laugh, I thought—the click of her heels on the stone floor—Chawton's tipsy giggle—a scuffling—Lucy's voice, "Roger, no—no—you've drunk too much—stop it—stop—" the note rising in fright—a tearing of cloth—a sob—feet running across the hall and up the stairs—the clatter of a falling chair—heavy feet pounding on the stairs—a stifled scream—

I ran into the hall. Halfway up the length of the staircase was a landing, and there, Lucy, the front of her dress ripped open, struggled with Chawton, his hand over her mouth.

I flew up those stairs. I grasped his neckband with my left hand and twisted it hard. He choked and struggled upright. As he came up he struck out at me. I hit him across the side of his jaw with all my strength. The blow spun him round. He stumbled across the landing, tripped off the top stair and somersaulted to the bottom. He lay motionless. The breath rattled hoarsely from his open mouth, and a thin trickle of blood tinged the slobber oozing from the corner of it.

"Oh, Philip," Lucy clung to the banister. She was shaking uncontrollably, tears streaming down her face. She looked down to the foot of the stairs and gasped in horror. "Philip—Oh, God, Philip—you've killed him!"

"It'll take more than a tumble downstairs to kill that thick-skulled brute," I said cheerfully; though I wasn't much taken with the way he was lying. "He can't be dead as long as he's making those pig noises."

Still she sobbed. "Oh, Philip, it's my fault—"

"Go and change your dress, girl," I said gently, "and leave this to me."

She seemed only then to realize that she was half-naked and scrabbled together the remnants of her bodice. She ran to the top of the stairs, then stopped for a moment to look down at Chawton.

"Poor Roger," she said softly, "Poor, poor, stupid Roger." And, without another glance at me, ran on. I suppose only women can understand women.

I turned over the unlovely lump with my foot, none too gently. It choked, retched, coughed some bloody spittle, rolled on to its back and began to snore. There was nothing wrong with Chawton that a bucket of cold water wouldn't cure.

Charles Fairleigh and the militia officers came crowding through the door. They checked, silent, on seeing me with Chawton at my feet. One of them asked, "What was all that noise?"

"Mr. Chawton fell downstairs," I answered nonchalantly. "He's unhurt and should recover in a moment. Would one of you get some cold water, please?"

As I had expected, these militia officers were really very pleasant young men. Without Chawton to lead them on they were polite and helpful—despite not being too sober. They poured water over Chawton—and more water. They dragged him into a chair, pulled off his jacket, slapped his face, undid his neckband wondering how it came to be torn at the back.

"By Heaven, he's got a lump on his noddle like a goose egg," they cried. "He'll be all right in a trice, Colonel, head's made of granite!"

Now Gist came in with Williams and Washington. I told them Chawton had fallen downstairs. They were not surprised. Williams examined the still unconscious hulk. He turned to us with a ghost of a smile. "Poor Mr. Chawton has bruised his face sadly," he said.

Washington sniffed. "Can only have improved it—not surprising if he came downstairs on it."

At that moment Chawton's eyes opened. He mumbled, "Lobster—ol' lobster—"

"Take him to his bed," said Gist.

Chawton lurched forward in his chair, spluttering, "Damned redcoat—he hit me—I'm going to . . ." His friends pulled him back into his chair. Gist took charge.

"Colonel Cato, is this true?"

"Yes, General."

"And, pray, why, sir?"

What could I say?

"Colonel Cato, I must ask why you struck Mr. Chawton?"

"I'm sure Mr. Chawton would prefer to explain."

"I see." He studied me for a moment. "Well—Mr. Chawton?"

Chawton spat out more blood. "Damn coward hit me—that's all I know."

"What were you doing that Colonel Cato should attack you?"

"Nothing—how should I know why? He's jealous, I s'pose, jealous of Lucy—"

"Lucy!—by God, where's Lucy, Roger?" Charles Fairleigh exclaimed.

"How the hell should I know?"

"Where's my sister, cousin Philip?"

"I advised her to go to her room."

"Was she in any way distressed?" said Gist.

"Yes, General."

Gist paced slowly across the hall to stand in front of Chawton. His voice grated like a saw on a nail. "Were you responsible for Lady Lucy's distress?"

Chawton's face, apart from a purpling bruise on his jaw, was now the colour of mud. He mumbled something.

"Speak up, man," rapped Gist, "You were loud enough just now."

"Didn't hurt her—was only play—"

"What sort of play?"

"Lucy's not hurt, Philip?" Charles Fairleigh asked.

"No—but why don't you go to her?" He went up the stairs four at a time.

Gist turned away from the sullen, but rapidly sobering Chawton. "Well, since no one is hurt but the one who deserved it, we can leave the matter there."

But Chawton was on his feet. "I'll have satisfaction first."

Gist turned to face him. "You'll have what?"

"Damned redcoat—"

"You will address Colonel Cato courteously and by his rank, or, by Heaven, I'll see you dismissed from the one you disgrace!" The loathing in Gist's voice snuffed out Chawton's bluster.

"He struck me, General, and I want satisfaction."

"I suspect you entirely deserved it. I certainly should not expect Colonel Cato to entertain your challenge. But after your vulgar impertinence I imagine he will welcome it."

Which I thought was a neat way of ensuring that I did. I turned to Washington. "Cousin William, will you act for me?"

He beamed. "Delighted—delighted, cousin."

"Well," said Gist, "tomorrow morning at seven o'clock?"

"Suppose so," grumbled Washington, "Never can understand why you have to get up so early to shoot a man. What's wrong with after breakfast? And who acts for Chawton, General?"

But the militia had already fled the field.

"That can wait," said Gist, and as he spoke Lord Fairleigh came in, beaming at us.

"What a lovely night it is, gentlemen—a lovely night!"

"True enough, uncle," cried Washington cheerfully, "and we'll have a lovely morning too. Our gallant cousin here is going to shoot that lout Chawton at seven o'clock sharp."

Fairleigh stared at me. "Did you challenge him?"

"No, sir. He challenged me."

"He challenged you? How in Heaven's name did you offend him?"

"Oh, he only knocked him downstairs," said Washington. "Let's find a little brandy and I'll tell you all about it. But I'm sending my principal off to bed. So off you go, cousin, and a good night to you."

I bade them all good-night and went to my room. Matthew was leaving it with my pistols, in their case, under his arm.

"Where are you going with those?" I asked.

"I just happened to be on the landing there your honour. So I thought I'd be after cleaning of them."

"I see. Well, you'll call me at six then?"

"I'll do that—and a good night to your honour."

Chapter Eleven

*In which I have an engagement at
seven o'clock in the morning.*

I woke early. A pale light lit the high ceiling of my room, throwing the wreathed fronds and flowers of the stuccoed frieze in clear relief. Through the parted curtains the autumn sky was milk-blue. My watch showed half past five; half an hour, I reckoned, before I needed to prepare myself. I knew I could not sleep again and lay on my back, hands behind my head, watching the shadows change in the brightening light among the stylised roses of the frieze, my thoughts changing faster than the shadows.

To stand within one stride of his grave hones a man's mind to a sharp edge of clarity. Familiarity with the experience can never lessen its effect. And, God knows, I am as familiar with it as most; before both battle and duel. At such a time the wildest and most serious thoughts, the most foolish and the dearest memories chase each other through your head, their separate voices whispering like a constant rustle of leaves in the gentlest breeze.

Before a battle you sit your horse in front of your troop with as much confidence and patience as you can muster, your mind a-fever. Your drawn sword lies before you across the pommel of the saddle or rests in the hollow of your shoulder. Now and again, almost unconsciously, you drop the point to tap your toecap or your stirrup-iron in an impatient rhythm. You shift your weight to and fro in the saddle to ease your back; you swing your sword-arm to take the stiffness out of shoulder and wrist; you twist your head about to get the crick out of your neck in the strangulation of your jacket collar; you mutter senseless things to yourself. And you wait.

You wait for the dawn to brighten and the long lines of enemy to stand out in their blue and their green and their red and their gold, whilst the steely sheen of the bayonets stretching the length of their array silvers in the morning sun. You wait for the batteries to stop their thundering. You wait for the enemy column moving steadily down the valley before you, its drums tapping in tuneless unison, to wheel slowly—oh God, how slowly!—until its unsuspecting flank lies open to your shattering charge. And you wait. You wait for the order.

And it comes. Then, for the first few occasions, you have no sensation for yourself, you have no measure of time. All is sudden, violent movement, confusion, shock. A surging, a crushing, a heaving, a stumbling—and over all and through all an endless, battering fury of roaring, clashing, screaming. The stink of burnt powder chokes your throat and through the swirling reek the bright blades thrust and slash. Then, as suddenly, all is over, all is quiet. Around you, in the smoke haze, men and horses move slowly, aimlessly about, stumbling over the dead and the dying. The harsh notes of the "Rally" ring inside your empty, echoing skull and sense and feeling return. You look for the standard and ride towards it. You are soaked in sweat, your voice croaks through a throat hoarse with shouting you cannot recall and your sword-arm hangs like a leaden bar. There is blood on your jacket, blood on your saddle-cloth, blood on your blade—none of it yours. Whose? You'll never know.

That's the way of it for the first few actions. Thereafter familiarity breeds an anticipation of events; even a sort of detachment. So that a man stays aware of what goes on around him in the scrimmage and can judge when and where to ride in and strike, and when to save his strength. And so lives to fight again—and again.

That's somewhat the way it is in duelling too—though quieter. In the duel the tumult of your own emotions replaces the turmoil of the battle. And because those emotions must be controlled if you are both to conduct yourself properly and—you hope—to live, they are the more oppressive. And anyone who deals satisfactorily with his first couple of opponents without the benefit of the self-discipline and confidence imparted by a careful schooling is a very lucky fellow.

You need to be a consistently accurate shot (that goes without saying); but you need to be a fast shot too. And there are tricks of the duelling trade to be learned from someone who has stood up and survived often enough to have learned them himself.

I have never called a man out—and I have my reason for that as I'll explain. But up to that morning I had, myself, been called out twelve

times. I know that's not enough to be in today's fashion, but when you
have earned what is termed "a reputation" even the eager and over-bold
will usually avoid an early morning encounter with you. I had dealt
satisfactorily—well, to my satisfaction—with all my opponents and hadn't
been touched worth the noting. Four died, six I wounded enough to
discourage them, and twice I held my fire until they'd missed, then
deloped—fired in the air—because the fools weren't worth the bullet.

I take no pride in any of this, knowing too well that I am able to say it
only because, from before my first meeting at dawn, I enjoyed a careful
instruction from an acknowledged master of the game.

He was the senior major of my Regiment when I joined it in Dublin in
1757. His name was John Manners—and no man was better named; his
were impeccable. So was his eye with a pistol.

"The settlement of a dispute by the duel," John used to say, "was first
devised by men of courage and a true sense of honour. Because it has been
debased by fools and murderers is no reason to ignore its principles. But
there are tricks worth the learning if you want to survive in your meetings
with the fools and murderers—and you'll meet them."

There were four of us who joined the Regiment together, and he taught
us painstakingly, with humour and humanity. "Understand, my lads, if
you are in the wrong you will admit it and apologize. That's rule number
one. And let fools call you coward if they wish. Rule number two is that
you never call a man out unless no other honourable course is open to you.
And going to law is not an honourable course; you'll find only knaves and
tricksters in a court of law. Rule three—be certain that the matter is worth
a life, yours or his. It would be a pity to die for a trifle to be laughed at
when tempers cool. Which leads to rule four." He paused and looked at us
very straight. "When you are face to face with him only you can judge
whether you should kill him or wound him—or not; let your
conscience—never your temper—be the arbiter of that."

He took us away from Dublin on three months' field training
immediately after we joined; and at our first bivouac, twenty miles outside
Dublin, he left us in no doubt of his reason.

"My lads, had you stayed there a week you'd have left it in a coffin or on
a litter. That murdering gang in the 6th would have had you out and that
would have been the end of you. They've killed more of their brother
officers than ever they'll kill of the King's enemies."

So, for three months, when we were not on duty, we practised and we
practised.

"Seat the stock of the pistol well into the crotch of your thumb and forefinger. Your hand has to fit like a glove around it, so it's a mere extension of your arm."

We tested our grips on the butts of every pistol we could muster. On the cob wall of an old ruined shebeen we drew outlines of men standing sideways on to us, and drilled and drilled before these impersonal, indestructible opponents.

"Stand twelve paces from the wall and face away from it opposite your man. When I say 'Turn' you turn and fix your eye on your point of aim; make it his groin to start with—no higher. As you turn, your arm comes up with your muzzle on the vertical line of your point of aim. As your barrel comes level in the line between your eye and your point of aim you squeeze the trigger—and mind those set triggers. If you're using a set trigger your point of aim is the centre of his groin; if you're not, then take it at the back of the groin because you'll pull to the right. Cato, as you're left-handed, you'll do it the other way around; but you should shoot the better than the right-handers for being able to steady and point with your forefinger along the barrel.

"Never let the muzzle lead your barrel up—if anything let it droop. The act of raising your arm will tend to make you throw high." He clapped his hands. "Come on now! Bigod, if you don't move sharper than that you'll not live long enough to do as I say!"

We didn't have long to wait before John Manners' instruction was put to the test. Hunting with Mr. Nicholson's hounds on the Saturday following our return to Dublin, I chanced to ride alongside a gentleman, unknown to me, in what I thought to be cheerful rivalry, at one of the great ditches found—all too often—thereabouts. My horse, lent to me by Mr. Nicholson, knew his business and flew the chasm like a swallow. Not so the other gentleman; he up-ended in its depths. I forgot the affair until, two days later, Major Manners informed me that a Lieutenant Ardloss of the 6th was demanding satisfaction from me for having, so he claimed, intentionally knocked him into the ditch.

"He didn't need any help from me into the bottom of it!"

"I don't doubt it, my dear fellow," said John Manners, "But he's very loud that you purposely disgraced him. I've arranged we meet tomorrow in the Park."

This was my first challenge, and to be called out for such a triviality shocked me in its mean senselessness. I was very green in those days. My concern must have shown for he slapped my shoulder. "Lad, I think Ardloss is in for a surprise. I'm pleased it's you he's picked on. And I'll tell you why. Tomorrow, when I give you your pistol, take it first in your right hand until you stand back to back. Then slip it across to your left."

"Will he care which hand I use?"

"Think, boy. Ardloss is right-handed. Think how awkward it is even for a right-handed swordsman to fight a left-handed one; he has to plan his attacks all the other way round. One in a hundred is left-handed and he is always fighting right-handed men. But when the right-hander meets the left-handed it always gives him pause, and if he meets him unexpectedly it can give him pain too. Of course, shooting with a pistol is a more instinctive action than fighting with a sword, and I've always taught you that a good shot will shoot to his mark and not at a mark he's learned. But present that mark to him suddenly and unexpectedly in reverse and unfamiliar form, and it can cause him a moment of confusion which could give you a quarter of a second or two inches either way; and they're both advantages worth the having.

"The first time I fought a left-hander I thought he was right-handed. When I turned to come up, for a moment I was lost. Thank the Lord I fired the faster; it threw him off."

"What happened?"

"I'd gone too far left. Knocked off his left tit. Anyway, pull your belly in and shoot fast tomorrow."

So the following morning I took my pistol from Manners in my right hand and, back to back with Ardloss, shifted it to my left. I thought I shot fast, but he shot faster, and I saw as he came up it seemed his hand jerked left, and the ball tore open the front of my coat and skinned my stomach; which, as ordered, I'd pulled hard in. The jerk and the sting of it sent my arm higher than I had intended and my ball struck him in the side of the neck below the ear. It broke his neck—like a hangman's knot. He stood for some moments, swaying, his pistol hanging by his side and his head sunk on his breast. He had an odd, inhuman look—like a dummy—hard to describe; "finished" I suppose you could call it.

I was seventeen and he was the first man I had killed. I had no regrets for it—nor have I. He was a murderer, like the other three I killed—and meant to—later. He had intended to kill me because I had—all unwittingly—ruffled his precious conceit. His sort are better dead.

Manners strode quickly to me. "God's life, boy, what the devil were you waiting for?—Christmas? You gave him time to load and fire again! Come on away now."

Ardloss' friends did not seem too distressed. I heard his epitaph pronounced cheerfully by one of them, as Irish as Ardloss had been. "Mother of God! The broth of a boy, so he was, and with him eight souls to his credit. It's terrible surprised he'll be to find himself dead—"

A gentle tap on my door roused me. Matthew came in with a steaming copper can. He pulled the curtains back. "Now," he said, cheerfully, "wouldn't that be a beautiful day for any sort of business at all? Will I be after laying out the black frock coat and stock then? And ye'll be wanting your white shirt with the lace cuffs and your black stockings—"

I got up and washed and shaved, with Matthew fussing quietly around, brushing my well-brushed coat and polishing my already gleaming shoe-buckles; talking about nothing all the time. I was glad to have him there, chatting away, and he knew it.

A second, more peremptory, knock and William Washington entered. "A good morning to you—and a lovely morning it is, cousin! I see you're up betimes. Had to order that cattle downstairs to shave and make themselves presentable! Been drinking all night—no novel occupation for 'em, I s'pose."

I had tied, a little higher than usual, my black military stock and pulled on my black frock coat and buttoned it close, so that I stood head to foot in black. Washington looked at the result a little disdainfully. "Very correct, I'm sure. We're not so formal in these parts. Don't think too much of dressing up to kill.'"

"I don't dress to kill," I said, "I dress to live." Matthew pulled out the lace cuffs of the white shirt sufficient to show but not to obstruct my grip on a pistol.

"Clever," Washington nodded, still a little sourly. "Haven't seen that before. Touch of white moving up distracts his eye of course."

"One hopes."

"Ay, well, young Chawton's a pretty fair shot drunk or sober, so they say. And been out a few times too. Well, now, if we're ready, shall we go down?"

Matthew said he would stay and pack for our departure. He had an excellent view of the lawn from my bedroom window.

In the hall James Fairleigh, Gist and Williams were grouped round Lord Fairleigh, who was bent over a mahogany box of all too familiar dimensions.

"My dear lad," Lord Fairleigh wrung my hand, "I trust you slept well. Now pray give me your opinion of these."

"These" were a very fine pair of heavy, octagonal-barrelled duelling pistols, their only decoration the silver bead of their foresights. Their stocks were curved to fit the palm and immaculately cross-hatched over the grips. They lay in sombre, ominous splendour in the blood-red velvet fitting of their case.

"They're an admirable pair, my lord," I said. "May I try the feel of one?"

I lifted one from its recess. The glove-like fit of my hand round the stock would have satisfied John Manners, I thought. And, at the thought, as I let the pistol come up effortlessly into the aim, another of his maxims reassured me: "It should come up lying in your palm as gentle as the fair hand of a trusting virgin." Picturesque but inapposite, I'd always thought; but this one fitted the bill.

Washington examined the pistols. "They're well enough," he said. "A little plain for my taste. The French make a pretty pistol."

"Indeed they do, my dear William," retorted Lord Fairleigh. "Inaccurate in its bore, imprecise in its action and damned useless in an affair of this nature. But very pretty." He snorted. "Now, let us proceed. William, you act for our kinsman—and who acts for Mr. Chawton?"

"One of his friends volunteered," said Gist. "The civilian—Mr. Secker."

I looked across at Secker, standing with the militia officers and Lucy and Charles Fairleigh by the front door, all, save Lucy, looking a little worn from the night's carouse. He gave me a half-smile and a half-bow.

"Have you known Mr. Secker long?" asked William, casually.

"I only met him here last night," I replied, as casually. Williams nodded. "Indeed?"

Lord Fairleigh raised his voice, "Will the seconds be so good as to observe me whilst I load the pistols. Mr. Secker, would you come, sir?" He turned to a task at which he obviously loved to show his skill, accurately measuring each charge, wrapping each ball in a little square of greased linen and tamping it gently down the barrel until it was seated firmly on the powder—"but not too firmly, gentlemen, else you will cake the powder, which will cause uneven burning and so inaccuracy of shot."

I sought to avoid further mention of Secker by asking William about Chawton. His reply was as chilly as the look he turned on the subject of it. "I know nothing of Mr. Chawton, sir, other than that he claims to be able to shoot better drunk than sober; though I can't vouch for this, never having seen him sober. But, judging from his conduct at the action at Camden, I can vouch he runs at least as fast—and as soon—as any in the Virginia Militia."

Chawton slouched against the frame of the door. His blue uniform coat hung wide open. His thumbs were hooked into the scarlet waistband of his breeches. His lace-frilled shirt gaped and his neckcloth was a dishevelled tangle. He stared at me with a sullen arrogance which, at first sight, might have been taken for drunkenness; but I noted that his eyes were clear and unbleared. The corner of his mouth dropped in a sneer and his slurred, hoarse voice was audible across the hall.

"Where's the lobster think he's going all dressed up in black? To his own damned funeral?" He cackled and, lurching upright, clutched at Charles Fairleigh's shoulder to steady himself. Charles looked at me shame-faced, but Lucy's glance, to see the effect of the taunt, was contemptuous.

"Mr. Chawton appears unfit to hold a pistol." Lord Fairleigh's remark was tinged somewhat with regret.

"Looks like it." The regret in Washington's voice was entirely undisguised.

That was when I should have observed John Manners' rule number three and agreed with them. The affair was not worth a life; certainly, in view of Lucy's contempt for me, it was not worth mine. But I didn't. I was angry. Angry because I had been schooled that these affairs are to be conducted with a courtesy, dignity and despatch, only to be achieved by a suppression—temporary maybe—of animosity and emotion; too much is at stake for such irrelevancies. Chawton's vulgarity annoyed me—and perhaps Lucy's expression had something to do with it. I said—to no one in particular—and my irritation showed in my voice, "I can't think why Mr. Chawton strives to appear drunker than he is."

There was a horrid stillness throughout the hall, and I got a moment's satisfaction in seeing the contempt wiped from Lucy's face. My remark struck home, as I had seen it do before with those who, afraid to finish what they had begun, feigned drunkenness or disability. Chawton's hand fell from Charles' shoulder and he stood straight, his head up. I thought what a fine-looking young man he could be if he had the guts to pull himself together. And I saw in his eyes that he was very afraid. Then he strode across the wide porch and stumbled down the steps to the green lawn beyond.

"Bigod," said Washington, happily, "he's moving sound enough. Let's get on with the business."

We went out on to the lawn. The morning breeze was cool and gentle. The lawn, close-scythed, was crisp and firm underfoot. The tall oaks stood still sentinels around the wide semi-circle of the lawn, their heads golden where the sun now touched them. And far away, across the mists of many valleys, the crests of the Blue Mountains stretched to the furthest distance, a rose-pink relief, sculpted along the pale blue edging of the sky.

Lord Fairleigh placed Chawton and myself face to face, a yard apart, in front of him. "Gentlemen, I shall give you the first order 'Turn,' on which you will turn about to face outwards and stand still. I shall then count slowly from one to six. On each count you will take one pace. After the count of six I shall give you time to complete your stride and give the order 'Turn' for the second time. On that order you will both turn about and fire in your own time. You may fire quickly or you may hold your fire, but when you do fire you will take only a natural aim. On no account will you take a deliberate aim. I shall myself shoot down either of you if I observe you taking a deliberate aim. Do I make myself clear?—Colonel Cato?"

"Quite clear, thank you, my lord."

"Mr. Chawton?"

"Yes—yes," hoarsely. Chawton's eyes were very wide now, the veins a little red, staring fixedly at me. At a yard, his breath stank stalely of brandy. His mouth twitched and the sweat dribbled down his ill-shaven cheeks to disappear into his jowls.

"Very well, then," Fairleigh nodded, "we'll have the pistols if you please, Mr. Secker." Secker came forward with both pistols levelled at Lord Fairleigh's stomach. "Good God, Mr. Secker, that's no way to offer a loaded pistol, sir! Careful now, please—"

Secker stammered nervously, "I do apologize, my lord—I'm not very experienced—in these things. I assumed—"

"Quite so. Never mind, sir. Just give me that one—I have it, sir, please take your hand away. Thank you. Now give the other to Colonel Washington for his principal. I'll give this to yours."

As Secker turned, Washington side-stepped smartly. "Damnation! Don't point the thing at me, sir! It's loaded—and cocked too, bigod! Here—" he grasped the pistol firmly by the barrel, "just—take your hand away now. Good. Much obliged to you, sir—" He turned his back on the wretched Secker, who slunk away. Breathing heavily, Washington offered me the butt. "Damned man's a dangerous lunatic—a lunatic," he muttered.

Since the Ardloss affair I have always taken the pistol in my left hand from the first, unless I reckoned I was facing a murderer. Today I took it in my left hand. Some sort of pity for this perspiring oaf in front of me

[*171*]

would not permit me to take any advantage. However, all appeared to be too distracted by Secker's stupidity to notice.

"Turn!" The first order. We turned and Fairleigh and Washington moved back from the line between us.

"One!" The first pace.

"Two!"

"Three!"

"Four!"

"Five!"

"Six!" I completed my stride, my heels apart, balanced for the turn.

This is the moment when a man is utterly alone, conscious only that his death stands twelve paces behind him and his life is in his own hand. He sees nothing—no trees, no sun, no sky. He hears nothing—no sound of any living thing—but strains only for the voice that says—

"Turn!"

I turned and the pistol rose light in my grasp. Lightly as the fair hand of a trusting virgin. Lightly up the vertical line from the foot, to the knee, to the thigh, to the groin, to the hip, to the shoulder—and I touched the set trigger. The hammer flashed, the flint clicked on the steel—and that was all.

Chawton had turned with me but his hand was not as fast as mine. I suppose he was all of a half-second slower. For all that half-second I watched the black hole of the muzzle from which my death would come follow the opposite line to that which my own useless barrel had just traced. And as it rose I saw the familiar waver of surprise and indecision. I watched without fear or any other emotion—there was no time. I watched with the detachment that experience gives you. I watched critically.

"You're confused by a left-handed target and you're overcorrecting— you're going too far left, lad—" that was all my thought in that interminable half-second. My concentration was such that I saw the black muzzle fill with flame as he fired. Too far left, as I had judged, and, because, in confusion, he had hung on too long, too high; but right enough and low enough to satisfy me—as this scar along my right cheek-bone and this notch in my right ear can witness.

I didn't mark the pain and I didn't mark the blood trickling down over my stock and collar; I looked down at my pistol. I pulled the hammer back to half-cock and examined the flint. It was sound, neatly cut and properly set. I looked at the face of the steel, touching it lightly with the tip of my forefinger. It had been greased. An old trick—a murderer's trick.

Washington ran to me, with Gist and Otho Williams. "Thank God you're all right!" No doubts on cousin William's sincerity.

Gist came round to my right side. "Let's stanch this bleeding, Cato. Here, I have a large kerchief." He took my arm. "By Heaven, but you're pale, man. It's the shock. Come and sit down."

"Not the shock, General." My voice must have sounded odd to them; it sounded pretty odd to me. As you may imagine, I was most damnably angry and, no doubt, white with it. Mostly I was angry with myself now. Here was pretty payment for my conceit. I had intended with a fair confidence only to knock a hole in this numskull's arm, that would teach him to mind his manners; and had near enough had a hole knocked in my own skull. But I had best discover who wished me dead before he—or she—should try again. "Thank you, I'm well enough," I said. "But what d'you think of this?" And I showed them the steel of the pistol. It was like setting a match to a cannon.

"Greased!" roared William Washington with the thunder of a thirty-pounder. "Greased!" he snatched the pistol from me, pulled the hammer to full cock, pointed it at the sky and pulled the trigger. Again the dull click of a misfire. "Damned soundly greased too, by God! Uncle, how did this happen? Damnation, it's inexcusable! But, cousin, Lord forgive me, I was your second and I gave you the pistol like that! Good God, it's unforgivable—"

"I'm as much to blame," I said, as cheerfully as I could. "I'm old enough to look to my own pistol!"

"No—no, it was my responsibility. Absolutely unforgivable! You're very generous—" He patted my shoulder gently; afraid I might collapse from my wound, I supposed, if he thumped as hard as he was wont. "But, damme, we must find how it happened."

It seemed clear to me that Chawton, loud-mouthed though he might be and a bit of a coward to boot, was no cold-blooded murderer. I doubted he had the wit to think of such a knavery or the resolve to execute it. I said, "Perhaps we should consult Mr. Secker. He took charge of the pistols after Lord Fairleigh had loaded them, you recall."

Lord Fairleigh, until now speechless with embarrassment and rage that the order of things—not to mention his precious pistols—had been so villainously deranged, quickly took charge again with a plaintive exasperation. "Yes, indeed. Quite right. Mr. Secker!" He spun round, frowning in every direction. "Now, where is he? Extraordinary conduct—leaving his principal unattended! Why isn't he here?"

[*173*]

No one had noticed Secker's going, but, after some shouting and searching, it transpired that Mr. Secker was not in the house. That Mr. Secker's valise was not in his room. And that Mr. Secker's horse was not in the stables. He had been quick enough about it.

"Must have been him," said Washington. "Must have done it while he was carrying them—you remember how he carried them? Bigod, d'you think the cunning devil put on that act to distract our attention?—I'll wager he did! But, then, perhaps he meant to grease 'em both so no one would get hurt!" I admired Washington's determination to think the best of all men.

"No," said Williams.

"But, good God, Otho, why should he want to kill poor Philip here? He don't even know him—well, hardly enough to want to do away with him, I'd suppose. By God! another thought," in a lower voice, "You don't think he got the pistols mixed up, do you? That I should understand!"

Williams smiled. "To your second question, William, again, no. But for your first," he looked at me, "perhaps Colonel Cato can suggest an explanation?"

I said, shortly, "I imagine he hoped to assist his friend."

"Oh, come now, sir. Why do you need to defend the fellow so resolutely?" Williams' quiet smile held more than a hint of suspicion.

My anger had not yet died in me. I met his tight-lipped, quizzical stare very straight. "Pray, sir, what do you infer by that?" I said.

For a moment Williams was taken aback; then his expression hardened. Washington saved the clash. "Now, whoa, for God's sake! What the devil's got into you both all of a sudden? Damme, one quarrel at a time is all we need, and we aren't finished with the last one yet!"

Otho Williams smiled at once and shook his head at me. "My dear Cato, I meant no offence. But, indeed, the quicker that two-faced villain is hanged the better for all of us, I believe! Forgive me, these damnable affairs put one out of humour."

"Oh ay," said Washington, "we're all having a deuced exasperating morning. And what do you suppose my dear uncle wants now?"

Lord Fairleigh approached us accompanied by Lucy and Charles and followed at a few paces by Chawton. Father and son looked acutely embarrassed, Chawton looked self-satisfied and Lucy was blazingly, beautifully triumphant. She had had her way over what was to happen next, I supposed. But we'd see.

Carefully not looking at any of us, Fairleigh began. "Er—h'm— gentlemen, if we could settle the matter." He half-turned in my direction and examined my shoes with close attention. "Er—nephew, you were the—er—the offending party in the affair, were you not?"

"If your lordship means that Mr. Chawton was right to require satisfaction when I rebuked him for his ungentlemanly conduct—then, yes, sir, I was the offending party."

"Quite so. Well—h'rm—Mr. Chawton—as the offended party—Mr. Chawton has declared himself satisfied with the—er—outcome and—"

"The devil he has!" gasped Washington.

This shamed poor Fairleigh into silence, but Lucy, with a furious glare at Washington, took up the tale at once. Her voice was as coldly contemptuous as her eye. "Mr. Chawton," she said, "considers he has sufficiently accomplished his purpose and requires no further satisfaction—other than that you leave here at once."

"Oh, generous, noble-hearted fellow!" Otho Williams' sepulchral comment and Washington's guffaw sprung Fairleigh into fury. He turned on his daughter, fuming.

"How dare you interrupt me, girl! Know your place! Hold your tongue! Charles—take the silly child away."

I don't suppose she had ever seen him so angry before. Charles led her a short distance off. Lord Fairleigh turned back to me, apprehensively, almost pleading, "Philip, I hope you will agree—that the matter should end there?"

"May I remind your lordship that I was prevented from defending myself against Mr. Chawton. Perhaps you should explain the situation as it now stands." I wondered what Manners would have said, but went my own way.

Fairleigh glanced at his daughter, then, turning to Chawton, said slowly, "Since Colonel Cato's pistol was tampered with—though I am assured you had no knowledge of that—and you had the benefit of an unopposed shot in your own time, Colonel Cato should now be given a fresh pistol—I should place you twelve paces apart—and you should stand and take his shot."

"No!" Lucy tore herself from her brother's grasp and ran to her father. "No—no, papa, please—he'll kill Roger! Please don't let him—"

"My dear," Fairleigh's voice was firm, but with a hint of desperation, "this is an affair of honour and it must be finished honourably. Charles—take her to the house."

As Charles pulled the distraught girl away, she looked back at me, "Philip—please—please—" I noted with some bitterness that there was no contempt now.

"Bigod, the silly chit dotes on that underbred boor," muttered Washington disgustedly. "You think she'd have better taste. Dammit, she's my cousin!"

But my own opinion of Roger Chawton rose somewhat. There must be some good in any man who could excite such devotion in Lucy.

"I'm prepared to accept that Mr. Chawton be given a fresh pistol, too, my lord," I said.

"A most generous offer. William, will you help me to load again? And who will act for Mr. Chawton?"

"Allow me." Otho Williams took the unhappy Chawton by the arm, led him to where Fairleigh had positioned us earlier, and—with a quiet word—left him standing fixed to the spot.

I walked to my position facing Chawton. His face was ashen. The drink had died in him. Now and again he shivered slightly. He sniffed and blinked and stared at the ground at his feet. He was mortally afraid true enough, and but for the sting of the weal across my cheek I might even had felt sorry for him; but the quaking, snuffling ninny disgusted me. Why the devil was he so fear-struck? He was reputed a good shot—deservedly so, as my face showed. He now knew I was left-handed and should be that much quicker this time. And he could have no idea whether I was able to hit a barn at five yards. And Lucy, watching now from the steps, must have seen all this—and still loved him. It made me sick of the whole business.

We were given our pistols.

"Gentlemen," said Lord Fairleigh, "remember, you turn on my word, take six paces on my count and turn again on my word. Are you ready?"

"M'lord," I nodded. Chawton's mouth opened and closed.

"Turn!"

Six paces. Those fateful six paces. I have never felt more relaxed or easy in my mind than when I walked them this time. "One—Two—I can kill this scrubby clown with a ball straight into his chicken heart—Five—and it's what he deserves—Six—Turn!"

And we turned.

Chawton's nerve failed him altogether. He flung round with his arm swinging like a corn flail and let fly—much too quick, all unbalanced—and the ball went winging off a foot or so in front of my face.

My point of aim this time was between his fifth and sixth ribs—as near as I could judge it in his fat side. When he fired my barrel was coming up nicely past his knee, and on it went—past the groin—the hip—and it checked on my point. Checked—and then, of itself, moved on. On past the sweat-stained armpit, past the creased shoulder, the stubbly jowl, the dank shag of his head—by God! in that half second I inspected his damned physiognomy closer than I've ever studied any trooper's on a parade—and on. On over his head into the bright morning sky. And that's where the ball went.

Why?

You may think it was Lucy Fairleigh's eyes. But I know it was the teaching of John Manners.

Chapter Twelve

*In which I learn of the death of an army
and witness the destruction of a family.*

Before returning to my room to prepare for my departure I informed Lord Fairleigh that I intended to begin my return to Charlottesburg that day.

"Ay," he said, "that would be the best for now. But ye'll come back, nephew, when all this is past?"

I made no reply to that but asked if James would be ready to accompany me.

"In one hour, cousin Philip," James said.

Matthew finished packing my saddle-bags as I changed into uniform and took them away downstairs. I was about to pick up my jacket off the bed when I heard a light step behind me. Lucy stood in the doorway, pale and subdued, no dominance or sparkle now. She said, nervously, "Papa said you were leaving." I nodded and waited in silence. I had had my fill of conversation with Lucy Fairleigh. She blinked and swallowed and pulled at a handkerchief she held. "Philip—I wanted—thank you for—for—"

"For not killing Mr. Chawton, ma'am. You need have had no fear. I never intended to." Blunt and cold—but I was surprised to see the effect.

Her eyes and mouth both opened wide with shock. "You never—oh, God—oh, God—" She swayed and the handkerchief fell from her fingers. I should have put my arm round her, sat her on a chair, picked up her handkerchief. Instead, I picked up my jacket and began to put it on. "You'll forgive me, ma'am, I'm late already."

She steadied herself with a hand on the door. "Must—you leave— today?" I buttoned my jacket. "Today, ma'am." Suddenly she stamped her foot and blazed at me. "Stop calling me 'ma'am!' " I stopped buttoning my jacket and bowed. "I beg your pardon, my lady. I'll not permit myself that liberty in future." And finished buttoning my jacket.

Anger brought the colour back into her cheeks and she blazed on. "You're a fool—a fool—a blind fool!"—stamping her foot with each "fool."

"Indeed, my lady. My dear wife is constantly informing me so." A flippancy, but she flinched as if I'd struck her. "Your dear wife—" she covered her face with her hands. This time I thought she really would fall, and moved towards her. She was shaking from head to foot. Her hands lowered a little and she stared at me over her fingertips, her eyes so full of pain that I was struck speechless and powerless. Then she was gone.

I don't know how long I stood there, staring at the emptiness of the doorway—and I don't know what I was thinking; perhaps I couldn't think. I heard my name called—and again—and a third time, before I could gather my palsied wits. I slung my sword-belt, picked up my hat and turned to the doorway. I stared again at the empty space and waited—hoping—hoping. It stayed empty. It was best so. I cursed myself, rammed my hat on my head and went back to the war.

Downstairs, in reasonable control of myself once more, I made my farewells to Gist and Williams. Washington enveloped me in a bear hug. "Cousin Philip, for God's sake, let's stay out of each other's way whilst this damned squabble lasts, hey?"

Lord Fairleigh's eyes were full of tears as he bade farewell to James and myself. He held my hand in both his. "God bless ye, Philip, and haste ye back. You are loved in this house and always will be." Again, too full of my own thoughts, I was unable to reply.

I climbed on to Williamson and gave the order to move off. They were all ranged on the steps behind Lord Fairleigh; young Charles, Gist, Williams, Washington and most of the militia officers—all rebels, all enemies. And they all waved—

"God speed!" they cried, "God speed!"

At the gates I looked back. They were all still standing there. And, high above them at an open window, a handkerchief waved.

"That's Lucy's room," said James, "I wondered where she was." And he waved back. I felt too ashamed—but still, too angry to do so.

We rode on for some while silent, lost in our own thoughts. I was still puzzled as to why Chawton had been so frightened of me, when no one in the company knew me. I asked James Fairleigh.

"Frightened?—he was terrified! Ask your soldier why." And he grinned at Matthew, riding behind me. Matthew looked sheepish as I called him up beside me.

"Why was Mr. Chawton so frightened this morning, Matthew?"

"Well, your honour, it might be because of one or two things I told him."

"What things?"

"You honour'll recall I took your pistols with me last night to clean them. I chanced to pass through the room where was this Mr. Chawton setting drinking with his friends and they demands to see 'em. So I opens the box on the table and they all crowds round to look. One of 'em picks a pistol out of the case. 'Well used, bigod!' says he. 'Well used?' says Mr. Chawton, 'How many times has he been out then?' 'Oh, sir,' says I, 'I've been with the Colonel for nigh on twenty year. I lost count long back.' 'And he's always successful?' he asks. 'Would I be cleaning them if he hadn't been?' says I. As I goes to put the pistol back, one of them says, 'How many men has he killed? I thought you notched the butt when you killed your man?' I smiles, sort of patient-like, ye know. 'Why, sir,' says I, 'No gentleman who goes out regular likes to spoil the balance of his pistols. And, sure, if the Colonel had notched 'em, they'd be no butts left on 'em at all!' And I shuts the box, bows all respectful and away off—with Mr. Chawton and his mates all setting there a-staring at me like I was Caesar's ghost. And that's all there was to it, your honour."

"And then you went and cleaned the pistols?" asked James.

Matthew looked at him, straight-faced. "Well—no, sir. After I'd seen Mr. Chawton there, I remembered I'd already cleaned 'em." And he reined back behind me.

James smiled. "You've got a man there, cousin Philip."

"And he's as good with his weapons as he is with his tongue," I said. "So that explains Chawton. But, by God, I'd like a word with that smily devil, Secker."

James laughed, then, all at once, grabbed my arm. "Well, now's your chance!" he exclaimed and pointed at a small clutter of cabins and huts—one of them a smithy—some fifty yards to the side off the road. Leaning against the door-post of the forge, smoking a short clay, was Secker. He saw us, straightened up, took out his pipe and waved it at us.

"Bigod, he's a cool one," said James. My hand had gone to my pistol. "Will you shoot him from here?"

"We'll have a word with him first." I drew the pistol and cocked it.

Secker was not at all disconcerted—either by my pistol or my

[*180*]

xpression. He smiled gaily. His face seemed somehow changed, his xpression relaxed, open—even honest!

"My dear Colonel, you can't imagine how relieved I am to see you vell!" His smile suddenly faded. "I hope—I hope Mr. Chawton is as vell?"

"He was well enough to put this across my face," I snapped, fingering ny scarred cheek.

"Indeed!—not bad!" He nodded. "Not bad for a boy who had never een out before, knowing he was facing a gentleman of your reputation. ir—he didn't know about—your pistol, Colonel."

"But Chawton claimed he had been out several times," said James.

"He claimed so, Mr. Fairleigh, but he's a callow, loud-mouthed youth, you'll agree. He just wanted to impress his friends."

I felt utterly ashamed. I thought myself a judge of men and, it seemed, nad entirely misjudged Chawton—if not the whole affair. The only thing I had done right was to delope—and thank God I had. I said, "Of course! He was drunk when he challenged. He didn't know what he was about. I should never have accepted it."

James was studying Secker closely. "To whom did Chawton confess his nexperience, Mr. Secker?"

"Why, sir—to me," Secker answered smoothly.

"And to my sister?"

Secker frowned and swallowed. "Well—yes—I believe he did—"

"And so she asked you to grease Colonel Cato's pistol?"

That floored Secker. It floored me too. Secker gasped and stammered. 'She asked me—how the Colonel's pistol—how it might—"

"And you explained how—and she asked you to do it—so you volunteered to be Chawton's second—and to take charge of the pistols after my father had loaded them. Is that correct, Mr. Secker?" Secker did not answer, but James was relentless. "Isn't that, correct, Mr. Secker?"

Secker shrugged. "Yes, that is correct."

"Because she was afraid that the Colonel would kill Chawton?"

"You're very perceptive, Mr. Fairleigh."

"I know my sister, Mr. Secker. Wasn't she concerned that Colonel Cato might be hurt?"

"Indeed she was—very concerned. But in view of Mr. Chawton's total inexperience and his—state of mind—he knew nothing of the Colonel's pistol, as I said—we decided it unlikely that the Colonel would be endangered. We appear to have misjudged somewhat—but—I thank God it was no worse—"

[*181*]

"Don't blame yourself, Mr. Secker," said James, "I can guess who did the judging and the deciding. So her only aim was to prevent Chawton being killed or hurt?"

"Exactly. She said she had used him—and could not let him come to harm because of it."

"Of course!" James slapped his thigh, "Of course, now it's all clear. She'd used him—"

"Used him for what?" I asked Secker. He just stared at me. I looked at James. "For what, for God's sake?" And James was silent too. "To kill me, I suppose," I said bitterly, "What else? She wanted me dead for all those things she accused me of—and she's been disappointed—"

"No!" said James and Secker, in chorus. They both looked at me as if they thought me mad not to understand. But I did not want to understand. I wanted to forget it all—and Lucy Fairleigh most of all.

I let the hammer of my pistol forward and put it back in the holster. "I've misjudged you, Mr. Secker, both here and in the past. I apologize."

"My dear Colonel, I aim to be misjudged; it's my stock in trade. I play a part—not a pleasant part—and I'm not playing it now. So long as I am mistrustfully trusted by all parties I can do my work. Which, sir, if you will believe me, is the King's business."

"I believe you," I said. "What did you do before the King's business?"

"I was a teacher, which gave me a good memory, and an actor, which gave me the ability to deceive my audience into thinking me someone other than I was. So I'm well equipped."

"And where do you go now, sir?"

"To Hillsborough, Colonel, for a word with my good friend Gates. Lord Cornwallis wishes to discover his intentions." He got on his horse. "I hope this fellow's shoes stay on. There seem to be as few good farriers in these parts as there are in Tarleton's Legion—" and he grinned at me. "Well, our ways part again, gentlemen. A safe journey to you." And away he trotted. I never saw him again.

For our return to Charlottesburg, James Fairleigh chose a shorter way, joining the road from Salisbury to Fort Prince George at the cross-roads below King's Mountain. East of this, according to James—but not to Henry Mouzon's map—there was a good ford over the main stream of the river by which we could come directly to Charlottesburg.

As we camped for our second night, the forage party, led by Corporal Mills, brought in five men. They were ragged, filthy, barefoot and in pitiful state. The light from the fire showed rope burns on their wrists and ankles. Two of them had rope burns round their throats—for these I felt a special sympathy. All bore wounds; one had an arm broken by a musket ball and the wound was festering; another, a great slash along the side of his head.

"Who are these men, Corporal Mills?" I asked.

"They say they was with Major Ferguson, your honour, and taken in a fight on King's Mountain."

I asked—and dreaded the answer. "Where is Major Ferguson?" The man with the head wound answered wearily, "He's dead, your honour. They shot him down—and then they—"

"Then they what?"

"They hacked him up—like they was gutting a beast—quartered him—and the women too, two girls—and others besides."

I sat down on a log by the fire and breathed deep to steady myself. Then I said pretty evenly, "Tell me all that happened."

"Well, we was set on top the hill, your honour, what's called King's Mountain, about fifteen miles south from here. We'd reckoned we was safe enough, but the rebels was all around us, a-firin' up at us from cover an' we couldn't fire down at 'em without showin' ourselves. We charged 'em with the bayonet and sent 'em back down the hillside twice. But they kept a-comin-and a-shootin' from every way. They was too many for us, and when the Major was shot we couldn't take no more of it. We threw down our arms and they come up the hill—then they just went on a-shootin' and a-shootin' us down whiles we was stood there unarmed."

"But weren't you reinforced with regular troops?"

"Not with regulars, we weren't, your honour. We had some King's American Rangers under a Captain de Peyster and some New Jersey Volunteers—but we didn't have no regulars, only provincials. The Major said he was expecting for some—but we never saw none—" There was an awful hopelessness in his voice as it trailed away into silence.

So Ferguson's celebrated militia, nigh on eight hundred strong, had collapsed when its commander, the only British regular soldier present, had been killed. The few provincial troops had been insufficient to bolster their morale.

"Did none escape?"

"None as I knows of, your honour. The rebels was all around us—like a fence they was—"

"And what are these ropes marks?"

"They tied us together, your honour, as targets for to shoot at or to practise their bayonets on. They had no use for us as prisoners they said, so they might as well improve their shootin' on us, or let their lads blood

theirselves on us. They tied a mate o' mine to a tree and let their boys
practise their bayonets on him—what they'd took off of us. They had
another as a mark for their throwing knives. They hanged a score—to
encourage the rest to behave, they said, though a few was cut down. Then
we was marched down the road—and they kicked us and struck us with
their butts to make us keep up—the wounded an' all. When a man fell we
had to drag him, or they'd kick him dead or bayonet him as he lay. When
they halted to feed or rest we was never give nothing—we was made to
stand where they could shoot at us if we moved, or just if they wanted to
shoot. I asked one of their officers for some water and food for my lads an'
he cut me across the head with his sabre—an' me with my hands tied
behind me back."

"How did you come to escape?" asked James.

"Well, after a couple of days they'd had their fill of campaignin' and
most left. Them as didn't were more often drunk than not. So most on us
got away at night."

"And what will you do now?"

"We meant to lie up in these woods and rest a bit, your honour. Then
try to slip home to Ninety-Six quiet-like; most on us come from
thereabouts."

"Why don't you come with us to rejoin the army at Charlottesburg?" I
asked. "You'll be safer with us than wandering around by yourselves. We
have food enough for you. You can get those wounds properly dressed at
Charlottesburg. I'll ask that you be given leave of absence to visit your
families."

They looked every way but at me.

"Come now," I urged, "we need brave lads like you—as guides—
scouts—couriers; you can do good service—"

Head down, one of them muttered sullenly,

"We aint' a-soldierin' no more. We're a-goin' 'ome and stayin' there.
Any bugger what wants can battle on—but it ain't a-goin' to be none of
us."

And that was the sum of the opinion of great numbers of the loyalists of
South Carolina after King's Mountain. And their despair was caused not
so much by the defeat of their militia, but by the callous massacre of those
who had surrendered and the bestial brutalities inflicted upon the
survivors by their fellow-countrymen.

We gave the militiamen such assistance as was in our power, arguing
with them still and encouraging them to accompany us to Charlottesburg
if only for their own protection. But they would have none of it and,

eeing no purpose pressing them, we left them to their own devices. The next day we rode on down to the cross-roads below King's Mountain and here turned east. Not a rebel did we see, though the litter of decaying orpses along the road, torn by bird and beast, bore witness to the militiamen's story.

During the day the wind changed and it became cold. Heavy clouds iled on the hills to our north and it began to rain. Huddled in our cloaks ve plodded on through the mud, the nauseous stench of death at times lling our nostrils from the refuse of war lying tumbled in the ditches.

Shortly before dark we came to a clearing beside the road in which tood a small, neat log house, with some low barns beside it. A light leamed through the cracks in the shutters, but no smoke came from the himney. I decided to ask for shelter for the troop.

I dismounted, took a pistol, cocked it, walked to the door and knocked. There was no answer. I knocked again, louder. No answer. I thought I eard a low voice inside the hut; not a whispering but a steady murmur, as f someone were reading to himself, or reciting, or praying. I tried the atch. It lifted and the door swung back, squealing on its wooden hinges. As it did so, the lowering clouds immediately above split in a blinding lash, and a terrifying, tearing crash of thunder shook the whole frame of he hut.

In the middle of the earthen floor a woman knelt beside the body of a oy. The dim, shivering light of a tallow dip stood at the boy's head. He ooked to be about fifteen. His fair hair lay back from his forehead, and his yes stared, unseeing, into the darkness of the thatch. He lay on his back, aked to the waist, and in his chest and arms I counted twelve vounds—bayonet and knife wounds—and round his wrists and ankles the ame rope marks I had seen on the fugitive militia.

The woman knelt still; never turning her head, never moving.

"Come ye in, murderer. Come ye in and finish your business. Ye've aught to murder now, save me." She spoke unhurriedly, unemotionally, vith the lilting accent of the western Highlands, every syllable distinct, ure and clear.

I took off my dripping hat and loosed the hammer of my pistol to the alf-cock. "Ma'm, I am no murderer—nor rebel. I am an officer of the King's army."

Still she never turned her head. "Rebel or King's man—King's man or ebel—ye are all murderers—all."

Again the lightning flared white through the cracks of the shutters and he thunder crash shook the dust from the thatched roof.

[*185*]

"Ma'am, we mean you no harm. All we seek is shelter for the night for ourselves and our horses."

"Take what ye wish. There's none to stay ye." Her eyes never left the dead boy's face.

I went outside and gave orders to take shelter, and for the woman not to be disturbed in any way. Corporal Mills said,

"There's a couple o' new graves behind the cabin, your honour."

"How new?"

"A month say—there's grass growin' on 'em. Crosses on 'em both too, but they ain't got no names on 'em."

I looked at the two graves, lying side by side; each with two sticks tied roughly together in a cross at their heads; each with a little posy of wild flowers on it, beaten down and draggled now by the heavy rain. A sense of death lay heavy all around this place.

I went back into the hut. The dragoons were making themselves quietly comfortable, as any good soldier does; laying down their cloaks, preparing the cooking pots and platters, drawing the charges from their pistols and carbines and drying and reloading them, cleaning their equipment and saddlery. But it was odd to see all these rough, veteran men of war creeping round the sides of the hut on tip-toe, whispering, out of respect for the Scotswoman and her grief.

I laid my cloak down on the floor and my pistols, sword and hat with it. Then I knelt by the boy's body, opposite the woman, and prayed. I prayed for him as if he had been one of my own sons; and for this poor woman who mourned him. And, dispassionate and dry-eyed, she watched me.

And, when I had done, a hand reached over my shoulder and laid a small silver crucifix on the boy's bare breast. I recognized it as the crucifix my wife and I had given her maid, Kitty, as a present at her last birthday. And Matthew knelt beside me now and prayed too.

At the sight of the crucifix the woman began to shake uncontrollably. Her hands rose to her throat, then to her face. A great sob tore through her body and she fell half across the boy, her lips on the crucifix. Very softly she began half to murmur, half to croon, "Oh, my little son—my little love—my light—my love—my little son—" Then she began to sob and sob, still very quietly, helplessly, hopelessly.

I thought it best to leave her awhile. Then Matthew and James and I raised her gently and sat her on a stool beside the boy. One of the troopers brought her some soup. She did not want it, but we made her take it, and a little rum and water besides. When she had supped these, I asked who she was and what had befallen the boy; though the latter I could guess very well. Her voice was cold, without any emotion.

"Our kinsman, Ferguson, came by here a month agone. The boy was mad to go with him. I could not stay him. There was a great fight on the hill nearby and he was taken. Taken by a William Campbell—a Campbell," she spat the word, as if for her there was no worse insult than that name, "—a Campbell and his kerns, who gave him—a boy—to their young men for their sport. And they tied him—and others with him—to a tree and flung stones and knives at them, and used the bayonets they took from Ferguson's soldiers on them until they wearied of their games. And let them die, still hanging on the tree.

"Then some of them who knew us, and were shamed, brought him here and sought to bury him beside his mother and father. But I would not suffer them—with their hands wet with his blood—I would not—" The words choked in her throat.

"Are these the graves of his mother and father—these ones here by the house?"

"They are the graves of my son and his wife, whose son this boy is—whose son this boy was."

"And they died recently?"

"My son died from the wounds he got in the fight by Camden. An officer of the militia came by here, taking every man he could lay his hands on, whether he would go or nay. He took him—my only son—from the field and put a musket in his hand. And when we heard of the fight, some said they had seen him die on the redcoats' bayonets. She—his wife—would go to him, for she did not believe he could be dead, poor lass. And she took the horse and went to seek him. And the boy here and I took a horse of a neighbour and went after with the cart. And, as God willed it, we found them both. She had found him—he had been wounded sore—and had brought him some way back. But then, the people said, she had fallen in with some evil men who had fled from the battle—and they took her. She was dead when we found her—and him beside her—dying. So we brought them home."

"And what will you do now, ma'am?"

"What is there for me to do, but die here?"

"But have you no kin hereabouts?"

"My kin are in my homeland. My husband's brother brought me here, with my son still in my womb, after the Rising. But he is dead of the fever long since and his wife gone back to her own folk."

"And your husband, where is he?"

"He lies under the bracken at Culloden. The Macdonalds of Keppoch came by our crofts taking every man, willing or no, to serve with the young Stewart Prince. They took men as those rebel officers took my son to serve with their militia. They took my man and his brother from out the byre and they marched with the Prince down into England against the German King. And they charged with Keppoch on Drummossie Moor against the redcoats—and my man lay where he fell for the crows to pick on. And after the battle, the Campbells burned our crofts, so that we had no place. Then, to live in peace, my man's brother took the oath to the German King and brought us here—to live in peace—"

Her hands lay in her lap and she stared at us, her face drained of all feeling, her eyes, sunk in their sockets, blank with sorrow. "Why could ye not let us be? Ye are all one—King's men and rebels alike—murderers and plunderers all. Ye took my man—ye took his son—and ye took his grandson. And not a one of them wished harm to anyone—only to live in peace. Why could ye not let us be?"

James said, "It's not of our will, ma'am."

Her eyes never moved. "If it's not of your will—then whose will oppresses us? If it was not by your hands—than by whose were my menfolk slain?"

We tried to get her to rest, but she would not. So we lay round the hut floor on our cloaks, listening to the drumming of the rain and the grumble and mutter of the thunder as the storm passed over. The tallow dip, at its end, flared and flickered out. But, now and then, the lightning blaze showed the woman, crouched on her stool, immoveable, staring down through the darkness at the dead boy.

After a while she began to keen quietly, in the manner of her folk, a slow chant—a lament—in the Gaelic. She sang, James said, of her husband, betrayed by his Prince, shot down in the charge of the Clan Macdonald at Culloden; of her son, deserted by those who had pressed him, left to die on our bayonets at Camden; of her grandson, beguiled into danger by his kinsman and foully murdered by his own countrymen. And she sang that more blood would run and more men die for these wrongs.

The day dawned grey and a thin rain still fell. I had asked the old woman if we, as soldiers, might bury her grandson, who had been a soldier of his King and our comrade-in-arms. And, as I hoped, this pleased her, touching her Highland pride; for, to the Highlander, the soldier's is the most honourable of professions.

In the cold morning light she seemed less distraught. She watched by the door as four dragoons carried the boy's slight form out of the hut on a hurdle. We had wrapped him in an old cloak of one of the troopers. He lay, quiet and serene, in its scarlet folds, his hands folded over Matthew's crucifix.

We had dug his grave, deep and neatly squared, by the side of his parents. We covered his face with the white cape of the cloak and lowered him gently into the depths. The old woman had come to stand at the foot of the grave and looked down at her grandson. She raised one hand towards him and said, "Fare thee well, my love—my little son. Go to God in peace."

She recited the Lord's Prayer in which we all joined. Then she looked up to the sombre skies and said, "Lord, receive into Thy love my son. Thy servant."

Her head lowered on her breast, she turned away from the grave back to the house. I would have read more of the burial service, but she forbade me. "He was a soldier, sir. He has done his duty. We'll not trouble him with more words. The Lord has no need of them."

We filled in the grave and put a neat wooden cross at the head. I asked the boy's name to put upon the cross, but the old woman would not give it. "Leave it plain, like the others. No man touches an unnamed grave for fear it may be a friend's. Leave it plain. I'd not want it defaced."

The rain had stopped and the clouds begun to thin. A pale sunlight lit the clearing. But as I stood before her, making my farewell, there was no light in her eyes. Her thin face still showed no emotion. She curtsied slow to me. To Matthew, standing beside me, she said, "I thank you, soldier, for my son's sake, for your gift of the crucifix. May God reward you." She hesitated a moment, then, standing straight, she let her gaze run over us all. "And God speed ye all to your loved ones." She bowed her head again, turned, and went into the house and closed the door. And we rode on to Charlottesburg.

As we rode across the ford of the Catawba River we were greeted with a cheer, and found ourselves among the green jackets of the Legion. Tarleton was sitting in his tent, looking very ill. His eyes were sunk in his head, his face haggard and his skin a sickly yellow. I commiserated with him and asked if he had news of Patrick Ferguson.

"Ay, I have. And I suspect you have too. He's dead, with those two girls of his, poor bitches. Some of his men who escaped have arrived here. They seem to have met with that noble patriotic fervour and righteous protest of their countrymen and haven't much enjoyed the experience—those that survived it."

"The real loss is Ferguson himself," I said.

[*189*]

Tarleton got wearily to his feet. "Yes. He was far too confident for his own good. Didn't like me and I didn't like him. We were too much alike in our own ways. Both of us rode for the fall and he fell first, poor devil. Hope when my turn comes it's not so mortal!" He swayed, clutched the tent pole and sat down unsteadily. "God's wounds!—this cursed fever— takes the blood, spirit and spunk out of you! But you're right. Without Patrick we'll get damned few recruits for any militia. He had a way with him. That's why those butchers wanted him dead—and gutted him to make sure he was, I suppose. And after what they did to his men there'll be precious few loyalists to be seen anywhere. Which means information is going to be harder to come by, damn it!"

In Charlottesburg we went straight to the headquarters, where I presented James to Cornwallis, informing him of Lord Fairleigh's request that James be given a commission in the militia.

"We've barely enough recruits from North Carolina colony to support a corporal's guard!" said Cornwallis, disconsolately. "I'd willingly grant Mr. Fairleigh a commission in a provincial corps—the British Legion, say—"

"My lord," said James, "I should be very grateful for that honour, but may I suggest that you allow me to recruit a troop from around Tryon County and further west, where I'm sure you will find yourself well received. Then, if I am successful, we could be attached to the Legion."

"Very well, Mr. Fairleigh," said Cornwallis, "as you suggest. If you can raise a troop of light cavalry we'll be in your debt." He looked at me. "Do you think you should accompany Mr. Fairleigh, to supervise the training of these recruits? I'm sure he would be grateful for your guidance."

James at once welcomed the idea. "Indeed I would, my lord! We could set up a headquarters for Colonel Cato at my home, Belhaven, and equip and train recruits there until we had formed a troop."

That settled it for me. I was not going anywhere near Belhaven again. "I've been away long enough I think, my lord," I said, "I'm sure Mr. Fairleigh is entirely competent to recruit and train his troop without my hindrance. I'm not needed at Belhaven."

There was an uncomfortable silence, with Cornwallis looking puzzled and James distressed. Cornwallis shrugged. "Very well, Mr. Fairleigh will have to manage alone."

After James had gone off with Richard England to discuss the supply of equipment for such a troop, Cornwallis slumped into his chair and groaned. "I've had the most damnable feverish cold for a week and now I feel the fever in me."

"You should go to bed and stay there."

"I can't, Philip. We must move from here. It was a mistake ever to come here. It's the most damnably dissident area in North Carolina. We'll be better off further south in well-affected, richer parts. I've sent a reconnaissance down into South Carolina, between the Catawba and Broad rivers—a good, fertile district and friendly."

"But we can't move with you in this state, Charles."

"We can't wait on my health, Philip. It would cost too many lives and we've lost enough already."

The army began its move from Charlottesburg on the evening of Saturday the 14th October and before the end of the month had settled in Wynnesborough, midway between the Catawba and Broad rivers. This station provided the dual advantage of a central position between Camden and Ninety-Six and from the rich and fertile countryside around, supplies of foodstuffs and forage in abundance.

At Wynnesborough the army built up its strength slowly from those recovering from fever and wounds, from recruits found in the neighbouring precincts and from deserters from the rebel forces. Parties were sent to bring in all manner of foodstuffs, forage, stores and horses; purchases, confiscated from rebel sympathisers or found abandoned by rebel troops. Carts, wagons and saddlery were all procured the same way and issued to replace those lost or worn out on the long marches. All was prepared for the renewal of operations against the rebel armies newly forming in North Carolina.

From here also, expeditions were sent regularly to overawe any defection in the northern precincts of South Carolina. I spent my time accompanying these expeditions; constantly witnessing the effect of such consistent malevolence and callous brutality inflicted by "patriot" against "loyalist" and "loyalist" against "patriot"—brother against brother, father against son, family against family and whole communities against each other, as I had never seen in all my service in Europe and Asia; and hope never to see again.

During this time I received the letter from my wife, telling me that Kitty was with child by Matthew. I taxed him with this and he admitted it freely. "Your honour, we love one another. We have done for some time, and that's the truth of it. It all come to a head when we heard you was away to these colonies and me with you. It was only a week we had and no time to marry." He looked at me uncertainly. "Maybe there's those that would think we done wrong. But we didn't mean it wrong, your honour, and—" he suddenly spoke out boldly, "and, as God's our judge, we don't think it wrong now!" And then again uncertain, "She'll not be sent away, your honour? She's not to blame. It was myself that persuaded her."

"Of course she'll not be sent away," I said angrily. "You know very well we all love her too much. But, Matthew, you'll marry Kitty when we get home."

"Sure, your honour, and that's the first thing we'll do."

"Then you'll write to tell her that. She may fear—she may think you mean differently—"

He smiled, a truly happy smile. "She'll not be thinking that, your honour. But I'd be thankful for you to put in a letter to her with your next letter to madam." And I did.

On Saturday the 9th December, a long-awaited convoy arrived from Charlestown, bringing every sort of supply, uniforms, shoes, saddlery, salt, rum and a host of other necessities which we had lacked for too long. This relief, together with a falling off in sickness with the colder weather, brought an improvement of spirit in the army which was further heartened as Cornwallis's intention to advance again into North Carolina became widely known.

Cornwallis had long argued unsuccessfully with Clinton's instruction to ensure the security of South Carolina, Georgia and the two Floridas by remaining within these bounds. To sit passively guarding this huge area with the force available to us could only lead to the loss of all three colonies piecemeal. Whilst in this way it might be possible to encourage the loyalist elements within the area in their support of the King's cause, and employ them in quelling rebellious factions, it could offer no inspiration or assistance to loyalists outside those colonies to do likewise. More important, it could not prevent rebel armies, based in Virginia and North Carolina, from invading South Carolina, from reinforcing such rebel militias as still existed, and from attempting to defeat our weaker detachments and overrunning our weaker outposts.

"If you want to stop the fox from killing your chickens you have to hunt and kill the fox," said Cornwallis. "And that's what we should be doing. Not just squatting on guard on top of the coop, hoping he won't find the holes in the bottom. We have to get after the rebel armies—get after the fox and hunt him down in his own earth—and that means Virginia.

"I've been at Pussy again and again about it, in letter after letter, despatch after despatch; but, of course, he doesn't see it that way. He wants me to hold the rebels down in the south, whilst he—in some sort of all-conquering, Hannibalian campaign, which he hasn't had time to plan et—subdues all the north. That might even do the trick if he could summon the energy to get off his backside and so do some conquering. The longer he is about it the less likely he is to succeed. With the war in India and the Sugar Islands going so badly, time is nowhere on our side. So if he won't start fighting—we must. I've written to Germain. I hope to God he can persuade Pussy to get his claws out."

Clinton had assured Lord Germain that he had left in Charlestown six thousand "effective" troops. A typical taradiddle!—for the figure included all sick and wounded, all prisoners known to be in rebel hands—even those officers and men on recruiting duty in England!

Cornwallis succeeded in persuading Germain that the only effective course open with his meagre force—the true figure was three thousand, six hundred—would be to advance into North Carolina and Virginia and to defeat the rebel armies there. Germain, in consequence, instructed Clinton—to his chagrin—to support Cornwallis' proposed advance to the north in pursuit of the rebel armies. Clinton complied, unwillingly, by sending Maj. Gen. Alexander Leslie with two thousand men to the Chesapeake, to join Cornwallis in Virginia. But, after the defeat at King's Mountain, Cornwallis ordered Leslie to join him in Camden. His plan was to leave Francis Rawdon in command of the garrisons in South Carolina and march with the rest of the force, which, with Leslie's reinforcement, would be around three thousand, north to Virginia.

This plan was accepted at a council-of-war on Thursday the 12th December, at which I was invited to propose ways of improving the recruitment of militia. With the reduction of loyalist support, which Tarleton had foreseen would follow the disaster of King's Mountain, the army was now suffering from a lack of information on the rebels' movements and, as important in this trackless area, a lack of competent guides. I suggested that this deficiency could be remedied by a strong recruiting effort in two areas in North Carolina where loyalist support was known to be vigorous—Tryon County and Cross Creek.

"And you think there are many recruits to be had in those parts?" asked Cornwallis.

"My lord, we'll gain no recruits unless we show our faces there. We should—we needs must—go and see. It can only do good."

"So what do you propose?"

"My lord, I propose that Major Fairleigh conducts an expedition first through Tryon County and then through Cross Creek with his troop." For having recruited a full troop with ease, James Fairleigh's commission now read as major of militia.

"And do you propose to accompany him this time—to give him guidance?"

"I should be most happy to go. I could perform a useful reconnaissance of the crossings of Broad River."

Cornwallis smiled. "Very well, Philip, as you propose. Let me have your plan and route. You had best take an escort if you want to move independently of Fairleigh."

And so, on the next day, with Charles Russell commanding a patrol of twenty dragoons of the 17th, I rode north from Wynnesborough for six days, past Fishing Creek and King's Mountain into Tryon County, in company with James Fairleigh and his troop of the loyal North Carolina Militia.

As James and I had suspected, there were many young men, mostly Scots and Irish, who looked only for opportunity to discharge the oaths they had taken to the Crown before sailing for the colonies, and came readily forward when that opportunity was offered. Indeed, so many came that I had Charles Russell and his dragoons form a convoy of them, and we marched them back to Wynnesborough, leaving James and his troop seeking further afield to the Catawba—and Belhaven, which I had avoided—for more recruits for his own command.

We marched to Wynnesborough in part by the way I had ridden back from Belhaven. And doubtless you can guess why.

We came to the cabin in the freezing dusk of Christmas Eve. The wind moaned through the pines, driving the snow and sleet into our faces. Our horses stood heads down, ears back, hating the sting of the sleet.

This time no light glimmered through the shutters. I dismounted, climbed the steps to the narrow porch and stood in the door. A rat scurried away. Within the cabin there was nothing, only a scattering of rubbish, the remnants of a poor man's wealth, littered the floor. There was no one now to light the lamp, to tend the fire, to open the door, to welcome the passing traveller.

I came out of the cabin and walked round to where the graves of the man and his wife and their son lay. They were undisturbed, the crosses held up their arms of mercy at their heads. Now, beside these three, there lay a fourth grave—there stood a fourth cross. But this grave was open; a shallow, uneven scrape. The snow had stretched its gentle blanket over the figure that lay within it. She must have dug it with her own hands and laid herself down beside her loved ones.

We filled in the grave, set heavy stones upon it to keep off the beasts, and drove in the cross more firmly at her head.

Death of an army—Destruction of a family

Four graves—four crosses; a family who sought to live in peace. Destroyed by men in Parliament and Congress whom they did not know, for causes they did not own, for reasons they did not understand. God rest their souls.

I climbed back into my saddle. And, as I did so, a gust of wind swung the door wide—then slammed it shut.

Chapter Thirteen

In which, being involved in disaster,
I am wounded and made prisoner.

On the afternoon of Thursday the 28th December I was summoned to Cornwallis' office. A sodden, weary, disconsolate Tarleton slouched in a chair in the ante-room.

Tarleton and I were not on the best of terms. He had complained bitterly that I should employ any part of the 17th Light Dragoons as an escort. He always claimed that the 17th were part of the Legion; though the 17th always claimed the contrary. Since Cornwallis preferred to deal with all cavalry matters through me, Tarleton had begun to resent me, though I had been careful to consult him whenever his interests were concerned. He thought himself slighted and being, for all his abilities, a selfish little fellow and vain beyond all discretion, he now criticized openly all that Cornwallis did and was off-hand with me. He resented James Fairleigh's successful recruiting and his own failure to gain any recruits other than those he extorted from other corps. He became solitary and surly, even with his own officers; and George Hanger, now sick again with fever, declared himself happy to be so, since he was able to avoid the company of his commanding officer.

Tarleton made no effort to rise as I came in, of course, but merely glowered up at me, his bloodshot eyes rimmed with red dust.

"This is the damnedest country I was ever in! One moment you're sweating a fever with your bowels running like a leaky tap. Next minute you're soaked to the skin and frozen solid, with your guts so numb and pinched with cold that you can't—"

"Come in and have a glass of brandy, Banastre," Cornwallis stood in the doorway of his room, smiling. "It'll unnumb your poor, pinched guts."

Tarelton drained a bumper draught in one, and, eyes watering, coughed and thumped his chest. "General, you're right—I'm unnumbing fast!" he croaked, and coughed again.

Cornwallis did not keep us long. "As you know, Gen. Nathaniel Greene took over command of the rebel army in the south from General Gates three weeks ago. His first act has been to divide his army into two parts. He himself has moved with one part to the Pedee River. The other part he has sent under General Morgan to threaten Ninety-Six. We are in no sort of strength to move against both parts of Greene's force yet, and I doubt he's prepared to attack us. But we can take advantage of his weakness in both parts and destroy one or the other. The more vulnerable part is Morgan's. And the force best placed and suited to destroy it quickly is yours, Banastre. Your strengths should be about equal. You have the battalion of the 71st and the light infantry companies and I'll endeavour to reinforce you further. He may have a few hundred militia, but they shouldn't count for much."

We agreed that I should support this operation by returning to Tryon County with Russell's detachment of the 17th. There, with James Fairleigh's assistance, we could seize any supplies moving to Morgan and any couriers passing between him and Greene, and delay any possible reinforcement moving to him. Tarleton, because confirmed in his independent command, entered with enthusiasm into the planning. He conceived the force I hoped to raise with James would be sufficient to enable us to trap Morgan between us. I had some doubts.

"If Morgan's force is eleven hundred, then the couple of hundred, which is the best I count on gathering from south of the Catawba, will scarce provide a secure lid for a mouse trap, let alone one for a Morgan."

"Colonel, you'll get five hundred and more from what I hear!" said Tarleton. He'd never got more than five from anywhere himself. "I'll drive Morgan against Broad River and, if you hold the fords, I'll hammer him to pieces!"

Cornwallis smiled. He liked enthusiastic, optimistic officers. So do I, but I prefer them to be practical too; which is why I have not been betrayed by their follies as often as he has.

"You should get more than a couple of hundred, Philip," he said. "And Tarleton's concept of the operation is sound. If Leslie arrives early enough, I'll move the whole army up the east bank of Broad River and close the trap myself!"

And so it was left. I knew Morgan only by his reputation as a doughty and experienced fighter. There were those who gave him—together with

Gen. Benedict Arnold—the credit for the rebel victory at Saratoga. In 1755, aged nineteen, he had driven a wagon in the column which General Braddock led to defeat at the hands of the French in the battle of the Wilderness, and had served bravely there. He had been commissioned in the Virginia Militia and during twenty years of service had gained considerable experience and reputation fighting on the frontier against the French and the Indians. He was certainly no mean adversary, but I'll admit that I thought Tarleton with a thousand regular troops a sufficient force to chase any rebel general with a similar command back to Philadelphia and beyond; and, if truth be told, such was Tarleton's reputation, so did every rebel commander, including Morgan. For he no sooner heard that Tarleton was moving against him, than he began to withdraw to the north.

Tarleton rode off to his command at Fairfield on Broad River, and the day after, Saturday the 30th December, I left Wynnesborough, again in a sleet storm, and headed for Tryon County. I was delayed by floods and rough roads and came up with James five days later. He had achieved more success with his recruitment and his command now numbered above one hundred and sixty, though many were untrained. We continued another nine days, riding slowly through the country west of the Montague Hills, enlisting new men and destroying the stores we intercepted on their way to Morgan.

During this time I maintained a reasonable communication with Cornwallis, but not with Tarleton. Tarleton moved so frequently and unpredictably, never giving information as to his planned direction, that it was impossible to communicate with him. But from information from Cornwallis' headquarters, from loyalists and captured rebel couriers and supply trains, I learned that Morgan was continuing to retreat, whilst Cornwallis, still awaiting the arrival of Leslie, had not yet moved from Wynnesborough.

There was now a danger that Morgan, if not prevented by an adequate force from crossing to the east of Broad River, would escape. So I ordered James to march his corps—now numbering over the two hundred I had expected—to the area of King's Mountain, whence he could move to harass and delay Morgan's force as it retreated. But I was stupid not to have thought of the associations King's Mountain held for loyalist militia. Though ideally suited for the purpose I intended, the place held little charm for James' troop and they moved only slowly; some even leaving him.

I am wounded and made prisoner

By Sunday the 14th January, Tarleton and Morgan were so close that battle was virtually inevitable. The knowledge that no blocking force opposed Morgan on Broad River haunted me that night as I lay sleepless, huddled in my cloak, on the floor of a ruined hut. I resolved to ride south the next morning with Russell's detachment of the 17th. If James' troop would accompany us, well and good. If not, in their uncertain state, they would be small loss.

It started to snow that night and, the wind dropping, it snowed steadily for the next two days. It was bitterly cold. James could not persuade his troopers to accompany me in any substantial numbers, so I thought it best not to take any. With Russell's dragoons we moved as fast as we dared over the ice and frozen ground, but arrived at the ford to the west of King's Mountain only on the Tuesday evening.

Here, on the west bank, in the dusk, we surprised part of Morgan's train, guarded by a few militia. They offered no resistance. They told us that Morgan, with a thousand men, was six miles south on the road to Pacolet Springs. We took their arms and their horses and such comforts as we could find in their wagons, smashed the wagon wheels and left them. They thanked us for not hanging them, as they swore they had expected—now what lying rogue had persuaded them of that? To send them scampering to Morgan with wild alarms and in the hope of persuading him to stand and fight, or disperse his force, where he was, I told them that we were the advance guard of Cornwallis' army, which was about to cross the river and, if it found them there, might not use them so gently. They took fright quick enough and disappeared briskly down the road to Pacolet Springs.

This done, I decided that Russell's detachment would be of most use with the troop of the 17th now with Tarleton. To avoid the rebel force, we kept to the path along the west bank of the river. It was narrow, rough, steep in places and deep in snow and, in the dark we moved slowly; but, at least, keeping to the line of the river, we moved certainly. We arrived at Thicketty Creek at three o'clock in the morning and turned off to ride along its north bank. We were rewarded, finally, in the grey glimmer of the dawn, with the sight of the tracks of a considerable force of cavalry and infantry moving north.

We followed the tracks and, as the day lightened, we came through a pine wood in front of which the battalion of the 71st Highlanders was moving into line in extended order, their plaids wrapped close around them to fend off the bitter wind. Two hundred yards to their right the cavalry of the Legion was forming in two ranks. I ordered Charles Russell to form his detachment on the left of the Legion dragoons, give the horses a small feed and take a bite and a dram themselves.

I rode over to where the tall, lean figure of an old friend, Maj. Archibald M'Arthur, commanding the battalion of the 71st Highlanders, stood, head bowed, leaning on his drawn claymore, while his men toiled wearily into line behind him. He looked up and nodded casually, without a word, as if we were met by chance strolling up the Royal Mile in Edinburgh.

"Where's Tarleton?" I said.

M'Arthur's bushy grey eyebrows drew down in a scowl and he jerked his chin in the direction of the main British line forming slowly, three hundred yards to our front. On the left of the line were fifty dragoons of the Legion, and on their right, the 7th Regiment—which dismayed me, for I knew that it comprised only two hundred raw, young recruits, fresh from England, who had never seen a shot fired in anger. Then, in the centre of the line, with a three-pounder cannon of the sort we call "grasshoppers" on either flank, were the Legion infantry. Beyond them were the light infantry companies and, on the extreme right flank, the troop—fifty strong—of the 17th Light Dragoons.

Across the open ground, five hundred yards to the front of our line, three long ranks of rebel militia were ranged across the front of a small hill. Behind them, where the hill rose higher, were four divisions of blue-coated Continental infantry, with more militia on their flanks. I could see no cavalry but, since these would be commanded by cousin William Washington, I suspected that they were properly concealed.

I said, "What are your orders, Archie?"

He slashed angrily at the bracken. "My orders? I'm the reserve!" He waved his blade contemptuously at the Legion dragoons, "Along wi' they green-bellied fly-slicers there!"

"And what's Tarleton's plan?"

"His plan?" M'Arthur's quick temper flared. "Ye'd best ask himself! Not a word has he said to me of any plan—nor to anyone else, I doubt. I mistrust he has no plan! 'Fore God! I fought my first battle or ever he'd sucked pap, the o'erweening, unlicked cub—yet he's ne'er deigned to ask my counsel! Look ye, Philip, my men are near starved and marched and frozen to death—but does he care for that? Not a whit! I know Morgan, ye mind. He's as old as I am and his bones creak like mine in this weather—like the wheels of an old wagon! But he's a bonny fighter—even if he is a Welshman! We taught him and he's learned well. And this unbreeched pup of a dragoon thinks to treat him like militia. He's forever complaining that no one can use his cavalry properly, but God!—look how the rattle-brained loon uses infantry!"

I turned Williamson to canter over to where Capt. David Kinloch sat his horse in front of the Legion cavalry. As I pushed the mare into a canter she stumbled—and I nearly came off—and I realized how tired the poor beast was, and how slow in my own weariness I had become.

David Kinloch had joined the Legion from the 71st Highlanders. He has a thin, hard mouth, a cold, blue eye and a wicked tongue. I like him. He speaks his mind.

"How do I find Colonel Tarleton?" I asked.

"I hope you find him in his proper senses, Colonel. He's out of them today, I fear. There's no battle to be won here awhile. I've hardly a man or horse that can stand, let alone fight—"

A cheer rang out from our right. Over the heads of the infantry, we saw a single line of fifty green-jacketed dragoons charge, sabres flashing, across the front. Since I had arrived on this field of imminent battle, a running fire had been maintained against our line by rebel skirmishers from positions in the long grass a hundred yards or so in front of the rebel line. At that extreme range their fire had no effect, other than to reveal their positions and their ill state of training. But, unless forced back, their fire could cause casualties when our line advanced. The way to drive them back was to send a company of light infantry forward in skirmishing order covered by a few rounds of case from the guns. But Tarleton—in too much of a hurry—had chosen to try to dislodge an unknown number of skirmishers from good cover with fifty dragoons in single line. Suicidal lunacy. The dragoons had galloped no more than a hundred yards before fifteen had been knocked into the snow. The rest swung back out of range.

"For God's sake!" I said. "Has he gone mad?"

I cantered on to the front of the troop of the 17th Light Dragoons, where Capt. Henry Talbot greeted me as glumly as Kinloch and M'Arthur. "What are your orders, Talbot?"

"To cover the flank, Colonel."

"That all?"

"That's all Colonel Tarleton's said so far, sir."

"I see. Well, I suspect Colonel Washington has his cavalry concealed behind the hill. Be prepared to charge them at once if they move towards you. Don't allow them to attack our line in flank when it advances and don't receive any attack stationary here. Let them come no nearer than five hundred yards, then go straight at them. They'll wheel away and fire their pistols. They're unused to fighting with sabres from horseback."

A smile now sat on Henry Talbot's usually cheerful, round face. A straightforward young man, he likes his orders clear. He arched his back and swung his short, fat legs free from his stirrup-irons to ease his stiffness and pushed the chin-strap of his helmet from under his double chin.

"Aaahh—that's better. Haven't been off this poor old sack's back much in the last two days, Colonel. We're both about done, old feller, aren't we?" He slapped his horse's neck. "Egad, I must say, Colonel Ban's in a bit of a hurry this morning. Wants to eat Morgan for breakfast."

Dulled by the wind and the snow, a staccato rattle sounded from the drums of the Legion infantry in the centre. The drummers of the light infantry and the 7th Regiment picked it up and began to beat the advance, though the line was still unformed.

"Bigod, we're off!" Talbot hitched his chin-strap back under his chins. "He's certainly rushing his fences today!"

An uneven scatter of shots rattled from the left of the line. At that stage of an advance such shooting, without orders, is a sure sign of near panic in the ranks.

"It's the 7th," I said, wheeled the mare and sent her flying across the front of the advancing line. I found Tarleton in the centre of it, waving his great sabre and cheering the men on. I call it a line, but it was never that. For the most part, particularly in the 7th Regiment, who had been slower than the other corps in coming up, it was a disordered straggle. I rode alongside Tarleton.

"Ban, for God's sake stop this attack! Can't you see the men arn't fit for it? There's no haste—Morgan can't move—you have him already. Give your men time to draw breath and we'll destroy him completely. It's madness to attack like this—you're in no sort of order—"

He turned on me like a rabid fox, spitting and snarling with rage. The stink of brandy on his breath struck foul half a length away and his Lancashire accent was thicker than I'd ever heard it.

"I'm not fighting your bloody Minden, Cato! I've no time for dressing the line ten times before I attack! I've got this gutter-born Welsh get where I want him—I'll crucify him on one of his own wagon wheels! If you've no stomach for the fight—get out the way! These men'll fight for me—" He waved his sabre and the weight of it nearly swung him out of his saddle.

A volley crashed out from the line of rebel militia. Not an even, regular volley, but steadier than I had ever heard from militia so far. It was at extreme range and did little harm, but it stopped the 7th in their tracks until their officers got them moving again. The poor 7th! All of them so very young—their thin white faces pinched in the bitter cold, the collars of their coats too big for their scrawny necks and the shoulders too wide for their boyish frames, weighed down by their equipment.

Now there was no semblance of any ordered line on the left. And battle was already joined. I was too late. Had we checked now and withdrawn, Morgan would—or should—have come straight down the hill and driven us from the field. Knowing his reputation, I was sure he would do exactly that; and very effectively. Common sense—and military expedience— dictate that only one commander should control an action; particularly an attack. Tarleton must be allowed to see this one through without distraction. But, foreseeing calamity, I sent Matthew to call Charles Russell and his troopers to join me, and rode back to the only troops upon whom I could rely to restore a ruinous situation, or, at least, shield what might be left of our little force from the worst effects of its commander's folly—the 17th Light Dragoons.

By the time I arrived there, our line—or what passed for it—had driven in the rebel skirmishers and was pushing back the first line of the militia. At first, the militia stood up well to the attack, before which, even as weak and disorganized as it was, they would earlier have fled without firing a shot. I was informed later that Morgan had told them they would be shot down by the Continental Line regiments formed behind them if they ran. As they began to fall back, Lieut. Duncan Munro came galloping across to us.

"Colonel Tarleton desires the 17th to charge and disperse those militia, sir!"

Talbot looked at me.

"All right," I said, "but remember Washington is probably round the corner with a hundred dragoons against your fifty. Keep your men together and don't go in too far. In fact, I'll come with you—"

I had guessed correctly. As we went into the militia who, again contrary to their custom, tried to resist us, Cornet Patterson, leading the right flank, shouted, "Rebel cavalry on our right, Colonel!"

I stood up, my sword over my head. "Ride straight on—straight on!" The militia were running every way now, and we cut our path deeper into them. I stood up again, waving my sword above my head. "Close up! Close up!" I dropped my point to the right. "Wheel right—and rally!"

This manoeuvre put a number of militia between us and the rebel cavalry, who, coming on all too fast, charged into their own militia. As they began to check, their rear files, galloping on, cannoned headlong into their front ranks. The 17th, holding well together, then rode out from the cover of the now panic-stricken militia, and charged into the flank of this confusion. The rebel dragoons, packed tight in a jumbled muddle, facing in all directions, could not defend themselves against us, nor prevent us from cutting our way through them and getting clear before they could do us much hurt. Some of them came after us, but the grasshopper guns turned to our assistance and knocked down a few of them; which discouraged the rest.

We had done what Tarleton had asked. We had driven the militia from the field. There would have been no sense in risking the troop of the 17th further. It would certainly be needed later.

The fight in the centre and left was now hidden by smoke. But in the middle ground, over which the line had passed, there seemed to be more men lying or crawling back, wounded, than I had seen at Camden. The fire of the militia had been more effective than usual.

We heard the pipes strike up and saw the 71st Highlanders move off in column to the left flank at a steady pace. Arrived there the column wheeled half-right, halted, turned to face front and formed into double rank at open files, all with the smooth, practised precision of a veteran battalion. The line advanced, halted, delivered its volley and advanced again as steadily into the smoke of the fight.

There was a sudden sound of cheering on the left. That side of our battle began to move forward quickly, though somewhat unevenly.

"Bigod, they're driving them!" Talbot was exultant. "There's Dick Corbet taking the left flank troop forward—"

Captain Corbet's move with his troop of the Legion cavalry had been noted on the other side of the battle too. Cousin William Washington, six hundred yards away on the hillside, looking enormous on an enormous horse, wheeled it round to lead his corps across the back of the hill, presumably to greet Corbet's troops as he had welcomed us.

I gave the order sharply, "Captain Talbot, advance your troop about a hundred yards at a trot, as if we're about to charge—at once, please!"

The troop trotted forward in line, swords at the carry, and halted—poised. A shout from one of his troop officers brought Washington back to stare hard at us, then across to the other flank, and back at us once more. I saw him pound his thigh with a clenched fist, then he slouched down in his saddle, one hand on hip, glowering across at us. I could imagine what he was saying. He dare not leave this flank uncovered, and, I can only suppose, he dare not leave one of his officers to command a detachment of his corps to face us whilst he went to command an action on the other flank. He had seen how the 17th fought.

Now above the confused roar of battle, volley after volley echoed from the left. There came a high-pitched, shrill yelling I had not heard before, and, all at once, there were men running back through the smoke towards the guns and the close-formed double line of the cavalry of the Legion in reserve.

"It's the 7th! God's death—they're running!" Disbelief and rage mixed in Talbot's anguished yell. Through the thinning smoke we could see the light infantry companies falling back—slowly, steadily and in good order—but falling back. With the 7th gone, a great gap was torn in our line, through which the blue-coated Continental Line infantry pressed, enclosing the ever-dwindling light infantry and the Legion infantry on both flanks. Away on the left flank M'Arthur and his Highlanders, alone and surrounded, fought on in a grim and hopeless struggle.

A tremendous cheer arose from Washington's dragoons. There was nothing to keep them on this flank now. It was clear that the day was won. Cousin William led them in a charge into the flank of the light infantry. There was nothing we could do to stop them.

Tarleton came galloping back towards the Legion cavalry, shouting and waving his sabre. David Kinloch, at their front, drew his sabre and signalled the advance. He and the other officers rode forward—but not another man moved. Tarleton halted, staring at the troopers, ranged in their well-drilled ranks. Again he shouted and waved his sabre. Kinloch and the other officers turned about to face the ranks: they seemed to be encouraging the soldiers. But, after a moment, some of the men in the rear turned their horses' heads and rode off into the woods behind them. More and more followed, until the whole herd—for they were naught but frightened cattle now—turned and fled headlong into the woods. And over on the left flank Richard Corbet's troopers streamed the same way.

"Tarleton's Green Dragoons!" scoffed Talbot, bitterly, "Tarleton's yellow mongrels!"

Our guns had opened their fire again, in an attempt to cover the withdrawal of the infantry. They were given little chance to do so. The rebel infantry came on in force—four hundred against two guns and twelve artillerymen. Here was something we could try to do to save the day—or, at least, the guns. We charged into the flank of the rebels as they came to the guns, and, for a few minutes, the fight swung crazily around them. But it was soon clear that we could achieve nothing and I ordered a withdrawal to save the 17th for what remained to be done. The artillerymen fought their guns until they could fight them no more; then they fought to defend them, until—to a man—they fell dead or wounded. Good gunners and proper men.

I re-formed the 17th, a bare thirty-five strong now, on the road back to
Thicketty Creek, to cover the escape of any troops which had fought free
of the rebels. As we withdrew slowly along the road, the rebel cavalry,
Washington well out in front, came hell-for-leather after us in column. By
now Tarleton had joined us with the officers of the Legion cavalry. I
ordered the troop column to turn about, form extended line and prepare to
use their carbines.

The rebel column came on straight at us. At close range we gave them a
volley and went straight in with the sword.

In the mêlée Matthew lost his place at my bridle arm and I found myself
hotly attacked by three rebel troopers. One missed me with his pistol and
the other two came at me with their sabres. They were not well practised
in the use of these but were engaging my attention assiduously enough
when something struck me in the back under my right shoulder blade. My
sword arm went limp and I fell forward on Williamson's neck. A sabre
flashed above me and bit all across my back. Barely conscious, I slid
sideways in my saddle. A man's knee then his stirrup-iron smashed into
my face as I felt myself falling—falling—into darkness.

I was lying face down. The snow under my face was red and my mouth
was full of blood. I could not move and I was cold—oh, so cold. Feet
crunched the snow. I heard a murmuring of voices.

"That's a nice 'orse—'Ere, this one's a bleedin' officer—" A boot toe
struck into my stomach and rolled me over. "Crimes—'e's alive!—Well,
he bloody soon won't be!—'Old up, not so fast! Let's 'ave a bit o' fun with
'im.—Nah, leave the poor sod alone. He's nigh dead a'ready—" They
were four militiamen. They had muskets and bayonets and two of them
began to roll me back and forth and over with the points of their bayonets,
laughing as my limbs flopped like a rag doll's. After a little of this the other
two protested—"That's enough o' that—leave 'im be.—Oh, pike off ye
soft bastards—'ere, Jack, what about 'is boots then?—Ah, look good.
We'll have 'em." And they began to heave at them.

There was a sudden thudding of hooves. A voice called, "What the hell
are you two doing?"—"Taking the twitchers off this bleeder—what's it
look like?" A sabre hissed and thudded home. One of the men heaving at
my boots screamed and fell to the ground beside me. Firm hands turned
me on my back gently. A Welsh voice said, "Ay, he's got Greys
facings—it's him. And that's his horse—the big mare there. Get the
Colonel—quick now, boy!"

My head was raised and the mouth of a canteen eased between my teeth. Neat rum, mixed with blood, burned down my throat. I coughed and choked—then darkness again.

I was lying on my back on something soft under a canvas tilt. I was wrapped in blankets. I ached everywhere, particularly my face and across my back and right shoulder; but I was warm. A dragoon, judging by his boots, sat beside me on a cask. I must have groaned as I became conscious, for he looked down and grinned. He put a mug to my lips—brandy and water—and I drank a lot of it.

"That's better, your honour." It was the Welsh voice again. "I'll get the Colonel now."

I saw I was in the back of a cart. Through the open canvas the stars glowed bright in a sky made blacker by the whiteness of the snow. A large man clambered clumsily into the cart.

"Philip, how are you now, lad? It's William Washington. God's sakes!—I thought we agreed to stay out of each other's way, cousin! I saw you go down. We came looking for you as soon as we could. Not too damned soon, Sergeant Thomas said. He's the one who found you—came to get me just now. I've put him in charge of you. He's a good man. I wanted you paroled and left with the rest of the wounded, but Morgan won't hear of it. He wants something to show to Congress besides a few colours, so, as the senior British officer present on the field, you're coming with us." He paused, then went on apologetically. "Be a roughish journey, I'm afraid. But we'll keep you as comfortable as we can. Our surgeons are pretty fair."

And a rough journey it was, what I saw—or rather, felt—of it during the time I was conscious. The surgeons were better than pretty fair and Sergeant Thomas was a ministering angel, but none of them could save me from the eternal agonies of jolting and rocking mile after mile up hills, down valleys, through creeks, over the rough tracks and trackless wastes which Morgan wisely kept to in his hasty flight out of Cornwallis' avenging reach. In mercy, they drugged me most of the time, so I have no knowledge of how long I spent in the back of that infernal conveyance; an apt term, for that's another of my conceptions of Hades—to be trundled, wounded and helpless, in the back of a farm cart, over the North Carolina hills in winter for ever.

I became conscious at dawn—on some morning or other. I was a little crazed in my mind, wondering how much longer I could last. I was now so weak that it was an effort even to move a hand. My various wounds—the pistol ball under my right shoulder-blade, which had entered my lung; the sabre cut laying open my spine and back ribs; my nose and cheek, broken, presumably, as I fell; the several holes made by the militiamen's bayonets as they pitchforked me about; all had been dressed by the surgeons as best they could in the night after the battle. Since then they had not been touched; there had been no time. Even to my drugged and pain-numbed senses they stank.

Washington climbed into the cart and knelt beside me.

"Philip, we're going to leave you. The surgeons have told Morgan that you won't survive another day if he takes you any further. So he has said to parole you and leave you where you can be cared for properly. He came to see you, but you weren't conscious. He was very distressed at your condition. I'm sending Sergeant Thomas with an escort for you to find some suitable place—where there's a good surgeon. There's not much round here, but he'll find somewhere." He took my hand. Until I saw it in his, I hadn't realized how weak and wasted it had become. "God bless you, Philip. I pray you'll recover well."

He tucked my hand back under the blanket and crawled out of the cart. There was a sudden scramble, a resounding oath and a heavy thud—followed by a groan.

"Why the devil can't they put some sort of step on the back of these damned machines? Might have broken me neck!" Then, suddenly anxious, "Hope I didn't jolt you, Philip?"

Even in the straits I was in, my dear cousin could make me smile. And, obviously very relieved, he nodded cheerfully, smiled back and hobbled off, swearing.

Then I was given a draught and I slept again.

Chapter Fourteen

*In which I am restored to life by true love and
meet with an odd recruit to the King's cause.*

I remember nothing clearly of what happened after Washington's surgeon had given me that last sleeping draught, until the agony as I was lifted
from the cart awoke me. My eyes were near closed in my broken, swollen
face, so that I sensed more than saw the flaring torches; heard voices loud,
then hushed and weeping; felt the gentle hands carrying me and laying me
on a bed—then terrible hands, butcher's hands, tearing off the congealed
and reeking dressings and swabbing the putrefying flesh beneath with
liquid fire. I screamed, I babbled, I raved, I begged them to let me die—to
kill me. But the hands went on tearing, torturing, until I could no longer
hear or speak; only feel—through my raw nerve ends. And then, thank
God, I felt nothing any more.

I lay near death for four weeks, they said. My swollen face shrunk into a
skull. My eyes would open but there was no sense nor sight in them. They
would feed me broth and wine and medicines and would speak to me, but
I made no recognition and never answered. They feared my mind was
unhinged by pain, for I would ramble and drivel in delirium, then shout
and scream and curse and sob all together. They feared I should die,
through no will to live. They underestimated the effect of their skills and
their patient care.

The curtains were half-drawn and the sunlight fell through them across
my face. My eyelids stuck together, unwilling to open. One eye
half-opened, painfully. A Negro boy sat by the window, reading. The
glare hurt my half-eye and I closed it again.

"Curtains—" A voice slurred somewhere, slowly, indistinctly. The boy exclaimed something and I heard him move to my bedside, so that he shielded my face from the glare. I opened the eye that worked.

"Curtain—close it," I muttered.

"Yes, sir—I'll close it." He did so and came back to my bed. "You better now, sir? You feel well now?" He was almost beside himself with excitement. "I get missus now, sir!"

He came back with a stout, motherly, middle-aged woman in an apron and mob-cap, carrying a bowl of soup and a mug of beer; the best beer I've ever tasted. She raised my head and gave me a few sips of beer and spoonfuls of soup alternately, crying all the time. I mumbled at her and tried to smile, and her tears came all the faster.

"Oh, sir," she sobbed, smiling and crying together now, "we've prayed so long—here at your bedside—so long—" then could say no more. The boy, neat in waistcoat and breeches, stood holding the soup bowl, only staring at me, his eyes big with wonder.

"Dr. Weekes comes tomorrow evening, sir," the woman said; she had a Lowland Scots accent. "Och, he'll be so rejoiced to see your improvement! See now, ye've finished the beer and the soup. Oh, ye'll be up and about in no time! Come away now, Andrew, we'll leave the Colonel to rest." She tiptoed out, followed by the Negro lad who, as he left, gave me a great beaming smile which cheered me wonderfully. I closed my one eye and, for the first time, slept without the aid of some narcotic.

Dr. Weekes, another Scot—from Edinburgh—is a sober, taciturn, little fellow. His hands are firm and cool, and his fingers close on you like a vice, relentless and deliberate in establishing the seat and cause of pain. I knew now who had stripped the dressings off my wounds on that first night. He and the woman cleaned and re-dressed my wounds this evening, with the woman exclaiming and chattering away and Dr. Weekes interjecting an "Ay," when she ran out of breath. After they had finished, Dr. Weekes stood looking down at me, hands on his hips.

"Satisfactory, Colonel. Ye're mending fine. Mind, it's as well ye've a good constitution." He nodded gravely. "A little broth and wine for the Colonel now, Mrs. Fraser, if you please, and I'll leave something to help him sleep, should he still need it."

Both my eyes were working today, and I looked around my room. It was small, square, plain and sparsely furnished with my simple, low cot, a truckle bed by the door, a table, chair and washstand. On the wall hung my uniform, cleaned and neatly patched. Through the one window I could see only the sky, but through the door I could hear the chatter and bustle of a kitchen and a laundry—and smell both; so the house could not be large, nor judging from the plainness of my room and Mrs. Fraser's dress, could it be wealthy.

After she had fed me the broth and wine, Mrs. Fraser set some water and oatcakes and a little bell on a table by my bedside. That I was incapable of using any of them didn't seem to occur to her. "Andrew will come in to sleep on the truckle later, Colonel, if ye wish anything in the night," she said.

"Thank you," they were the first intelligible words I had been able to mumble at her and she smiled delightedly. She put a warm, plump hand on my brow. "Och, ye've no fever the now," she said brightly, and left me.

I tried to stay awake. I wanted to find out from Andrew where I was and how long I had been here—I wanted to know what had happened to me, who had brought me here and why. Where was the army and Cornwallis? Had Anne been told of my wounding and capture?—and was I still a prisoner?—or had I ever been made prisoner? Who were the Frasers?—and was there a Mr. Fraser? Why had they shown me such care and kindness? My mind, still fevered, was wandering aimlessly through a fog of questions when I fell asleep.

This time it was the moon that waked me. Andrew had opened the curtains. The moonlight showed him as a heap of blankets on the truckle bed; nothing could have awoken him. At the foot of my bed, in the shadows, knelt two figures, a man and a woman, praying. "We've prayed so long at your bedside—" she had said. Tears come easily when you are very weak. As mine traced down my cheeks, I wondered at, and thanked God for, the care of those who had tended me here.

Next morning, when I woke, Andrew had already gone and the truckle bed with him. My uniform too had disappeared. Mrs. Fraser bustled in with a bowl of porridge. It was an effort still for me to speak, so I could never break into her steady stream of chatter; nor, since she spoke so fast and it was an effort too for me to attend to all she said, could I take in much of what she did say. I gathered that now I was conscious and sleeping normally, I was to be moved to where the kitchen noises could not disturb me. Until now, whilst I had lain insensible, it had been more convenient to keep me where my needs could be most easily met. She would give me a physic which Dr. Weekes had left to make me sleep soundly, and they would move me whilst I slept, so that I should not be distressed by the motion.

When I awoke in the early evening I was in another room altogether. Through the two high windows I saw again the crests of the Blue Ridge

Mountains, snow-covered and shimmering in the sunset glow; and the light through the curtains tinted the fronds and flowers of the same frieze I had studied lying there that morning when I had met Chawton at seven o'clock on the lawn below. I was at Belhaven.

Mrs. Fraser hushed me when she came to feed me and tend me that evening. "No, no, Colonel! Dr. Weekes says ye must not exert yourself in any way—not until ye're stronger. Now, hush—or I'll not say one more word to ye." But she did, more than one; again I could never get one in edgewise.

That night I woke again in the moonlight, but this time it lay the length of my bed. I recognized the same two figures who knelt to pray at its foot. One was Lord Fairleigh—the other, Lucy.

As they rose, I mumbled "My lord—"

"Philip!" he hurried round the bed and bent to kiss my cheek. "My dear lad! Oh, this is joy to hear ye speak again and see ye better. Lie still, ye must not speak or move. God be thanked that ye recover! Now, we'll leave ye. Ye must rest." He patted my hand. "Lucy dear." He went to the door, opened it. "Lu—"

Lucy still stood at the foot of the bed, looking down at me, her back to the moonlight. She never moved. Fairleigh went out, closing the door quietly behind him. Lucy came up beside me. She took my hand in both hers. She said, "Philip." It was all she needed to say.

I whispered, "I can't see your face."

"Good," she whispered too, "it's got old and ugly." She ran the tip of her forefinger down my mended nose. "Your new nose suits you."

I tried to turn my head and pull her hand to my lips, but hadn't the strength for it. A tear splashed on my hand. She bent and kissed me lightly on the nose. "Poor nose!" she whispered. She hung over me for a moment and another tear splashed on my cheek, then she kissed me again full and softly on the lips. "Poor Philip—sleep well." She flitted, silent as a white moth, across the room and out of the door. And Andrew snored quietly on his truckle bed below the window.

The next day I was able to silence Mrs. Fraser in full flow. Lord Fairleigh had called in to see me twice during the day, but Lucy had not come near me. I determined to ask Mrs. Fraser why. When she brought me yet more broth in the evening, I raised my hand—slowly and with much effort. It struck her dumb. I beckoned her and she bent over me. I strained out, "Where is Lady Lucy?"

It threw the poor woman into a proper state. She started to babble something about Lucy going away; busily straightening my sheet, tucking

1 my blankets, settling my pillows and getting more and more scarlet in
e face the more she fibbed. I managed to catch and hold her wrist.
Where?" I husked. She looked at me like a rabbit looks at a fox—pop-
yed.

"Lawks, Colonel Cato—she'll be sore angry with me, sir!" But I could
ee she was dying to tell me, so I husked again and she sank down on a
hair at my bedside, her handkerchief to her eyes.

"Och, Colonel, the poor lass—she's resting. She's scarce slept a wink
ince ye were brought here, and when she has its been on yon truckle bed
eside ye in your old room. She was the one who held ye while Dr.
Veekes stripped off the dressings on that first night; she'd let no one else
ouch ye, and I thought her heart would break with sobbing. She's been
he one who tended ye, fed ye, washed ye, changed the dressings—
verything she's done. Only let me help when she couldn't manage
erself; until ye came to yourself, that is. Then she said she looked so
owdy she couldn't bear ye to see her. She's wasted away these last weeks
lmost as much as you—the Lord knows how she kept her strength.
Perhaps she may come this evening, when you're asleep. She and I—and
is lordship—used to pray every evening by your bed, and you mumbling
nd gabbling on like some witless bairn. She held all her grief and pain to
erself, never impatient, never irritable; never giving up hope—even
hen the rest of us had—"

But Lucy never came while I was awake. Though each morning on the
ble by my bed there was a little vase of flowers, fresh cut every day; and
n my pillow, the faintest breath of her perfume.

And so there passed another two weeks and I grew strong enough to
alk, with the aid of Andrew's shoulder and a stick, to a chair set by the
indow to watch the mountain snows melt and the early spring flowers
atch the outworn, wintered drab of the nearer hills. I took my meals
itting there and the truckle was removed to make place for my table. And
t the end of the second week I was able, again with Andrew's assistance,
o descend the stairs and walk out upon the lawn in the spring sunshine.
hen I realized the extreme joy of being alive. I, on whom the door of
eath had so nearly closed, was permitted to live again. And all this—the
eauty I saw around me, the freshness of the air I breathed, the joy of my
ecovered strength, my very being—I owed to Lucy. To what purpose?

That night I lay awake as I had lain awake before in this room. The
urmoil of thoughts in my mind was as strong as at that September
norning; and so lost in them was I, that I never heard the opening of the
oor. But as the glow of a candle lit the doorway I instinctively closed my

eyes. I sensed her come to my bedside and stand there for a moment, shielding the candle from my eyes. I heard her put down the fresh vase of flowers on the table by my head. Then her perfume came to me—nearer—nearer—and I felt the softest of kisses on my cheek. I opened my eyes. She started back.

"Oh! Why—you're awake!"

She put down her candle on the table with the flowers, stepped back a pace and stood looking down at me, her hands clasped in front of her. Her auburn curls fell loose over the green shawl covering her shoulders. A green ribbon tied the lace collar of her white nightdress.

"Can't you sleep?"

"I've too much to think about."

She shook her head. "You must sleep well to get really better."

I said—I had to say, "The sight of you will mend me quicker than any sleep."

She was silent for a moment. Then she smiled slowly and whispered "Will it, Philip? Why?"

Her smile stopped the breath in my throat. I could not answer; only gaze and gaze at her. She said, still very softly,

"You've always slept before. I've been every night to see. What are you thinking of now that won't let you sleep?"

She stood so still, her eyes in mine. The moon, half-hidden in a cloud, set a silver halo on her hair. There was no world beyond the candlelight.

"You are all my thoughts, Lucy—only you—and always you."

She gave a little gasp—near a sigh. Her eyes grew wider, draining my mind of all senses but my love for her. I stammered, foolishly, meaninglessly,

"How shameless—to come every night—into a gentleman's bedroom."

Her lips parted. She whispered, breathless,

"Philip—I am shameless."

She let the green shawl slip from her shoulders. "Shameless—" She pulled the ribbon at the throat of her nightdress. It fell in a foam of folds at her feet. The moonlight streamed softly down the whole smooth line of her body. Her eyes were lit like great stars by the candle flame; the full curves of her breasts rose and fell slowly in its gentle glow.

I stretched out my hand to her. "Lucy—"

She snatched it in both hers, kissed it and held it between her breasts. pulled her towards me and she came into my arms, her lips eager on mine her tears wet on my cheek.

"Lucy—my love—my love—"

I took her slowly and gently, as I had dreamed I would, and then she
y soft and warm and wakeful in my arms. Her fingers traced again and
gain the lines of the dressings I still wore on my wounds. Suddenly she
lung fiercely to me, shuddering and sobbing,

"Philip, hold me—hold me! Oh, my darling, I was so frightened—so
ightened that I should lose you—"

I kissed her and comforted her, murmuring loving nothings; my lips on
er hair, the nape of her neck, along her eyebrows, down her cheek and
he soft line of her throat to her breast. And we loved again. Then she
ghed—the longest and happiest of sighs—and fell asleep, like a child, in
ry arms.

he days that followed—oh, those days—I remember only as pure
aradise. I knew that I wronged Anne—and Lucy—and that all the
xcuses I could find were nothing but shabby, contemptible evasions. I
ad been away from home for a year, I told myself, and hadn't touched a
oman in that time. In the next battle I might well be killed outright, I
ld myself, or die of fever. Having been so near death I should grasp
oldly the happy present—and so on and so on. A bad excuse is better
han none the cynics say; but all cynics ignore the truth, the heart of the
natter, because they fear it. The only real comfort I found—because I
new the honesty of it—was in Matthew's simple admission of his love for
itty—"We love one another—we didn't mean it wrong—and we don't
nink it wrong now." In that light—and I mean this in truth—our love did
ot seem wrong. And when I say it was a time of pure paradise, I mean
xactly that.

Lucy was always with me, day and night. We lived, and loved, as man
nd wife. Fairleigh saw this, accepted it and delighted in the true and
nreserved happiness of the daughter he adored.

"These things are foreordained," he said once to me when we were
lone. "In my heart I've always hoped it might happen. I rejoice to see
our love and your joy in each other—as my Katharine would have done.
only wish it may not bring you—and your own family—any unhappi-
ess. How will it end?" He put his hand on my shoulder. "God will
rovide. 'Things future are the property of hope.'"

Only once did I see Lucy distressed. It was my fault, but it confirmed
or me the rightness of our love. We were stood together, hand in hand, on
nat fateful lawn beneath the oaks, now spreading their first pale green

leaves above our heads. I said—and I can think of no reason for saying i
other than, I suppose, the lawn put it in my mind, "Why did you think
should ever want to kill Chawton?"

She dropped my hand as if it burned hers. She stared at me, deathl
pale. "Philip, don't torture me. I tortured myself enough. I tried—I di
try so hard not to love you, or not to show it. I tried so hard to make yo
hate me. And then, when you quarrelled with Roger—I thought—he sai
you had killed so many men—and he said he had never fought a due
before. Philip, he tried to be brave, but I could see—he was so afraid.
thought because you must hate me for what I had said, that yo
would—and it was all my fault, because I had used him. I couldn't let i
happen. I asked Mr. Secker to help—to stop it; he understood—and ther
was no one else I could ask—who would listen—and be able to help. An
then—I was so frightened for you. I wanted to tell you everything when
came to your room afterwards—but then—I saw you hated me—and
wanted to die." Her hands writhed agonizingly together. "Silly—wasn
I? It was what I wanted—nobody was hurt—and you hated me—" He
voice trailed away. The awful pain I had seen in her eyes before was ther
again. "Philip, please—I know I'm silly—I know I was stupid—and I'r
sorry—and I love you—please, haven't I been punished enough?"

There, before Belhaven, before all the world, I took her in my arms an
held her. "Lucy, I love you. And as long as I have breath and life I'll lov
you—and after—and always."

I needed no excuses now. In my heart I knew from that moment tha
whatever the world might think, we loved and it was right.

On Tuesday the 8th May, whilst Lucy and I had ridden over t
Brindletown to visit Dr. Weekes, James Fairleigh arrived home with
detachment of his corps and a hundred or so new recruits he had collecte
from the settlements along Broad River. Loyalist enthusiasm had bee
strongly revived by the news of Francis Rawdon's defeat of Genera
Greene—with Gist and Otho Williams and cousin William, I supposed—
just north of Camden, on Hobkirk's Hill, two weeks before.

James was relieved to find me alive. "Cousin William wrote to me to sa
he had arranged to leave you here, though in very poor state and like t
die. He thought you would be well enough tended if you survived, and
judging from what father tells me, he seems to be right!" He grinne
happily and embraced me. "Thank God you did survive, Philip—or do
call you brother-in-law? I brought your baggage in the hope that—well, i
the hope that you would need it and Matthew is in your room now

waiting you. The—situation—has been explained to him, but I believe
e's in some doubt as to how it affects his usual duties!"

But Matthew was in no doubt. Everything was arranged in its normal
lace; except my miniature of Anne, which remained in my saddle bag.

"It's good to see you again, Matthew," I said, "And how are you?"

"All the better for seeing your honour well—and happy with her
dyship." He hesitated. "Your honour, I never saw you go down. I
as—"

"Leave it," I said. "There was nothing anyone could have done. It's all
ast and finished with and I'm alive."

He shook his head. "I failed your honour—and I did at Camden too. I'll
ot do that again." And I knew he meant it. There are few friends like
Matthew.

"How did the fight end, Matthew?"

"Well, the 17th held together, your honour, and we punished them
ragoons enough to make them hold away. So then we got off and
e-formed at the wagons." He looked down at his boots. "They all said that
ou was dead—and that there was naught I could do—"

"And they were right; there wasn't. And what did you do then?"

"I stayed with the 17th and, bigod, for the next two months, sure it was
s hard soldiering as ever I did. I've rid over every inch of North Carolina,
our honour, and you can have it all. It's all pines and mud—black pines
nd red mud. We fought and we marched and we fought. We beat old
Greene at a place called Guilford and a bloody battle that was. We spent
ll night in the worst rain I remember a-collecting all his guns and his
agons and all his wounded too—though some of the poor sods was
rowned in the mud afore we could get to 'em. Then off we marched
gain, all the way down to Wilmington, on the Cape Fear River, near the
oast. And we lost many good men on the way, of the wounds they got at
he Guilford battle."

"Why Wilmington?—why not Camden?"

"I wouldn't be knowing that, your honour. But we was reinforced and
eplenished from Charlestown there and, bigod, we needed it. Most of the
nfantry were barefoot by then, and in the cavalry we was all in rags and
he horses done. We'd been there but a few days when his lordship had
he letter from Colonel Washington to say you had been taken to Belhaven
nd might be alive. He'd written so back in February, but it seems the
ourier he sent had been killed by some militia and he didn't hear this until
fter the Guilford battle. So this time he sends and officer of his with an
scort into our rear party, under a flag, to make sure we got the letter."

"What did his lordship say?"

"Well, he sent for Major Fairleigh and me straight away. He tells u<
what's in the letter and says Major Fairleigh's to away and find recruit
from around these parts because we needed them if we was going t<
Virginia. And he says to bring you back if you was alive and wel
enough—"

"The army is going to Virginia?"

"That's the talk, your honour. Colonel Tarleton there, he don't think <
should. He's in a proper bad way, the Colonel. Lost most of his right han<
from a rifle ball at Guilford—just at the start. But he wouldn't not fight
though he'd no hand to fight with at all. He leads us all, the 17th an<
Legion, all through the battle—all the day—and all he could do was t<
ride his horse. He's the brave one—but he's no easy man to serve!"

"Have you heard from home, Matthew?"

"Devil a word, your honour. Major England in the headquarters say
there was letters for you earlier. But they thought you was dead and sen<
'em home again, with a letter from his lordship to madam. He was goin<
to write again directly he had Colonel Washington's letters, but then h<
thought better not. Not until he was sure you was alive."

I had written to Anne as soon as I was able; and told Lucy I had don<
so. I had addressed it to Francis Rawdon in Camden and sent it by hand o<
a loyalist farmer going to do business there; but there was no means o<
ensuring that he would be able to deliver it, and he had not returned befor<
I left Belhaven.

I said, "Unpack my wife's picture, Matthew."

He looked at me and nodded, smiling. "I'll do that."

That night, as Lucy and I lay together, I told her I must return to th<
army. Her arms crept round my neck and she held close to me. "Phili<
darling, you're not well yet. Dr. Weekes says—"

"If I wait for Dr. Weekes' permission I'll never go. He's too keen t<
please you."

"But haven't you done enough? You've been badly wounded. For al
they cared you might have died."

"They cared, my love, but there wasn't much Charles Cornwallis coul<
have done, not knowing where I was, or even if I was alive."

"But can you go back? Aren't you—what do you call it?—you give you<
promise not to fight again—"

"Paroled. No, they didn't bother to parole me. They were so sure <
would die. No," I kissed her softly. "I must go back with James. He leave<
the day after tomorrow."

She lay still and silent for a while. Then, from the curve of my shoulder a small voice said, "You'll come back, Philip—to see our child—"

I had expected this. I had hoped for it; for, surely, any man rejoices to have a child by the woman he truly loves—and I rejoiced. Now I lay silent, savouring my own joy. My silence alarmed her. Her head came up. "You're not angry, are you?"

I slid my hand down her body. "My sweet, how could I be angry when your body holds all our happiness here? I'll come back." I kissed her again. "Please God I'll be here when the child is born." She was happy then, and later, after our love-making, lay close and still in my arms. And, in her sleep, she smiled.

I left Belhaven on the morning of Thursday the 10th May. The whole settlement came to see us go—James and his soldiers and recruits, and Matthew and Andrew and I. Andrew had begged to be allowed to accompany me, so James had accepted him as a recruit, equipped him and attached him to me. From the start the lad got on famously with Matthew, who was at great pains to teach him the use of sword, carbine and pistol. Being a natural horseman and horsemaster and an excellent shot, Andrew learned quickly; and so thoroughly did he master his swordplay that, as often as not, he could discomfit both Matthew and me in our training bouts.

Before I left Belhaven, Lord Fairleigh called Lucy and myself into his study. We stood before him and he took my hand and put in it a plain gold ring. "It was my mother's wedding ring. She left it to my Katharine, who wanted it used for Lucy's marriage."

I put the ring on Lucy's third finger. It fitted exactly. I kissed her hand, the ring and her lips.

Fairleigh said, "Farewell, my dear son. Haste ye home." And I rode away again to the war.

I was poor company for James for I scarce said a word, my mind always too full of thoughts of Lucy. But he was very understanding, giving me time to awake from my dreams.

We rode straight for Virginia, by way of Salisbury and Hillsborough, meeting no offence at any place. Cornwallis had marched from Wilmington on the Cape Fear River to Virginia with his whole army—about three thousand—setting out on the 17th April. The army had been strengthened by General Leslie's reinforcement; though Leslie being incapacitated by illness, his place as second-in-command to Cornwallis was now held by Brig.-Gen. Charles O'Hara.

James and I arrived at Petersburg, on the Appomatox River, on Monday the 22nd May. The army was encamped here and, back among its familiar sights and sounds, I came alive again to events. On its arrival at Petersburg the army had been further reinforced by the raiding party which had been operating in Virginia since January, commanded by Brig.-Gen. Benedict Arnold, one of the best of the rebel generals, who had defected from the rebel cause: and by another force of two thousand men, which had arrived in Virginia in early April under the command of Maj.-Gen. William Phillips, who died of a fever ten days before I arrived at Petersburg.

Cornwallis greeted me as you would expect—genuinely and without superlatives. "Thank God you're safe and well, Philip. You are well, aren't you?—you know, I've lost too many good friends in this damned war. Well, lad, you'll have a good deal to do now. John Simcoe has joined us from Arnold's force with his Queen's Rangers; they're a legion, like the British Legion, but largely cavalry. Then James Fairleigh's corps is well recruited now, and, of course, Tarleton's much the same as ever. So there's your brigade of cavalry at last—see you keep them busy! Charles O'Hara is delighted that you are here—he's looking for you. By the way don't mention his son—the one in the artillery—the poor lad was killed at a fight we had at Guilford two months ago. Charles doesn't show it—well you know him—but he hasn't got over it properly yet."

Charles O'Hara enveloped me in a great bear hug. "Philip, my old chum, they told me you'd been put to bed with a shovel! What's resurrection feel like? God bless you—I told 'em it would take more than a rabble of lousy rebels to do for old Cato!"

Charles O'Hara is a very old friend. He had always epitomised for me the best sort of guardsman; large in every way except in girth, of great courage, humour, kindliness and regard for his soldiers—and always utterly imperturbable. When I first met him he was a 3rd Dragoon, but there were few horses big enough to carry Charles and all a dragoon officer's impedimenta at seventeen, and as he went on growing they got fewer still and the more expensive. So he transferred to the Coldstream Guards, which was his father's Regiment.

There is a story that, at the assault across the Catawba River during Cornwallis' pursuit of General Greene, Charles O'Hara's horse was knocked over by the force of the current. At the time, he was characteristically, leading his guardsmen in the attack by several lengths. He and his horse rolled over and over down stream for some way in a fond embrace before Charles found his own feet; and then, his guardsmen swear, to the acclaim of both sides, he picked up his horse, set it on its feet, clambered aboard again and the attack continued and succeeded—how could it fail?

He took my arm. "Come and meet our newest recruit—you'll never meet an odder one. There he is, talking to Prudence—"

The man talking to Richard England was a thick-set, broad-shouldered fellow, sallow-faced, with a big beak of a nose and a jaw like a ship's prow. He wore no wig but had his hair tied back in a club; its jet blackness gave him a hard, humourless look. His eyes were the coldest I have seen in any man, very steady, very confident—critical, impatient, imperious. And he had the voice to go with the eyes, strong and harsh; a voice for giving orders and a voice to be obeyed. His name was Maj.-Gen. Benedict Arnold.

A strange man. I knew him for just four days, and all his conversation during that time was of power or money—or both. He spoke brilliantly, wittily, cynically. He would never admit the character or opinion of any other man to be estimable, or his own to be anything less. His concern was only within the compass of his own interests. He is a most competent, determined and courageous man. But a man I would not trust and could never esteem as a friend.

He left the army on the Friday following to return to New York and thence to London. On the evening of the Thursday we dined together—Cornwallis, O'Hara, Arnold and I—in Westover, a house belonging to a Mrs. William Byrd; a magnificent house in a beautiful situation.

The army had been ferrying across the James River from Mr. Mead's plantation on the south bank to the landing below Westover. I had been all day ordering the swimming of the horses of the cavalry. We lost no horses, though it's a long swim, but many of us, including myself, had to swim a little to achieve this. Arnold, with typical efficiency, had foreseen the need well beforehand and had prepared some excellent boats. These had served the rest of the army well and everyone had enjoyed a pleasant day's boating; except the cavalry. I was very tired and a touch irritable.

Arnold had been holding forth on the incompetence of the British commanders in the earlier stages of the war; criticizing Howe for failing to destroy the rebel army—and so, the whole rebellion—when, Arnold claimed, he could easily have done so; and Burgoyne, for his over-ambitious plan which ended in the disaster of Saratoga. He, of course, would never have been so—respectively—dilatory or misguided. Perhaps not.

Cornwallis sat listening patiently. Charles O'Hara was dozing off,

bored and full of wine. He had taken his fair measure of it at dinner and so
had I. He said he was making up for time lost in the Carolina wilderness; I
was homesick for Belhaven. Arnold was at full rant on the importance of
the part he had played at Saratoga. Hardly tactful. I cut him short.

"Why were you a rebel, General?"

The silence which followed was so deafening it even woke O'Hara—
screwing up his eyes and snuffling. Cornwallis stared at me wide-eyed in
embarrassment, and Arnold—well, in my fuddled state, I thought he
looked amazingly like a frightened, angry cat, glaring at me with those
cold eyes, yellow in the candlelight. He really had his ears back. Then he
suddenly relaxed and, leaning his chin on his hand, stared at me intently
across the table. He attacked at once, and hard. He was going to give at
least as good as he got.

"Because, Colonel Cato, at that time His Majesty's government cared
for nothing but what it could wring out of these colonies. It never gave a
thought to the colonists' real needs, nor their aspirations—it never
expected them to have any! A blind, pig-witted looby of a government!"

"Ay, we have a good few of those. And what made you change your
mind?"

"Because successive governments—having learned a little—have made
reasonable proposals which we could with honour, and profit, accept.
Because our army is made up in the main of fumbling, undisciplined
cowards, officered by place-seeking incompetents, who are ruled in all
they do—at every point—by the unprincipled, ignorant, illiterate,
covetous peddlers of windy, idealistic rubbish who now sit in Congress."
He smiled sourly. "I quote General Washington's opinion exactly, and I
have a great regard for his opinions."

"And why do you hold him in regard?"

"Because he is a gentleman—a very rare property in the rebel
community; and a man of honour—even rarer. He is one of the few rebels
who seek nothing for themselves in this squalid dispute. The rest cannot
understand this and so don't trust him."

O'Hara squinted owlishly at Arnold. "And does he hold you in high
regard, sir?"

Arnold's ears went back again, and who can blame him in the
circumstances, but he answered steadily and quietly. "He did."

O'Hara nodded portentously. "He did? And did no one share his regard
for you?"

"Few."

"Ah-ha, I see. Few. And pray, sir, could this be the reason why—the reason you are here?"

"Not 'could be,' sir. It is. One of the reasons. The others I have already given—except one."

"Except one? And can you give that one too, sir?"

"Certainly. I detest and mistrust the French."

O'Hara snorted. " 'Ecod! Who doesn't? But they're your allies—h'm, beg pardon—they're in alliance with the rebels. They can't afford to distrust and mistest 'em. Does Washington dis-mistrust 'em?"

"Yes."

"Does he now? And does he detest 'em too?"

"How should he not? You will recall he has fought them, and suffered at their hands, more than any of you."

O'Hara was taken aback. "H'm, never thought of it like that. Yes—that's true. Have you ever fought the French?"

"Yes. But in no way as often or as desperately as Washington—or Morgan and some others."

"Do they all hate the French?"

"Yes, all. Morgan can't stand the sight or smell of them. And he stinks like skunk most of the time himself!"

O'Hara hiccuped with laughter. " 'Egad—what a happy alliance you'll all have—oh, beg pardon—"

"It's been a disastrous one so far," said Arnold bitterly.

There was a silence. Cornwallis, leaning back in his chair, slowly traced with his fingertip a design in some spilt wine. He said quietly, "But surely, General, Washington must have a great deal of business to do with the French commanders?"

"Indeed, my lord, he does. But he has a more equable temper than I—No—" he rubbed his face with both hands for a moment, "No—that's not enough." He looked straight at Cornwallis. "He's a far greater man than any of us—" then, with a slight smile, "I mean, my lord, than any rebel—or past rebel."

Cornwallis smiled too. "And tell me, General, upon whom else in your opinion does this rebellion depend other than Washington?"

"Upon a few, my lord, a very few. But upon no one as much as he. He is the one crutch upon which the whole unhappy affair hobbles. And were he to break—" He shrugged.

Half asleep again, O'Hara mumbled, "H'mph—pity Patrick Ferguson didn't shoot him when he had the chance—saved us all a lot o' trouble."

[*223*]

Even Arnold laughed at that. He got to his feet and asked to be excused since he was to leave early on the morrow. Cornwallis and I rose, and O'Hara heaved himself up, clearing his throat and pulling his jacket straight. Cornwallis bowed.

"General, I fear we have kept you late and catechised you hard. Pray, forgive us and accept our thanks for your patience and courtesy. I hope I shall have the pleasure of seeing you before you depart tomorrow?"

Arnold smiled at Cornwallis, but not at O'Hara or me. "My lord, I'll report to you before I leave. I've much enjoyed our conversation. Goodnight, my lord—gentlemen." He bowed and left us.

O'Hara and I mumbled and bowed—and sat down again. Somehow the air seemed lighter. Cornwallis stared down at us disapprovingly.

"You ought to be ashamed of yourselves—you two!"

We both gaped at him and he burst out laughing.

"You were both very rude. You've both had too much to drink." He glowered, grinning, at O'Hara. "Oh, for God's sake, Charles, get your stock from behind your ear and tuck your shirt in! You are the most congenitally dishevelled officer I've ever known! How in heaven the Coldstream ever accepted you I'll never know!"

O'Hara grinned back and belched from his boot heels. He loves to be teased in this way.

Cornwallis dropped back into his chair. He looked across at where Arnold had been sitting and was silent for a moment. Then he said,

"But you know—that man—extraordinary. Washington admired him enormously and trusted him implicitly. It near broke his heart when he learned that Arnold had betrayed him. He wants to destroy him now—desperately. He knows better than anyone what Arnold could do—if Germain and Pussy will let him. He was probably their best general. Washington and Greene are sound—but Arnold is bold and brilliant and ruthless; he'd run rings round any of them—if we let him. Washington wanted him to command an army, but Congress was too frightened of him—he's too sharp for their liking; he's not a man of honour, as he described Washington, and they can't use and dupe him and still depend on his loyalty the way they do with Washington. D'you mind he said Washington was the one crutch on which this rebellion could hobble? Well, he could have been the other, if they'd let him. Thank God they didn't. With two crutches like those—working together—this rebellion would have moved a damned sight quicker than a hobble!"

Chapter Fifteen

*In which I travel through Virginia in good company
and the Marquis de Lafayette, becoming for once
unusually bold, is discomfited.*

A council of war met in the drawing-room at Westover on Friday the
25th May, the day after Arnold left us, to discuss Cornwallis' plans for
the future actions of the army. Cornwallis sat at a little sofa table with
Maj. Alexander Ross, his senior aide, sitting beside him taking notes of
our discussion. Cornwallis spoke quietly, his head in his hands, looking
down at some papers lying in front of him.

"Gentlemen, as some of you are aware, a month ago I wrote to the
Commander-in-Chief and Lord Germain recommending that this year, as
our prime aim, we should concentrate our chief force and our greatest
effort in this colony and so isolate the rebels in the southern colonies from
all source of support. Of course, I have as yet received no reply to either
letter.

"Until I do have some acknowledgment of my recommendation I must
discharge the orders given by the Commander-in-Chief to Generals
Arnold and Phillips. These orders conform to General Clinton's strategy
of conflagration. That is to say, he proposes we should establish at some
place within the Chesapeake a defensive post which can serve as a base,
both for our naval operations and from which we can conduct harassing
raids into the interior of the colony."

He stopped and looked up at us, then said slowly and deliberately, "I
believe this policy of conflagration, which involves dispersion of our
strength into indefensible bases and relies entirely for the security of those
bases upon command of the coastal waters of this continent, is at all points
contrary to sound strategic principles and can only result in our forces

being beat in detail. And I have said as much in this letter I have written to the Commander-in-Chief protesting his orders—" he held up a paper, "which, in the meantime, will, in course, be obeyed. General Arnold departed yesterday to New York bearing my letter on this matter to General Clinton."

He picked up another paper. "I have dispatched General Leslie to take command at Portsmouth and to prepare and fortify it for use as a base for naval operations. I have my doubts on its suitability as a base for anything, though it is the one which Sir Henry Clinton himself selected. Lieutenant-Colonel von Fuchs, who commands there now, reports that the works are but slender and the sandy soil too unsubstantial material for defensive works; apart from that, the place is a fever haven. I have written to the Commander-in-Chief to that effect.

"I have also said that I propose to dislodge the Marquis de Lafayette from Richmond and destroy all magazines and stores in that town. After that we will withdraw to Williamsburg; by which time I shall hope to have his reply to my suggestions for our plan of operations."

He asked for comments on what he had said, but the council being in agreement with him, he picked up a letter,

"Here is Lord Rawdon's report on his defeat of General Greene at Hobkirk's Hill. He says he had to use men still sick or with unhealed wounds in hospital to make up his strength to even half that of the enemy. Any man who could move with a little aid moved himself to the battle, he says—and these were his provincial and militia soldiers—and all volunteered to do so." He looked up at us, smiling. "Brave men, brave men! It was one of His Majesty's ministers—Sandwich, I believe—who claimed that the American colonists were raw, undisciplined, cowardly men. God knows, we've been shown enough spirit and courage by our own provincial and militia corps—and by the rebels too—to make that idiot eat his words! Well, that's all I have for your information, gentlemen. Does anyone wish to say anything?"

"My lord," I volunteered, "on Tuesday you ordered that the cavalry should investigate an assembly of four hundred rebel militia reported to be at Warwick Courthouse. Colonel Tarleton took a patrol of dragoons for the purpose and routed them, taking around fifty prisoners. These say that the Marquis de Lafayette has a force of one thousand Continental troops between Richmond and Wiltown, awaiting the arrival of General Wayne and the Pennsylvania Line regiments and some local militia."

On the strength of this information, and other to the effect that the approach of General Wayne with his brigade of the Pennsylvania Line was delayed by yet another mutiny in those regiments, Cornwallis decided to march north with all speed to prevent their junction with de Lafayette's force; and, if possible, to destroy each in turn. But though we moved fast, de Lafayette ran faster; and Cornwallis gave up the chase when we arrived at Hanover Courthouse on the North Anna River on Friday the 1st June.

I had sent Tarleton ahead to search for the rebel army, ordering him not to become involved in any action beyond a skirmish. He rode around Lafayette at will and came back to meet us at Hanover Courthouse with some prisoners and letters taken from one of the Marquis' couriers. One of these letters was directed to Mr. Thomas Jefferson, the rebel governor of Virginia, and another to General Steuben, who commanded the rebel arsenal and garrison at Point of Fork on the James River.

It was clear from their contents that the rebel General Assembly of Virginia, whom we had chased from its proper seat at the capital of Richmond, was at that moment in session at the small town of Charlottesville; and also that General Steuben had collected a great quantity of military stores at the arsenal of Point of Fork, which were intended for the support of General Greene in South Carolina. Both Charlottesville and Point of Fork were about fifty miles from Hanover; and Cornwallis was delighted with the news.

"Even Pussy would approve of these as fitting targets for one of his conflagrating raids! Jefferson's house at Monticello is only a few miles outside Charlottesville—to bag a governor would make good reading in our despatches; though, from what I hear, we'd do no great harm to the rebel cause in Virginia by bagging theirs. The stores at Point of Fork are more important. It would be best for both raids to be done together."

"I'll have to use both the Legion and the Queen's Rangers then," I said. "Fairleigh's North Carolina troop stands at around a hundred and sixty now. They can provide a reserve here and they'll give a good account of themselves in any action."

"Yes, I think you should send both Simcoe and Tarleton. Who goes to which?"

"Simcoe with the Queen's Rangers will go to Point of Fork to roust out the Prussian drill-master, Tarleton and the Legion to Charlottesville to bag the Monticello fox. And a good detachment of mounted infantry to go with both, if you agree?"

"Certainly. That's a very fitting appreciation of the relative importance of the missions." He grinned quizzically, "and you'll leave me here with a mere handful of militia dragoons to fend off the dreaded Marquis?"

[*227*]

"Well, yes. Tarleton needs some supervision—we don't want the whole rebel Assembly and Jefferson hanged, I suppose? And I'd like to watch Simcoe work; I've not served with him before. Fairleigh's troops are sound enough."

"Enough of excuses!" Cornwallis laughed. "Of course you should go. But—don't get caught, Philip," he was suddenly serious, "and don't get hurt again. I need all my cavalrymen."

I sent at once for Simcoe and Tarleton, and for Captain Champagné, commanding the 23rd Regiment, and Captain Hutchinson who commanded the 2nd battalion of the 71st Highlanders.

Fortunately Hutchinson was the first to arrive at my tent. I had intended that the 71st should accompany Tarleton to Charlottesville, but the bitter resentment of the Highlanders at what they claimed to be Tarleton's betrayal of their 1st Battalion at Cowpens had not faded. Hutchinson begged for his battalion to be excused the duty and volunteered to accompany Simcoe instead. So I left it like that and, when the rest arrived, ordered Champagné and the 23rd to march with Tarleton.

Both parties left before dawn the following morning—Sunday the 3rd June. With Tarleton rode the Legion and the 17th Light Dragoons, and, mounted on captured horses, seventy rank and file of the 23rd, amongst whom I noted my old acquaintance from Charlestown, Sergeant Lamb; about two hundred and fifty in all. Simcoe with the Queen's Rangers, the 2nd battalion of the 71st and one 3-pounder grasshopper cannon, had around four hundred.

I had kept with me Charles Russell, who acted as my aide, and an escort of dragoons of the 17th, commanded by Sergeant Mills. I rode with Tarleton, since he would be the first to strike, and, being closest to the rebel army, was in the greater danger of being brought to action by a superior force.

We moved fast through unfrequented ways. The weather was now very hot and we stopped at midday for two hours to rest and feed, for which I was grateful. The hole in my lung I had acquired at Cowpens still made itself felt when I exerted myself immoderately in the stifling, humid heat.

We pushed on, not halting until eleven o'clock that night at the plantation of a loyalist gentleman at Louisa. Loyalists abounded in Virginia, so we were generally well provided with information, reliable guides and good hospitality.

I shall always count myself fortunate to have visited Virginia. There is something in the character and temper of that dominion which encourages an ease of manner, a generous hospitality, a perceptive appreciation of the essentials for the enjoyment of life and a genial dismissal of the trivialities. In short, a very civilized society at all its levels, which conducts its affairs with the leisured and philosophic calm I find in my own county of Somerset; where things are done—or not done—at much the same pace.

We rode on again at two o'clock the following morning, guided by a small party of Loyalist gentlemen. Our route joined with the great road which, skirting the Blue Ridge Mountains, was the chief line of supply for the rebel armies in the south. As we approached this junction in the still, grey twilight before the dawn, our scouts reported a column of military wagons approaching from the north along the great road.

Closing to the junction, Tarleton dismounted the infantry and placed them in ambuscade along the sides of the road. Then he and Russell and I advanced, under cover of the roadside trees, towards the head of the convoy. The long column of lanterns on the wagons came slowly nearer and nearer. As they approached, we made out the figures of five men riding a few paces in front of the first wagon.

"No scouts and no point," whispered Tarleton, "and that guard too close to the wagons to serve any useful purpose. Must be militia. Two men on the buckboard of the leading wagon—and on them all, I'd think. Can't see any more guards down the line."

"Probably be in the middle of the column and at the back," I murmured. "I count twelve sets of lights—twelve wagons—"

"They're asleep," whispered Russell. "Look—all of 'em—fast asleep." And so it seemed. The guards, heads bent, chins sunk into their collars, rocked inertly with the movement of their horses, plodding along at the pace of the oxen teams which drew the wagons. The two men on each buckboard were huddled at either end of it under the hood. Not a sound save the shuffle and thump of hooves and the steady rumble of the wheels. The whole convoy drowsed, secure in the knowledge that the royal army lay forty miles to the east.

"Say twenty guards and two men on each wagon—forty-four in all," I said. "Banastre, you and I and a few others can take the front guard, McLeod anything in the middle, and Charles Russell the rear party. As each guard passes we'll each ride down, quietly and slowly, and fall in just behind them. Until Charles rides down himself behind the rear guard, he can send pairs of dragoons to deal with the crews of each wagon as they pass. No hurry and no noise; though I doubt they'll suspect that we're not members of the guard. No swords, only pistols—and no firing unless they resist; otherwise an alarm might get to Charlottesville. Charles, take a trumpeter with you and when you're in position behind the rear guard, have him sound the halt. Then we close to our guards and everyone covers his man all down the line. Understood? Then let's all play Dick Turpin!"

We rode back to the ambuscade. I gave the orders, and the whole thing went as painlessly as I had hoped. Only one of the rearguard, less dozy than his mates, peered at these phantom troopers who suddenly materialized behind him with some doubt. His doubts were confirmed on squinting into the muzzle of Russell's pistol, but fortunately for us—and for him—he appreciated at once the folly of any attempt to warn his drowsier companions.

Up in front—and by now the slow plod had near sent us to sleep as well—we heard the trumpet. Each of us rode alongside a member of the guard and made our pistols apparent to their bleary gaze. I found myself addressing the officer commanding the convoy. He stared at me vacantly, half asleep, "What d'you wan'—wha' th'devil—?"

"I'm an officer of His Majesty's Army," I said cheerfully. "And I'll be obliged if you will halt this convoy at once." He still gaped at me, so I added, "Or I'll blow a hole through your thick skull." Which persuaded him.

There were twelve large wagons, loaded with arms, powder and uniform clothing. We took what we needed. Then we ran the wagons together and set the lot ablaze. We loosed and drove off the oxen and took the horses of the guard. From the guard we took their boots, breeches and weapons and flung all these into the fire. Then we marched the poor fellows, fast, for a mile on our road to Charlottesville, apologized for the inconvenience we had caused them, thanked them for their company on the march, and left them to their own devices. Some of them thanked us for not shooting or hanging them. I was glad we had no cause to harm them.

We rode on at a fair pace and, shortly after dawn, six miles from Charlottesville, Tarleton decided, on the advice of our guides, to split the force into two. He rode with one column to a house named Castle Hills, the home of a Dr. Thomas Walker, where he took prisoner from their beds some of the most prominent rebels in Virginia.

I rode with the other column, commanded by Capt. David Kinloch, to a house named Belvoir, the home of Dr. Walker's brother John. Here, too, all were a-bed. We turned them all out in their nightshirts. One attempted to slip away into the garden. David Kinloch shouted, "Bigod, it's my cousin Francis!" and gave chase, bellowing to the fugitive to stay to breakfast. Congressman Francis Kinloch, becoming quickly persuaded that early morning exercise in a nightshirt was uncomfortably chilly and hard on the bare feet, accepted the invitation. I've yet to meet a politician possessed of any stamina.

We rode on to Charlottesville and, at a little distance still from the town, Tarleton ordered Capt. Kenneth McLeod to take a party to Governor Jefferson's house, Monticello, standing on a hill overlooking the valley along which we approached the town. I rode with this party, firstly, because I wished to ensure that, should we succeed in taking Mr. Jefferson, both he and his family were treated with respect and courtesy, and that neither his people nor his property suffered abuse. And, secondly, because I was eager to make the acquaintance of a gentleman who, despite the poor opinion his fellow Virginians held of his abilities as their senior executive at that time, is, by all reports, a charming, cultured and modest person and an accomplished horseman; a true Virginian.

But alas, we drew the Monticello covert blank, the fox was not at home. Nor was Mrs. Martha Jefferson, whose carriage it was, I suppose, which, possibly by accident, blocked the road and delayed our approach to the house. We searched the house and surrounds, but we found nothing of interest save a few state papers. This done, we cantered on into Charlottesville.

David Kinloch went to report our failure to Tarleton, whilst I rode round the town, a pleasant, small place, little more than a large village; with, perhaps, a dozen houses of size and quality, a score or more of the meaner sort, an inn and a courthouse, where the Virginia Assembly had been daily in session until our arrival.

Tarleton stood in the shade of an oak tree by the main road through the town. "Welcome, Colonel." He waved the half-eaten leg of a chicken at me. "Sorry to hear you were disappointed at Monticello. But according to these gentlemen—" he waved the leg at some Continental and militia officers captured in the town, "the distinguished owner of that property would be small loss to them. Come and have some breakfast."

"Where are all the members of the Assembly?" I asked.

"A lot of 'em flown the coop, damn it! Apparently they were warned by a militia officer who spied us back in Louisa and guessed what we were about. But we've got a few of 'em under guard in the courthouse."

We spent the whole day searching the town and the surrounding houses for rebels and stores. We discovered quantities of arms, powder and uniforms; as well as a party of escaped prisoners, our own soldiers, members of Burgoyne's army, taken at Saratoga, who shouted for joy at the sight of the red coats of the 23rd.

[*231*]

We rode south out of Charlottesville towards Point of Fork, and on the road I spoke with both the captured Congressmen and members of the Virginia Assembly. All had expected to be maltreated, even to be hanged on the spot as traitors—I was interested to hear them describe themselves as such; and all being immensely relieved and grateful to be treated with courtesy were the readier to talk remarkably freely. They bemoaned the state of the rebel cause and, as all politicians do, blamed their ills on everybody but themselves, and chiefly on the stinginess and greediness of their colleagues in the northern colonies. They foretold disaster and defeat unless the French—whom one and all distrusted—could be persuaded to act more effectively. For, if the French failed them yet again, so they all assured me, Virginia would be content to forsake the alliance and enter into honourable treaty with Britain. "And where Virginia leads," they asserted, "the rest will in due course follow."

"And what will your leaders say to such an end to their labours?" I asked.

"Oh, sir, every cobbler will return to his own last," replied one cheerfully. "Jefferson will retire into his books—he's the visionary and the idealist; Washington will go to his estates and hunt his hounds—he's the farmer and the practical man; and Henry will make an impassioned speech on the text of all's well that ends well and look for his next brief—he's the lawyer and the realist!"

This frankness took me a little aback. I remarked—tactfully, I thought, "Sad we can't enjoy the learned Governor Jefferson's company." Out of the frying pan into the fire.

"Learned Governor Jefferson be damned!" They all hooted with one voice. "He's no longer Governor, thank God! His term expired two days ago, and for all he did during it he might as well have served on Lord Cornwallis' staff. We're proposing an inquiry into his conduct of affairs. So if you don't hang him—we may!" And they all laughed merrily.

It seemed these self-styled statesmen possessed all the powerful intellect, breadth of vision and stubborn loyalties characteristic of our own native breed of politician.

I left Tarleton at mid-afternoon to continue his way to the main body of the army, and rose to find the other raiding party—John Simcoe and the Queen's Rangers and the 71st. I came upon them early that evening on the north bank of the Fluvanna River, opposite the arsenal of Point of Fork. Simcoe was directing the laying of his one 3-pounder gun. "Welcome, Colonel, you're just in time to see the fun. Fire now!"

The little gun leaped and roared and the shot whipped through the trees on the far bank.

"That'll wake 'em up! They've been too quiet for too long."

"How are you deployed?" I asked, somewhat puzzled, for I had seen no formed body of troops.

"I'm deployed to make a hell of a noise and every man seems five. The 71st are marching down to the river by platoons, then creeping back up the draws and marching down again. Every man's going to light three separate camp fires in an hour's time. The baggage wagons are driving round in circles, making dust. A couple of local friends will tell Steuben he's got the whole of our army across here, ravening for his Prussian guts. And this old grasshopper will spit into his evening beer a few more times."

"D'you think he'll run?"

"I want him to run so fast that he won't think of opposing my crossing or have time to take anything with him. And I want him to run so far that he won't think of coming back to stop me destroying everything I find in the arsenal, or of creeping back to attack my rear-party when I withdraw to their bank again."

The difference between the characters of my two senior cavalry commanders was, at once, very clear. Tarleton would have done it all with sabres, swimming the river at night, and suffered casualties we could not afford. Simcoe did it all with bluff and a few rounds from the grasshopper; and Steuben, though stronger than him, fled with his whole command without firing a shot, deserting everything for which he was responsible.

Simcoe ferried all the stores, guns and other equipment he was able to transport across the Fluvanna River and destroyed the rest of the arsenal. Steuben made no attempt to attack him or harass the ferrying, and neither the Queen's Rangers nor the 71st had a man hurt.

By the 7th June both my raiding parties had re-joined the army at Elk Hill, four miles from Point of Fork. Here news came that Gen. Anthony Wayne had subdued his last mutiny with his customary thoroughness, by shooting seven of the leading mutineers, and joined with Lafayette at Racoon Ford on the Rapidan River.

"Good," said Cornwallis. "We've played at touch all the way across Virginia and got very little for our pains. Now we'll play grandmother's steps all the way back. And as he's got Mad Anthony with him now to bolster his courage, perhaps the Marquis will be a little bolder at this game."

[*233*]

But, regrettably, Lafayette showed boldness only in the claims he made in every despatch which fell into our hands, of chasing the fleeing enemy from Virginia. His chasing was most restrained. He was very careful—and rightly so in his circumstances—never to come up with our rearguards except with his light troops, though we offered him every inducement to do so.

We marched from Elk Hill on Friday the 15th June on our way back to Richmond and Williamsburg. Cornwallis had received no reply from Clinton on his proposals for aggressive operations in Virginia, and since Lafayette refused to come to battle, he was left with no alternative but to follow Clinton's original orders and establish the base at Portsmouth, raiding from there into the interior of Virginia; as ineffective and uneconomic a use of our army as the rebels could wish.

On the evening of Friday the 22nd June after having fled headlong—Lafayette's words—from Elk Hill for seven days, with a three-day wait in Richmond to allow the galloping Marquis to catch up, we lay at two days from Williamsburg. Early on the Saturday morning, Simcoe, who was doing rearguard, reported that Lafayette's main force was closed to within twelve miles from us, apparently believing us closer to Williamsburg. We were preparing to mount and move on.

"Let me take Fairleigh and some light infantry," I said, "I'll draw their main body on to you. You could move through us against it and Tarleton and I could get round their flank. Simcoe's already there as a reserve."

Charles O'Hara slapped his thigh and clambered on to his horse. "Ay, that's the way of it! What are we waiting for?"

"He's a cunning little fellow that Marquis," said Cornwallis, "I don't underestimate him."

"Och, the timorous, little twiddle-poop!" O'Hara's accent gets broader as he becomes excited. "He's hung his poxy frog arse all across Virginia and back—only got it this far for Wayne's kicking it!—"

Cornwallis nodded at Maj. Alexander Ross. "Have the march delayed for an hour, Ross." He grinned at O'Hara. "Get off that horse, Charles. You're not going anywhere for a while. We'll wait and see if the Marquis wants to dance."

But he didn't. And we marched on to Williamsburg with Charles O'Hara in a great sulk and cursing all the way.

The next morning, around dawn, I was riding with Tarleton to reconnoitre the best crossing for the army over the James River at Burrels Ferry. One of Cornwallis' aides came thundering down the road to us. "Colonel—Lord Cornwallis' compliments—you're to return with the

Legion—rebels attacked Colonel Simcoe in bivouac this morning—he's driven 'em off—but there's a larger body drawing up to him—lordship's marching with the main army to Colonel Simcoe—wants you to move fast round his left to catch the enemy in flank. He's keeping the 17th with him—Major Fairleigh's troop will meet you on the way—"

We went like the wind. But it was all over. Simcoe looked very pleased with himself and his Rangers. "Came in on us just before dawn, Colonel. My picket gave the alarm, but they were on us damnably quick. Dragoons—and they got in amongst us, but after the yagers had knocked a few from their horses they went off. They attacked again, with some infantry, but my infantry held them in front whilst I went into their flank with my hussars. They didn't like that and left!"

"Well done—pity Tarleton wasn't here to help."

"Oh ay, together we'd have cracked them like a rotten nut."

Cornwallis was as pleased as Simcoe with the outcome of the skirmish, but for another reason.

"It looks as if this attack was really intended, but if it was it wasn't very cleverly done—all too hurried. Those dragoons—charging in all unsupported—got what they asked for. But their infantry came on well—late, of course, and they weren't used boldly enough; they should have overwhelmed Simcoe. But, at last, they did try to attack and must have moved fast to do so—that's what disorganized them, I expect. The spirit's there! I see the hand of Wayne in this sudden aggressiveness."

There was a mutter behind us. "I see his boot in the backside of that lackadaisical frog-eater!" O'Hara was still in a sulk.

As we rode back to Williamsburg, Cornwallis scanned through some letters delivered by courier that morning. He sighed and shook his head. "God save us!—Pussy's been at his sums again. He reckons that we have eight thousand regulars against the Marquis's two thousand Continentals and a paltry rabble of ill-armed peasantry. Pussy alone knows where he gets his figures from—I'm damned sure God doesn't! Anyway he says he has only—note that only!—eleven thousand effectives in New York against the rebels' twenty thousand—unbelievable!—besides the expected French reinforcement and the militias of five colonies, and he fears a siege. Well, I hope nobody tells Washington that he commands twenty thousand men or he'll start getting inflated ideas! 'Fore God, I wish it was that crafty old pock-face commanding us in New York—I honestly wish it! He doesn't suffer from Pussy's hallucinations and vapours! He'd be sending me reinforcements, not grabbing back my soldiers like some old washerwoman snatching her drawers off the line before the rain."

"Where does Pussy get that expression 'paltry rabble of ill-armed peasantry' from?" I asked.

"Oh, that's how the noble, egalitarian Marquis de Lafayette describes his militia in his official despatches. They'd be interested to know that he thinks so highly of them, wouldn't they? Anyway, Pussy wants three thousand men back—Queen's Rangers, your 17th Dragoons—"

"When does he want them?"

"Oh, the day before yesterday, of course. They'll have to embark at Portsmouth. However, since we've got to cross the James River to get to Portsmouth and the Marquis is become a little bolder, we'll encourage him to attack us while we're crossing it. He might get a bloody nose."

I was sorry to leave Williamsburg, a clean, pleasant, little town with some fine buildings and pleasant vistas, amongst which we spent nine days of our headlong flight. On Sunday the 1st July I attended divine service in the parish church of Bruton, in Williamsburg, which was named, so I was informed, for our Somerset town of Bruton—which gave me the greater affection for the place. At Williamsburg too, most received letters from England, but there were none for Matthew or me. So neither he nor I had any news from home since the letter received in December informing us of Kitty's pregnancy. I had written to Anne again immediately on my arrival at our headquarters at Petersburg, but this would scarce have reached her by the time we came to Williamsburg. This total lack of any news of Anne and the children was for me the most distressing of all the discomforts of the campaign. And my depression made me value the more the letters Lucy and I exchanged through those of James Fairleigh's troop who came and went between the army and their homes in Tryon County. These letters I read and re-read until I near had them by heart.

We marched out of Williamsburg on Wednesday the 4th July, and on the Friday encamped on Jamestown Island, where the first colonists from England had landed to found this lovely dominion of Virginia.

The withdrawal of an army across a large river in the presence of a formed enemy is one of the most hazardous operations of war; and to encourage the rebels in their efforts to seize upon what we hoped they would consider an easy prey, we sent out two men professing to be deserters—a dragoon of the Legion and a Negro servant. These were instructed to persuade the rebel advanced guard that only our rearguard—the Legion and a company of light infantry—now remained on the island, to embark after nightfall. Loyalist friends asserted widely that Cornwallis had been seen on the south bank of the river with the entire army. And, as a final decoy for the rebel scouts, we left a 9-pounder gun—from Steuben's arsenal at Point of Fork—unattended, as if abandoned in the swamps which enclosed the island along its north shore.

The Island of Jamestown is joined to the north shore of the James only by a narrow and insubstantial causeway and road, passing through a morass. It is nowhere more than a few feet high, and is everywhere uneven and covered with reeds, rank grasses and a scattering of pine, oak and birch. The ground on the island at the end of the causeway is open, but broken and uncertain under foot, with many patches of bog.

At around two o'clock in the afternoon the rebels began to press more eagerly against Tarleton's patrols. This rearguard fell back slowly through a picket holding the northern end of the causeway. The picket itself then withdrew across the causeway under heavy fire. Long before this, Cornwallis had deployed in two wings what force the small area available for manoeuvre could carry, and between the wings had posted a battery of 6-pounders. The entire force were standing or lying under cover of the broken ground, with the guns concealed with reeds and brush.

After the withdrawal of our picket, the rebels began to move only warily across the causeway in pursuit. Then, finding the resistance continued still as from a small rearguard, they gained confidence and pushed the harder. The rebel force on the island now numbered around five hundred—one Continental battalion facing our left and a mass of light infantry and riflemen moving against our right. Behind these were two more battalions of Continental infantry, picking their unsteady way through the mud which the passage of our army had churned up.

Tarleton came stumbling over the hummocks. "I've got Fairleigh's and my dragoons formed behind the left brigade as you ordered, Colonel. Dismounted, of course. We might be able to get forward and do a little chopping up if it doesn't all end too late. Don't relish the idea of charging through this stuff, in daylight or dark." He kicked a sodden tussock of yellowed grass, "We'll all end on our arses in the bog."

"Just be ready to move," I said, "And if you're needed, move at a trot, no more. This will be carbine and pistol work, so see the men all look to their weapons while they've time."

Tarleton gave the order. Then he stared across at the Continental battalions slowly forming line on the rebel right, and sniffed, "Not hurrying, are they? Do they think our rearguard's waiting to kiss 'em goodbye?" He suddenly smiled. A large, stout, smartly-dressed officer on a big bay horse rode with a fine, bold air among the front ranks of the Continental line, encouraging them forward. "Ah ha! Here's the bold

Anthony himself. Now things may liven! Those are his Pennsylvanians, I suppose. Poor bastards!—he's flogged and hanged and shot them to get them into some sort of discipline, and they say they still like him, so he must be a good soldier! He must give the poor little Marquis the bloody flux for fear of what he'll do next! We could do with him."

"That's Anthony Wayne?" I said. "Yes, we could do with him—he's almost the twin of Charles O'Hara."

A party of rebel light infantry ran forward to the gun we had left as bait. Wayne waved his hat and cheered them on as they ran—straight into the waiting ambush.

Cornwallis said, evenly and unemotionally, "Have the men stand up. Uncover the guns and engage."

The drums beat. The line stood up. The front ranks presented and fired their volley. The guns thundered their grape and canister, tearing great holes in the Pennsylvania battalions. The rebel light infantry took one volley and the survivors scattered into the mob of riflemen behind them. These took fright at once and fled in a confused mass over the causeway or struggled through the swamps to the safety of the north shore. With nothing now to withstand it, the right wing advanced to outflank the Pennsylvanian brigade.

The battalions of this brigade, torn by the fire of the guns and the volleys from front and flank, began to break. But now we saw how "Mad Anthony" Wayne had earned his *nom de guerre*.

His sword high above his head, he cantered forward from the line and, turning to face his battalions, roared at them. Almost at once they steadied, and, stepping over the dead and wounded, they reformed, presented and returned our fire. Two guns lumbered and splashed off the causeway and were swung to bear on our line. They blazed at us, and as they did so Wayne led his brigade in a charge, straight into the murderous storm of our fire. He must have known he'd overplayed his hand and had to withdraw, that he needed to hold us to give time for Lafayette to cover him, and, for that time he must pay with men's lives—his own, if need be. I doubt his men thought of this, or anything—other than that he led them. And they came at us at a run, halted on his order, gave a volley, levelled bayonets, and came on. Brave men, led by the bravest.

But, despite their courage, the Pennsylvanian line finally broke—shot to pieces. And when the left brigade went in with their bayonets and the light infantry closed on their flank, the Pennsylvanians straggled back across the swamp, with the yagers picking them off as they went. The teams and the greater part of the crews of the two guns were killed, and the guns left in our hands. But all this had taken time; and, what was more important, the last of the fading daylight.

I mounted Williamson and ordered up the dragoons. There might still be time to cut off the remnants of the advanced guard of the rebels from their main army and destroy them. I rode over to where Cornwallis stood beside the captured guns. As I came up he shook his head. "No, Philip. It's too dark for the cavalry to do any good. There weren't more than a thousand there, and the Marquis has another two thousand he hasn't used yet. You'd lose men I can't spare. I need all my cavalry. Tell Tarleton to bivouac—they've done well today."

And he walked off to talk to the wounded. It was a hard decision. We might have destroyed Lafayette. And I believe that if Clinton had not demanded those reinforcements—for which he later admitted he had no need—Cornwallis would have taken the chance. But I suppose it was the right decision. Black night and bog are no proper conditions for a cavalry action; even against a beaten enemy.

The following day we continued our crossing of the James River with no further interference from the rebels. Indeed, the whole operation was conducted in as peaceable and leisurely a manner as if it were a mere military exercise without an enemy; which it was.

We arrived complete in Cobham, on the south bank of the James, on the 7th July; where yet another instruction from New York awaited Cornwallis. I have never seen him so angry, but his voice was as calm as ever.

"His Excellency the Commander-in-Chief appears to have forgotten that in his last four letters he has urgently demanded that we should send him reinforcements to aid him in beating off a siege threatened by Washington with twenty thousand Continentals, a great French force and the entire militias of five colonies. Now—for God's sake!—he says he needs them to assist him in seizing Philadelphia! I can only suppose he's thinking of cutting his way through Washington's twenty thousand—and the French—and the militias—and back again—having reduced Philadelphia to ashes. Or perhaps the rebel and French forces have all deserted. God!—he makes me doubt my own sanity!"

So we prepared for the embarkation of the troops Clinton had demanded. Whilst continually, by every packet, instructions poured in from him, each one contradicting the last, and all of them critical of what we had done, what we proposed to do and what we were ever likely to do. At Charlestown I had thought him unconfident and unsettled in his mind; now I thought him out of it. For no other description can fit the constant inconstancy of his directions. I was finally convinced in my opinion when having, after great labours, embarked all the troops and all the horses, and with the convoy forming to sail, we received yet another instruction. It revoked every previous one.

We were now not to despatch the troops to New York. Instead, we were to establish a base and naval station at Old Point Comfort, and were to employ the entire army in constructing the post and securing it from attack by any rebel force. This was patently the worst of all compromises as well as the most ridiculous. It reduced this army of seven thousand veterans to a corps of sentries and labourers; to be allowed an occasional "desultory expedition," as he called it, in the summer—to stretch our legs, we supposed, for it could serve no other purpose.

Lieutenant Sutherland, our engineer, and the commanders of the chiefest ships-of-the-line in the Chesapeake were unanimous in recommending that both the post and the anchorage were unsatisfactory for the purposes of the Navy, and most difficult to fortify in any adequate strength.

Cornwallis was despondent. "I'd like to send him the reinforcements he asks for and take the rest back down to Charlestown with me. If he won't let me do what we should do here we might as well begin all over again. But he won't agree to that. So that leaves the only possibilities for his plan as York and Gloucester. I looked at both while we were at Williamsburg; neither look suitable or I'd have gone there sooner. Now there's no alternative. Admiral Graves says he needs a station in the Chesapeake. So he'll have to have York and Gloucester—they complement one another. And I hope to God he never loses control of these waters, or we shall be in sad trouble."

"When I saw him in Charlestown, Pussy assured me that that would always be his chief and constant concern," I said.

"Small comfort in that," gloomed Cornwallis. "Anything Pussy ever gets his fractious, fidgety paws on is bound to end in confusion and disaster!"

So, on the 29th July, Cornwallis and I sailed from Portsmouth aboard the frigate H.M.S. *Richmond*, leaving Charles O'Hara the task of evacuating and destroying our post at Portsmouth. And on Friday the 3rd August we stepped ashore at York.

Chapter Sixteen

*In which I arrive in York, lose two friends
and am aided by an old opponent.*

York was a pleasant, prosperous place two years ago—in August 1781. Most of the Virginian tobacco trade passed through it. The wharves and warehouses were set on the shore of the York River, at the bottom of a low, steep, sandy cliff. On this cliff, overlooking the river, stood the main town, very clean and neat with some fine houses well laid out with shade trees, wide walks and delightful gardens. It held three thousand souls, so I was told; but a few of these had fled before we arrived there.

The York River there is at its narrowest, about a mile in width, with a good channel of five fathoms, convenient for ships-of-the-line. Across the river, on Gloucester Point, is the village of Gloucester, which, together with York, commands the passage of the river at this place. Above these narrows the river widens again to form an anchorage, comfortable for ships of any burden.

Immediately on our arrival we began to construct small works based upon the two creeks which almost surround the town; at that time expecting to be attacked only by militia. The village of Gloucester, on its point, lies between a creek to its north and the river to its south; the approach to it being along a narrow peninsula. Here also we planned works similar to those at York. But in both places the soil was so light and sandy that the defences were in constant need of repair from the effects of the weather alone. The work was largely done by our soldiers, who were hindered by a lack of proper tools; and the stout and voluble Commissary Perkins, the senior member of that department, was near beside himself with vexation when he reported the deficiency to Cornwallis.

"They got very few spades or picks, m'lord. Left 'em littered all round the Carolinas o'course. Damaged by enemy fire, Mr. Perkins, they say—wore out in the service they was, they say. So I tell 'em now they're a-goin' to have to wear out their bleedin' hands in the service; for I can't find 'em no more tools."

"But there must be some about, Mr. Perkins. What do they use in the local agriculture?"

"'Oes, m'lord, nothing but bloody 'oes! You wouldn't get any of the lazy bastards what live round these parts to lift a spade—nor even to lean on one neither, which is about all they can manage with their bloody 'oes!"

Cornwallis smiled at him affectionately. They had served together in many places and were firm friends. "I'm sure you'll find a way, Mr. Perkins."

Perkins gave a snort and grinned morosely at him. "Ah well, m'lord, needs must when the devil drives, as they do say."

Cornwallis smacked him on the shoulder. "And they also say—the Army needs must when Perkins drives!" Which piece of gentle flattery sent Perkins off in a roar of laughter and a better humour. But even he could not find enough spades for our needs, and this lack was one of the reasons why our defences at York were later so ineffectual against the enemy's artillery.

Cornwallis' headquarters was established in the house of a Mr. Thomas Nelson, a charming old gentleman who had been the Secretary of the Governor's Council for the colony and was still addressed by all as Mr. Secretary Nelson. His nephew, another Thomas Nelson, was elected Governor of Virginia by the rebel Assembly eight days after we had chased his discredited predecessor out of his house at Monticello. Mr. Secretary Nelson, studiously polite and hospitable, was immensely proud of his nephew but disapproved strongly of his revolutionary inclinations. He was stout, short in stature and breath, and very fond of port; of which he had none left and we had a fair amount. So we got on very well.

On Wednesday 22nd August, Charles O'Hara arrived from Portsmouth, having demolished that post and evacuated it entirely. He was accompanied by a great number of loyalist families, and we were soon to regret their presence. Together with the residents and the army they raised the total population of York to around nine thousand; which overcrowding brought on many ills—fevers, the flux and even the pock. So that, in a short time, our sick outnumbered those still fit to bear arms.

For some time Cornwallis had seemed to smile less and talk less with us, though always showing a cheerful air and a ready smile when amongst the troops. But after O'Hara's arrival with the rear party he became more cheerful and communicative, and the reason was soon apparent. He had invited me to dine with him, and on arriving at Mr. Secretary Nelson's house I was shown into a small drawing-room. A young lady, most elegantly gowned, sat at the window embroidering a handkerchief. I bowed and wished her good-day and she rose and curtsied.

"Good-day, sir," she answered; she had a delightful, soft voice with a touch of Irish in it. I couldn't think of whom she reminded me, but then, all at once, it struck me—Jemima Cornwallis!—the same hair, the same colouring and cast of feature, the same poised, slender form. I stood gawking at her, until she said gently, "Are you well, sir?"

I scrabbled my startled wits together and stammered, "Forgive me, ma'am. You reminded me—so intensely—of a lady I knew."

"And who is the lady, sir?"

"Why, ma'am, the Lady Jemima Cornwallis. You're so alike—you must be related—?"

She coloured up, charmingly. "You do me a great honour, sir. No, I was not related to her." Then, in quaintly childlike gesture, she put her hands together, as if pleading for my approval. "I am Mrs. Katharine Harlow—I am his lordship's mistress—" And she broke off, watching me with the same droll, fearful look which Jemima would use after she'd said something quite outrageous and wasn't sure—or would pretend so— whether you would laugh or be cross with her. She quite captivated me; but then Anne always says I'm the simplest-hearted gull for any scheming woman—and she should know. I bowed again.

"I'm delighted his lordship is so fortunate in his companion. Col. Philip Cato, at your service, ma'am."

Then Cornwallis came in and was a little surprised to find me there, having forgotten that he had invited me to dine; understandably. I thought dissimulation to be the better part of discretion and said hastily, 'I must have mistook the day, Charles. Forgive me, ma'am, for having trespassed upon your time."

But they would have none of this and made me stay. Charles O'Hara was sent for and old Mr. Secretary Nelson joined us, and we spent a most pleasant evening together. Mrs. Harlow played upon the spinet and sang, most enjoyably old songs we all knew; and Charles O'Hara joined her in some, which was not so enjoyable. But Charles Cornwallis was a different man, and I rejoiced to see him so.

As we walked back to our quarters O'Hara said, "Thank the lord he's got a woman. A man like him needs a woman. Well, any man does—'less there's something wrong with him."

"She's charming," I said. "Where did he find her?"

"In Portsmouth. Don't know what she was doing there. I heard her husband is in the rebel army—a deserter."

"And what about you, Charles? You never have much trouble in finding yourself a warming pan. Did you find one in Portsmouth?"

We had stopped outside the house where I was quartered. O'Hara said "Philip, you mayn't believe it—bigod, I know my reputation!—but— well, d'you know I haven't been near a woman since leaving Hillsborough. It's that lad of mine—my eldest son—lying in his grave at Guilford—that bloody battle. You've been kind enough not to talk of him He was a good boy. We could have done so much together. I could have shown him how to enjoy life, the way I have—well, perhaps he'd have let me. But now—I miss him—God, how I miss him!"

I couldn't leave him to brood over his heartaches, so I walked on slowly with him to his quarters in the Swan tavern.

"Tell me about Guilford," I said.

"Guilford! I want to forget it! The messiest, bloodiest scrimmage I was ever in! We'd been chasing Greene for months and at last he summoned up the guts to fight. He outnumbered us by three to one—some say more—so it wasn't a hard decision for him. We thrashed him—though not so thoroughly as you thrashed Gates—he ran, and left all his guns and wounded in our hands—and it rained all bloody night while we were dragging them out of the mud, poor sods. But we didn't destroy him—if we'd had half as many as him we might have done. But, being so few, we had to pay too much for it. And I paid more than most."

We paced on in silence for a while, then he suddenly stopped and faced me. "But, Philip,—y'know, I don't like our situation here. You've heard of the French reinforcements coming from the Indies to support the rebels, haven't you? Well, Pussy's got enough men to see 'em off, but what if they come at us here? We can't defend this place. Look at our works—they won't stand up to rook-shot!"

"That's true, but surely their aim will be to unite with Washington against New York—our main base. If they do attack us here Pussy will certainly have to create some sort of diversion."

"The devil he will! The only creative act that puff-guts is capable of is fornication—and he's not too reliable at that either, they say! I honestly believe he'd like to see Charles beat. He loathes him—you know that."

"Yes, I know. But it's fool's talk to say that he'd like to see him beat."

"Fool's talk maybe, but a lot of people talk it and they're not all fools. ou know very well that a good few at home would like to see us beat, so 1at they could get into power again. What the devil do politicians care for ur lives? And who's to say that Pussy isn't in with them? He's Jewcastle's man, don't forget. What about the brothers Howe? Whose 1terests were they serving? Not the Army's and Navy's, bigod!"

I knew that O'Hara's pessimism was based on sounder foundations than ool's talk. For now we had emerged from the Carolina deserts to the astern seaboard, news from England—and rumours from everywhere lse—were quickly in our ears. And nearly everything we heard depressed ur hopes for success in this way. We learned that Baillie and Munro had een defeated in Mysore by Hyder Ali supported by the French, that iibraltar was besieged by the Spanish, Minorca was threatened and lorida fallen again into Spanish hands, and in our struggle with the rench and Spanish in the West Indies our losses outnumbered our gains. .nd to cap all this tale of woe, a week later, Captain Symonds of the igate *Charon*, commanding all His Majesty's ships within the Chesaeake, reported a French fleet of over thirty sail entering within the capes. Vhich fleet first proceeded to blockade the York River and then to isembark the French reinforcements Charles O'Hara had mentioned at 1mestown Island.

I rode out on each of the next four days to observe the movement of the rench troops, and, during this time, Lafayette joined forces at Villiamsburg with the Comte de St. Simon, who commanded the French. In returning from reconnaissance on Thursday the 7th September I ound a council of war in progress. Alexander Ross came out and asked me o join it. Cornwallis was questioning two naval officers, the captains of 1e frigates *Richmond* and *Iris*, and the sailing-master of the *Richmond*. The pproach of a British fleet had been reported on the morning of the 4th nd we had observed the French fleet, which we now knew to be ommanded by Admiral de Grasse, sailing out to give battle. Gunfire had een heard all day on the 5th and 6th, but no British ship had entered the :hesapeake save only the two frigates, which had slipped into the bay nder cover of the confusion of battle and the dark.

The frigate captains perched nervously on the edges of their chairs. :ornwallis was grim-faced. "You say Admiral Graves is repulsed. How as that?"

"My lord, the Admiral was outnumbered and outgunned. In the main ction his flagship and the others of his van were sore battered. And

[*245*]

though only half the fleet have yet engaged, it is the same for the French
for the wind failed half their line and they never came up. So he is still a
disadvantage."

"What will he do?"

"That depends a great deal on how badly his ships are hurt, my lord
He may need to return to New York for repair."

Cornwallis frowned impatiently.

"Well then, what can he do?—can he come into the bay?"

The captains both looked at the sailing-master; a short, thick-set
slow-spoken West Country man.

"M'lord, 'er's like as the captain says. 'Pends much on what damage th
admiral's got. 'Er's got the weather-gage on they Frenchies as 'er lies—w
a good sea-way 'twixt 'em, nigh on three leagues an' mebbe more. But th
wind's a-backin' to nor'-east and freshenin'. That'll take the lot on 'en
down 'long Cape Hatteras. As for comin' into the bay—well, what wi' th
damage an' the wind an' the French a-lyin' close in—" He shook h
square, close-cropped head gravely, "Nay, I don't see it, m'lord."

"Indeed," Cornwallis leaned back in his chair and pursed his lips. "We
then, gentlemen, it appears we have lost control of these waters, an
cannot say when—or even if—we shall ever regain it."

The two captains looked very glum. "We fear that's about the measur
of it just now, my lord."

Cornwallis glanced at me. "So much for our friend's 'constant and chie
concern,' " he said and smiled bitterly. He got to his feet. "That is all
wished you to hear, gentlemen. You will realize that until we can again b
supported by the Navy, we must exercise the greatest restraint on th
consumption of all munitions, stores and foodstuffs. The Quartermaste
General's staff and the Commissary will ensure that proper measures ar
put in hand at once." He turned to the frigate captains. "You gentleme
will be attempting to rejoin the fleet?"

"Yes, my lord, when we can. The wind's not favourable now."

"Then I'll wish you good fortune and a safe passage. Pray tell Admira
Graves that he cannot come too soon."

Everyone left except O'Hara and I. There was a moment's gloom
silence. Then Cornwallis said disgustedly, "What price Pussy's damne
conflagration now!" He slumped back in his chair. "God save us!"

O'Hara smiled at him disarmingly. "It'd be better, I'm thinking, to pra
that he won't need to!"

"Charles," I said, "I'm just back from Williamsburg. We still have th

rength—and the opportunity—to beat Lafayette and these new French
oops. But we must do it now, before they are reinforced."

"Where do you propose that we attack them?"

"At Williamsburg—a direct attack with any outflanking movement
om the north—" and I outlined my plan.

"Yes—" He studied his map for a few minutes, measuring with the little
ory rule he always uses. "Yes—let me have their positions and numbers
id have the approaches reconnoitred. We'll plan on that."

And so we planned for such an attack and the orders were written.
hen the express arrived from Clinton. He said he had four thousand men
nbarked, and that he waited only for Graves' nod to sail. The letter was
gned on the 6th September.

Two days after the arrival of the letter Cornwallis sent for O'Hara,
ommissary Perkins and myself. He sat with the letter in front of him on
e table. He sounded tired and strangely uncertain.

"You are aware of the contents of this letter. It is a great responsibility
iat rests upon us." He spoke slowly, hesitantly. "If we should mistake
:re—it could cost us this war. We must not take unjustifiable risks at this
ncture. The balance of our fortunes is too fine." He looked up to see
ow his words had affected us; and saw they hadn't. He spoke now almost
; if he found it difficult. "If I had no hopes of a quick relief I would risk
ich an action as we have planned. Because, as you know, this town is
defensible against any force such as now begins to threaten us." He bent
wer over the letter and his hands, lying at either side of it, slowly
enched. "But—the Commander-in-Chief—promises speedy and certain
ipport. With such an assurance—I do not think myself—I am not
istified—in risking the fate of this war—this whole war—on any such
tempt. I am confident we should succeed—but—now, with regular
rench troops engaged—it might be at a greater cost than we suffered—at
uilford." And that last word came hard drawn out of him, like an old
ail out of oak.

I had already realized what the Guilford battle had cost the army; I
idn't realized, until that moment, what it had cost Charles Cornwallis.
here was a horrid, chill silence. None of us moved. His voice was hoarse
ow, muffled.

"But, if we are not relieved soon—then I fear the worst." He looked up
iddenly and his tone sharpened. "But you must understand—no one
iust know that!"

Now he relaxed, resting his elbows on the table. He moved his head up and down between his hands, letting his fingertips gently rub his temple He said quietly, "Mr. Perkins, I'd be grateful for your views on how w can ensure an even stricter economy of all our stores. And your be estimate of how long they can sustain us." Then he dropped his hand looked up and smiled wanly at us. "Thank you. I'm writing to th Commander-in-Chief to this effect this evening."

A dismissal. In silence we got up, bowed and left him. O'Hara said n a word until we were out of the house. Then he rammed his hat on, kicke the gate, swore and said, furiously,

"We're beat—beat!"

"He's beat," I said.

"That's it—that's it exactly! But why?"

"He's sick. He looks like a chewed gob-string. Probably got the fev again."

"Ay, could be—" He stopped short. "Bigod! You don't suppose th woman of his has persuaded him?—an agent?"

"No, I don't. You know him better than that."

"He's amazing fond of her, Philip. But, no, it wouldn't be that."

"If he's ill, thank God for Mrs. Harlow, say I. She'll nurse him bett than any of our sawbones."

And so she did. For he was sick indeed, though never admitting to nor yielding to it. Every day he rode through our outposts and every d walked through the defences of York. His calm confidence and cheerf words encouraged the whole army in its endlessly filthy, sweaty task building defences. The army drew its strength from him as it had alwa done, and as soldiers always will do from such a commander. Bu perhaps, just then, he drew some of his from this Irish girl.

By Wednesday the 26th September, the rebel forces, now commande by General Washington and composed entirely of Continental Li troops, except for a brigade of Virginia militia and the French troops, no commanded by the Comte de Rochambeau, were united arour Williamsburg in a great army of sixteen thousand men. From then on the began to probe forward and reconnoitre our outer lines.

On the evening of the 29th a general council of war was summoned f ten o'clock that evening. All the senior officers attended. There was an a of expectancy and excitement. Clearly all supposed that some form attack was to be made upon the enemy's extended and unprepared line. guessed otherwise. When all were present Cornwallis began at once.

"A letter arrived from the Commander-in-Chief this afternoon. He sa the fleet will sail on the 5th October with five thousand men embarked,

lieve us." He smiled cheerfully round the table; but I thought the smile a
ttle too fixed. "This is very satisfactory news."

There was a murmur of approval, but it sounded a little disappointed.
bviously he was not planning to attack the enemy armies. Cornwallis
rned his chair towards a map of the defences of the town, hung on the
all behind him. He looked over his shoulder at us. "Our prime
sponsibility now, gentlemen, is to maintain this post until it is relieved;
hich I expect to be in a reasonable time." He turned to face the map
gain, his back to the council. "I have for some time been concerned about
e extent of our defences in the outer line. The enemy has now the
rength to concentrate for an attack upon that line at several points at
ice. And we lack the numbers to defend everywhere in the strength we
ed. So—to ensure that we are able to maintain the post for as long as is
quired, I propose to withdraw from our outer works tonight."

There was an audible gasp of amazement—even of horror—around the
ble. Cornwallis ignored it.

"All guns will be withdrawn from the outer works at once and mounted
nder the direction of Captain Rochfort within the inner line." Captain
ochfort commanded the artillery in York, and did it very well. "Every
an available will be employed to improve the inner line. Sufficient
atrols will be maintained to prevent observation of our movements by the
nemy before daylight."

He swung round to face us, his whole demeanour admirably composed,
ominating. "If there are no immediate questions I wish you to repair to
our commands at once. There is no time to be lost. We must all act
uickly and secretly. That is all, gentlemen." And, for the first time that I
an remember, he rose at once and left the room before any of us.

O'Hara sucked his teeth and called for a large brandy.

"You're right, Philip, it's him who's beat. He's going to let 'em so close
ey'll be able to concentrate their guns damned near wheel to wheel, at
ght hundred yards! And they haven't come all this way to play taws.
ou ever been in a siege before?"

"Never."

"'Ecod, you've been lucky! Well, I'll tell you—they'll batter us to a
udding in ten days—less maybe. They've twice our iron, and all of it
eavier. What the devil's got into Charles Cornwallis? He marched us all
e way up here without Pussy's leave, why in Hades can't we have a bit
f a battle without it?" He slammed his empty glass on the table. "Ah, to
ell with it! Don't know I've much to live for anyway. Might as well die
heerful. Better go and see my lads." And he heaved himself up and

[*249*]

stamped out. But his two questions were the ones the army repeated dail
during those last tragic days in York.

I repeated Cornwallis' orders to Tarleton and Fairleigh, and aske
Lieutenant-Colonel Dundas, who commanded in Gloucester, to infor
Simcoe, whose Rangers were stationed in Gloucester. I said I intende
eventually to move the whole force of cavalry across the river
Gloucester. We had over two hundred cavalry horses in York and no u
for them when the allied armies were closed into their siege positions;
for every reason—supply of forage, health, labour to care for them—ar
for the sake of the horses themselves, it was better that they should be
Gloucester. It was also at the back of my mind that, all else failing, th
army might escape through Gloucester to New York; and, so placed, th
cavalry would be better able to cover the move. But I made no mention
this.

The next day, of course, the enemy began to move at once into o
deserted works. Our guns opened on them whilst the Legion ar
Fairleigh's troop ambushed and skirmished with their reconnaissan
parties. And, from one such patrol, Matthew Ryan did not return.

He had asked to be allowed to go out with James Fairleigh to make u
numbers. "I'm getting out of practice, your honour," he'd said, "I've ne
forgot which end of a sword ye hold!"

James himself had commanded the patrol and I went out at once wi
him, under a flag. We were challenged by troops of the New Yo
Continental Line, and their commander, Lieutenant-Colonel Hamilto
conducted us to his surgeon's tent.

"A brave fellow, Colonel," said Hamilton, "but—" and he shook h
head.

Matthew was lying on his cloak. His eyes were closed. I saw the dea
in his face. I dropped to my knees beside him and took his hands. The
were ice cold.

"Matthew—Matthew—it's me—" My voice choked in my throat and
felt the tears running down my cheeks. I loved this Irish soldier. He ha
ridden beside me in battle after battle, he had served me in campaign aft
campaign; loyally, bravely, cheerfully for near twenty years. He ha
saved my life a dozen times or more. He was part of my family. I love
him like a brother. I could not let him die. He was the father of Kitty
child. He must not die.

His eyes opened. They were glazed with pain and there was n
understanding in them. I looked into them closely. "Matthew—it's me—

He seemed to make a great effort. His eyes cleared and he recognize

e. He tried to speak. The blood dribbled from the corner of his mouth. He coughed, spattering my face with blood.

"Ahh—aahhh—Kitt—Kitty—child—" His eyes closed.

"Matthew—I'll care for them as my own."

His eyes opened again, suddenly, very wide and clear.

"Kitty—"

Then the blood filled his mouth, he retched, his back arched and then relaxed. His head fell back. He was dead. And I had lost my right hand—my right arm.

Williamson and I brought Matthew back into York. I led her and she carried him strapped across her saddle. Andrew was waiting for us. Stony-faced he took the mare's reins from me.

I gave him Matthew's sword. "You're my soldier-servant now, Andrew. Matthew would have liked you to have this." He stood very stiffly at attention, reins in one hand, the sword held tightly against his chest with the other, staring at me.

"I try be like Matthew, your honour." Then, all at once, his face crumbled. He bowed his head and led Williamson away. And we buried Matthew Ryan, private soldier of the 2nd Royal North British Dragoons, in the yard of Grace Church in York, Virginia.

By the 2nd October there remained no ground between the lines sufficient for the operations of the cavalry; and we spent that night shipping all the horses across to Gloucester. I went myself and Williamson with me, for the surrounds of Gloucester and the wide deployment of the enemy force opposing it still permitted action by cavalry.

The following morning I rode out with Dundas and all the cavalry except Simcoe to cover a foraging party. It was reported that the enemy commander, Brigadier-General de Choisy, intended to close in upon our defences to prevent us foraging outside our lines. So Dundas wished to make hay while the sun still shone. The Legion formed the forward screen, covering the road which runs north out of Gloucester, whilst Fairleigh's troop extended through the rough, close country to the west, down to the river bank, to protect the wagon column being cut off from that flank.

It was a fine, warm day and after the sodden, enfeebling heat of the summer the air was delightfully fresh. The leaves had begun to turn scarlet and copper and gold—lovelier and in greater profusion of colour and shade than anywhere I can remember. It was a joy to ride out that morning. All proceeded well and the column, fully laden, had returned to within a mile of Gloucester. Dundas, Tarleton and I were riding together at the head of the main body of the Legion, following the column. A trooper bent low over his horse's neck came galloping in from the rearguard. He pulled up beside me.

"Lieutenant Cameron begs to report, your honour—enemy—cavalry and infantry—on the road behind us—mile or more back."

Dundas and Tarleton looked at me. Here, at last, was a fight—a fight the whole army had been wanting. I halted the Legion.

"Banastre, take the Legion back along the road and repulse the cavalry. Send the 17th out to your right and have them scout forward to find the enemy's flank and drive into it when you attack in front. Dundas, get the column moving at its best speed. Send an officer to bring an escort from Gloucester to take it safe in. Have Champagné deploy the light company of the 23rd in the skirt of this wood here, to cover the cavalry if they're pushed back. You've got the Legion infantry as a reserve. I'll leave you in command here. I'll go to the left and find Fairleigh and bring him in to strike from the left—so keep an eye open for us. And Banastre—don't get in too deep!"

I knew Dundas and Tarleton were entirely capable of handling any situation likely to arise in these circumstances. But I was not so sure of James Fairleigh, nor was I even sure where he was. If his command was to be used to best effect I had to find him myself.

I sent Williamson flying across the pastures to the west of the road towards a small wood, with Andrew tailing along a few yards behind me. As we neared the wood I heard him shout. Instinctively I ducked in my saddle and swung the mare to one side, just as a rifle cracked to my front and a bullet whined past. A rifleman ran from bush to bush in the edge of the wood, but not quick enough to avoid Andrew's blade.

"You be more careful, your honour," Andrew shouted. "Be more rebels for sure." He had the acute instinct and reflexes of a cat. Twice more he shouted at me as we cantered on, and twice more went in at a gallop, swerving his horse from side to side, to cut down the rifleman I had hardly time to see before Andrew was on him. We rode on a quarter of a mile to the far edge of the wood.

"Three men, Andrew," I said. "Scouts for a patrol most like. Now where's the rest of them?—and where the devil's Major James?"

Andrew shook his head. "Never hear nothing."

Pistols and carbines crackled behind us where Tarleton was engaged on the road.

"We must find him, and quickly," I said.

A narrow track with deep ditches and banks on either side ran for fifty

ards from the north corner of the wood to disappear into a copse. There
were many new hoof marks in the dust.

"Stay here and cover me into that copse," I said. "I'll wave you forward
from there. And don't move before I wave."

Andrew wiped his blade on his hand, returned it, swung down from his
horse and, hitching his arm through his reins, unswivelled his carbine,
checked the priming and cocked it. He nodded at me sternly. "Ready.
You be careful now!"

I had my sword drawn, but, as an added precaution, I opened the caps
of my holsters and took a pistol, half-cocked, in my bridle hand. I trotted
down the road to the copse. At its edge I sensed rather than saw a
movement in the long grass under the trees. I pushed Williamson into a
canter. A rifle cracked. Williamson checked, stumbled and cantered on.
Another shot. A red-hot talon scored over my left shoulder. A half-dozen
strides and, all at once, the mare collapsed under me, flinging me into the
ditch and rolling over me.

It was soft falling, but I was stunned for a few moments. When I came a
little to myself I saw blood on my jacket—Williamson's. She was quite
dead. Only her courage had saved me. Had she dropped when the first
struck her, the second shot would have killed me too.

I could not move the lower half of my body. At first I thought, hazily,
that my back was broken—that I was paralysed—about to die. Then I
realized the mare was pinning me down. I struggled to free my legs.

"You're bleedin' lucky to be alive-o, aint' yer, bloody-back?"

I looked up. Standing by the ditch with his rifle levelled at my head was
a rifleman, in a torn, shapeless, buttonless, brown smock and an ancient
tricorne with a dirty white cockade. He grinned down at me evilly.
"Reckoned I'd knocked you off. Me mate up the point got yer 'orse, but
she run on and that saved yer. I didn't swing fast enough. Anyways, that
don't matter now, do it?"

He ran his eyes over my patched and faded jacket and poor
Williamson's cobbled saddlery. "Crimes, not much pickin's on you! You
ain't in much better state nor me, are yer?—proper ragged arse the pair on
us. Got any lurry on yer? British guineas, French guineas, joes,
doubloons—I'll take anythin' 'cept Continental crap—'ere, that's a
spanker yer got there in yer neckrag!"

He reached down with his free hand to grab the gold pin with the ruby
which Anne gave me to wear in my stock. I knocked his hand away. He
swore at me and grabbed it again, trying unsuccessfully to disengage the
pin from its catch with one hand. He laid down his rifle and knelt to peer

closer at the action of the catch. I seized him with one hand and struck him as hard as I could in the face with the other. He tore himself free and fell back, cursing. He got to his feet. "Right, you bastard, you can 'ave it!" He cocked his rifle and levelled it at me. Then, suddenly looking over his shoulder, seemed to think better of it. He tugged out a bayonet and clumsily lashing it on to his barrel, grinned savagely at me.

"Best do her quiet-like or the bleedin' orficer'll be at me!"

He stepped to the edge of the ditch above me and jabbed viciously down at me. I was just able to twist aside and the point only tore through the side of my jacket. He nearly overbalanced on top of me. "'Old still, ye squirmy shag-bag!" He poised for a second thrust. I waited for the point. There was a sudden movement of blue behind him and the butt of a spontoon cracked across the side of his head, knocking him sprawling.

"You damn murdering rogue, get back to your post!"

I heard the spontoon thud again and a cry of pain follow it. The voice of the officer seemed somehow familiar. He looked down at me. It was Roger Chawton.

"Colonel Cato! God in heaven! Here, sir, let me help you."

He took hold of the mare's front legs, braced his big shoulders, and heaved. I slithered out from under her. I looked at my saddle but the tree was broke. I remembered my second pistol and pulled it from the holster. I looked up at Chawton, cocked it and fired. He leapt back, wide-eyed with horror and anger.

"God damn you—!"

Then he looked where I was looking. The rifleman stood on top of the bank behind him, his musket at his shoulder, the muzzle still levelled at Chawton's back. In the middle of his forehead there was a neat hole. From the hole to the muzzle of my pistol was, I judged as I lay in the ditch, twelve paces. In the circumstances, had he been able, he would have appreciated the shot. He toppled slowly forward off the bank into the track. Chawton stared down at him, then, still a little white and wide-eyed, helped me out of the ditch.

What do you say on these occasions? I said, "How do you do, Mr Chawton? I'm obliged to you, sir."

"I'm delighted to see you well, Colonel. By God—I'm obliged to you too, sir—" He began to brush the dirt off my jacket.

"Don't brush too hard," I said, "It will fall to pieces."

We both laughed at this silly joke, shakily and stupidly, gratified to find ourselves alive, and something embarrassed, remembering our last meeting. And I thought what a change a year had made in him. He was slimmer, harder-looking, maturer, more confident; a fine-looking young man. I picked up my hat and knocked the dust off it. "Well, Mr. Chawton, I suppose I'm your prisoner."

"Great Heaven, no, Colonel! I'll get a horse for you to get you back to your lines."

He shouted orders and his men brought me a horse—a nondescript, solid troop horse. They put a saddle on it and fitted my threadbare saddlecloth and pouches and holsters to the saddle. They found my sword and my other pistol lying in the ditch. One of them reloaded both pistols and set them in my holsters. I thanked them for their help and mounted. They all stood smiling. Were these the Virginia Militia that had run at Camden?—they seemed a very different breed—smart and soldierly, brisk and cheerful.

I offered Chawton my hand. "God be with you, Mr. Chawton, and I thank you, sir. I look forward to meeting you in—less depressing circumstances." Then I rode off, whilst Chawton and all his soldiers saluted. I began almost to wonder which side I was on.

I hadn't looked again at Williamson. I knew I couldn't bear to do so. I didn't try. His horse is the half of a cavalryman—the better half. The patient, uncomplaining, unselfish half. In battle, they say, a horse draws its courage from its rider. But in battle and out, in all dangers, through all weathers, at every stride of the endless, weary miles of the marches, I had drawn strength from the gentle patience and courage and beauty of that mare. A brave horse—a soldier's horse. And as I jarred along on the militiaman's chop-actioned beast, I wept for her unashamedly, like a child in my loss.

I found Andrew in the wood where I had left him. A sergeant and some dragoons of James Fairleigh's troop were with him. "We was just about a-coming for you, your honour," he said; but he was staring at the horse. His eyes filled with dismay—"Will'mson—?"

"Dead."

His face distorted with grief. I had loved the mare. Andrew, who had tended her at Belhaven and after, worshipped her.

I said to the dragoons, "Where's Major Fairleigh?"

"He's taken, your honour."

"Taken?—by whom?"

The sergeant shrugged. "Don't rightly know who they was. Some on 'em was a-wearing green jackets, so we thought they was Lee's Legion at first. They give us a volley and run and we chased 'em. But they run too fast and we couldn't come up with 'em—'cept the major and a couple of others. They come back, but not the Major. He's—"

The crash of a volley from the direction of where I had left Dundas interrupted him; another followed—and another.

"Where's the rest of your troop?" I asked.

"Between here and Gloucester, your honour. We're part of the rearguard."

"Go to the commander of your rearguard and tell him to fall back on Gloucester now. And say I am taking these men of yours to join Colonel Dundas. You lads—follow me."

I kicked my beast into a shambling canter and we joined Dundas and Tarleton on the road. Dundas greeted me composedly.

"Had a bright little affair here, Colonel. Tarleton charged the French and got rolled in the mud. Then the French charged us and the 23rd sent them packing. Then the infantry took a poke at each other but sensibly decided to call it quits. And that's how we stand just now. The column's all safe into Gloucester."

"Many down?"

"Young Moir of the 23rd was killed, Tarleton had some hurt." He looked at the litter of dead and wounded, men and horses, in front of the wood, "And there's a few that won't see France again. Honours even, I'd say. We've got what we came for."

The patter of musketry died away as the scouts on either flank slowly disengaged. Neither line moved.

"Looks as if everyone's had all the fun they want for today," said Dundas. He looked at his watch. "Ah—if we started home now, Colonel, we'd be in nice time for breakfast." So, unharassed, we returned to Gloucester.

The following day I rode out, under a flag, to the headquarters of Brigadier-General de Choisy to inquire after James Fairleigh. The General was out of camp, but I met with Lieut.-Col. John Mercer commanding the Virginia Militia. I explained the circumstances and asked if James was held by the Militia. Mercer shook his head.

"No, Colonel, much to my regret, otherwise I'd gladly be entertaining him. I know his family well. But I'll certainly send a patrol to search for him and let you know if we find him."

I crossed to York that night to report to Cornwallis. A depressed looking Ross met me. "He's asleep, Colonel. And there's no point in waking him, because the fever's on him and he's not making much sense

He had your report of your action yesterday. He wished you now to stay in Gloucester in command of it and send Tom Dundas back to command his own brigade here under Colonel Robert Abercrombie. He's divided the town's defences into two halves; General O'Hara commands the right half—he's got his Guards brigade and Colonel Yorke's and the Hessian and Anspach regiments—and Colonel Abercrombie has the left, with Dundas' brigade, the light infantry and the 71st." He smiled a sad smile. "So now all we have to do is wait for General Clinton—or General Washington."

Chapter Seventeen

*In which, again, I witness the cost of
being over-matched.*

I returned to Gloucester that night. My chief concern now was t
ensure the safety and condition of the horses, both in the cavalry and fo
such wagons as I had there; for it seemed to me inevitable that the arm
must escape through Gloucester.

On the afternoon of Tuesday the 9th October, John Simcoe and I wer
inspecting the defences of his stabling, when, of a sudden, the air shoo
with a thunder from the other shore.

Simcoe groaned. "Now the fun's begun. They've emplaced thei
batteries. 'Ecod, look at those houses!—falling like packs of cards! Poo
devils, how long can they hold out against that?"

As the evening drew on, more guns joined the cannonade, and whe
night fell, from all round York the lightning flicker of the gun flashes, th
slow, curved flight of the shells with their sparkling fuses, the crash an
the flame as they burst and the garish glare of the burning town made
ghastly spectacle.

I crossed to York early in the morning and went straight to th
headquarters, which was already much damaged by the enemy's fire
Alexander Ross met me in the hall, calm as ever.

"The general's just left, Colonel. He's at his cave."

"Cave? What cave?"

"The cave he had made for—er—for his use, some days ago, Colonel; i
the cliff above the wharves."

"I see—well, I want a word with General O'Hara too. When th
General returns, tell him I wish to see him, will you?" A thought struc
me. "Mrs. Harlow—is she safe?"

"Mrs. Harlow?—safe? Why, I believe so. She's at the cave too, Colonel—" Ross seemed suddenly ill at ease and I wondered why.

I drew blank again at the Swan Tavern and began to make my way back to Mr. Secretary Nelson's house. To walk through a constant fall of shot and shell may sound rash, but experience tells you that an artillery bombardment has more effect on the nerves than on the body; at least, it is comforting to think so whilst having to walk through it. In the centre of the town I was hailed from one of the houses.

"Colonel Cato! Bigod, sir, this is no time for our valued senior officers to be walking around exposed to the malice of the enemy! Come and take a moment's shelter and a glass of wine for breakfast!"

Maj. John Conyngham and some officers of the 33rd were gathered in the dining-room of a house beside the road. All were red-eyed with weariness and covered in dust. Conyngham handed me a silver tankard of claret.

"'Pologize we've no glasses, Colonel. All broke last night when they hit the roof. What Mr. Digges—fellow who owns this house—decided to look for quieter quarters when he heard the rebels were coming—what he'll say when he finds all his best glass broke—not to mention his roof—I hate to think. Been up all night waiting for an attack. Seems they want to flatten the place first. Well, here's to an end to this damned war; after seven years I'm getting bored with it!"

Through all our campaigning John Conyngham had never lost either his sense of proportion or his sense of humour; which is why I found his officers all of the same spirit, and why they showed a gayer, more defiant mood now that the real fight had started.

"You heard the 76th had some people hurt yesterday afternoon, Colonel? They were at dinner. Robertson, their adjutant, was wounded and poor old Commissary Perkins was killed—he was dining with them. They say Cornwallis was very distressed when he heard about old Perkins—rest his soul." He drained his mug in honour of the old Commissary, and refilled it. "Got us this claret—God knows where from—"

A shell roared into the garden opposite the house, rolled a few yards and exploded, blowing the wooden fence flat and showering the house with earth. One of the officers dropped a bottle of wine and swore.

"Hell and damnation! Look at all that good claret gone to waste! Where the devil's Sir Henry bloody Clinton with all those reinforcements he prates about?"

John Conyngham hiccuped. "Lying in state between a couple of those

slutty old muttons of his! 'Ecod, when he's been up the poop of one o
those nymphs all night can you wonder the randy little goat hasn't th
strength to untangle his hooves from the sheets—"

A tremendous crash shook the house, and a large piece of the ceiling
plaster fell on Conyngham's head. The whole company fell off their chair
laughing.

"There, John," they cried, "there's heavenly retribution for you! That'
teach you to criticize your senior officers!"

Conyngham peered through his plastered eyebrows into his tankard
"The Lord be praised I had me hand over me mug," he said.

When I returned to Mr. Secretary Nelson's house, Charles O'Hara wa
standing at the door, tired and dejected. "Thank God you're here," h
said, "come and help me talk to Charles."

"What's the matter?"

"He's demented. Never seen him like this. Ross says he was like i
earlier this year—around the date of Jemima's death." He paused. "Th
poor Harlow woman was killed by a shell this morning, just outside th
cave he had made for her. He went rushing down there. Dundas has jus
brought him back. I was here when he came in. Shaking like i
leaf—sobbing—muttering to himself—" He put his hand on the door
handle of the little drawing-room. "Come on, now, Philip. We must di
something with him—we must!"

We went into the room. Cornwallis sat in a chair facing the window
staring fixedly down towards the shore; towards the cave. O'Hara put hi
hand on the back of the chair. "Charles—" Cornwallis made no move
"Charles, for God's sake—" Still silence. O'Hara looked at me anc
shrugged.

I walked round the chair and halted in front of Cornwallis. For i
moment the shock of his appearance confounded my tongue. When I hac
last seen him on the Friday he had looked tired and sick. Now, five day:
later, he was decayed into an old man, defeated and hopeless. There wa:
clearly no point in trying to coax him into remembrance of hi:
responsibilities. He would have to be provoked. This was no time fo
humouring despair.

"Charles, I've come to report all's well in Gloucester. And I've come fo
orders."

His eyes never moved. He muttered. "Is the fleet in sight?"

"No."

"Is there any news—any more promises from Clinton?"

"No."

"Then I've no orders."

This wasn't the true Cornwallis. I rasped. "God's sakes, Charles! For aught we know Clinton may be dead. In which case you would command all His Majesty's forces in these colonies. Is this how you'd do it?"

That brought his head up. But then he slumped back to stare down at the cave again. Dully, he said, "Philip, in the last two years I've destroyed everything I've ever loved. Jemima—whom I loved better than my life—my friends—so many of them—Patrick Ferguson, James Webster, Charles O'Hara's boy, old Harry Perkins yesterday, and now, today, this poor child Kate. All dead for my mistakes—all dead at my hands. And now, day by day, I destroy my soldiers. Don't you see I'm not fit to command now? I'm worthless—useless. And—" a despairing mutter, "too much of a coward to end it all with a bullet—" He was silent for a moment. "Can't you see that, Philip?"

I had to be ruthless, callous. "Yes—yes, I understand all that," I said, full of impatience, "but the army understands that you command here at York. And they won't understand why you don't."

He heaved himself to his feet, very upright. He pulled his jacket straight. There were tears on his cheeks—from weakness, grief, despair, what you like. He made no effort to brush them away. It was agony to watch him struggle to gain control of himself. He swayed a little on his feet and I put out a hand to steady him. He knocked my hand away and glared at me.

"Yes, you're right. I command here." He drew in a breath sharply, like a sob. "I have no orders for you except that you hold Gloucester."

I hadn't finished with him. I said, quietly now, "Charles, a year ago in Charlestown I asked you why you and I were fighting in these colonies. Do you remember your answer? You said, 'We have our duty as soldiers. What is left for us?' Do you recall that?"

The grimness left his face and it twisted into a sort of agonized smile. He took me by the shoulders and shook me gently.

"Damn you, Philip! You wring a man's duty out of him as you'd wring the neck of a chicken!" Then he said wearily, but more in his usual, level tone, "Well, let's go and talk to my soldiers."

So we walked out into the thunder of the cannonade. Cornwallis appeared as calm and cheerful and confident as ever. He fended off Col. Robert Abercrombie and a few others who remarked that he looked unwell with jokes about the noise affecting his unruly liver. No one was deceived and all thought the more of him. For, sick or no, he gave every man something of his own spirit and courage; and God knows whence his came at that moment.

We went first to the Fusilier Redoubt, sited to protect our right flank on the river. The Welch Fusiliers set in the shelter of their parapets, their weapons clean and ready beside them, patching again their much-patched jackets, rough-cobbling their worn equipment, re-dressing their wounds, smoking, playing cards and—the veteran soldier's inveterate occupation—cooking. In the Hornwork, the centre of our line and the most exposed to the heavy siege-guns of the French, the light infantry companies were similarly engaged, as imperturbably as the rest of the garrison. And the Germans—the Hessians and Anspachers—who, though forming the reserve held in the centre of the town, had no more respite than those in the forward line, gathered in groups round their cooking fires and cheered us, and all others within earshot, with their songs, most of them sung with great gusto in swinging chorus.

In the line supporting the two redoubts—Numbers 9 and 10—defending our left flank on the river we found the 71st Highlanders repairing the damage done to their works. Officers and soldiers, stripped to the waist, all laboured together, re-setting the gabions and fascines and piling earth and rubble to raise the height of their parapet. James Macdonell was in charge of these operations. He greeted Cornwallis breezily,

"A Sisyphean labour, my lord! The game is to see how high we can build the parapet before they knock it down again. Would you care to hazard a few shillings?" A shot thudded into the parapet, sending earth and stones flying all around us.—"Hell and Hades! I've lost another shilling!—Well, my lord, now's your best chance to come in on the game!"

Cornwallis smiled. "I'd like a better knowledge of the odds, Captain Macdonell." And he walked on to talk to some of the soldiers.

"Where's Alexander Fraser?" I asked. "Surely he's the man to build a tall parapet?"

"Och, that idle young devil's lazing about in our redoubt there, Colonel, Number 10. He's waiting for Lafayette to attack it—swears they'll never take it while he's alive." He wiped his brow with the back of a dirty hand. "He's become a good soldier, the bashful young laird, the best of our ensigns. A lion in sheep's clothing, a fearful executioner with his claymore!" He grinned his wicked grin. "But ye can still make him blush like a maid!"

I turned to follow Cornwallis. "Look after yourselves, you and Alexander, Jamie."

"We'll do our best to, Colonel, never fear! But it seems the enemy have a great mind to do it for us!"

Everywhere we walked, throughout the town, there were houses burned and ruined, men killed and wounded. Civilians too—men, women and children—inevitably suffered. We endeavoured to pass most of these poor people out through the lines under a flag. Mr. Secretary Nelson, fortunately unwounded, was one; though only consenting to quit the town after his house had been near brought to ruin—and the headquarters had run out of port.

The hospitals were set up on the shore below the cliffs and the sick and wounded were taken to these. The wounds from splinters of shells quickly turned gangrenous, and, since most were wounded this way, many more died than would be the case in a normal campaign. There were many too, who were injured or burned as the houses fell or caught fire. All these were in addition to those who fell ill of the fever or the flux. So that there was a steady traffic by cart and litter, day and night, from the town to the hospitals and thence to the cemeteries. And the cemeteries grew in proportion as the town fell more and more into ruin.

I had never been in a beleaguered town before, so had never witnessed such desperate misery, agony and despair amongst a civil population; and found it the more distressing.

We walked along the shore and past the entrance to Cornwallis' cave. A little to one side of the entrance a blanket covered a body. Cornwallis saw it and checked in his stride; then, bowing his head, walked on.

As we came to where my boat lay, I thought it time to suggest to Cornwallis the plan for a withdrawal through Gloucester. I had discussed it with O'Hara, Abercrombie, Dundas and Ross. We proposed to withdraw the army from York to Gloucester in the course of two nights, leaving a small rear party in York to deceive the enemy by a constant and determined fire. Then to break through the small enemy force encircling Gloucester and march to New York. With no cannon or large train to hinder us we should move faster than any possible pursuit.

O'Hara and I put this to Cornwallis; but though he listened attentively he seemed not to hear us. His eyes were on the blanket by the cave. He nodded abstractedly.

"My lord," I said, "it is imperative that the decision on this plan be made before the enemy parallels approach nearer and we suffer casualties which will weaken us excessively for the march to New York."

[*263*]

He nodded again, looking straight at me; not a vacant gaze, but full of thoughts—though I doubt a damned one touched on our plan. As he turned to go, I grabbed Ross by the arm.

"Ross, you and General O'Hara have got to make him see the sense and the need for haste in this plan—and quickly. Or we're lost."

Ross nodded. "I understand, Colonel, but," he shook his head at me reproachfully, "he's far sicker than you think."

I spent the next three days and nights in more and more of a fever of frustration. On the night of Friday the 12th October, Charles O'Hara came across to see me. The strain of the constant bombardment was telling on him. He was slow and stiff and clumsy, his eyes bloodshot and every line of his face deep-etched. He looked weary beyond bearing. He drained half a glass of brandy.

"Philip, we haven't a gun that hasn't been unbreached at least once, and the most are damaged beyond any repair we can attempt. They'll have their second parallel within three hundred yards of us soon. We outnumber them in one thing only—casualties. We've had a hundred and forty men killed and wounded in the last few days, and of the civilians—God knows how many! We've nigh on two thousand sick and wounded now—near half our strength. We're down to a couple of days' ammunition for what cannon and mortars we have left."

"Has Cornwallis decided on the withdrawal plan?"

O'Hara shook his head dejectedly. "No. Charles Cochrane arrived on—what's today—Friday?—yes, then he came on Wednesday night. Don't ask me how he got here. Brought an express from Pussy and some other letters—one for you, that's it. Pussy said he hoped to sail on the 12th—"

"That's today!"

"Ay, so it is. Well, let's hope he does—but I doubt he has. His letter said something about possibly not coming until the middle of November. What the Hades does he think he'll find here then?"

"What did Cornwallis say?"

"Since you were last there he's said damned little at all. The sight of Cochrane cheered him, but Pussy's letter bitched the effect of that. And then, of course—" He broke off and re-filled his glass.

"Then, of course, what—?"

"Well—" He looked into his glass. "Cornwallis took Cochrane out to see the light infantry. Cochrane was a light infantryman himself, you remember—"

"Was?"

"Yes—was. Shot took his head off—standing right beside Cornwallis and covered him with his blood. You can imagine what that did for Cornwallis. Poor old Cochrane." He shook his head sadly. "Brave fellow. Well, nice quick way to go—"

"And Cornwallis is worse?"

"Well, he's certainly no better. Might help if you came to see him again. I've tried to get him to make up his mind about marching to New York. But it's no good—he won't. Says he must wait here for Pussy. And Pussy's waiting for bloody Christmas. Why don't you come and try?"

"I'll come tomorrow."

O'Hara finished his second glass, sighed and gave a great yawn. "Good. Well, I must get back to the fair. Everything ready to march here?"

"Everything. Horses ready, wagons loaded, forage cut—everything."

"Good." He got up stiffly and stretched. "You come and tell Charles that. If we don't go soon there'll be none left to go at all."

In the perpetual glare of the fires across the water, I watched his boat picking its way back, through the blackened hulks of the frigate *Charon* and the transports destroyed by the fire of the French batteries on the river bank, back into the inferno which had been York.

"Glad you moved us when you did, Colonel." It was Tarleton; a more modest, even-tempered, restrained, likeable Tarleton now. War and wounds and sickness and command can finally tame the wildest, and the past year's bitterness and pain had had their effect on him.

"Come in and have some brandy, Banastre," I said. "You'll excuse me while I read a letter from my wife—first I've had for nearly a year."

It was the one dated New Year's Day, 1781. It said the trap carrying Kitty to visit her mother had overturned on the icy road. Kitty had been thrown out. The next morning, in her mother's home, she had given birth, before her time, to a child stillborn. And that same evening— Christmas Eve—had died.

I must have said something. Tarleton looked up and leapt to his feet. "Colonel! sit down here—not bad news—?"

I said, "You knew Matthew Ryan?"

"Of course. Who didn't? I was so grieved to—"

"Read that."

Tarleton read the letter. "My God—" He put the letter on the table, sat down and read it through again. He held the letter down with the remains of his right hand and smoothed it out slowly with the left. He looked up at me, down at the letter, and up again. He said quietly, "Colonel, it's a hard thing to say—but perhaps, in the circumstances, it's as well it happened."

[265]

I said, unreasonably, "If Matthew had been home she'd not have gone to her mother's."

Tarleton leaned across the table. "How can you know that?" Then pushed himself back in his chair and nodded. "Yes, I know. This damnable, damnable war! It reaches deeper and deeper into all our lives. And so much happens because of it that need never have happened." He picked up the letter. "D'you know the song—

> 'Into the pool of life is thrown
> A stone,
> And none
> Can tell how far the ripples run—?' "

I walked out again on to the shore. I paced slowly along the river's edge. The smouldering fires of York turned the smooth, black waters to blood. The only thought in my mind was—had I not come to these infernal, God-forsaken colonies, two people who had served my family well, two whom we all loved, would that day be alive and happy with their child.

The following morning, at dawn, whilst I was going my round of the defences, Col. John Mercer of the rebel Virginia Militia rode up, under a flag, to the main redoubt. He was escorted by four troopers. They had two led horses with them. On one, a man, bareheaded, in a green jacket, his hands tied behind his back. On the other, a roll of blankets. I went out to meet them. Mercer saluted and dismounted, his expression set and grim.

"Colonel, I have to report that I have discovered the whereabouts of Major Fairleigh." He nodded towards the roll of blanket. "Unload it." His men laid it gently on the ground. I lifted the corner of the blanket. It was the body of James Fairleigh, still in his uniform. As I looked, dumb with horror, I felt my throat constrict, for around his neck—now shrivelled and livid—was the raw, red scar of a rope.

I let the blanket fall back. I stood up. I felt myself shaking with rage and disgust. I said—and my voice shook too,

"Who did this?"

"A gang of which this fellow here is a member." Mercer pointed at the man in the green jacket. "He is twice a deserter, once from your army and once from ours. I leave him with you to do what you will with him." He stretched out his hand to me. "Believe me, Colonel, I mourn the death of this brave, young man as much as you. I've sent Roger Chawton with his troop to search for the gang. He wished you to know that."

"Thank you. Pray give him my best wishes for his success. I'm very grateful, Colonel Mercer."

He nodded silently and climbed back on to his horse. Then he said, "Pray God we may see an early end to all this misery and bitterness, Colonel."

"Amen to that," I said. And he saluted and rode away.

The prisoner stood between two dragoons of the Legion. All green jackets together; a colour I used to like. I looked down at the roll of blanket at my feet for a long time. Then I looked at the prisoner. That was all he needed.

"It weren't me, your honour! God's truth, it weren't me! We was ordered to do it."

"You will tell me the truth—all of it."

"I will—I will, your honour—" He stared at me and swallowed hard. His face was the filthiest shade of grey and, even in the chill morning air, he sweated. "Well, see, your honour, we'd all been in a village down on the river, when we heard the French was a-coming to attack Gloucester. So we comes in on the side like, waitin' for a few pickin's—a loose nag, weapons, powder and such."

"Why don't you draw your horses and powder from the rebel quartermasters?"

"Rebels!" he cried, to my astonishment, "We ain't rebels! Well, that is—we're independent like—"

"Independent to loot and murder who, where and what you like?"

Head down, he muttered sullenly, "We ain't the only ones."

"Is that your excuse?" He kept his head down. I said between my teeth, "Go on, man, tell me what happened."

He started again. "Well, your honour, these fellers a-comin' sharpish down the track, with scouts out an' all, they sees us. We 'eard 'em shout we was Lee's lot, and they come at us. We was dismounted, and, anyways, we don't want no fight with proper troops and such, so we gives a volley to slow 'em, gets on our prads and off."

He peered up now and again to see how I was taking his story.

"Seems the officer's 'orse took fright. It bolted with 'im, right through us. Some of the others come after us, but they didn't come on too far, 'cause the fight started up away be'ind 'em. Then this officer tried to get back—and—we took 'im."

He looked up at me and licked his lips nervously. "I said to let 'im go. I didn't want to—"

[267]

"Go on," I said. And his head ducked down again.

"He were 'andy with 'is slicer and done us a fair bit of mischief. We didn't knock 'im off. We could see he were an officer, and on a good 'orse. We reckoned we could get more for 'em both alive, one way or another. He 'ad an arm broke an' a bang on the noddle, your honour, that's all—and I didn't give 'im neither—"

"What next?" I said.

"Well, we wouldn't 'ave done no more to 'im. But when we got back to the village the Major said as 'ow 'e were a traitor and to 'ang 'im. 'Course, the Major only said that to butter the Congressmen as were with 'im—"

"What Congressmen are these?"

"Oh, they ain't proper Congressmen, your honour, they're commissioners. The Major's been lushing 'em up for two or three days now to get a proper commission. That's what 'e come 'ere for. Give 'em some loot too—they didn't mind getting their mauleys on that neither—"

"And so you hanged the officer?"

He seemed to shrivel. "Weren't me, your honour—"

"And where's the rest of your rabble now?"

"Off back in the 'ills, I'd think, your honour."

"Then how were you caught here?"

"Well, me and two mates 'ad a woman in the village—an' we got left be'ind somehow. Then these rebel militia come to the woman's house, an' one of my mates what 'ad just cut 'is stick from 'em, lets fly at 'em with his pistol. They knocks 'im off, and t'other one too. I was with the woman at the time, an' they grabs me an' takes me back with 'em. They'd found the officer. So then the Colonel asks me what I knows—and that's it, your honour."

"What do you call this band of yours?"

"Ain't got no proper name—no more nor any lot like us. Most we call ourselves the militia of what colony we're in—then you can act rebel or loyal to suit yourself."

"And what are you called now?"

"The Major calls us Virginia Militia when he's talking to the commissioners, your honour."

"Indeed? And what's he call himself, this major?"

"Major Cook your—"

"Cook!" My sudden fury set the wretch snivelling again.

"It was 'im what told us to 'ang the officer—"

"How long have you been with him?"

"'Bout five months—"

"And where before?"

"I was in the 9th Regiment at the start, your honour. We was taken at Saratoga—the Convention Army. Them yankees don't treat prisoners right. I got sick of bein' kicked around by the bastards, so I volunteers for the Pennsylvania Line. That weren't no better than bein' in clink. They give us naught to eat and less to wear an' only that Continental crap for ready. They'd mutinied before I joined 'em and come this May they 'ad another. General Wayne 'ung some for it and ordered some others on us five 'undred lashes. But I cut me stick with 'em before they could tickle my back. Been on the smout ever since—"

All this came in a rush. I said,

"What's your name?"

"Thorn, your honour."

"Well, we'll not hang you Thorn—yet. I may have need of you."

I sent for the officer commanding James Fairleigh's troop. "Put this man in irons," I said. "He will make a full account of Major Fairleigh's death and swear it before the chaplain."

We buried the body of James Fairleigh of Lochdearn that same morning, by the little chapel in Gloucester. It was a grey day and the mist still hung on the river, deadening the sound of gunfire from the opposite shore. His own men from Belhaven—his friends from boyhood—carried him. They laid him in his grave, wrapped in his cloak, booted and spurred still, his sword on his breast under his folded hands. As they lowered him, they closed the collar of the cloak to cover his face. The carbines volleyed in salute and we turned away and left him; far from Belhaven and the true home he longed for in the glen of Strath Dearn.

That afternoon I crossed again to York in the hope of seeing Cornwallis. I reported first to O'Hara, who was virtually commanding the army whilst Cornwallis was incapacitated. I accompanied him and Robert Abercrombie on their rounds of their commands. A depressing experience—and yet heartening.

The men moved slowly and uncertaintly, near exhausted by the unending labour of repairing the defences and remounting the guns and by the long hours of watching, deafened by the constant thunder of the enemy cannon and the bursting shells, sickened by the sight of their comrades struck down or blown to bloody offal by their side. They staggered as they carried powder and shot to the embrasures, and the wounded from the embrasures to the hospitals. They stumbled blindly into the graves they dug. Relieved from watch, they dropped to the ground by their place of duty, to twitch and groan in the restless sleep of an endless nightmare.

Every hand—soldier or civilian—was pressed into serving the men or the defences and the poor wretches in the hospitals. The surgeons laboured day and night, tending the broken bodies. The chaplains lived in their cassocks, their only office the burial of the dead.

The whole town stank of death. From the tumbled ruins which had once been homes came the bitter reek of powder smoke, of red-hot metal, of charred wood, of burnt brick: from the rubble-piled streets, the stench of the rotting, flyblown carcasses of animals, lying unburied; and from the hospitals, crowded to overflowing, the obscene plague-stink of the puddles of blood and ordure and vomit soiling the floors, and of the heaps of amputated limbs, piling higher and higher, putrefying and crawling with maggots, on which the birds and beasts scavenged and fought and gorged.

But through all this wretchedness and horror the spirit of the army still remained high. Every man—all veterans—could see clearly enough what a bad box we were in; outnumbered, outgunned, a small, concentrated target open at every point to the fire of enemies who, with the aid of their fleet, completely surrounded us. They all asked for news of the arrival of our fleet and the reinforcements promised by Clinton. Of course, we could give no answer. Some asked why Cornwallis was not to be seen on the works now. We said he was sick of a fever; but we did not add that among its symptoms were the agonies of indecision and despair. There was little cheer for them in our replies and they accepted them non-committally. They showed only a grim-faced, weary determination to see the affair through. Under Charles Cornwallis they had suffered in all the weathers of the dreary wastes of the Carolinas, and the dust and heat of the long marches to and through Virginia. They had driven and chased every army that had stood against them. Cornwallis had never failed them yet; he would not fail them now. Nor would they fail him. It is a great privilege, and a greater responsibility, to lead such an army.

When we had done the rounds we went to the cave. Ross met us at the entrance. "General, I regret his lordship's in no state to receive you. He is delirious. The physician says his fever should increase tonight and, if it breaks, he might be able to receive you tomorrow."

I murmured: " 'Tomorrow and tomorrow and tomorrow, Creeps in this petty pace from day to day, To the last syllable of recorded time'; and that's just about when we'll get a decision out of him!"

"Bigod, Philip," exclaimed O'Hara, "I never thought to hear you quote Hamlet!"

"I never thought to hear you recognize Shakespeare, Charles, and it's Macbeth."

I spent the night in the headquarters. Mr. Secretary Nelson's house having been reduced to a shambles by the enemy fire, the headquarters had removed to his nephew's—the Governor's—house; a solid red-brick affair, not so large nor so elegant as his uncle's, but more stoutly built and less exposed to the guns. The rooms too are smaller, but Governor Nelson had not spared expense in furnishing them, so we were comfortable enough.

Charles O'Hara had ordered all provisions to be put in the care of the Commissary, to be stored and cooked centrally in the cellars of some ruined houses; whence the food was taken regularly to all troops in the lines. So all, including the headquarters staff, ate the same food. This daily, well-prepared meal, together with a regular and generous ration of rum, did much to maintain morale. I had my share with the rest and spent the evening listening to Richard England playing Governor Nelson's excellent new pianoforte and accompanying Charles O'Hara on his visits to the outpost line.

I waited all the next day in the hope of seeing Cornwallis, but his condition was unchanged by late afternoon and I decided to return to Gloucester. As I embarked at around six o'clock that evening, the firing suddenly slackened.

"An assault!" said O'Hara. "You'd better hurry!" He turned on his heel and raced off to his own headquarters. I ordered my crew to pull their hardest. About half way across we heard heavy firing around the fort at Gloucester. After some minutes this too slackened almost to silence. Then, clearly and distinctly, we heard six guns fire, one after the other, on the York side. Immediately the cannon again began their thundering, on both sides. After some moments, from the eastern end of York, around the two redoubts which stood there—Numbers 9 and 10—there came a great rattle of musketry and shouting even above the noise of the cannon.

The firing at Gloucester stopped before I came ashore. I climbed to higher ground and looked across the river. The two redoubts were still under fire; but now the fire came from the parapets of York.

I went at once to my own forward posts, where Tarleton was conducting affairs as calmly as if he were directing a pheasant shoot. "Mere diversion, Colonel. You could see that from the start. Nice peaceable lot on this side. Don't want to cause any trouble. Hardly worth leaving my dinner for—and I'd just mulled some rum too. Be cold now, damn it."

But things were not so well in York. I crossed again before dawn and found O'Hara and Col. Robert Abercrombie in the headquarters, even wearier and grimmer than before.

"We've lost those two redoubts," I said.

Abercrombie nodded. "Ay, and they're extending their parallel into them now. Never known such people for digging. Like a lot of bloody moles. It will bring their guns within a couple of hundred yards of us."

"How's Cornwallis?" I asked.

"Better, thank God," said O'Hara. "The fever broke last night and he's making sense this morning. Better still, he's agreed to the plan. We start transporting across to you tomorrow night and should finish it by first light."

"All in one night? Is there time?"

"Yes, just—allowing for all the sick and wounded we'll have to leave behind. We'll do it in three trips. Robert here is going to spike their main batteries before dawn tomorrow; so we may even get a bit of peace."

"Is there anything I can do?"

"Go and chat to himself. And for God's sake make him stay in bed. He's too weak to be anything but a nuisance."

I ordered the boat back to warn Tarleton and Simcoe to prepare for the march, then went to the cave. Cornwallis was in a neat little room, curtained about with green baize and furnished with a bed, a washstand, cupboard and dressing table; borrowed, I suppose, from Mr. Secretary Nelson's house.

He was lying propped up on cushions, his campaign writing-table on his lap. His skin had that bloodless pallor which follows a fever; his eyes were deep in dark sockets. He was writing slowly and laboriously, but stopped as I came in and stretched a hand to me—all fleshless tendon and bone, like one of da Vinci's anatomical sketches. He has never carried much weight, though Gainsborough's new portrait of him shows him plumper now than he was wont to be, but, that morning, he looked like an animated skeleton. I took his hand. "This is better. You had us very worried." I looked at the hand I held. "There's no meat on you at all."

"Oh, I'll get that back quick enough. I'll be up tomorrow."

"If you get up tomorrow you'll fall flat on your face. We'll get a litter to carry you for the crossing tomorrow night."

"I shan't be with you."

"What do you mean? You'll be fit enough to move with us. It will be uncomfortable but—"

"But I should just have to stand it—is that it? D'you think I couldn't, for God's sake? But what if I become more ill?"

"We might have to wait a bit—"

"Yes—to wait a bit—maybe to stand and fight a bit, and not escape free to New York—for me!" His breathing was quick and shallow. "Exactly. That's why I can't agree to come. I got the army into this mess because I was stupid, and I'll not have it sacrifice itself for me because I'm sick. I won't—"

"Do I interrupt?" O'Hara poked his head between the curtains closing the entrance of the little room.

Cornwallis grinned. "I smell conspiracy!"

"Charles," I said to O'Hara, "he doesn't want to come with us to New York."

"Because," Cornwallis broke in, "—I shall be a burden and a cause of delay, which we can't afford. If the enemy take me here, with the rest of our sick, they may not be so urgent to pursue you."

I said, "Do you remember the chief reason you gave Prudence at Camden that we must fight Gates and not retreat?—eight hundred sick in hospital that you would not leave? D'you think the army's forgotten that? Charles, if you order it to leave you here, it will die of shame."

He glared at me angrily, plucking at the edge of a blanket with wasted fingers; tears of frustration at his weakness ran down his thin cheeks.

"And that's the bloody truth!" said O'Hara.

Cornwallis knew he was defeated. He sank back on his pillows and rubbed feebly at his tears with the back of his hand. He nodded. "Very well—very well." He picked up the paper on which he had been writing and held it out to me. "I want you both to read that, then have Ross copy it and dispatch it. I expect it will be my last letter to the Commander-in-Chief."

With O'Hara looking over my shoulder, I read—"Sir, last evening the enemy carried two advanced redoubts on the left by storm . . . My situation now becomes very critical . . . we shall soon be exposed to an assault in ruined works, in a bad position, and with weakened numbers . . . I cannot recommend that the fleet and army should run great risk in endeavouring to save us . . . ."

Cornwallis said, "I now have no hopes for this place. Take the letter. I have another to write. If I am to leave the wounded and sick of my army—and not to stay to defend their interests; if I am to leave a force in this town—and not to stay to command it, then I must write, personally, to intercede with the allied commanders for both. I shall do that now."

As O'Hara and I bowed and went to the entrance curtains, Cornwallis added, "Charles, tell Robert Abercrombie, from me—to go in fast and hard with his sortie to spike the batteries. Tell him not to tarry in their lines. He is to spike the guns to stop the killing—not to kill. Tell him."

"I'll tell him."

"And Charles—tell him from me—God keep him and his men."

O'Hara blinked. "M'lord."

The preparations for Abercrombie's sortie and the evacuation of the town proceeded side by side securely and successfully. And, in both cases, fruitlessly; for both failed completely.

Abercrombie's sortie went out at three o'clock next morning. The storming companies penetrated unobserved to the enemy's second parallel, surprising the French defenders. Then all went awry.

You spike a gun by blocking the touch-hole—the little, round vent in the breech of the gun through which the main charge is ignited. You use a small spike, like a round nail, of a metal hard enough to resist a drill and of a size to fit tightly into the touch-hole. You hammer this spike into the touch-hole and cut off and file down any part that you cannot punch in below the level of the lip of the hole until it is level with the lip; so that the spike cannot be gripped with pincers and withdrawn.

The spiking party was to follow the storming companies. They did. But they lost their way in the darkness and had to fall back.

So the enemy guns, spiked with the bayonet points of the storming companies, broken off and hammered in with their musket butts, were unspiked and in service again by noon.

At ten o'clock that night the first embarkation, the light infantry, the Guards and the 23rd Regiment, began to cross. I travelled with them and disembarked at Gloucester a little before midnight, returning the boats immediately to York to embark the second party. The enemy, on both banks of the river, remained entirely unaware of the movement. At about two o'clock a sudden, violent squall swept up the river, drenching us and swamping the two dinghies moored at the jetty. It lasted only a few minutes and we hoped it would not long delay the second embarkation. We waited a dark, shivering, dank eternity. At last, around half past four, a boat ground on to the beach. A sodden Alexander Ross clambered out and saluted. "The troops are to return to York, Colonel. We've not time to get the rest across before dawn."

"Return! Why, for God's sake? Where are the boats?"

"They're coming across now, Colonel—what's left of them. We lost half, and a good few men, in that storm."

"But, in God's name! Why drag these troops back? We could get clear way to New York if we started now! Whose orders are these?"

"His lordship's." Ross' face was expressionless.

"But, Ross—"

"Those are his lordship's orders, Colonel." His unfailing composure failed suddenly and explosively. "Colonel, General O'Hara has argued, Colonel Abercrombie has argued, we've all argued—but—those are his orders."

There was a silence—except for the never ending cannonade. I said, "Well, if we're all to die, at least we'll go to hell in good company." And I went for the commanding officers.

It was drizzling now. The heavy clouds, splashed crimson by the blaze of the guns and the flaring, smouldering ruins, hung bloodily, ominously over the desolation of York.

The commanding officers came, one by one, wrapped in their cloaks, tumbling down the beach to where I stood by the boat. When they were all arrived, I said simply, "Gentlemen, we are all to return to York." The worst moment of my military career.

One of them said, "All? You mean all of us—and our soldiers, Colonel?"

"All."

I could not see their faces, but I could sense—and, in some cases, fear—their reactions. It was clear to everyone that surrender in York was now inevitable. One of them said—"Colonel, couldn't we—?"

"No," I said, "we could not."

A long sigh. It seemed to come from everyone there. The one who had spoken said resignedly, "No, I suppose we couldn't—not and leave the General and the other lads."

And that was the end of that plan. If we had done it only twenty-four hours before—but what's the use? There's never any comfort to be found in "If only—." War is a matter of realities.

I gave orders for the re-embarkation and, after it was completed, returned to York myself. I took with me what few possessions I had left; which now amounted to little more than the uniform I wore, my sword, my pistols, my razor and the miniature of Anne. No soldier ever travelled lighter. I handed over command to John Simcoe. There would be little more commanding to be done in Gloucester.

Ashore in York, I sent Andrew to find us room in the new headquarter
in Mr. Secretary Nelson's nephew's house, and went straight to the cave
Cornwallis was lying on his bed, part clothed in shirt, breeches an
stockings. He looked sicker than the day before. He smiled faintly. "Goo
morning, Philip. Well, Heaven has ordained that you should not carry m
off to New York in a wagon." His tone was almost gay. "I've sent for th
others. We must have our final council."

His apparent pleasure that our plan had been frustrated by the weathe
angered me, and his easy acceptance of the prospect of surrende
infuriated me. I had never in my service been party to any surrender
Only the enemy surrendered.

"Where's the need for a 'final council'?" The disgust and anger in m
voice took the smile off his face. "You've made up your mind. You'
surrender us like a flock of witless sheep. What's there to discuss?"

He smiled again, patiently; which infuriated me all the more.

"Terms for the surrender of the sheep?"

"What terms?" I spat the words. "The same terms as King's Mountain
To be targets for their rifle practice—for their bayonet practice—for thei
knife throwing—to be stabbed, burned, hanged at their pleasure?—kicke
into a ditch to die when they've finished with us? You'll be content wit
those terms, I suppose? By God, Charles—not three hours ago th
commanding officers of the Guards, the 23rd and light infantry and all th
garrison of Gloucester would have marched with me to New York had
agreed." My voice grew harsher and harsher. "I would to God now I ha
agreed!"

"And why didn't you?"

"Because I had your orders. Your orders to return to York—like loya
sheep to the fold. To be surrendered for slaughter or sold into slavery lik
their Congress sold the men Burgoyne surrendered at Saratoga. But, o
course, they let Burgoyne away to England on parole!"

That roused him. It was a vicious and unpardonable thing to say to hir
of all people, but I was sick at heart with the shame of surrender. He sai
coldly, "And had you tried to march to New York, what do you think yot
could achieve?"

"We could fight—which is what we were sent here to do! We wouldn'
surrender tamely to an enemy we've always thrashed no matter what th
odds! If we died, then at least we died fighting like soldiers—not waiting
to be butchered like cattle."

He lay on his pillows, staring at me; a supercilious stare. I raged on
"Can't you realize this army wants only a chance to fight—to fight! You'v

[*276*]

ven us all our fill of sitting as targets for the enemy's guns. Now you'd
rrender us to be targets for their recruits' muskets and bayonets. If we
ght and we die—"

"If you die—and with three thousand only now fit to bear arms against
ore than fifteen thousand I can see you doing naught else—if you die,
hat benefit will fall to your country—to anyone—to anything? Do you
ink Anne wishes to see you die?—do your children? Do you think that
e families of these soldiers would prefer that they died in a final,
peless assault—or that they returned home, alive and well?"

He pushed himself up from his pillows and levelled a thin, shaking
ger at me. "You know if I thought there was now the slightest chance of
trieving this situation I would take it. You know that!" He was
eathing short and hard now—as angry as I was. "I know I've been
rogant in my opinions, mistaken in my judgments, weak in my
ill—and a little sick. These have resulted in our present desperate strait.
one little week five hundred souls—men, women and children—who
usted me, have died through my folly and weakness. Is this too light a
rden for me? And do you want now to add another three thousand—
d more women and children—to it? Why? To justify my judgment—
hich I own to have been mistaken? Or to gratify your pride—which you
ow, in your heart, to be blind and selfish?

"As for terms—the enemy here are professional soldiers and their
mmanders are gentlemen. They're not the rabble of brute beasts who
urdered their prisoners at King's Mountain."

He was right, of course. Nothing could be remedied now; least of all by
major assault by our few troops against the united strength of the allied
my. There was nothing to be done. I slumped into the chair and the fire
me burned out into the bitter ashes of frustration and shame.

Cornwallis leaned back on his pillows again. His tone softened. "Philip,
u know well—everyone knows—my opinions on the futility of this civil
ar. I remember you said on your sick-bed in Charlestown that, if you'd
en a colonist, you would have resisted the King's authority. And I
member I said that I believe I should have ridden with you. Well, I
lieve now that—after this—the King may be so discouraged that he will
gree to end this futile struggle which benefits only our mutual enemies."

"But what will happen to those who stayed loyal to the King—the
egion, Queen's Rangers, New York Volunteers, Loyal Americans—all
e provincials and militias—thousands of them and their families, and all
e others who supported the King in every colony? What will they do?"

"What did our—and their—ancestors do, a hundred and thirty years

[*277*]

ago after our civil war, those who remained loyal to the Crown?"

"They survived after a fashion."

"Exactly—and so will these. Oh, there'll be persecutions, and many ⬦ the best will fly the country—to Canada—to England—as their forbea fled here from England and Scotland. But most of them are men (character and ability, and what country can do without such men? Th fever will pass."

The curtains over the entrance were pulled aside and O'Har Abercrombie, Dundas and Ross came in, followed by Colonel vo Seybothen, the senior officer of the Hessian regiments, Captain Rochfo of the artillery, Lieutenant Sutherland, the chief engineer, and Commi sary Stedman, who had assumed the duties of Commissary Perkins aft he had been killed.

"Good morning, gentlemen," said Cornwallis, "I'll not detain you lon You'd better sit on the end of the bed, Ross, if you're going to wri legibly." He eyed Rochfort's face, blacked by powder and streaked wit sweat, his burnt and torn jacket, his bandaged hands. "How many gu do we have left in action, Rochfort?"

"One at the moment, my lord—and I doubt that's for long. But we'll g more back as we can."

"And crews?"

"We're training a few more to replace casualties as we go, my lord The young artillery officer's face was impassive, past all emotion.

"And ammunition?"

"If we had all guns in action, I should estimate—say, two days, m lord."

"Thank you, Rochfort," Cornwallis gave a little bow from his pillow "Thank you. And Sutherland—?" He groaned compassionately. "Poo lad—I'm afraid you'll have to wake him; he may have something we nee to hear."

The engineer leant against the wall, asleep on his feet. Dundas shoo him gently by the shoulder. "Sandy, wake up, lad!"

Sutherland jerked awake, blinking. It took him a few moments ⬦ remember where he was, as always with men stretched beyond all natur limits. Cornwallis said kindly.

"I'm sorry to wake you, Sutherland. If anyone here deserves a rest yo do. Will you please describe the condition of our defences?—and ad anything else you wish."

Sutherland screwed his eyes tight shut, then opened them very wid le shook his head once—and again. His voice was slow and the words urred. "M'lord—very sorry, m'lord. Defences—yes—not much left of m—assailable most places—" He blinked a few times, and the last time is eyes stayed shut for a few seconds. He swayed, then his eyes opened ;ain and he tried to take a firmer grip of himself. "We can't keep them in ıy satisfactory state of repair. We've worked—rebuilt—hundred mes—no good. Abatis—all thrown down—ruined—put up some aizing—never lasts more'n an hour—thrown down. My men— khausted, m'lord—"

"Thank you, Sutherland," said Cornwallis. "Go and tell your men to et some sleep. There's no more for you to do."

Sutherland stumbled out.

"Gentlemen," Cornwallis began quietly, "I do not intend that the army ıould continue to suffer this bombardment until the enemy decide to ssault, and then for those still able to fight to defend indefensible works gainst a force already five times their number. I have written the ollowing letter to General Washington, who commands the allied forces:

" 'I propose a cessation of hostilities for twenty-four hours, and that two fficers may be appointed by each side, to meet at Mr. Moore's house, to :ttle terms for the surrender of the posts of York and Gloucester.' " He ıid the letter on his knees and looked at each of us in turn. "Are there any bjections or comments on that letter?"

No one spoke. Cornwallis nodded.

"Thank you, gentlemen. I've no doubt General Washington will hasten ıatters to allow the Comte de Grasse to leave with the French fleet before superior British fleet arrives. I intend to request the customary honours; nd that the entire force be paroled and returned to England and ìermany; and that all provincial troops, militia and civilians who have ıined us are protected. I have appointed Colonel Dundas and Major Ross) act on our behalf—who better than two hard-headed Scots? Does ıyone wish to add to these proposals, or amend them?"

Again no one spoke. Cornwallis handed the letter to Ross, who copied :, sealed it and returned it to him. Cornwallis said,

"We must signal the enemy from some foremost position to show we ʋish to parley. I think the horn work would be best." He offered the letter o Abercrombie. "Robert, since those defences are within your area of esponsibility, will you please deliver this personally to General Washing-on?"

Abercrombie took the letter with obvious distaste. He turned it over in

his hands. Then he shrugged, bowed stiffly and strode out of the cave.
thought he could do with some moral support, so I begged to be excuse
and followed him. We paced through the reeking, smouldering, stinkin
ruins side by side. Robert Abercrombie is a man of few words. He sai
gloomily,

"What a damned thing to have to do."

And that was all that was said until we reached his light infantr
positions. The men on duty were digging steadily, repairing the parape
above their trenches. They were filthy and ready to drop with fatigue
Their officer, his head and one arm bandaged, came to report. Aber
crombie cut him short.

"D'you have a drummer?"

The officer, as exhausted as his soldiers, stared uncertainly a
Abercrombie. "A drummer, Colonel?"

"Yes, a drummer. D'you have one here?"

"Why, yes—a drummer—yes," the officer mumbled confusedly. "Yes
there's a drummer—" He turned and staring round vaguely, shouted
"Drummer!"

A thin little lad heaved himself wearily out of the trench in which h
had been huddled asleep. His jacket and breeches were stained with eart
and the blood of men he had tended; his face was the colour of chalk. Th
sergeant brushed him down with a heavy hand and rammed the boy'
grenadier cap down on his head. He was one of the boys who ha
volunteered to join the army as drummers at Hillsborough in Nort
Carolina. Brave little lads they were.

Abercrombie looked him up and down—it wasn't very far either way
"Up to the top of the parapet, lad, and beat for a parley."

The boy blinked. "For a parley?—yes, your honour." He begar
clumsily to stumble up the crumbling, shifting slope of the parapet. A
round shot roared over his head and thudded into the back of the parado
on the opposite side of the work. The boy ducked—far too late. He
turned, still crouched, to gaze fearfully at Abercrombie. "The—the top o
the parapet—your honour—?"

Abercrombie's grim face relaxed into a grin. He took out a white
handkerchief, drew his sword and tied the handkerchief to the hilt.

"Come on, lad, up behind me."

He scrambled up the steep slope to the top and held the sword, by its
blade, above his head. The drummer clambered up awkwardly after him
carrying his drum on his hip. On top of the parapet he hooked his drun
on its sling, came to the attention, head up, chest out, squaring his elbow

with his sticks held horizontal, level with his mouth. Then, he began to eat.

And, with the rattle of that drum, barely audible even to us above the roar of the guns that still fired on the flanks, there ended, to all intents and purposes, that most futile of all civil wars, the American Rebellion.

Chapter Eighteen

In which, in surrender, I meet with a cousin.

General Washington and Admiral de Grasse were in a tearing hurry to get the matter done. Understandably. Both feared the arrival of a British fleet. For Washington it could mean frustration of his strategy of concentration against York. It could force him into assaulting the town before we were reinforced; which, though he might have succeeded, could have cost him dear in casualties. For de Grasse it could have meant an earlier date for the day, six months later, on which his fleet was shattered, his flagship captured and himself made prisoner.

So, whilst General Lincoln, hoping to be relieved, had been allowed to bumble on for five days before surrendering Charlestown to us, Dundas and Ross were accused by the enemy commissioners of procrastination after a mere ten hours.

Cornwallis summoned a council that same evening. He was still in the cave; there was no point in moving him from it whilst the possibility of a renewal of the bombardment remained. We were joined at the cave by Capt. Thomas Symonds, the senior naval officer in York. Dundas and Ross were already there, having brought the draft of the terms of the surrender treaty.

Cornwallis, still very pale, turned at once to business. "I have the draft of the terms here. They're not as generous in some aspects as I hoped—however—" and he began to read them through. You will have seen them in the newspapers, so I shan't repeat them here. When he had finished he said, "Are there any comments?"

Commissary Stedman spoke first. "My lord, in respect of that article about the handing over of arms and stores an' all, I suggest we pays each man as much of his back pay as possible, which the terms allows 'em to

ep. That'll give 'em all a bit of the ready while they're prisoners. And
other thing is that I got a good store of new clothing—jackets, breeches,
shirts an' all—what'd be a pity to hand over. We could give all the lads a
good, new coat for their backs, and what with winter a-coming on, I'd
think they'd be glad of it."

Cornwallis nodded. "Well thought on for both points, Mr. Stedman.
Please do as you suggest."

"D'you have any clothing an officer could use, Mr. Stedman?" O'Hara
asked hopefully.

The Commissary shook his head. "No, General, I'm sorry, 'tis all
soldiers' clothing I got. Don't think I can do nothing for officers."

O'Hara looked dejectedly at his frayed cuffs and the patches on the
knees of his breeches. "What about a hat?"

"Got no braid for it, General. Leastways, not for a general."

"Haven't got any braid on this floppy old piss-pot I've got now,"
grunted O'Hara. "Oh, well, never mind. They'll just have to think us a
damned shabby lot—"

A sudden thought struck me. "Have you got a dragoon jacket, Mr.
Stedman?—17th Light Dragoon or such?"

"I got a Scots Grey jacket, Colonel, for your fellow what was
killed—and a hat and breeches besides. Bit on the small side for him, he
said, which is why he didn't draw 'em."

"Good. I'll send my servant for them. They'll fit him."

Stedman looked mystified. "Your servant?—d'you mean that black
fellow of yours?"

"The terms say I'm permitted to keep my servant. If he's dressed as a
militiaman he'll be thought to be an escaped slave—which he's not—
and I'll be damned if I let them drag him off to be flogged or hanged. If
he's in the King's uniform he's a soldier, and my soldier-servant, and they
can't take him. And I can make sure he returns to his proper home at
Belhaven."

Cornwallis said patiently, "Perhaps we might return to our consideration of the terms?"

I said, "My lord, what's to happen to my provincials and militia? The
terms imply that if they are given any trial at all it will be in rebel
courts—which means they will be murdered either way, out of hand. And
there are other loyalists here in York as well."

"I have instructed the captain of the sloop *Bonetta*, which will carry my
despatches to New York, to conceal as many loyalists—of every sort, but
specially soldiers—on board before he sails. The terms state it will not be

searched. I shall ask the Comte de Grasse to provide a guard to stop the rebels from interfering with anyone boarding the vessel. More I cannot do."

"I may inform them of this."

"You may."

"And I shall instruct them to escape in any other way also."

Cornwallis shrugged. "I believe that their disposal affords an embarrassment to General Washington of which he will be happy to be relieved."

There was some discussion of other points. When all was done, O'Hara leaned well back in his chair, out of Cornwallis' view and winked at us. He said thoughtfully, "My lord, since when we march out tomorrow to surrender our arms you'll not be fit to stand, let alone ride a horse, I propose to the council that I command the troops during the ceremony."

Cornwallis flared up at once. "That's unthinkable! I must command at such a time—of all times! What the devil will my soldiers think if they don't see me at their head tomorrow?"

"What the devil will they think if they see you fall off your horse on your head?" O'Hara rejoined. Even Cornwallis laughed.

"Charles," he protested, "I'll be well enough tomorrow. It can't be far to ride—"

"Away!" said O'Hara. "Ride? You can't even walk across this room! He turned to Ross. "What do the physicians say?"

"They advise most strongly against it, General."

"And I should damned well think so. Well, my lord, you'll please be ruled by your council on this." O'Hara glanced round at us. "Are we all agreed on it? Colonel von Seybothen, I should ask you especially, do you agree, sir?"

The commander of the Anspach battalions nodded. "You should command, General."

Cornwallis fretted still. "What will General Washington think—?"

O'Hara thumped his fist on his knee. "Och, to the devil with Washington and his thoughts! He's getting his pound of flesh isn't he? Philip, will your cousin have fits because his lordship doesn't tip his hat to him in person—hey?"

"I can't believe any of the allied commanders would wish you to distress yourself, my lord."

Cornwallis looked at me, then nodded briefly. "Very well. I shall abide by the decision of the council." He pushed himself up from his pillows. "Ross, would you give me my sword, please?"

Ross brought the sword. A workmanlike, well-used weapon; the gilt fittings on the guard and the plain, steel scabbard dulled and chipped, the ivory grips yellowed with use, the gold cord of the sword knot tarnished and frayed; and the blade, bright and keen as new. Ross looked at it doubtfully. "You didn't mean your dress sword, my lord?"

"No," said Cornwallis, "I didn't." He held out the sword to O'Hara. "Here, Charles, take it."

O'Hara took it uncertainly. He cocked an eyebrow at Dundas. "Tom, there's nothing in the terms about surrendering swords?—"

"Nothing, General. My lord, the terms clearly state that we keep our sidearms."

"Yes, I understand, Dundas," said Cornwallis. "And I'll regret to lose this faithful old friend. Nevertheless, Charles, you will please take it and present it personally to General Washington—and to General Washington alone."

O'Hara nodded.

"You will say to him—" Cornwallis' voice shook, "you will say—that as I am not able—myself—to be present—I send him my sword."

O'Hara got slowly to his feet, the sword lying in both hands. He looked down at it and then at Cornwallis. He started to speak but shook his head. He bowed jerkily, turned on his heel and went out. There was nothing more said. We left Cornwallis lying there, staring, blankly, at the blank wall.

The article governing the surrender ceremony required us to march out from York at two o'clock the following afternoon. We formed in column of regiments, though they looked more like companies their ranks were so thin; about three thousand in all, with the music of each regiment at its head. Robert Abercrombie was at the head of his light infantry, Lieutenant-Colonels Yorke and Dundas at the heads of their brigades, with the Anspach and Hessian commanders at the heads of their commands. Which left O'Hara and myself with Ross and a few others of Cornwallis' staff at the head of the column. Hardly a soldier in the column did not have a new coat and hat and O'Hara remarked on it.

"Make us look a lot of scarecrows! Stedman's done 'em well. First time anyone's got something for nothing out of that tight-fisted old bastard. Been generous with the rum too, I see."

He pulled up by the 23rd Regiment. "Why have you lads got your knapsacks packed? Where d'you all think you're away to?"

A sergeant grinned up at him. "I was with the 62nd at Saratoga, your honour. The bastards marched us straight off to clink from where we stacked our arms so's they could pinch all our kit what we'd left in our bivouacs. They're not catching us like that again!"

It wanted ten minutes or so of two o'clock. The commanders came up to report their corps. O'Hara said sourly, "There's a few men look as if they'd been bit in the head by the tavern bitch. Put 'em out. I'll have no damned rumtitums fuddling along on this crusade."

Robert Abercrombie said, "And what sort of rumtitum do you wish the music to play on the march, General?"

"They can play the 'Rogue's March' for all I care—No!—I'll tell you what we'll have! Old Washington's twisting our tails, so we'll give his a tweak. Play 'When the King enjoys his own again.' "

"They may not all know it," said Abercrombie.

"Then they've got ten minutes to learn it! They may know it by another name." He grinned. "I know some splendid words to it!"

"We do not know this music, General," said von Seybothen.

"Of course not. What do you suggest for yourselves, Colonel?"

"We have a song 'Ich sah ein schiefflin fahren'—you would say 'I saw a ship a-sailing,' I think—"

"Very appropriate," murmured John Yorke, "dedicated hopefully to Admiral Graves, Colonel? Well, that would go very well with what the 71st wish for their pipes, General."

"Oh, bigod, I'd forgotten the sheep-gut squeakers! What do they want to inflict on us?"

"They've an old song they wish to dedicate to the Commander-in-Chief. Its called 'Ye're o'er lang a-coming'—"

The enemy hearing the laughter that followed, must have thought it strange that the British should be so merry on such an occasion. O'Hara gave a great sigh,—"Well, it's a brave heart that can laugh at its own wake—" he stopped short and stared with amazement at the figure which now approached us. "Now who in the devil is this pompous, little vinegar-pisser, d'ye think?"

It was a French officer, utterly immaculate in his gold-braided white uniform and plumed hat. He halted his horse at some thirty paces from us and stared at us with infinite disdain.

"Faugh!" O'Hara wrinkled his nose, "I can wind him from here!"

After a brief examination, the officer came slowly towards us. It is not easy to appear mincing on a horse, but he managed it very well. After many years of encountering them in and out of battle, I have the highest admiration for the French army and its officers. But if they have many more like this fellow, they have some cause to fear for the future. He reminded me much of the dandiprat whom Clinton had wanted in my place—his cousin, Percy Pelham, being short, stout and wearing a permanent sneer below a bulbous nose and a threadbare string of a moustache. He eyed us haughtily. We were plainly of no importance.

"Where milord Cornwallis?" His tone was as disapproving as his eye.

O'Hara said coldly. "Lord Cornwallis is ill and cannot present himself. am his deputy—Brigadier-General O'Hara."

"No understan'. Where milord Cornwallis?"

I started to explain in my sort of French. Frowning, he waved a white-gloved paw at me. "You no speak French—" at least he recognized my efforts as such—"I speak well English." He nodded vigorously and pounded his padded chest. "Well English! Where milord Cornwallis?"

"Oh God!" groaned O'Hara, "Cornwallis ill—ill—"

"Malade—" I said.

"Ah!" the fellow squeaked. He raised a finger pontifically, his eyes and mouth wide and his eyebrows disappearing under his hat-brim. "Il est malade, milord Cornwallis!"

"Eureka!" breathed O'Hara.

The pontifical finger lowered to point at him. "Who you?"

O'Hara took a deep breath. He was getting a little red around the gills. "I am Brigadier-General O'Hara. I command here."

The look of disdain was compounded with an expression of utter disbelief. O'Hara was inspected minutely in detail—every stitch in his patches, every fray on his collar and cuffs, every flop of his fuzzy, braidless hat-brim. Finally—"You—General?"

"Yes—oui—General!"

An expression of doubt now improved the officer's features. "You command?"

"Oui! I command!"

O'Hara's fluent French had effect. The officer shook his head incredulously, shrugged, removed his hat and bowed. "Please—General—you follow?"

O'Hara nodded to Abercrombie. The drums beat, the fifes shrilled, and we were off.

It was all a bad dream; made worse by the clown who guided us. He was prepared to speak French to me now and volunteered with pride that he had asked to be our guide because of his command of English and his wide knowledge of the etiquette of surrender. I informed O'Hara of these excellent qualifications. He grunted. "Well-practised in surrendering, I suppose. Can't think who would surrender to him—'cept some desperate ancient virgin. Why isn't there a guide from the rebels?"

I asked our mentor. His sneer contorted. "The Americans? You joke sir. What do they know of etiquette? As the Marquis de Lafayette says they are mere peasants."

I translated this for O'Hara. Again he grunted. "I'd swap old tallow-guts there for a peasant any day."

We were riding between the ranks of the French and rebel armies; the French on our left, and the rebels on our right—with Continental troops in front and the militia behind them. The French were as smart, as well-drilled and as impressive as ever. I found it almost comforting to see their familiar uniforms. The Continental regiments were not so well arrayed—though, in my threadbare state I was in no condition to criticize them—nor so well drilled; but I liked their air. They had a confident open manner which was impressive.

O'Hara said to the French officer. "Who is the Commander?"

The Frenchman frowned. "Monsieur le Comte de Rochambeau."

O'Hara looked puzzled. "But surely General Washington is the Commander?"

"Mais oui. Monsieur le General Washington—commander, et Monsieur le Comte de Rochambeau—commander—"

"Very helpful," said O'Hara. "But, Monsieur, who is—the—er—the big Commander? General Washington or Count Rochambeau? Do I present myself to Washington or Rochambeau?"

"Oui—Monsieur le Comte de Rochambeau—commander."

"Man's a bloody parrot!" said O'Hara despairingly. "Philip, d'you think Washington would ask Rochambeau to take the surrender—as a gesture? Maybe that's why they sent this idiot instead of an American?"

"It's certainly the sort of diplomatic gesture he might make. I'll try this fellow again."

And I tried. By now we were very close to the serried ranks of enemy generals, ranged on the furthest flank of their troops. Our guide was become highly agitated and, for me, totally incomprehensible. O'Hara rode close alongside him and ground slowly and distinctly into his ear, "Monsieur, please, do I present myself to Count Rochambeau?"

The officer stared at him vacantly and waved wildly. "Voila le Comte de Rochambeau—"

O'Hara looked at me, shrugged, and rode up to Rochambeau; an excellent commander of cavalry and a gentleman of great charm. O'Hara removed his hat, carefully, and bowed. "Your Excellency permit me to present myself. I am Brigadier-General O'Hara, deputy to Lieutenant-General Lord Cornwallis—"

At this point Rochambeau gently interrupted him, "Pardon, mon General, the Commander-in-Chief is there." And he pointed to where Washington sat his horse, facing us on the other side of the road. At the same time, our guide—or misguide—now near apoplexy, pushed his horse roughly between O'Hara's and Rochambeau's, shouting at O'Hara. Unmoved, Rochambeau muttered something at him which sent him slinking round the back of Rochambeau's staff like a whipped puppy.

O'Hara bowed again, "I'm grateful for your Excellency's correction. Forgive me." He rode over to Washington and again removed his hat and bowed. "Your Excellency will please forgive my error. Not so much a case of the blind leading the blind, as the uncomprehending being misled by the incomprehensible. However, sir, may I present myself. I am Brigadier-General O'Hara, deputy to Lieutenant-General Lord Cornwallis, who has instructed me to offer you his compliments and sincerest apologies that he is unable himself to wait upon you, being sick of a fever." Then he slowly took Cornwallis' sword from his saddle-bow, and looking very straight at Washington, said, "Your Excellency, his lordship also instructed me to say to you personally, that since he was unable to be here himself—he sends you his sword."

Washington met his gaze steadily, then looked down at the sword. He is a soldier and recognized the sword for what it was; and what it meant to Cornwallis. He touched—almost reverently—the worn hilt with his fingertips. Then, smiling at O'Hara, he shook his head. "Never, General, never from such a good hand. Pray give his lordship my sincere wishes for his early recovery. Now, sir, would you be good enough to receive your instructions for this—er—business from my deputy, General Lincoln?"

I saluted Washington. He is a bigger man than I had thought. A long, lean fellow, holding himself very erect, with a good length of leg. He sits a horse better than most and, what's more important, they go kindly for him. He has a long, lean, pocked face too, as well as a long straight nose, and the deepest set eyes of any man I've ever seen. His manner, in general, is calm and cold, but, when he wants, he can smile. And he smiled then, taking off his glove and stretching out his hand to me. Delighted to see you well, cousin. I feared for you."

"I'm very honoured, your Excellency. May I ask how you knew me?"

He smiled the broader. "William told me you were here. And Lady Katharine Fairleigh was forever showing me her miniature of you and telling me what a good soldier you are. Rightly so, of course, but I found

it irritating not to be told that I had some talent for soldiering too!" Th
smile disappeared. "I mustn't keep you now—but we must talk about poo
James Fairleigh later—"

I saluted again and rejoined O'Hara who was still being instructed b
Lincoln. General Lincoln is stout, solid, kindly and jovial. Having himsel
experienced the same ordeal, he was too embarrassed and sympathetic t
our discomfort than to attempt any conversation, and guided us, ir
silence, about half a mile to a field where we delivered our arms an
colours.

As we marched back to the gay tunes of "Over the hills and far away
and "The girl I left behind me," the troops we passed, French and rebel
all smiled cheerily upon us and exchanged jokes with our lads. It was to b
expected, for it was finished between us. Only amongst the civilia
spectators—hundreds of them—did some still glower and jeer at us as w
passed. But, of course, they would be glowering and jeering soon enoug
at their own soldiers, whom they now hailed as heroes.

Charles O'Hara and I rode down to the cave to report to Cornwallis. H
asked, "Was any remark made on my absence?"

At that moment, Ross came into the little room. "My lord, a Col. Davi
Cobb, an aide to General Washington, is here seeking General O'Har
and Colonel Cato."

Cornwallis smiled bitterly. "Let him come in. Let him come an
confirm what he has been sent to determine."

O'Hara blazed furiously, "Charles, I don't believe that either Washing
ton or Rochambeau doubt your sickness for one moment. You misjudg
them—"

Cornwallis raised a hand. "My dear Charles, I believe as you do. Bu
there'll be others less generous in their judgment."

Ross held the curtains aside. "Colonel Cobb, my lord."

A short, square-built officer in immaculate blue and buff uniforr
entered and bowed. His voice had the nasal twang of a New Englander. "
hope your lordship will forgive my intrusion. I came to extend to Genera
O'Hara and Colonel Cato General Washington's personal invitation to d
him the honour of dining with him today in his quarters."

"We'll both be honoured," said O'Hara briskly. "Food's not so good ii
the 'Swan' in York nowadays."

"Excellent, the General will be delighted. At five o'clock, then
General." Cobb paused, then said hesitantly, "My lord, I was als
instructed by his Excellency to assure you that Dr. James Craik, the Chie

physician of the Army, would most willingly offer his services to your lordship. He is particularly skilled in the treatment of fevers."

Cornwallis smiled, suddenly more relaxed. "Thank you. Will you convey to General Washington and Dr. Craik my gratitude for their generous concern. I'd be happy for him to examine what's left of me—say, tomorrow at this time? It's my staff's intention to move me to my headquarters in the town. This place is—is—" his eyes flicked round the cave—too many ghosts—too many agonizing memories—all at once the distress showed clearly on his haggard features. "This place—is inconvenient."

Cobb bowed again, a little less stiffly, his eyes on Cornwallis' face. "With your permission my lord, I'll return now and inform the General." Then he added gently, almost apologetically, "May I wish your lordship a speedy recovery."

I pulled the curtain open for him and, as he passed me, he said. "May I have a word with you, Colonel?"

We left the cave together. Outside he said,

"Surely his lordship is a little sick in mind as well as in body?"

"Hardly to be wondered at in the circumstances."

"No—I suppose not." He stood silent, fiddling with his gloves, looking so embarrassed that I began to think that he had indeed been sent to confirm Cornwallis' sickness. He nodded at the cave. "He's a great general. You know—he's much admired in our Army." He sighed, then pulling himself together, said, "Colonel, General Washington wished to know whether you had any knowledge of the manner of James Fairleigh's death. Colonel Mercer of the Virginia Militia reports that he handed over a man to you who confessed to be a member of the gang responsible for it."

"I have the man Colonel Mercer brought in. He has written a full confession and sworn it. I'll have him brought over from Gloucester and General Washington can question him."

We had come to where his orderly waited, holding two horses. Cobb climbed up on one. "Good," he said, "I'll tell the General. Tomorrow morning would be best." He looked down at me and suddenly smiled, for the first time, "Colonel Mercer told the General that you had had a lovely mare killed a few days ago and had been given one of his troop horses. The General remarked on the beast you were riding when you met." He took the reins of the second horse from the orderly. "He sends you this—one of his own—with his compliments. You're to treat him as your own as long

[291]

as you have need of him." He grinned now. "He said, even if Our Blessed Lord did consider a donkey sufficient transport to ride around Jerusalem his gallant dragoon cousin shouldn't be required to make do with one in York. So there you are!" Without waiting for my reply, he saluted and trotted off. Leaving me with this most generous gift. It was a handsome well-mannered creature; but it could never replace my poor, brave Williamson.

I rode over to the headquarters and found Andrew looking the model of a Grey Dragoon, even to the dour expression. Whilst in the clothing store he had discovered—despite what Stedman had said—a few items which I could use and which fitted me; a pair of dragoon boots, breeches, shirts, gloves—for all of which I was in sore need. And with these, and my new horse, I began to present a less dilapidated appearance.

Whilst waiting the following morning for Thorn and his confession to be brought over from Gloucester, I walked through the town to visit my soldiers in the hospitals. In one I found a number of wounded from the 71st Highlanders, and James Macdonell amongst them. He had been wounded in the back and legs by the splinters of a bursting shell and was in great pain; but as coolly and distantly courteous as ever. He said "You'll have heard about Alexander Fraser, Colonel."

"I heard he had been killed at the taking of Redoubt Number 10."

"Ay. They took it over his dead body—and over a few of their own dead, too. He saw to that."

"How did he die?"

"Sergeant Duncanson was with him."

Sergeant Duncanson had two bayonet wounds through his chest and spoke only in a hoarse whisper.

"As a chief's son, your honour—the claymore in his hand and his face to the enemy. God send us more like him."

"Amen," they all said.

"Where is his grave?"

"They wanted to lay him in one of these bit cemeteries, Colonel," said James, "but we said to bury him where he fell."

I walked out to Redoubt Number 10; now, a tumbled mudheap of no consequence. There, in the midst of it, they had buried this chief's son, with a guard from the enemy, who had admired his courage, and another from his own Highlanders. A long and lonely cry from the Lovat hills of his own country. He had given of his best, as he said he would.

Back in the town I found Corporal Mills awaiting me with two troopers of the 17th Light Dragoons and the man Thorn. We went at once to

eneral Washington's headquarters, and were led into his pavilion; a large
adorned, plainly furnished tent, most unlike those of the senior French
ficers, which were very handsome and most elegantly furnished.

Washington was reading a document which I recognized as a copy of
olonel Mercer's report on James Fairleigh's death. He got to his feet at
ice and came to meet me, giving me his firm, hard hand. "Good-day,
usin. This damnable affair distresses me immeasurably and at the
oment there's not a thing we can do about such rabbles. In time—in
me, we'll settle with them." He picked up the document and walked
owly to tower over Thorn.

"So, you are the self-confessed murderer of Major Fairleigh?" Washing-
n's expression was pitiless. Thorn made no answer, staring sullenly at
e ground. Washington's expression and tone softened. "Look up, fellow.
ou were a soldier once, weren't you?"

It touched some hidden spring in Thorn. Slowly his head came up and
looked Washington in the face, though still apprehensively. His
oulders straightened and he stood as tall as his escort of dragoons. He
cked his lips. "Yes, your honour. I were a soldier. I were in the 9th
egiment."

Washington nodded. "Yes. I can see you were now. And now you can
iswer my question."

Thorn stood as on parade now, head up, his voice still hoarse but more
nfident. "I were ordered, your honour—me and me mates—we was
dered."

"So you say here." Washington slapped the report with the back of his
ind. "Ordered by this Major Cook. That is the truth?"

"God strike me dead if it ain't. I swore it on the Bible, your honour."

"I see. You said you were part of the Virginia militia."

"That's what the Major calls us."

"But you're not."

"No—your honour."

"And you knew that."

"Yes, your honour."

"So you knew that Cook was not a major—or any sort of officer—and
iat his orders were not military orders."

Thorn hesitated. "'E'd 'ave shot us else, your honour."

Washington turned and, his hands under his coat tails, began to pace
owly back and forth in front of Thorn and the escort. "You are a deserter
om the 9th Regiment of His Majesty's Army—and from the 1st
egiment of the Pennsylvania Continental Line—as well as being, at least,

[*293*]

I suppose, guilty of a number of acts of looting, burning and murder.'

Thorn stood like a ramrod, looking straight to his front, ashen-faced b absolutely steady.

"So there are no less than three charges on which you could justifiab be hanged." Washington still paced on, but, suddenly stopped in front Thorn and faced him. "So what's to be done to you, fellow?"

Thorn blinked. He gave a little shake of his head. "It's—it's as yo honour pleases. But—as God's my judge, sir—I'd not 'ave 'armed th officer—" he paused, then burst out angrily, "I never run from th 9th—an' I never would—an' that's God's truth too. I run from th 'ell-fired prison camp where we was being treated like slaves—that's r offence. An' I run from the Pennsylvania 'cause we was being treate worse than the bleedin' prison camp! An' you know we was, yo honour,—we 'eard you spoke for us." He nodded defiantly at Washing ton, looking far more of a man than he had ever looked before. "What done since, well—that's as you says." He stopped, and the flame died him. Still standing straight, he shrugged. "It's as your honour pleases.

"Hmph," said Washington. He stared silently at Thorn for som moments. "Does this Major Cook have any place to which he retreats avoid pursuit?"

"Yes, your honour, it's in the 'ills by the Dan River, over from Dix Ferry."

"I see. That's difficult country. Could you guide a troop of the re Virginia Militia there to seize him and his gang?"

Thorn frowned. His head bowed and he shifted uneasily. "Some o 'em's my mates. I'd not want—"

"There's no question of not wanting!" All at once Washington's voic cut like a whip, then slowed, "The only question—which you must as yourself—and answer—is, which do you prefer—to guide a troo there—or to hang?" Thorn's head stayed bowed. Washington said, "Yo may have twenty-four hours to consider it. Take him away."

Corporal Mills marched Thorn off, and Washington relaxed.

"That's no bad soldier. I doubt his loyalty to his gang-mates will matc his loyalty to his Regiment—let alone to his neck. He'll guide Charle sure enough."

"Charles?—Charles Fairleigh? Where is he?"

"He was very sick of a fever two months ago. I sent him home t recover. I had word from him that he hoped to be back here b tomorrow. He's one of my aides."

"Do they know at Belhaven of James' death?"

"Not yet. I thought Charles should be the first to know. Then he can find this villain Cook and settle with him before going on to tell his father and Lucy."

"Yes," I said, "I suppose that might help a little." And I wondered how little. Would the knowledge that James' death had been avenged really console his father?—or Lucy, my Lucy? And I should not be there to help and comfort.

I thanked Washington for the loan of his horse. "I'm glad you like him." He smiled. "He's a good sort of beast. Jump anything and very sure-footed, as a horse needs to be in our Virginian hills. I hope you'll enjoy him." He sat down on the edge of the table, his hands on his knees, and looked at me a little uncertainly—a little shyly. "And now you can do me a favour, if you will. Our chief physician, Dr. James Craik, is shortly going to call upon Lord Cornwallis to examine him for his fever. D'you think his lordship would receive me if I accompanied the Doctor? Is he well enough to do so? I'd prefer to avoid a pompous, official visit—"

"I'm sure he'd be delighted to see you. He's improving slowly. We've moved him into Governor Nelson's house—a much better place for him to be. We dine in an hour's time—and thanks to the generous assistance of your larder, and General Rochambeau's, our table's much improved! So you and the Doctor must dine with us. I'll go on ahead and warn them."

"If you think so,—yes—thank you." He still looked a little uncertain. "D'you know, I've always wanted to meet him; one of the ablest commanders in any army. Pity he couldn't serve these colonies as well in the field as he served them in Parliament. He could have led us—Fairfax and Fairleigh are too old, and neither of them are soldiers." He smiled bitterly. "He could have dealt with those self-styled gentlemen of Congress. The whole affair would have been over in half the time." He sighed and shook his head sadly. "I'd have very much liked to fight under his command."

He stretched out a long arm and put his hand on my shoulder. "Charles has told me about Lucy and you. I share her father's joy in her happiness." His hand gripped harder. "You're fortunate, cousin. It must be a man's greatest happiness to have a child by the woman he loves. It was never granted to me—" he was looking down now, speaking to his own thoughts, emotionless, expressionless, his unseeing eyes staring at a memory. "But then—I could never have the only woman I ever loved."

Chapter Nineteen

In which I see an Englishman lost to England.

I had sent ahead to our headquarters to give warning of Washington⟨⟩ visit. To allow time for some preparation to be made for his reception⟨⟩ conducted him on a tour of the ruins—architectural and human—of Yorl⟨⟩ I took him through the shambles of every street, past every shattere⟨⟩ house, into every hospital tent and each spreading cemetery—where th⟨⟩ dead, men, women and children, were being buried now in pits, the⟨⟩ being no time nor sufficient room nor labour to provide more decer⟨⟩ burial. I thought he should witness the fruits of the labours of the allie⟨⟩ guns; see it all, smell it all, suffer it all. And I made sure he did. And h⟨⟩ thanked me for guiding him on this grim inspection.

"I have never been in a besieged town. I never conceived such horror⟨⟩ Soldiers—yes, they must accept such perils and devastations. But thes⟨⟩ wretched civilians—and the children. The cannon is an impersonal an⟨⟩ indiscriminate assassin." The tears were in his eyes. "A blind, senseles⟨⟩ futile waste—it must never happen again in this country!"

Ross was waiting for us at the door of Governor Nelson's house. Th⟨⟩ French grenadiers on guard, immaculate, saluted punctiliously. I pr⟨⟩ sented Ross, who bowed and said, "I am to bring your Excellency to hi⟨⟩ lordship's bedchamber at once."

Washington looked at the house and smiled. "Governor Nelson aske⟨⟩ me to say that he is most honoured that his lordship should have hi⟨⟩ headquarters in his house. And much relieved to find that it withstood th⟨⟩ attentions of our artillery so well!"

The window of Cornwallis' room looked out towards the defences. H⟨⟩ lay on the bed, wearing a shirt, breeches and thick woollen stockings⟨⟩

opped up on pillows. A table with books and maps stood beside his bed.
n another table, set against the wall, were dishes and bottles of wine;
fts from Rochambeau and Admiral de Grasse.

Washington came into the doorway and, distressed at the sight of
ornwallis' gaunt pallor, forgot all formal courtesies.

"My lord!" He strode forward and took Cornwallis' welcoming hand in
oth his. "My lord, I never thought to see you so prostrated! I'd never
ave suggested that I impose myself—you're clearly in no condition to
ceive any visitor—Heaven above! Forgive me—I forget all my man-
ers!"

Cornwallis smiled cheerfully and pulled him by the hand.

"Pray sit down, your Excellency. Your concern for my health is very
ind. They say I'll be on my legs in a couple of days."

At this time I was standing in the door with Dr. Craik. He asked for
ow long Cornwallis had had the fever.

"Around four weeks, doctor."

"Indeed—indeed?" He had the Lowland Scots manner of speech. "And
as he been much cast down then?—dejected?—melancholy?"

"Yes—sadly so."

"Would ye say—suicidal even—Colonel?"

"It wouldn't be an exaggeration."

"Indeed?—Ay." He sighed and nodded; which he did the entire time he
atechised me.

"But we thought that to be caused by the death of his wife—and certain
riends."

"Indeed?—ay, that could be so. But in this particular form of the fever
which, I believe, I observe in him even from here, this depressive mania is
 clear symptom. It dulls the judgment, so that the patient considers
aught but the cause and extent of his own melancholy." He pursed his
ps and nodded on. "And when was the crisis of the fever?"

"Three nights ago."

"Three nights ago?" He looked at me pityingly, and this time shook his
ead. "Ay—at such a time! Of all times! Man, the Lord himself was agin
e! Ay, well, all I shall be required to do is to speed the recovery and
nsure that there is no relapse. That should present no difficulty. It will be
 rare honour and pleasure to attend his lordship. He's obviously a
entleman of great strength of character and resolution." He took me by
he lapel and murmured in my ear. "Not like the General's step-son who
uffers from this same fever. A nice, young man, but indeterminate—

weak-willed—not robust—the sort who succumb most easily to th
fever." He sighed and shook his head again, "As I very much fear h
may."

"Does the General know that?"

"Ay, though he doesn't show it." He took me by the lapel once more
"I've known him since we were lads. Most think him a cold, hard mar
needing little affection. But I tell you the withdrawn and meditative mar
such as he is, needs as much as anyone; perhaps more in the position th
General now finds himself. He loved unhappily early in life. I believe h
still feels the pangs. Since that time I've seen how he has put on this chilly
self-restrained manner. But it is a mere mask to the true nature of the ma
behind it. He is married, of course, but—well, neither of them wer
young. She had a son and daughter by her first husband—and th
daughter's already dead of a fit, poor little lass, and if this lad, Jackie, die
of fever—" He shrugged. "He and Martha have no bairns of the
own—nor like to have. There's affection there right enough, but he need
the love of children—"

Charles O'Hara had now joined Washington and Cornwallis and wa
making them both laugh. Some colour was come into Cornwallis' thi
cheeks, the first for many days. He waved at the table of dishes. "You
excellency, I thought we might dine here—"

Dr. Craik stepped forward. "My lord, if you permit—"

Washington leapt up. "Oh Gemini! I'd forgot the leech!" He seized th
Doctor by the arm. "My lord, permit me to present the best physician o
this continent. He asked if he might have the honour to advise on you
fever. Dr. James Craik."

Cornwallis gave Craik a skinny hand. "My dear Doctor, this is ver
good of you. Perhaps it would be convenient if you examined me after w
have dined?"

Craik bowed and rubbed his hands in the speculative manner o
physicians. "Oh, that will not be necessary, my lord. I've been examinin
you the while from the doorway there. And Colonel Cato has kindly
advised me of your symptoms."

"Ah, yes," said Cornwallis, dryly, "Colonel Cato kept them under th
closest observation."

"Indeed he did, my lord, as a good friend should. And from his advic
and my observation I am able to diagnose most confidently that you
lordship has been suffering from a peculiarly melancholic malignancy
Such a fever frequently proves fatal, but I rejoice to see that in you
lordship's case the crisis of the fever is passed. But to assist your recovery

[*298*]

nd avert the danger of a relapse, I recommend that you should take
ow—yes, now, my lord—this draught I have prepared. It will refresh
ne blood and renew your strength."

He poured a dark brown liquid into a little glass and gave it to
ornwallis, who sniffed at it. "Faugh! It stinks!"

"Indeed, my lord, most foul. Drink it up, if you please."

Cornwallis sipped it. "Ugh! It's vile!"

"Just so, my lord. Very vile. It's best to drink it quickly."

"Can I have a little wine to take away the taste?"

Dr. Craik clucked, chidingly. "Wine, my lord? Merciful Heaven! That
would react against the efficacy of the draught. No wine, my lord. Some
roth maybe—and a sop of bread. Well—perhaps a little wine later, to
ettle the stomach."

Cornwallis held his nose and gulped down the draught. "Brrr—ugh!
What the devil's in that witches' brew?"

"It's a distillation from the bark of the cinchona, my lord. Regarded by
he natives of New Spain and the Indies as the sovereign remedy for most
orms of the fever."

"I'd rather have the fever," murmured Washington.

Craik smiled patiently, "The general will always have his little joke. I
hall leave another measure for you to take this evening before retiring,
ny lord. And six more—" Cornwallis groaned, "to be taken three each
lay—morning, midday and evening—tomorrow and the day after. We
hall have your lordship up and about in no time."

And so we dined all together, sitting round Cornwallis' bed, on chairs,
on tables, on the window-sill and on the floor. Very merry and
nlightening it was; with O'Hara and the seemingly sedate Dr. James
Craik vying with one another in stories uproarious and outrageous, and
Washington telling of journeys in the western and uncivilized parts of
Virginia and on the Ohio River, and battles against the French and
ndians. And, as the afternoon drew on, their duties called most away,
until there were left sitting around Cornwallis only Washington, Dr.
Craik, Charles O'Hara and I.

At length, Cornwallis, silent during most of the conversation, said,
"Your Excellency, I'd like your views on two points I've been considering.
Some years ago, in Parliament, a few gentlemen and myself opposed
certain acts restricting the colonies in various ways. We did so because we
believed the acts to be unjust to our fellow-countrymen—the colonists—
and because we feared that they would result only in resentment, division
and even bloodshed in the colonies. I believed, and do so still, that what

[*299*]

those acts made inevitable could have been avoided. Is that your opinion
And, if it had been avoided, for how long could the King's authority ha
been maintained over the colonies? For five years?—for fifty?—for eve
Or are our ambitions too diverse and exclusive?"

Washington leaned back in his chair and looked down at his boots. "M
lord, you'll understand, I've given these matters some thought myself. N
rebellion is lightly undertaken by reasonable men, who are the strength
any such movement if not its spirit—and, I believe, we are reasonab
men. All of us who undertook it consciously—and the most of
unwillingly—put our necks in the noose. Despite these last few days, th
noose still hangs there. And, as Dr. Johnson says, the threat of hangin
concentrates a man's mind wonderfully."

He took a sip of his wine. "As to whether division was inevitable—why
no, my lord it was not. Well-intentioned men could—no doubt at all—b
reasonable discussion have arrived amicably at some acceptable arrang
ment. But there were men on both sides who made this impossible. O
your side by their ignorance, prejudice and stupidity. On ours by the
greed, their selfishness and their lust for their own advancement at an
price, so long as it was paid by others.

"But I believe, in time, some disruption would have been inevitable
any case. Our ambitions and those of our mother country are too much
variance. In Europe you look into Europe for the springs of power; an
England, in pursuit of her ambitions, strives against nations, for he
empire. We, in these colonies—" he checked himself and smiled wryly
"You see? I'm still a colonist at heart! We strive only against nature to wi
our empire. This opposition of influences alone would bring dissensio
between us; the resources of the one side being unwilling to support th
ambitions of the other. And, sadly, we don't lack for other causes
contention.

"But beyond that, my lord, some rupture, by force or by agreement
would be inevitable in the very nature of things. No active young man
content to sit idle in his father's house. He will want to be up and away
stand on his own feet, make his own decisions. And he will suffer n
hindrance. Not that your politicians offered hindrance by their restrictiv
acts—which you so adamantly opposed, my lord, and will always be hel
in high regard in these states for that unselfish service. It was those act
that thrust the young America out of doors, all unready.

"And if, after all that's passed, some agreement was imposed upon us
then, I believe, if unwillingly accepted, and I cannot see it otherwise—i
could not last.

'He who by force is convert 'gainst his will
Stays of his contrary opinion still.'

hink I misquote—I'm much given to it—but it will do to illustrate my
·int."

"It does very clearly," said Cornwallis. "And if you gain your
dependence, what of a reconciliation—in the interests of both—after
is war is done with?"

"Some agreement on trade will be essential to our economy, and our
clinations are, naturally, all towards England. We have little to expect
·om any trade with France. Indeed, we may have much to fear from
·ance and Spain, and will need to seek assistance from England until we
·ve sufficient strength to fend for ourselves.

"So, despite whatever's said and done now in public—yes, we needs
·ust seek some sort of reconciliation with our mother country. But how
·elcome such advances are to her will depend on her generosity. No
·ubt we shall have to await her recognition. But we shall hope that His
·ajesty's ministers recall the recommendations of Mr. Burke that 'A great
·npire and little minds go ill together,' " he frowned. "It was Burke, wasn't
·?"

Cornwallis laughed. "Let's take it as Burke. Now, one last question.
·hat of the divisions between the colonies—and within the colonies
·emselves? How will you persuade all men to work to achieve a true
·nity—which is your only course if you are to be secure against all
·nemies?"

There was a silence while Washington, leaning forward, studied the
·epths of his glass. Then he said, slowly and heavily,

"My lord, you have unerring skill in hitting upon the weakest point of
·ny position—tactical or political. Yes—unity will always be our greatest
·eed. Without some form of union—some central government to direct
·ur policy, we shall drift apart. We shall be thirteen lost lambs, strayed
·rom their shepherd and their safe fold, an easy prey to any predator.

"Ask these people what we have gained from all these years of
·iscouragement and agony—what we have won here at York. They will
·ry 'Freedom!'—but never know what they mean. Oh, we're all so jealous
·f our freedom—so hell-bent on what it will give us—so damnably blind
·o what it will require of us. Too many honourable men—in Congress and
·utside—believe this freedom decrees the rights of their own states to be
·aramount, and a restriction of them by any other government to be
·nathema. And beside such honourable men are those who find their
·mbitions dissatisfied and thwarted, even by so feeble an authority as

Congress. Others, more evil still, see in disunity and disorder room
prey upon their fellow men. And all cry they fight for freedom!"

His voice was now wearied and bitter. There was no other sound in the
little room.

"I will confess, my lord, that in these long, sad years I have feared—and
despaired—and persevered—and hoped again. I have feared that we have
cast off the restraints and strengths of our unity under the King only to fall
into disunity and despair. I have feared that if scoundrels combine under
the banners of honourable men to dismember and destroy our fledgling
unity, only disaster can follow. For they will see in this debauchery of
Freedom occasion to cheat and conspire, to rob and murder, until all we
have fought for, all we have suffered for, all we have planned and prayed
for—is lost in anarchy.

"Only in unity can we find security. And if we cannot come by it in
counsel, then we may need to come by it in blood. And this—this—I fear
most of all. For it could bring upon us a civil war more vicious, more
bloody, more terrible than this we fight now, or that which our ancestors
fought under the Stewarts more than a century ago. And, as God's my
witness, my lord, I tell you when I have thought on this, then I have
wished I had no part—no hand or part at all—in this whole unhappy
affair."

There was a long silence after this. It was as if all five of us in that room
were asleep and dreaming the same dream. Finally, Cornwallis gave a long
sigh, as if waking from a dream, and leant forward off his pillows.

"Your Excellency—I must thank you—for your opinions, so clearly and
honestly given—" He spoke abstractedly, still considering what Washington had said.

Washington bowed in his chair. "I'm very glad your lordship was able
to receive me. My best thanks to you and your officers for such pleasant
hospitality. And may I wish you a speedy recovery, my lord—?"

I sat listening with half an ear to these civilities. Conventional
manners—conventional words. So unreal, so irrelevant, so damned
banal—after what had been said before.

Washington pushed back his chair. Then, of a sudden, he fingered his
chin and looked a little askance at Cornwallis. "My lord, if I may trespass
a moment more on your time—if it will not tire you—"

"Your Excellency, I have nothing to do and grow very weary doing it.
Your conversation is a tonic to me. I'm sure Dr. Craik would approve."

A little hesitantly, Washington said, "You will, of course, be discussing

[302]

ith others our conversation of this afternoon, and are entirely at liberty
quote what I have said—though preferably not to the French. My lord,
point occurs to me—relating to what I have said—on which there may
 some doubt." He took a deep breath, then slowly rubbed his knees
ith his great bony hands as he spoke. "A point on which I would prefer
.ere to be no possible doubt—or misunderstanding." He looked hard at
ornwallis from under his heavy brows. "You're aware I held a
ommission in the Virginia Militia from the Governor, Lord Dunmore, in
.e wars against the French and Indians. I served with General
raddock—"

"And was largely responsible for saving the remnants of his force at his
sastrous defeat at Great Meadows," said Cornwallis. "Yes, the whole
rmy knows that, and it regrets too that your courage and ability on that
:casion—and on others—were never adequately recognized."

Washington flushed. "Your lordship's very gracious. I'd not intended to
:mark on that. My sufficient reward was that I'd served His Majesty and
.e Army as best I could.

"Well—you'll know too, I'm sure, that I sought eagerly—perhaps too
1gerly—a regular commission in the Army; which I was never granted.
1y lord, I must say, in all honesty, that at the time, I resented that I was
ot granted what I thought I had earned; an ambition I held dearer than all
thers. I thought myself ill-used, slighted. But now I must state honestly
1at I am glad that I was not granted that ambition. For had I been so
ewarded, I should still have acted as I have done—only—I should have
one so with an even sicker and sadder heart." He looked hard at
Cornwallis again. "That is what I wished you to know, my lord." He got
o his feet. "Now I shall say farewell."

Cornwallis stretched out his hand. "I'm honoured by your Excellency's
onfidence. I hope I should have as much courage at such a time. I admire
ou the more for it."

Washington took his hand, very moved. Cornwallis said,

" 'A hard hand—the sign of a brave mind.' "

Washington answered, his voice a little muffled, "God send I see your
ordship well soon—" He bowed quickly, turned and, head down, ducked
is big frame out through the door.

There was a silence in the room while the boots clattered down the
tairs. Then Cornwallis said, "Help me up!"

O'Hara and I lifted him and took him to the window. Washington and
Dr. Craik were riding along the lane leading out from the town.

[*303*]

Washington turned in his saddle to look back at the house. He saw us
the window and, smiling, took off his hat and held it high above his hea
Cornwallis waved a hand.

"He sits a horse well. I'm told he rides very straight across country—a
and elsewhere too, no doubt." He shook his head and gave a deep sig
"My God—what an Englishman is lost to England in that man!"

Chapter Twenty

*In which, to solve my dilemma, I seek my
death—and fail; and return home.*

That night I could not sleep. The weather was too hot and oppressive
again and the stillness after the long bombardment seemed unnatural,
unnerving. These were the excuses I made for myself. But I knew the real
causes of my disquiet; they had nothing to do with the weather or gunfire.
They were the two thoughts in my mind—the one joyous, that I might
now be paroled and given leave to visit Belhaven for the birth of our child,
Lucy's and mine; the other, black despair, that whatever I did now,
whether I stayed in Virginia or returned to Somerset, I could only destroy
the happiness of someone I loved—either Anne and our children, or Lucy
and her father and our child.

If only I had been killed in York. If only that rifleman's bullet at
Gloucester had cut me down, instead of Williamson. If only I had never
gone to Belhaven. If only old Croachy had never heard of my
appointment—God! if only I had never accepted it!—Matthew would not
be dead, Kitty and her baby would not be dead, James Fairleigh would
not be dead—and poor Williamson.

God in Heaven, what should I do?—what could I do?

Put a bullet in my head. But that's the easy—the coward's way out;
leaving grief for everyone except myself, who most deserved it.

Could I not get killed honourably?—leaving some pride to relieve the
grief of those who would mourn me? But do women find comfort in such
pride when distraught with grief at the loss of a loved one?

Perhaps—but that was it!—by God, a chance! If I was allowed to
accompany Charles in his search for Cook—then if I were killed avenging
James Fairleigh—what better cause? But would they let me go?

[*305*]

Feet thundered up the stairs to my door, and it swung back with crash.

"Philip!—Philip—are you awake?—where's a light?—"

I lit a candle by my bed. Charles Fairleigh, haggard, covered in dus his clothes all travel-stained, stared down at me.

"Philip, where's that man Thorn?—the Virginia militiaman deserter?—I want him—"

"Thorn? He's in his cell, I expect. Charles, you can't do any goo seeing him now. I'll bring him to you first thing in the morning. Don worry, we'll make him lead us to his gang's hiding place—I think he'll t willing to. We'll settle with that devil Cook. I mean to avenge Jame myself—"

"You mean to come?" Charles sat down on my bed, still panting "You'll come with us?"

"If I'm allowed to. I'm a prisoner—"

"Philip, you've got to come—you've got to! I'll tell the General—you'v got to come! Philip, that man Cook—he—he's got Lucy—"

The world stopped. I felt sick—horrified—terrified: and then coldly bloodily, murderously furious. "Lucy—how—Lucy?"

"Cook's gang attacked Belhaven a month ago. They wore gree jackets—called themselves Virginia Militia. They rode up to the gates We had no warning—but we keep the gates closed lately, because som people have been attacked—"

"What do you mean—he's got Lucy?"

Charles babbled on, distractedly, "They rode round the settlement trying to break in. But we drove 'em off. They left a few dead an wounded. We took 'em in and found out they were a gang of deserters—led by this man Cook—"

"Charles—for God's sake—Lucy—"

"Yes—yes—then we remembered that Lucy had driven to Brindletow that morning—with Mrs. Fraser—to see Dr. Weekes. And she wa driving back that afternoon. She had a groom with her—to drive if she fe tired. I took some men with me—we rode towards Brindletown. Halfwa there we found the groom—badly knocked about—tied to a tree. He said gang—like Cook's—had stopped them and taken Lucy and Mrs. Fraser o in the gig. They left the groom to tell us that they wanted ten thousan guineas for Lucy's safe return—"

"You know where she is then?"

"No. The money was to be left at an inn at a hamlet calle

estfield—about thirty miles from Belhaven. We took some money and
wels there, but the innkeeper has been scared out of his wits by the local
ilitia who were looking for Cook to hang him, and he wouldn't touch the
oney. I swore I'd hang the innkeeper if he didn't tell me where Cook
as, but, even with the noose tightening round his neck, he swore he
dn't know where Cook hides up. So we don't know where Cook is—or
here Lucy is."

"Thorn knows—or I believe he does."

"That's what the General said. I've already spoken to him. He said if
horn decides to tell us, he will release me to go in pursuit of Cook with
e local militia—Virginia or North Carolina—or both." He stood up.
'll ask the General to let you come with us—" Then he slumped
ejectedly back onto my bed. "But you're right. I won't get him again
night. I've just arrived and I woke him up at once." He grinned
namefacedly. "He was very civil and sympathetic, but he clearly thought
could all have waited until morning. But then it's not his sister—and not
is brother."

I lay back. "Go to bed Charles," I said, "I'll bring Thorn over to the
general's tent at seven in the morning. Be there."

He went, slowly and wearily. I blew out the candle. I was now
ompletely calm. The only answer for my problems had been presented to
e. I should save Lucy and our child, I should avenge James—and I
hould die honourably doing so. Lucy would know of it. Anne would be
old of it—though not of the child. There would be grief, but it would
ass. Anne was young enough and attractive enough to marry again—she
ad never lacked for admirers—and I hoped she would; and the
hildren—well, they were young and would soon forget. Lucy—certainly
he should marry.

So—all was clear; if that was the way things could be made to go all was
ettled. And—after I had prayed for my loved ones—I slept soundly.

I reported to General Washington's tent, together with Thorn and
Corporal Mills' escort, at seven. Thorn had already assured me that he
was ready to act as guide, and I informed Washington of this. He looked
t Thorn steadily for a moment and Thorn looked as steadily straight
back. Washington said, "Understand that you will be on trust. You will
ot be guarded." He paused. "And you will not desert, though,
nevitably, you will have opportunity to do so. If you behave honourably,
n your return you will have the alternative of joining the prisoners of war
from York with a report from me that you have behaved honourably and

should in no way be punished or penalised; or you may join the tru
Virginia Militia and be given a grant of land here in Virginia—as many
your fellows have done. D'you understand?"

Thorn nodded. "I understand, your honour. I'll be going back to tl
9th."

Washington nodded back, with the slightest of smiles.

"Good," and added, as if an afterthought, "Captain Fairleigh
Belhaven here will command the troop you will guide. It was his broth
you were ordered to hang—"

"Belhaven—Fairleigh!" Thorn gaped at Charles, stammering, "I nev
knowed—I never put 'em together—Fairleigh—o'course." He pulle
himself together and the words came in a torrent. "I was at Belhaven, you
honour. Me and me mates told the Major to leave the lady alone—yo
could see she was with child. Anyways it was too dangerous—we was o
the run already and she'd only delay us. We said leave 'er, but 'e wouldn'
The old dame wanted to come but 'e didn't want to take 'er—but we mac
'im—to look after the lady like. We tried to get the Major to leave 'em bot
at Westfield, at the inn, but 'e wouldn't 'ave that neither. What with tl
Fairleighs bein' well-known and well-liked we 'ad the whole country o
our back in no time—nobody'd do nothing for us—didn't want to s
us—which is why we shogged up 'ere for a bit. But Major Cook left '
there—at Shadlock's—"

"Shadlock's?" said Charles.

"That's the little farm—on the Dan River—where we 'ides up like
said. Shadlock was the name of the farmer—but 'e's dead. I'll lead yo
there. I'll not fail your honour." He glared at Washington, "An' I won
run neither—"

Unmoved, Washington said stonily, "Take him and wait outside." An
when Thorn and the escort had gone he smiled at us. "Well, I like hin
better now than when I first saw him. He's got some spirit. Will you tak
him, Charles?"

"He's our only hope of finding Lucy, General." Charles paused
embarrassed. "General, do you think I could—would you permit—"

"Would I permit cousin Philip to go with you? Certainly I would. H
has an interest. He must be paroled first though."

"I thank your Excellency," I said. "Would it be possible for m
soldier-servant to accompany me? He came from Belhaven, but is now
private soldier in my Regiment."

"Of course. Will you allow for that in your demand for provisions
Charles, and he'll need his usual weapons, I suppose? I've ordered Colone

Mercer to provide a troop. You are nominally in command, but I think our cousin the Colonel should do the commanding; I'm sure it's all very improper, but I think it would work better." Washington turned to me. "You'll understand the essential task of this force is to destroy the band entirely. You have authority to execute them—any or all of them—at your discretion. And if, in the course of action, you are able to save Lucy Fairleigh from them, so much the better, but it is not the prime purpose."

"I understand," I said.

"Very good. Charles you should start your preparations now. Mercer said he'd have his troop here by tomorrow midday, so you could leave tomorrow afternoon."

That evening I asked Cornwallis' permission to accompany Charles Fairleigh in pursuit of Cook's band; and explained the reason why.

"Of course you must go," he said. "Pity you can't take the 17th with you, that would suit them better than sitting around in a prison camp." He looked down at the papers on his little writing desk. "Have you thought what you will say to Anne?"

"Every day for the last seven months."

He smiled sympathetically. "Poor Philip—

> 'It lies not in our power to love or hate,
> For will in us is overruled by Fate.'

And what straits Fate can land us in! And I suppose you've come to no decision?—no, I thought not. Well, anyway you must go. And when the business is done, come back to us in New York."

So we left the following afternoon—Sunday the 21st October; Charles Fairleigh, a troop of forty mounted infantry of the Virginia Militia commanded by Roger Chawton, Thorn, Andrew and myself. Foreseeing casualties—and for the care of Lucy—I had asked for a surgeon to accompany us, but the Virginia Militia could not provide one. So, with the consent of his commanding officer, I had asked for James Hawkins, the surgeon of the 76th Regiment who had accompanied me aboard the *Union*, to be paroled and released to join us. This was agreed; there now being sufficient surgeons to tend the sick and wounded in York.

Roger Chawton had lost trace of Cook's crew to the north west of Williamsburg, near Spencer's Tavern, where Simcoe had had his skirmish at the end of June. Thorn ignored this northern route and led us by Westover and Petersburg to the Roanoke River, along it to its junction with the Dan and on to Dix's Ferry; where we arrived late on Tuesday the 30th October.

[*309*]

So that Cook should not be warned of our true purpose, we put about that we were sent to guard the ferry and patrol the road to the south. The following morning, as would be usual with a patrol of such strength, we sent out foraging parties. One such party included Charles, Chawton, Thorn and myself. I had taken two green dragoon jackets from the Legion store for Andrew and myself to replace our conspicuous scarlet ones, so that we passed unnoticed by the civil populace, a great number of rebel troops being clothed in green.

I had Thorn draw me a rough plan of Shadlock's Farm and its approaches, and, with this in hand, and Thorn left well out of sight, we rode into the farm, ostensibly to purchase hay, and had my hat well down over my eyes and my chin well sunk into my collar, but there was no need for either, for we saw no sign of Cook. We were met by a couple of surly churls who told us they had no hay nor anything else for us, which was clearly the truth for the barns were empty, though in good state. Whilst Roger Chawton engaged them in conversation as to where we could find forage of any sort in those parts, Charles and I had time to examine the extent of the farm, estimate distances and amend the detail of Thorn's map.

Shadlock's Farm lay on the hillside above the south bank of the Dan River. The main fields of corn and tobacco ran down the hill to the meadows along the river bank, and were only partly and roughly harvested. The track on which we approached the farm ran above it, following the rising crest of the hill. A rough stone roadway led from the track through a cluster of barns and cabins to the small square farmhouse. The house stood apart at about fifty yards from the barns in a garden, now neglected and overgrown; the bottom half of the house being built of stone and the top of clapboard, roofed with shingles. From the far side of the house a path, screened by trees, led above the headlands of the fields to join a track running up from a summer ford on the river.

Before we withdrew, I asked whether they had seen or heard of a deserter called Thorn and gave his description. I said he had escaped from custody and was reported to have ridden this way. They pricked their ears at this, but assured us—and we believed them—that they hadn't.

That afternoon I asked Thorn to approach the farm by the way from the ford, to show himself to the gang and discover which buildings were occupied and by whom, and, in particular, where Lucy and Mrs. Fraser and Cook were accommodated and if they were guarded.

Thorn had changed remarkably in manner and appearance since his first interview with Washington. He had gained in confidence and now spoke up cheerfully and did everything briskly with a will; in short, behaved like a good soldier. But now, to my disappointment, he bit his lip.

"If they catch me out they'll kill me."

I thought to test him. "I know. But you're the only one who can find out such vital information unsuspected." I let a touch of scorn come into my voice. "But you don't have to go."

He gave me a half-grin. "I'm glad to be trusted, your honour. I'll go."

He had passed my test, so I added, "I don't think you need worry too much. They're far more likely to tell you that this morning we asked if they knew where you were, because you had escaped and were thought to be around here. They'll either tell you to sneak off before we find you there, or—being what they are—they may even arrest you and hand you over to us!"

Thorn grinned the broader. "Thank'ee, your honour! I'm glad we're on the same side! I'll go now."

"Before you do," I said, "you'd better make yourself look more of a draggle-tail deserter and less of a regular dragoon, or they'll think our tale about your escape a little odd."

"I'll make meself look a right villain—" he nodded, "'ad enough practice—"

When he had gone, Charles Fairleigh said, "We can't just let him go like that. They might kill him. We must be there to help him if he needs it."

I had thought that Charles lacked the character of his elder brother; now, his concern for Thorn made me wonder if I had misjudged him. I said, with an air of surprise, "Have you forgotten he helped to kill your brother?"

Charles looked down at his boots. "Yes. I know. But—all the same—I think we should go. He's working for us."

"He may well be betraying us."

"Possibly—" he looked at me with a sort of doubtful stubbornness, "but—I think not. I'll take a file of militia and go and—"

"We'll take the file of militia I've ordered to be ready, Charles. Roger is to stay here and come for us if he hears firing."

Charles stared at me open-mouthed. "Why did you order?—"

"Because, like you, I think Thorn's a good soldier at heart. But, if he's not, then we'll be forewarned, won't we?"

So we rode up into the woods above the farm, dismounted, crept forward to the edge of the track at the entrance and waited. We heard them greet Thorn's arrival with shouts and laughter. He went into one of the cabins. We waited silent, all weapons cocked, for half an hour. No sound came from the cabin. Then Thorn came out, carrying a full haversack. They brought him a horse and he got on it and rode out of the farm and up the track over the hill, with a number of the gang shouting and waving farewells to him. We waited to see whether any of them might be suspecting Thorn of betraying them and follow him; but none did and we rode back to camp.

Thorn had very sensibly gone off in the opposite direction to our camp to disarm suspicion, and made a wide detour to come back to it; arriving well after us. He was gratified to hear from the militiamen that they had been watching over his well-being, and informed us gleefully that he had been able to discover everything that I had asked of him. He took delight in ensuring that we appreciated his success to the full; understandably, in his circumstances.

"First thing they says is the militia is a-looking for me—an' you was too, wasn't you?—ha!" and he rocked with laughter. "So they gives me some food—" he held up the haversack, "and the 'orse and tells me to pike off quick and not go leading the militia on to 'em. I tried to stay, but they wouldn't let me. Ain't in too good a mood, they aren't. Near 'ad a mutiny 'gainst Cook couple o' days back, 'cause of the women, an' now they got the shites 'cause of the militia sniffin' around."

"How many are they?" I asked.

"Thirty-two—not countin' the Major."

"And where are Cook and the women?"

"In the farm'ouse, your honour. Been there all the time since they got 'ere. Cook'd never let any of us near 'em. Took a shot once at one of the lads what was climbin' on the porch roof to get in their window."

"Has he ever—molested them?"

"Dunno. I'm sure, your honour. But she's a fine-lookin' piece, the young 'un—an' 'e ain't the sort to just sit on 'is arse admirin' of 'er. She's got 'erself a good pudden in 'er belly, o'course, but whether that's Cook's or another's I couldn't say—" He saw my expression and stuttered into silence, "—Meanin' no offence like, your honour—"

"What else did you discover?"

"Well, some on 'em was fair lushed up and talkin' of doin' for Cook and gettin' the women and the loot what 'e keeps for 'isself. Got too bleedin' 'igh and mighty, the Major, with 'is private residence and 'is private bit o' puss." He glanced at me uncertainly, but I controlled myself sufficiently to show only casual interest, and he babbled on. "'E lives all comfortable in the 'ouse there, while they 'as to muck it out in the barns. 'E said there weren't no more room in the 'ouse, but 'e got a couple o' black blowsies in there to clean up and cook for 'em. 'E didn't let us get any niggers 'case they runs off and splits on us. 'Tweren't reasonable—'im living snug as a duck in a ditch with 'is women an' servants and them lads a-piggin' it in the shite. Funny thing, though, 'e's 'ad a fair run o' molls, the Major, an' kicked 'em all out quick when 'e's done with 'em. But 'e's 'ad this Belhaven bit longer than any and ain't 'ad enough of 'er yet it seems—"

"Thank you, Thorn," I said. "You did well and bravely. Go and make yourself look like a soldier again—or you may get shot." Then I gave them my plan. Chawton and half his troop would approach the farm in the same way as we had done that afternoon. They would be in position, under cover, prepared to attack the barns by first light. Charles Fairleigh and I with the other half of the troop would cross by the ferry to the north bank of the river and, guided by Thorn, would approach the farm on foot by the path from the ford. The signal for Chawton's troop to open fire was to be a single shot fired by me when my party were fifty yards from the house. Whilst the attention of the gang was held by the fire from Chawton's half-troop, Charles, Thorn, Andrew and I would break into the house, and bring out Lucy and Mrs. Fraser, sending them back with Charles and five of the militia to the ford. When they were clear, the rest of my party would fire upon the barns from the house. Attacked from front and rear, I had no doubt that Cook's men—those who survived our fire—would either ask for quarter or try to run. Finally, since my party would be the one most likely to suffer casualties, I ordered James Hawkins to accompany it.

It was all very straightforward and simple. And nothing went according to plan.

The early morning before first light was clear and cold with a sharp breeze down the valley. We had given sufficient time for Chawton's half-troop to get into position and had begun to approach the ford, when we heard a shot from the direction of the farm. We halted, listening. Another shot—shouting, then a clatter of single shots and the shouting grew louder. I pushed past Thorn and began to run towards the ford, the others following. The firing continued—more evenly—single shots, spaced out, like a skirmish line picking its targets; it couldn't be Chawton's party. The gang must be fighting amongst themselves.

As we came to the ford, Thorn shouted, "House is a-fire!" The breeze was drifting a trail of smoke above the trees around the house. A sheet of flame flared into the sky and died. I began to stumble across the ford. The water came almost shoulder-high, deeper than we had thought it—and

[*313*]

colder—and we struggled across holding our weapons and powder horns above our heads. We ran, soaked and breathless, up the track from the ford, tripping and slithering on its stony surface. At the junction with the path to the house I halted. We were in no condition or order to attack an enemy already alerted. I allowed the whole party to close up, ordered them to stay so, and led them at a slower run along the path.

We could see now that the whole length of the porch, most of the clapboard front of the house and the front roof shingles were now all a-fire. Just then a ragged volley crackled from Chawton's position and the shouting re-doubled. I halted my party in the shadow of the trees at the end of the path. I ordered them to extend in single line down the hill, facing the house, kneel and check their primings.

In the glare of the fire we saw a rabble of men milling uncertainly in our direction, through and around the garden. They were firing up at the house and back at the barns, halting to load and fire, then stumbling on a few more paces towards us. They had not seen us. I ordered my militia to pick their man and prepare to fire a volley; in the roar of the flames and the din of firing and shouting I had to yell myself to be heard, but none of those in front of us heard me. At thirty paces I shouted the order to present. This the mob did hear, and turned, startled and aghast, to face us, and receive the very model of a volley. My Virginians had picked their men well, for around half the gang fell where they stood, whilst the rest staggered or ran back towards the barns; straight into another volley from Chawton's party. I reckoned that these volleys had achieved Washington's definition of the prime purpose of the operation; Cook's band was destroyed. But there was still Cook—and Lucy.

I had noticed that the wooden shutters of the front windows on the upper floor of the house were open, and that from each window someone was still firing at the few members of the gang straggling about in front of the house between Chawton's half-troop and mine. Thorn, at his own request, had taken no part in the fight as yet, but now I grabbed him by the arm.

"How can we get into the house?"

"Back door's solid—an' bolted all the time. Up there, your honour, on to the water-butt—then on the roof of the 'ut—"

We clambered up on to the sloping roof of a lean-to against the side of the house. A single window, still shuttered, faced us. We tried to prise the shutters open, but they were too strongly secured. Sparks and tatters of burning shingles from the roof fell around us. Thorn thudded the butt of his carbine against the shutters, then heaved at them. One flew open, knocking me off balance and nearly off the roof of the hut. On my hands and knees, I saw the room within, lit by the glare from the roof through the broken ceiling, and Cook, his face streaked with blood, crouched beside the window in the front of the house, a pistol in each hand. He whipped round to face us.

"Thorn—you whoreson bastard—betrayed us—"

One of the pistols blazed. Thorn staggered, his feet slid from under him and he rolled down the slope of the roof to the ground.

My pistol was raised. Cook saw me and recognized me. He made no effort to shoot. I saw his mouth open. I heard him yell, "Don't shoot!—she's here—she's all right—" and at that moment the wooden front of the house behind him and the floor where he stood crumbled and fell away in a great gust of flame—and he with it.

I clambered in through the window. The room was empty. The ceiling sagged as I ran to the door, across a small landing at the head of the raging furnace of the staircase, and flung open the door of the room on the other side. It was full of smoke. A pistol exploded in my face, the flame burning my cheek and the ball tearing through my stock and collar, scorching my throat. The smoke cleared for a moment—and Lucy stood before me.

"Philip—Oh God!—"

She dropped the pistol and stood, her hands over her face. Mrs. Fraser was standing by the front window, loading a pistol. I shouted to her to come away and flung open the window at the back of the room. The flat roof of the outhouse beyond it was already smouldering. I pushed Mrs. Fraser through the window first, and together we helped Lucy through. I scrambled out and, as I slammed the shutter behind me, the ceiling of the room crashed down.

The house being built into the hillside, the drop from the edge of the outhouse roof was no great height. I leapt down and lowered them both to the ground, then, with an arm round Lucy, brought them up to the main track.

The firing had stopped now. Some of Chawton's men were on the track, guarding a few prisoners; with James Hawkins tending those who were wounded. Chawton came back with the rest of his party and reported that they had found the gig from Belhaven in one of the barns. I ordered it to be brought up for Lucy and Mrs. Fraser. Mrs. Fraser said that they had poured water over themselves as protection against the fire, but their hair was singed, their dresses burned and their faces and hands were black with the powder of the pistols they had been firing from the windows.

I had kissed Lucy, filthy and exhausted, in my arms. She had only murmured,

"Philip—oh, thank God—you're safe—"

And then, as Mrs. Fraser was speaking, she fell against me in a faint. I laid her down on a cloak, her back against a tree, and took my arm from around her. My hand and sleeve were soaked in blood.

James Hawkins cut away Lucy's blood-soaked gown and examined the wound. A ball had struck obliquely just above the right breast and torn through the flesh of the armpit in a horrid, jagged tear. He cleaned and padded the wound and bandaged her arm tightly to her side. "Be all right if we can stop the bleeding," he said casually. "Let her lie quietly and keep warm." And he turned back to the other wounded.

Of the gang, twenty-one were dead, and we had eleven prisoners, six of them wounded. None, they said, had got away. Thorn was our only casualty; Cook's pistol ball had struck the buckle-plate of his shoulder-belt, breaking his collar-bone, and he had cut his head open in his fall. Of Cook there was no sign, nor could we have searched for any until the fire had burned out. I thought it unnecessary to wait.

We returned to Dix's Ferry, informed the local authorities of the true purpose of our visitation and its consequence, and handed over the prisoners to them for trial. Chawton provided us with an escort of a sergeant and ten men, and, as we sat our horses, side by side, before going our separate ways, he said, "Please God all goes well with Lucy and with you, Colonel."

"We'd never have saved her without your help," I said. "You command a good troop—which means they have a good officer. Tell Colonel Mercer that from me."

"I will, Colonel." He saluted, smiling, and took his troop off. They looked almost good enough to join the 17th. We sent Thorn with them, in a cart, with a letter of thanks from me to General Washington, recommending that Thorn's wish to be returned as a prisoner-of-war to the camp of his old Regiment be granted, as Washington intended.

Then Charles and I started a long, slow journey to Belhaven, and James Hawkins came with us to care for Lucy. It took us eight days. We made a tilt to cover the gig, the weather growing colder and wetter. The roads became difficult and Lucy suffered—as I had done—from the incessant jolting and lurching of the carriage. So I rode in it and held her in my arms, and, with the help of the opiates that James gave her, she slept most of the way. I took turn about with Mrs. Fraser in driving the gig and holding Lucy; and talking to Lucy when she was wakeful.

What Lucy and I said to each other can be of no interest to anyone else. It was as simple and as repetitive as any other lovers' talk, and would be tedious to read. To us, it was all our life—all our world.

And when Lucy was asleep, I learned about Cook from Mrs. Fraser. "A strange man. So uncertain in his moods. He'd no intention of taking us captive until Dougal, the silly man—our groom—told him we were from Belhaven, to impress him. He fired up at that. We only learned he had attacked Belhaven later. I suppose he thought to avenge his defeat. Lady Lucy had her veil down of course, so he never recognized her until she took it off that first evening at the inn in Westfield. He was cursing at us until then; but that struck him dumb at once. That changed everything. He stayed close to us all the time himself after that. They told us he swore to hang any man of his who offered offence to Lucy. He never offered any himself. He told me he owed her his life—that she'd nursed him on board ship. Is that true, Colonel?—you wouldn't think a man like that would remember, would you?"

"Did he allow you any privacy?"

"Oh, ay—except—well, and this is strange—if she slept at any time in the day, he would often come, on tip-toe, and sit and watch her—just staring at her. At first I thought he might—well assault her. But no, never. I do believe, Colonel, he was in some way a-feard of her. It was always 'my lady' to her and very mindful for his tongue to us both. D'you know, he told me his mother had been the mistress of a lord, who had disowned her and him—well, maybe there was some truth in that. I could never question him on it—or on anything else for that matter. He wasn't a man for conversation; he talked and you listened. If I interrupted him or disagreed with him he could get very vexed."

"Did he know who was the father of Lucy's child?"

"I told him."

"What did he say?"

"Oh, he just nodded and said 'He's very fortunate to have a child by the woman he loves—' nothing more."

"Did he, indeed? Odd—those were General Washington's own words exactly. But, Mrs. Fraser, why did he keep you so long?"

"Oh, he hoped for a ransom at first. But when we had to flee from the inn at Westfield he knew he could not come by that easily. Then he thought his lordship could use his influence to get him a commission with the rebel militia; ay, he used to say he could command men, so should have the authority that was his due by his birth. And then he would go on about him being as noble a bastard as Brig.-Gen. Charles O'Hara and he

[*317*]

was a Brigadier-General of Foot Guards! Well, anyway, that failed too
He was very angry; and then he could be terrible. He would not come
nigh us then. You could hear him cursing his men and ordering them
punished—flogged. They were terrified of him. They only stayed with
him because, being so many, they could rob and loot easily and safely
They were well rewarded with what they stole. He had over sixty with
him at one time.

"But he could be gentle and thoughtful too. Those two black women
who looked after us—they were slaves—he took them as his share of the
loot from some place, for our benefit. It shames me to say it. Then he used
to get us milk and the best meat—really for Lucy and child of course—and
good bed linen and such—"

"Do you think he would ever have harmed Lucy?"

"Och, no, Colonel, never!" Mrs. Fraser was truly shocked. "Why—he
died defending her—and the child she bears for you!"

Which I found a strange thought.

We arrived at Belhaven in the afternoon of Saturday the 10th
November. Lucy's wound was very painful, the shoulder was swollen and
she was feverish. Dr. Weekes came that evening and he and James
Hawkins examined her together and reported to Lord Fairleigh.

"She has lost a great deal of blood, my lord, and has clearly been in
poor state of health for some time—the conditions under which she had
been living, of course—and the journey has aggravated this." Weekes
shook his head gravely. "Were it only the wound I should not be so
concerned. She has as strong a constitution as the Colonel there. But the
child draws on her strength. However, with complete rest and quiet now
and proper food—we can be hopeful."

Three days later, early on the morning of Tuesday the 13th November
a month before her time, Lucy bore our daughter. And died in my arms
shortly after.

We buried the body of Lady Lucy Fairleigh in the little cemetery of the
settlement. But her grave had no meaning for me. For I know that the
Lucy I loved is with me, and I see her now in the eyes of our daughter.

At first, I determined on suicide. Why not? The child was safe, and
would be happy at Belhaven. They could tell Anne that I had been killed
at the fight at Shadlock's Farm; she need never know of the child.

I suppose my resolve showed in some way, because Charles and his
father watched me like hawks; never letting me out of their sight. But it
was Andrew who found me early one morning, after another heartsick

leepless night, with my pistol—which I'd taken from its box in Charles' oom—in my hand. Unknown to me he had slept every night since Lucy's eath at my door, with the door just ajar. He didn't shout or try to take he pistol from me. He looked at me with his dark eyes wide. He shook his ead slowly, "Lady Lucy would not want that, sir—not never," is all he aid. And all he had to say.

For it cleansed my mind of my self-pity, and recalled me—worthless as was—to my responsibilities to those I loved; Anne and my children— nd my child. I would willingly have died to spare Anne the pain I knew I hould cause her; but would she wish that? And I could never forswear or esert Lucy's child.

Lord Fairleigh and Charles begged me to leave the child at Belhaven; er true home, they said. But her true home is with me and Lucy, and either of us would be at Belhaven. So we found her a foster-mother, the vife of one of James Fairleigh's troopers, whose release from prisoner-of- var Charles obtained on condition that he returned to Strath Dearn and is own people; to which, as an alternative to lying in gaol—or being anged by the "patriots"—he was happy to agree. They and James Hawkins and Andrew travelled with me to New York, escorted, for our afety, by Charles Fairleigh and the file of Virginia Militia which had idden with us to Belhaven. We sailed, with others paroled from York, on Saturday the 19th January, 1782, and arrived in Portsmouth eleven weeks ater, after a most difficult passage, on the 6th April.

We took four days travelling through Winchester and Salisbury and Shaftesbury and Sherborne to arrive at the top of Snow Down and the ight of the roof of my home. All around us, as we rode, the colours of the arly spring had begun to show us welcome; the pure whites, the golden ellows, the gayest pinks and the palest greens, and above us the spring ky, as blue as the eggs of the English sparrows that greeted us from their edgerows; and all the fleeting scents of spring and the smell of the dark ed soil of Somerset, new-turned by the plough, came to us fresh on the gentle, westerly breeze.

It was two years to the day that I had ridden over that hill to London nd Horseguards, to learn of the stone, thrown clumsily, and misguided- y, into the pool of my life, to set the ripples running.

We came to the house. We had been seen from a distance, and all were here to greet us. It's a wonderful thing, to be welcomed home with love.

After the first greetings were done, I took Anne alone into the drawing-room. I called for the foster-mother and she came in carrying the little girl and her own child. I took the girl from her and sent her out. I said, "Anne, this is the grand-daughter of Katharine Fairleigh—whom w both loved. The child's mother—Lucy Fairleigh—died in childbirth There was no one to give her proper care—love—"

Anne took the child in her arms, smiling. The little girl laughed an gurgled and patted her cheek. Anne said, "Of course—those eyes— they're Katharine's. Oh, you sweet, little lamb—" And she kissed th child and smiled at me over its head.

Smiled—until she read what was in my eyes. Then I would to God th hurt in hers had struck the sight from mine.

I said, "Her mother—Lucy—saved my life when I was wounded— should have died but for her. She was captured herself—and wounded She died—bearing the child—she near died saving me—"

I bowed my head. I could not bear to see her pain. I forced the word out through my clenched teeth. "Anne, I would have died—rather tha hurt you so. I swear to you—but for my love for you—but for th child—I would be dead by my own hand—so that you would never hav known. As God knows—that is the truth."

She sank to her knees, holding the babe tight against her. She hid he face deep in the child's shawl. The little girl cooed, her hands clutchin and twining in Anne's curls. The long-case clock in the hall ticked away slow stillness, silent save for the gentle babbling of the child. Then Ann said softly, her voice muffled by the shawl,

"Shall we call her Katharine—or Lucy—our daughter?"

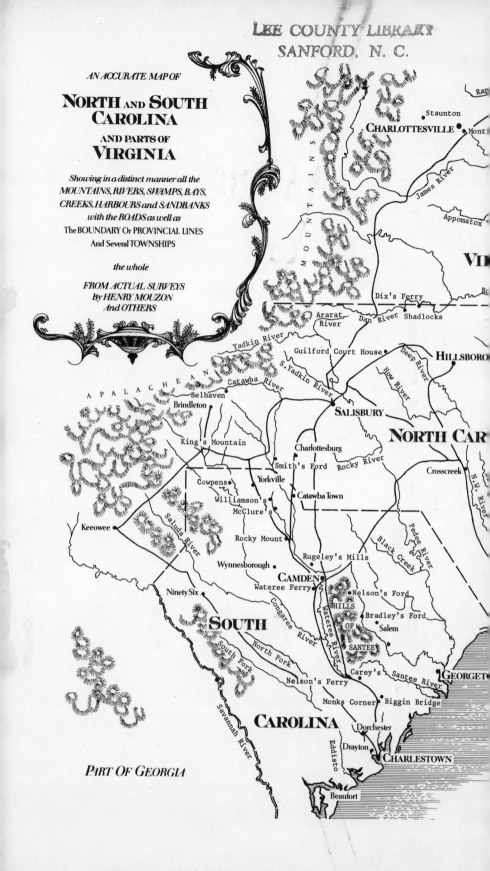